IN THE LAP OF THE GODS

IN THE
LAP
OF THE
GODS

LI MIAO LOVETT

A LeapLit Book
Leapfrog Literature
Leapfrog Press
Teaticket, Massachusetts

A LeapLit Book
Leapfrog Literature

Published in 2010 in the United States by
Leapfrog Press LLC
PO Box 2110
Teaticket, MA 02536
www.leapfrogpress.com

Distributed in the United States by
Consortium Book Sales and Distribution
St. Paul, Minnesota 55114
www.cbsd.com

First Edition

Library of Congress Cataloging-in-Publication Data

Lovett, Li Miao.
  In the lap of the gods / Li Miao Lovett. -- 1st ed.
      p. cm.
  "A LeapLit book."
  ISBN 978-1-935248-13-2
  1. China--Fiction. I. Title.
  PS3612.O867I5 2010
  813'.6--dc22

      2010028866
              Printed in the United States of America

For David Miao,
who remembers the world he once knew

Last night the wind raged furiously,
And broke the trees on the riverbank.
The river flooded over,
The waters were boundless and dark:
Where were you then, O my beloved?

—Li Po (701-762), Tang Dynasty poet

THE WAVES LAPPED AGAINST THE NEW SHORE, MUFFLING THE baby's cries. As the water advanced, it threatened to swallow the wicker basket resting on a spur of limestone. The river, now a growing lake, crept up the fields inch by inch. Now the ripening ears of wheat disappeared, their spikelets resisting the current before being pulled under.

The baby in the basket squeezed her eyelids shut and cried. It was a plaintive cry, like the sound of gulls circling above misty waters on a steel gray day.

The last inhabitants had cleared out several hours earlier. In the morning, there was a light rain, and the couple moved quickly. They loaded their furniture onto the boat, leaving the rickety beds behind. By early afternoon, the kitchen pots and pans, a handheld radio, *po-chai* pills, and tiger balm had found their way into the nooks and crannies of the wooden vessel. The fog hovered in the valley, casting a ghostly pall on the outlines of the man, woman, and boat. When the river rose up to the mooring, the man released the little ark, his wife took one last glance at their unharvested vegetables, and they sailed away.

But the baby remained. She was swaddled in a wool sweater, bundled twice over with the man's old cotton trousers. She lay in the basket, sleeping soundly, lulled by the sound of the waves swirling closer to the rocky outcropping.

The wailing began when the baby's slumber wore off. Dusk was approaching, and she was hungry. A cold mist descended on the land, smoothing away the peaks and terraced hills in a miasma of gray. Even the little nubs of broad bean shoots poking out from higher ground looked gray. But the creature was too young and too closely bound in her swaddling cloths to seek nourishment.

The river rose steadily, crawling uphill at a centipede's pace. In the faltering light, it found the dirt path to the old house. Still the swollen river advanced, until the water leapt up and played against the cradle. The baby's cries turned shrill and inconsolable, like those of a wailing widow unable to summon the spirit of the recently departed.

• • •

LIU RENFU KNEW THE TERRITORY WELL. HE STOOD ON THE promontory overlooking the terraced slopes of Emerald Gorge. He had watched the couple darting like little mice between their house and boat. Now the village was completely deserted, and soon it would be submerged by the vast and growing reservoir that crept up the riverbank.

Over the past few days, the river had risen more than forty feet, and the fast-flowing current became slack. The lower villages were no more, having surrendered every remaining brick, stone, and swath of fertile land to the Yangtze's new dam.

In the abandoned houses and shacks, Liu would find a forgotten trinket or a salvageable jug, and if he was lucky, he might come across hidden savings, perhaps for a wedding or a flock of goats. The ghost villages were eerily quiet, with the residents gone and the pigs and chickens long ago sold. On occasion, he would find a dog wandering around the fields, whimpering.

Liu made his way downhill on lanky legs, skirting boulders and shrubs on the slopes, bounding across the leveled plots where radishes, spinach, and red peppers grew in neat rows. He stopped by an old banyan tree to survey the last family's plot. The house stood some two hundred yards away, its roof stripped of tile and covered with a patchwork of tarp. If he moved briskly, he would have just enough time to comb the interiors before the water claimed it.

As he drew closer, he heard a baby's cries. They pierced through the fog in shrill gasps. Picking up his pace, Liu turned toward the wooden shed across from the house. He kicked aside a broken shovel and rounded the corner.

There the baby lay, crying so fiercely that her face was red and contorted. The makeshift crib rocked from the commotion.

"A little kitten," the scavenger muttered, shaking his head. "Left for the river god."

He had a sudden urge to light a cigarette, but the river licked his toes. He knew he had little time left. He scooped up the baby bundle and trotted along the path to the house. Only twenty paces. The baby squirmed, crying louder. The wind had picked up, rattling his trousers and seeping through the holes in his shirt. He was determined to reach the house before the water did.

A low shrub snagged his pant cuffs, but he tore on, all the while holding onto the infant with a bony hand. The louder she cried, the more tightly he clenched the bundle against his ribs. The wind streamed against his face, forcing him to pick up his knees and dig his toes into the loamy soil.

The river showed no mercy. It swallowed the landscape in slow, heaving gulps. The surrounding fields had all but disappeared, digested over the course of the day in a pulpy mass. An odor arose from the surface of the new reservoir, a slightly sour smell resembling fermented cabbages.

When Liu reached the house, the water had already submerged its base. The front door had been torn out and salvaged, but the frame remained intact. Liu hopped over the threshold, banging his shin against the raised wooden ledge in his haste. "Damn," he muttered. He spat into a small eddy on the dirt floor.

Designed to keep out evil spirits, the ledge could do nothing to keep out the approaching deluge. Liu always felt a little pang as he crossed the thresholds of other people's homes. But fate and simple bad luck had taken so much away from him; that was how he justified his living.

The baby fell into muffled sobs. Dusk had cast an ominous

gloom on the house, whose mud brick walls were crumbling with age. Liu turned toward the adjoining kitchen. The surfaces were blackened with soot. A pile of wood lay stacked against the stove, and wilted vegetables sat on the low counter. A few earthenware dishes remained unwashed.

Beneath the grime Liu could make out the images of blue carp etched into the plates. He felt a sharp contraction in his stomach and grasped the infant a little tighter. His wife used to serve the New Year's meal on plates decorated with fish, which signified bounty and prosperity for the coming year. He wanted to take the dirty plates, but thought better.

The incoming tide shook Liu out of his reverie. The water had risen over the threshold and covered the floor with a slippery, moving carpet. Liu kicked away twigs and debris floating on the water's surface, his toes cringing from the cold. He rummaged through the kitchen for anything of value, but all that remained was a broken table and an odd assortment of items—work gloves, soiled mop heads, old socks used for window insulation.

Liu sloshed back into the common room, his knapsack still empty. The infant renewed her wails, dousing his shirt with snot and tears. With each spasm, she would cry in ever sharper tones as if to admonish Liu for trespassing.

The encroaching lake had risen to his shins. He glanced at the ramshackle door opposite the entrance. It was risky, he knew, to enter. The water was advancing up the walls, charcoal gray in the dim light. He pressed on, feeling the resistance of the tide against his cloth shoes. He yanked the door open and stepped inside.

Here lay two cots, their hard, bare surfaces stripped of bedding. Liu crooked his elbow and held the baby's head against his breastbone, but it was less a loving gesture than an attempt to muffle her cries.

He spied a chest in the far corner. The water tugged at his trousers, but curiosity propelled him forward. Setting the baby down, he bent over the chest and wrestled with the lock. He tore at the rusted hinges until the lid gave way. Inside, beneath layers of crumpled fabric, was a lacquered box with gilded letters on the cover. He could not read the characters, but one looked auspicious, like the bold red posters hung upside down during New Year's to chase away evil spirits. He stuffed the small box into his knapsack.

He grabbed the baby, holding her high against his chest. The lapping sound of the waves had calmed her down. But the new lake was gaining ground. The door to the bedroom slammed shut from the outside.

Liu cursed himself, rushed toward the door, clawing wildly at the latch with his free hand. The old door refused to budge. The veins bulged in his arms, sinewy from years of carrying coal. He kicked, then threw his shoulder against the door, but still it would not give. The infant bared her tiny teeth, protesting in furious howls.

The cots were now covered with a thin layer of water. No perch for the baby, except on top of the chest. The river was icy cold, and Liu could not move fast enough. He rattled the window; it was sealed shut. His knapsack scraped against a raw, bleeding spot on his arm.

Fear seized him suddenly. A fleeting image, of a body lying prone, embalmed with river slime. "Prosperity does no good to a drowning man," he muttered. Liu refused to die; he'd lived through too much sorrow to surrender just now. Fate had swept him up in its inevitable tide, had once left him homeless and wifeless. But maybe there were forces even greater than fate.

"Heaven help me," he cried.

And then he seized upon an idea. He plowed through the water, murky in the semi-darkness, and groped his way toward one of the cots.

Liu bent down and pushed, aiming the corner of the cot toward the door. The wooden legs scraped against the floor, wobbling slightly. He breathed hard, grunting and praying, steeled by the will to live.

"Heaven help me," he groaned, slurring the words between breaths.

His aim was true. The door splintered on impact, and a heaving wave of water swept through the cavity. Like a great sea monster, it washed over the chest and threatened to devour the baby. She screamed, and Liu shuffled back through the water, now above his knees, to fetch her. With the infant in his arms, he leapt through the broken door into the front room, and scrambled over the cursed ledge. The baby's shrieks became hoarse, and even she seemed weary of complaining.

Outside, Liu caught the sweet fragrance of citrus trees. But the landscape was awash in fog, blurring the edges where water met land. He tried to run, but the mud beneath his feet threatened to suck away his shoes.

Night was falling, and he felt the chill traveling up his legs. The wind picked up from behind and propelled him through the water. But the lake was a greedy monster, reluctant to let him and the baby go. At length, he emerged with his trousers dripping onto a patch of dry land. He was exhausted, but he feared that the lake would soon consume the hillside above him. He drew in a deep breath, slung the baby higher up on his shoulder, then marched up the hill, stumbling on wild grasses and crumbling rock. On the slopes, the prickly shrubs of gooseberry tore at his clothing. He forged on, knowing that he could only stop when he reached the promontory. The baby hiccupped, and Liu patted her on the back.

When at last he reached the top, the sky had turned indigo, but a heavy fog kept the stars from view. Liu stumbled toward a sturdy tree, collapsing against the trunk with the baby beside him. He stared back down the hill, but the hazy darkness had devoured everything below him: the house, the hungry lake, the exposed slopes waiting to go under. His numbed feet came back to life, and as he stretched out his legs, he fell fast asleep.

Sharp gusts blew across the ridge, and the baby tossed her head as if wasps were stinging her. She whimpered, longing for the warmth of mother's milk, and her cheeks were wan and lifeless.

Liu awoke to a rustling sound in the trees, not knowing how long he had slept. The night was damp and chilly, and he checked to see how the baby was faring. He pulled off a damp cotton layer, but the old wool sweater beneath had kept her dry. Concerned she might be cold, he took off his trousers and stuck the infant into the cavity. The trouser legs flapped against her tiny head.

A smile crept over his face. "Little scarecrow, scare away the river birds."

His delight was fleeting, now that he was sufficiently alert to assess his surroundings. His moped, left at the top of the ridge, was nowhere to be seen. His search yielded nothing, only more scratches on his bare legs. He would have to wait until morning. He curled up beside the baby, all belly and no legs in his tattered trousers, as the night wind whistled up the rising lake.

2

STREAKS OF SILVER LIGHT STREAMED ACROSS THE YANGTZE RIVER valley. The jagged shapes of boulders stood like sentinels on the flat ridge where Liu had made camp. He found his moped nearby, behind a thicket of rhododendron.

He stared at the sleeping baby and wondered what he should do with her. He had found a few valuable items over the past few months, but he never expected to come across a baby. He was not surprised, however, as unwanted girl infants were left on more than one occasion near roadsides and market stalls when the farmers came into town.

Liu had almost been a father, but when his wife died, the unborn child died with her. That was a year and a half ago, just before the lunar New Year. He hadn't known whether the baby was a boy or a girl, but it didn't matter to him the way it would have to his parents. Liu shared his wife's excitement about the baby, but he knew that the carefree life he once lived was over. He felt a sense of duty as a new father, and he worked harder so that they could save some money before the child was born. As a day laborer, he hauled coal from the shoreline to ships docked in Fengjie's harbor. He found extra work inland making deliveries for local merchants.

Traditional work was becoming scarce in the river towns. New highways were being built, and the coal-carrying jobs that Liu was suited for—tough, gritty jobs that required neither skill nor schooling—were disappearing. After the sudden death of his wife, Liu was rudderless for some time, taking the small amount he had saved to the old town of Wushan. It was a seedy place, but unlike the other laborers, he didn't spend half his earnings on prostitutes.

Liu was a resourceful man, and a diligent one under the right circumstances. He learned about the building of the Three Gorges dam and found a new job for himself, combing through deserted houses when villagers moved to higher ground. Scavenging was not officially sanctioned, but it filled his belly. He knew where to find his pickings as each of the villages and towns along the Yangtze became vacated. A local official had tipped him off on the schedule of evacuations.

"The dam will tame the Yangtze," said the official. "From here to Chongqing, the river will become a giant bathtub." The size and reach of the dam was of a magnitude that had never been achieved, that Liu could not comprehend. The residents of Wushan, unlike the villagers, were eager to move to the new town, which was built on the slopes above the old. But after his wife's death, Liu had not cared one way or another. He had nothing to look forward to, or run away from. His forays provided a reprieve from loneliness; as long as he kept moving he didn't have to remember.

But Liu still thought about his wife. In the quiet hours of night, pleasant memories seeped into his thoughts. They had lived a fairly simple life in the town of Fengjie, a short boat ride up the river from Wushan. He called her Fei Fei, from the part of her given name that meant "to fly." Liu always thought of his wife in flight, her limbs graceful and swift like the wings of a cormorant.

It was a clear spring day when he first laid eyes on Fei Fei. Her father's barge pulled into the harbor at Fengjie, and she sprang from the boat without touching ground, it seemed. He was hauling coal in two sturdy baskets he had bought from a village weaver. He could cover the distance from the coal pile to the waiting ships faster than anyone else. At twenty-six, he was in his prime.

Coal portage was a fairly lowbrow profession. But Liu felt a certain sense of pride in his work. The other men who crowded the harbors wore sleeveless shirts, in flamboyant pink, revealing their wiry arms and gnarled muscles, but Liu was more reserved. In the heat of midday, the sweat on his back and arms formed rivulets that streaked down his gray undershirt. On a good day, he could make 25 *yuan*, more than his father could ever have dreamed of.

When Liu spotted Fei Fei coming up the dock, he stopped and stared at her. Blood rushed through his temples, his chest and loins. Two bucket-loads of coal weighed down his shoulders, but he did not put his carrying pole down. He saw the way her long hair flew back in the breeze, and noticed that her shoulders were bare. He admired the shape of her figure; she had sprightly but flared hips and legs like a gazelle's, lean and strong. She saw him staring at her, but instead of turning away, she smiled. When at last he had the courage to approach her, he put down his pole, straightened his shirt, and wiped the coal-dusted sweat from his brow.

Their romance was somewhat rocky, though not for a lack of affection between them. Like the treacherous shoals that pulled the Yangtze's barges and sampans under, her parents threatened to sabotage their plans for marriage. Liu managed to win her father over with his hardworking ways, and a certain intelligence that he learned from surviving on his own since youth, although he'd had very little formal schooling. He had left home at seventeen, estranged from his parents, who were farmers in Daxi village.

Fei Fei's mother was more discerning. No man could ever be quite good enough for her flesh and blood. Unlike the parents who prized only their male children, Fei Fei's mother looked out for her daughter's future as much as she did her son's. Liu could never win the approval of her mother, but he was intent on winning Fei Fei's hand, and that depended as much on her free-spirited ways as on his staying power.

"I'll run away with you, if she keeps refusing," Fei Fei declared.

And so it was that she chose to marry him, despite her mother's fervent hope otherwise. They would have six peaceful years together, at least when her parents weren't visiting, before she died. Marriage had rooted him, but Fei Fei's untimely death cut his ties to Fengjie, the place where, for the first time in his life, he had truly found home.

Old Wushan provided a brief respite from the memories. It was not so much a home as a roosting spot between Liu's forays into abandoned villages. What he found in those peasant homes, baubles and household items and the occasional heirloom piece, did not fill his coffers or prop up his pillow at night. They merely gave him money for rent and his next meal at Tai's. He would have been content to pitch a tarp of plastic and bamboo by the riverbank. But old Wushan was a lawless place, so he kept an apartment to store the goods before selling them.

• • •

NOW THAT LIU WAS IN POSSESSION OF A BABY, HE FELT SOME-what responsible for her. He couldn't see treating her as salvaged goods, although she'd be worth something on the black market. But how could he possibly take care of her? Perhaps the child might afford him assistance for poor families. His friend Tai did say, though, that the government program wasn't much help anyway.

In the light of the day, the child appeared to be an apparition, a wild creature he'd encountered in the thick of night, that had somehow possessed him, snatched his trousers, and wrapped them around itself.

"Little scarecrow, who's gonna want you?" Liu sucked on his cigarette, the air hissing through a gap in his teeth. He wasn't sure how he could give her up without arousing suspicion.

He leaned his moped against the small spruce tree where the baby lay asleep, then walked a short distance to relieve himself in the brush. He felt a curious impulse toward modesty, which he'd reserved for his mother-in-law, who balked at the immodesty of coal porters and their kind.

The baby stirred, a yelp escaping from her scabby lips. He had a little water, but nothing to feed her if she awoke. He'd have to get back to town. He lifted her by the folds of his trousers and settled her into the wooden crate hanging from the moped. And then his gaze alighted on the lacquered box.

He fingered the embossed gold character on the lid. He could fetch perhaps 30 *yuan* for the box. Not bad, he thought. A good day's work. Inside was a black and white photograph of a couple, and beneath that, an embroidered cloth pouch. The edges of the photo were scalloped and worn with age. The man was perhaps in his mid-thirties, about Liu's age; the woman appeared to be younger. The man was dressed in a drab Mao jacket, but he conveyed a certain dignity in the way he held his chin and braced his legs. The woman had a broad face, and her hair was pulled sternly into a bun. In the blurred contours of black and gray, Liu could make out a pensive look in her eyes. The photograph seemed of a different era; there was a distinct rigidity in their stance, an air of hardship and forbearance.

Liu fingered the faded print, wondering if the man and woman were still alive, if the mementos were indeed forgotten, or cast aside. And the baby—had she been too much trouble to keep? He wondered what kind of folks would leave a baby and a good chest by a rising river.

Lifting the photo, Liu removed the pouch underneath. His pulse quickened in anticipation of a good find. It might be worth another month's rent, and a round of drinks with his friend Tai to spare.

When the clasp gave way, a gold chain fell into his hands. Etched on the thin pendant was a cluster of peaches. He took a deep breath, caressing its rounded surface. It reminded him of pictures of fat, cherubic boys bearing giant peaches who boded good luck and fortune for the New Year.

Liu stuffed the chain back in the pouch, afraid that someone would be lurking in the bushes, ready to steal his good fortune. Sure, such discoveries were exciting, but Liu knew that whatever wealth one possessed could easily be taken away. He would take the gold chain to Ol' Fang, who had brokered some of his more valuable finds.

"No, I don't really trust him," he muttered. "Maybe I'll ask Chen to appraise it."

Liu shook his head. Chen would ask questions. He was a nosy fellow who would divulge secrets to a local Party leader in exchange for a tax break or kickback.

Grabbing his knapsack, Liu climbed onto his moped with the baby in the back. In his distracted state, he'd forgotten he was partly naked, wearing only a pair of briefs, stained by dirt and the morning dew. He grabbed the tattered cotton pants he'd unwrapped from the infant the night before. They felt a little snug, and the stitching barely held together between the patchwork of holes. But he didn't want to take back his own trousers, lest he awaken her into a crying spell.

Setting off for Wushan, he pondered his next move, where to take the baby. She rocked in her makeshift cradle as the moped skidded over rocks and bumps on the mountainside trail. Liu made his way to the main road, going more slowly than usual. Old trucks and construction vehicles shared the road, but they did not seem to notice him.

The wind whipped through Liu's hair, still tangled with brush and burrs from the night before. The barrel-tiled roofs of farmhouses flew past against the jagged outlines of the deep gorges. Barking dogs guarded the growing fields of wheat and corn, while sun-browned men struck the earth with plows, and elderly women hunched under the weight of babies on their backs. Liu felt a sense of ease as he sailed through the countryside. In these moments, little weighed him down. Old memories and longings retreated like shadows.

He gunned the bike to pass a slow-moving truck, sending up a wave of dust behind his rear wheels. The baby stirred a bit, but remained asleep in sun-induced stupor. Absorbed in the motions of life swirling by, the sensation of moving through space, Liu's ruminations ceased. He knew what he needed to do.

He'd keep the gold chain for now, and take the baby to Ol' Fang. The old broker had connections, even if he couldn't be completely trusted.

FANG SHUPING OWNED A ONE-STORY BRICK HOUSE ON THE outskirts of Wushan. He lived a rather reclusive life when he wasn't making deals for his clients. When the new town of Wushan rose up above the old, Fang had pulled strings with county officials to get a fairly nice house away from the hubbub and chaos.

He had been the son of a Shanghai tycoon, but the gods of fate had treated him unkindly, reducing him to a jack-of-all-trades. Whenever he could find an opportunity to broker a deal, Fang would seize it. The old businessman knew most of the merchants in town. If a tobacco shop owner complained about the cost of goods from Hong Kong, Ol' Fang could get him a better deal from Nanjing. He knew what came into the city and what went out.

Because of Fang's connections outside of town, small-time businessmen in Wushan agreed to the premium he extracted for his services. He knew port authorities in Shanghai, hoteliers in Chongqing, factory owners in Wuhan and Wanzhou, and he even had connections to a Communist Party leader in Beijing, hundreds of miles to the north.

"The sky is high and the emperor is far away," his father used to say. Fang stood by the old adage. For dealers like him in the vast interior of the country, the authorities were far enough away that they could keep out of trouble, but close enough to call on when a client got into a pinch.

Liu didn't exactly enjoy doing business with Ol' Fang, but he had few connections himself. Now that he was engaged in scavenging, he needed somebody above ground to find buyers for the goods. He had enlisted Ol' Fang's services half a dozen times. The broker had gotten him a price of 150 *yuan* for a pair of jade bracelets. Liu suspected, however, that Ol' Fang made a handsome profit from the deal. A ceramic bowl he salvaged turned out to be an artifact from the late Qing Dynasty. Ol' Fang insisted that this was a national treasure, and had to be turned over to the authorities. Liu didn't get a single *fen* for the piece, but he wondered if Fang was really telling the truth. He had an unsettling feeling that Fang had taken advantage of his ignorance.

Still, Liu had to rely on the old broker. Fang boasted of his dealings with commercial boaters, retailers, medicinal shop owners, as well as brothels in old Wushan, and orphanages in Chongqing city. Those babies abandoned by market stalls and roadsides often did find a new home, thanks to people like Fang.

● ● ●

IT WAS MIDMORNING WHEN LIU ARRIVED WITH THE BABY AT Ol' Fang's house. He eyed the peephole, wishing he could peer inside, into the old man's brain. What was Fang really thinking when he made his deals? With some hesitation, Liu knocked. No answer. Liu shifted the baby's weight in his arms. She was getting restless. Her small body seemed heavy as lead, although Liu had carried her up a steep mountain path the night before.

Today, he was anxious to let go of the baby. When he'd found her, it had seemed natural to pick her up and take her away to higher ground. She had been crying. She was a living creature, left alone by a rising river. Now he thought about the fact that she was worth something.

In Tai's noodle shop, Liu once overheard a mother talking with an American tourist, who was journeying upriver to the big city of Chongqing. The foreigner, in halting Chinese, explained that she had come to adopt a baby girl. The mother, strapped with a wan-faced girl at her side, asked how much people paid the orphanage for healthy children. The girl's eyes darted nervously from her mother to the stranger.

There was a market for abandoned infants because people from faraway lands would pay to adopt a child. Liu was puzzled by the tourist's motives, but like the mother, he had begun to wonder how much a human life could be worth.

He braced himself, then knocked again, this time a little louder. Fang would try to take the lion's share of the profits, but Liu wasn't going to let him have the upper hand.

Not this time.

Ol' Fang opened the door and greeted Liu with a hearty pat on the shoulder. "My friend, what brings you here?" He stared at the baby bundle, nudging Liu with an elbow. "Been busy, eh?"

Liu stepped inside and set the squirming baby down in the sitting room. She had wet his old pants, but he couldn't blame her for the sour smell on his hands. Those pants were worse than soiled diapers, after his forays in the flooded villages.

"Where'd you find this one?" Ol' Fang asked. He wrinkled his nose, and promptly dug out a handkerchief from the pocket of his wool vest.

"Suchien Village," Liu replied. He leaned over the infant, and a spark from his cigarette fell on the dimple in her little elbow. Her cries reached a piercing crescendo, her thin arms flailing about. Her torso threatened to burst out of the swaddling cloths. Liu grabbed her arms with a callused hand, stroked her forehead with the other. The infant wriggled like a trapped rabbit. But Liu would win this battle of wills, calming the creature until her cries subsided into a whimper.

"She was left by the river," Liu continued. "The last of the villagers took off yesterday. The crops were already under water when I got there in the afternoon."

"She's a skinny one," Fang said, pinching the creature's flesh. "Starved little rascal. Folks would have let her die anyway, dam or no dam."

Liu batted the old man's hands away. "Hey, don't make her start bawling again."

"Bring her in here," Fang said. They headed into a smaller room where a large portrait of Fang's ancestors graced the walls. Laid out on a pinewood cot were three other infants fast asleep. Only their heads poked out from the edges of a wool blanket.

"Where'd they come from?" Liu asked.

"Mrs. Lung brought them over. Folks left these two girls at the market. Refugees lightening their load," Fang mused. "The boy's parents knew she took care of unwanted babies, had a soft spot for them. All of 'em were howling like wolves when she got here. I put a bit of rice wine in their gruel. It works wonders. Good for this old louse, too."

"Hasn't dulled your wits, Ol' Fang," Liu remarked. "How much do you fetch for the healthy ones anyway?"

Fang lit his pipe, ignoring the probe. "Any good loot in the houses?"

"Nope, not really. Just found the youngster. She must be worth something."

Liu flicked his cigarette up and down in his mouth as the infant's eyes followed his movements. He was not going to let Fang have the pendant. "There was an old chest. Too big to carry. And uh . . . a mah jong set. I'll take that to Big Chen."

"His store is full of cheap bric-a-brac. That stingy bastard won't give you anywhere near market value." Fang waved his pipe in an arc, creating a contrail of gray smoke.

"Well, sir, I wonder sometimes if you do." Liu stared directly into Fang's placid eyes.

"My good man, have I ever given you a bad deal?" The broker rose from his chair. "Look, I'll give you 80 *yuan* for her. She's skinnier than the rest." He gestured toward the sleeping infants. The male had a hawkish countenance while the twin girls had more rounded faces, but all were less gaunt than the new arrival.

"That one's got a harelip," said Liu, pointing at the boy.

Fang walked over to the cot, took the pipe out of his mouth and stuck it into the fleshy gap beneath the boy's nostrils. The creature wriggled and sputtered, then fell back into a fitful slumber. The two flaps of his upper lip curled, as if remembering the warm flesh of a mother's breast.

"He'll fetch 70 *yuan*," Fang said. He drew a long puff from his pipe. "Who would have guessed that girls would be worth more than boys?" The old man glanced at Liu, then lowered his voice to a soft growl. "I tell you, there are young women in the city who think they're good as the men, with their college education. They don't know what it's like to eat bitterness. Their flesh is soft, just right for a man's hands, but not for hard labor."

Liu nodded. Perhaps life had indeed gotten easier for the younger generation. In hushed tones, Fang had once told him that he'd been sent to the countryside as a young man to be reeducated. He had borne the stain of a capitalist background during the Cultural Revolution. After his affair with the daughter of a high-ranking leader, he had been flogged and publicly ridiculed. Somehow, his life was spared. The girl must have pleaded with her father—nothing had happened, really, and they had a reputation to maintain, just send him far away from the commune. And so, Fang took flight to Badong, deep in the Yangtze's Three Gorges, to labor in a munitions factory. Down by the harbor, he remembered watching the trackers along the Yangtze's riverbank, dozens, sometimes hundreds of men yoked to barges like oxen, pulling the boats through treacherous rapids. More than once, he had seen the lines break, and several men would be swept away like flotsam. But now, even the great river would be tamed by man. As the Yangtze's banks rose steadily, swallowing the sweat and blood of a bygone revolution, it too would become soft and flaccid.

"Yes, they're soft nowadays," Liu agreed. "Except for this one." He pointed to the new arrival, now sedated by the slumber of her companions. "I tell you, old man, she's scrappier than a stray dog."

"All right, 90 *yuan* for this little pup," said Fang.

"My friend, that's a pittance for found treasure. Fatten her up, and she's worth much more than that." Liu stroked the black wisps on his chin. "I even fancied keeping her for myself."

"Hah! Why taken an abandoned pup when you've fathered more than a few little bastards in the shed?" Fang snorted. "Why, I've seen a youngster or two in the village upriver with a big Western nose like yours. Little Liu, I call 'em. Liu's little pups!" The old man slapped his thighs, howling with laughter.

Liu dug his heels into the floor. "Mr. Fang," he said evenly, "we have done business, you and I, for some time now. A little respect for your comrade, please."

"Of course, of course, my friend! You deserve no less." The old man chuckled. "Why, you're the best scavenger of them all. Not just for heirloom chests and the like. That's dead, heavy stuff. These ten-kilo gems are worth more than their weight in gold. You know where to find the live treasure."

"Then pay me what she's worth," Liu replied in a steely voice. The old man claimed they were business partners, but he always seemed to have the upper hand.

Fang stroked his pipe. "All right then. You want a fair cut? I'll tell you what, you come with me to Chongqing. That's right, my friend, I'll take you to the orphanage, and we'll get a good rate for these pups."

"What's in it for you?" Liu furrowed his brow.

"Simple, Mr. Liu," the old broker replied. "You keep me supplied, and I keep your trust." He patted his partner on the back. "Trust. Now that's hard to keep around nowadays, even harder than pocket money."

The two stepped outside to where Fang's vehicle was parked next to his neighbor's chicken yard. The late afternoon light played against its metal hull. The lettering on the side looked like chicken scratches in the dirt. "What does that say?" Liu asked.

"Chongqing Taxi and Transport." The old broker smiled. "At your service. I bought it from a cabbie who's doing a little time in jail."

For what, Liu wondered, but dared not ask.

Fang opened the door on the passenger's side. An odor reminiscent of pickled cabbage wafted out. Liu stared at the seat, the stains on its fuzzy fabric. This would be his first trip to the big city of Chongqing. It'll be an adventure, he decided. Even more than wading through half-drowned homes for treasure.

"You sit here," the old man said. "We'll put the babies in the back."

THE BABIES HAD AWOKEN, ONE BY ONE, AND FIRST IT WAS the new foundling who cried from hunger. The others sensed her distress and joined in like a chorus of baby sparrows. Each crying mendicant had its own pitch, each raspy voice chimed in where another faltered to catch a breath. They did not know that Mother would never come again, and for better or worse, their fate rested in the hands of a mercenary old man who knew how to make deals.

The cacophony of cries brought the men back into the house. Fang stirred up some gruel in the kitchen, a thin mixture of rice, chicken stock, and bone marrow. As the mixture came to a boil, he added a capful of *daqu jiu,* a pungent blend of sorghum liquor that chased away ailments and sorrows. It was a sedative for even the youngest of souls.

Fang poured the gruel into two soup bowls and returned to the sitting room. "Grab those pillows and prop the babies up," he said, handing Liu a spoon. Fang raised his own spoonful of gruel and took a whiff.

"Ah, when I'm really old and toothless, I'll have a maidservant feed me like this." Fang smiled. "With much more alcohol, of course."

Liu stared at his spoon and dipped it into the porridge. "Will she be able to take this?" he asked, pointing to the infant he had rescued.

"She's sucked on a woman's breast enough. Sooner or later we all have to be weaned." Fang edged close to the boy infant, yanked opened his jaw, and released the spoonful of gruel into the baby's mouth. The little boy sputtered, then swallowed the mixture. Traces of gelatin clung to his severed upper lip.

Liu didn't have as much luck. He offered porridge to the foundling, but she turned her head away. He tickled her chin to get her attention. She only writhed in protest. He nudged at her lips with the spoon, but she gritted her three tiny teeth until he backed off. The foundling let out a vengeful yelp, and in his haste Liu spilled some of the gruel.

In the meantime, Fang had finished with the two other girls. He tossed Liu a towel, grimacing at the small puddle on his rug. "Trying to starve her, Liu? She'll be worth less than a sparrow egg."

Fang hustled Liu out of his chair and fed the rebel infant. A few quick motions, and the gruel went down without fuss. Liu stared on, shaking his head.

The broker grabbed a small bag and filled it with medicines, a toothbrush, a comb, a change of clothes, and playing cards. Outside, he lined the back seat of his car with a pile of old newspapers. It would be a long trip, and those diapers could give out. From the front seat, he scooped up an old radio and a pile of magazines. He wrinkled his nose at the faint perfume of glossy paper. The cover model was too thin and primped up for his tastes. He was a refined man, but he preferred the stocky type, a sturdy peasant woman. Like the one he used to know. He shoved the heap into the trunk, and kicked the dust off his shoes before going back inside.

Fang stared at Liu's pants and frowned. "Been sleeping in a bed of mice, Liu? Better look presentable in the big city." He threw the scavenger a pair of cotton trousers. "Grab two babies, will you?" he said.

The two men emerged from the house with a baby in each arm and placed them in the back seat. Fang started the car. The engine whined like a dentist's drill for several seconds before cranking up.

Liu climbed into the passenger's seat, and scratched his crotch unceremoniously. "Uh, these are too tight."

"Sorry, my friend, it's what I've got." Fang nudged his companion.

"Besides, we don't want you making babies when we get to Chongqing."

"Chongqing? That's really far, Ol' Fang."

"You think this old buggy can't make it?" Fang said, letting out a puff on his pipe.

"No, Fang, it's not the car," Liu replied. "I thought we would have to go by boat."

"Too risky." Fang lowered his voice. "Four babies on a small boat would draw the attention of authorities. On a big boat, there's too many people, too many nosy questions. Besides, there's a highway now. Trust me; it'll be quicker by land."

"Is it safer?"

"You're safe in my hands," said Fang. "Of course the river's easier going now, with the new dam. But you have to wonder. All that rubble at the bottom of the river, like drowned souls."

The scavenger recoiled, a look of horror appearing his eyes.

"Don't worry, my friend," said Fang. "There's no ghosts in the mountains."

•   •   •

THE DEADLY SHOALS OF THE THREE GORGES, WHICH HAD gutted ships and pulled sailors to their watery graves for centuries, were no more. They had created fearsome rapids and whirlpools, a scourge to the boatmen of the Yangtze's fiercest stretches. But they were also the stuff of legends. As a child, Liu had learned that rocks were gods and magical animals that protected humans, or caused them misery.

Nestled in Wu Gorge, the Goddess Peak was famed for slaying dragons and protecting the ancient wayfarers on the Yangtze. She had been a fairy, more interested in human affairs than life in the heavens. As she receded from view in the car's mirror, Liu wondered if the goddess would be bored again overlooking the tamed river. It seemed as if a new world had been created over the course of a day, a week, six years since the great Yangtze had been dammed by the authorities. Now they, like gods, controlled the river.

As a boy, he had stood on the edge of the mountains, gazing

down at the river from old trackers' trails. He had climbed high up on the slopes, feeling the swirl of the gales that could hurl a child into the depths if the spirits were angry. But never before had he been in the interior of these mountains, populated by the spirits and legendary warriors of his boyhood. Now that new roads sliced through this rugged landscape, perhaps the spirits, like the people of the Yangtze, would be forced to move.

On the outskirts of Wushan, the car sputtered into a lower gear as it ascended into the mountains. The new highway offered a smooth ride, although the engine twanged like a poorly tuned instrument when the car accelerated. On the roadside, giant honeycombs of concrete braced the slopes, holding back the slippery earth. There was no goddess, no benevolent spirit, around to watch over the luckless traveler.

"How do you suppose people make a living out here?" Liu asked.

"Just as they've done for thousands of years," said Fang. "Wasn't your father a farmer?"

"Yes, and my folks died poor. I learned that years after I left."

"Anyone with a romantic idea about the countryside should spend a week out there." Fang grunted. "I did, for six months. Nearly killed me."

"I don't miss it," Liu replied. "But don't you ever have an urge to live a simpler life? You must deal with a lot of crooks."

"That's why I'm good at what I do," said Fang. "I know which wheels to grease, which ones roll straight and which send you off a cliff."

"Ever get tangled in them yourself?"

"Why, of course, my friend. Why else do you think I live as a broker in the shadows?" Fang waved his pipe with a flourish. "Why, I could have been a rich tycoon with factories in the city, fancy cars and big houses in the country. Like my father."

"Your family screwed you up, too?" Liu did not elaborate on his past, but felt a curious impulse to hear the old broker's musings.

"No, the government screwed us, all of us." Fang's voice was gruff and devoid of emotion. "There are some things, my friend,

31

you are too young to know." And Fang proceeded to tell Liu about his family.

•   •   •

FANG SHUPING'S FATHER WAS A SHIPPING MAGNATE IN THE 1930s in Shanghai, on the eastern seaboard of China, where the Yangtze meets the ocean. The city was a major center of trade that, on its bright face, glittered with wealth and foreign influence. His father owned factories producing silk, iron, and tung oil, and boasted an impressive fleet of steamships that cruised the lower Yangtze. An imposing man whose mustache never went untrimmed, he was the envy of Shanghai businessmen. His profits helped the struggling Nationalist government in its war against the invading Japanese and the Communist underground. Fang said his father had met Chiang Kai-shek, not just once, but on several occasions.

When the Communists took over the country, the elder Fang was thrown into prison along with other capitalists from the old regime. The government seized his factories and vessels and ordered him to turn over his other assets. He was jailed for a year, living on thin gruel flavored by the spittle and snot of the guards, who were merely peasant boys conscripted to the cause. By a twist of fate, the Communist government released Fang's father and put him to work in the state-run shipping industry. The man had a wealth of experience, and Party leaders knew that they couldn't get by on Communist aphorisms alone. But still they kept their eyes on him.

"You see, my friend," Fang said, glancing at Liu, "in those days I could not tell you what I knew, what I really thought. Why, you could turn me over to the Party officials. You couldn't trust anybody."

"But somebody like me, from a peasant family, what could I do? Turn a plow into a weapon?"

"Maybe so. It was mad enough in the cities." Fang grunted. "When I went off to Nanjing University in 1965, the paranoia spread like a disease. Why, anyone who stuck their head out could be an enemy of the revolution, not just an old shipping tycoon, but his son, his wife, his dog."

Fang told of the feverish battles that raged during the Cultural

Revolution. His friend's father, a prominent Party leader, was tied up and paraded through the streets, then dumped outside town in a trough of pig slop.

"The man was kind of a pig himself," said Fang. "Ate well while the rest of China starved. But tell me, Liu, what did he have to confess? That he actually had some ideas of his own about government? That he wanted to give farmers a real incentive to produce more crops? Back then, it was blasphemy. And for that, he nearly lost his life."

Liu thought for a moment. "Today the man would be paraded around town like a hero."

"That's right. Too bad he didn't live long enough to enjoy the changes."

"Did you ever get into trouble?"

"What, with women? Wine? Creditors?" Fang poked Liu in the ribs. "I'm indulgent, you know, but I watched my tongue during those years. I had a black capitalist background, as they called anyone who wasn't a poor wretch before Mao took over, so I chose to study a perfectly innocuous subject, math. I stayed away from things that could be labeled *bourgeoisie*." Fang paused, choosing his next words with care. "I did get into hot water once."

"You talked too much?" said Liu, chuckling to himself.

Fang raised an eyebrow, and gave Liu a wry smile. "Hey, I may talk nowadays, but believe me, I was not about to throw more ink on my black background. But the revolutionary frenzy was growing, and in the fall of 1966, some of my classmates talked about starting a faction of the Red Guards. They slapped on the red armband, the signature cap, and they turned into different people. Truth is, they weren't the sons and daughters of Party loyalists. They had that capitalist stain, you know, but these rascals went around smashing statues and burning books. And denouncing their parents, as custom dictated. Think about it. They disowned their parents!"

"Why didn't the government send in the cops?"

Fang curled his lip. "Don't you see? The government was behind it all. Stirring up the coals. I minded my own business, steered clear of trouble."

Liu was silent, trying to imagine a younger Fang, a less talkative one who didn't call the shots.

"And I was doing a good job of it," Fang continued, "until a rival faction came to town. They arrived early one morning with big banners, marching lockstep like soldiers to the university gates. They raised their little red books in the air and shouted, 'Surrender. . . . All class enemies! Long live Chairman Mao!' My friend Chiu and I heard the commotion in the courtyard. We went outside to join the growing crowd. Professor Shen was the target of ridicule. He'd taught pre-Communist history, God forbid, so he was an enemy of the revolution."

"What did they do to him?" Liu asked.

"Well, our school's faction of Red Guards came out. At first, they joined the struggle session. It was a good time to beat up on your teachers. After all, Professor Shen had given those kids a few bad grades.

"Until now, we'd seen bonfires and charred books and the like, but nothing violent had happened. That day, the outside faction grew more aggressive after they had their fun with Shen. They formed a line and advanced toward our group. 'You're too soft for struggle. Must be children of capitalist pigs!' they shouted. Some of our classmates began throwing rocks at them. The rival Red Guards whipped out pistols hidden under their uniforms. One fired a shot into the air. We were stunned; nobody let out a peep. And then all hell broke loose. Chiu and I started to run, but an enemy guard cornered us. He was armed. He told my friend to drop to his knees, pressed his boot into Chiu's spine, then grabbed me by the wrist.

"I was terrified. I wanted to run, but he turned my wrist until I cried in pain. I looked at Chiu, my dear friend humiliated by this devil. And then, in a bold move, Chiu turned around and smacked the guard. The boy's pistol clattered to the ground, and I broke free. 'Fang, run!' Chiu cried. I ran hard, ducking through the chaos, until I got to the countryside, where I collapsed in an abandoned shed."

"What happened to your friend?" Liu asked.

Fang paused, and for the first time, Liu could sense a heaviness in the old man, undisguised by sarcasm or wit. Fang did not take his eyes off the road, but his gaze seemed fixed on an unseen horizon.

"He was killed," said Fang. "I found out when I returned to school two days later. My friend had saved my life." There was a catch in the old man's throat, almost imperceptible.

Liu stared ahead, saying nothing. He fidgeted with a pack of cigarettes and offered one to Fang, but the old man declined. His own suffering seemed to pale in comparison with the travails of an earlier generation. These were matters the older folks rarely spoke about. Old injustices were hidden like rot under the skin of over-ripe plums. In time the fruit would fall and the old tree wither away, but the poison would remain, potent for generations to come.

It puzzled Liu that someone as smart as Ol' Fang wouldn't use his connections to become a *da lao ban*, a prosperous businessman above the ground. Now Liu realized that while he never fully trusted Fang, the old man had long ago lost his trust in others. Perhaps it wasn't the common folk that Fang despised, but rather the people in power, who could stir up such hatred between father and son, brother and brother. Liu wondered if there was more to the loathing he had felt toward his own brother.

After some time, Fang resumed his story. He had wanted to leave Nanjing after this incident. The revolutionary flame was turning into a forest fire. And then, in 1968, the violence had gotten so bad that the government sent millions of Red Guards to live in the countryside, to be sobered up by hard labor. Fang managed to get deported with a gang of Red Guards to a remote commune in Sichuan.

"Life was hard. Those bad boys, the sons of high officials, had gotten soft in a generation, too soft to carry firewood for hours and sleep in the freezing cold of winter." Fang sneered, exhaling a ring of smoke. "But after another year of hell at Nanjing, not knowing who would be exposed or ridiculed or killed next, I found peace in the countryside. In the morning the sun would rise over the flood-plains, and everything sparkled, like a thousand jewels. We grew rice and wheat. I would stand on the muddy ridges between the rice paddies and watch wild ducks and geese sailing by overhead. I lost touch with my family, but so had many of the other young people."

"Did you ever hear from your parents again?" Liu asked.

"Ah, yes, but that's a story for another day." Fang's voice became very soft, almost gentle in a way that surprised Liu. "That day I learned my friend was killed, some part of me went with him. I lived like a troubled ghost for many months. Nobody puts up an altar for the living dead, eh?"

Liu shook his head. "When I left Nanjing with those scoundrels, I was thrilled to be sent away," said Fang. "It was a second chance at life, and I seized it."

AS THE AFTERNOON SLID BY, FANG BLEW LAZY RINGS THAT filled the car until they wafted out the window, where the air was tinged with the faint aroma of pine and cedar.

The diorama of peaks unfolded in an endless jagged line, marking a silent pulse. Silhouettes of distant mountains rippled in the stillness, but Fang felt a nagging unease amidst the calm. The babies in the back seat slumbered, and the only noises the men heard were an occasional burp or cough, and the rapid breathing of an infant when an unpleasant dream must have invaded sleep. As the car groaned up a steady incline, Liu dozed off and began snoring softly.

Fang thought about some of the things he had told Liu. He asked the ancestors to forgive him if he'd spoken too much. Out of habit, he wondered what the younger man could do with these stories. Was there a prying official eager to turn in old misfits? Could criticisms of the government be used against him? Fang played with his pipe and looked at his sleeping companion. Liu's head was propped up against the window, and his tongue lolled to the side, framed by a set of crooked, yellow teeth.

The old man grunted. It was a guttural sound that almost gave way to a laugh, enough to shake off his paranoia. He's just a peasant's boy, Fang thought to himself. And besides, his life is in my hands right now. Just like those babies in the back.

Fang approached a steep incline, gunning the engine. The car kicked into lower gear with some reluctance. Then it slowed down, although he sank the pedal as far as it would go. The engine whined furiously, like a sick infant. The ancient sedan barely crested the hill before sputtering to a halt. Fang pumped the pedal, cursing and pleading for divine intervention. Still, the car would not budge.

He got out of the car and surveyed his surroundings. Down the hill, he spotted some construction trucks a half-mile away. The mountains gave way to a fertile plain to his right. In the distance, he saw a tiny cluster of buildings surrounded by farmland.

"Son of a eunich." Fang kicked dust at the tires. He popped the hood, and stared at the array of wires and tubes and casings. The car would not reveal its troubles.

Liu had awoken and stuck his head out the window. "What's the matter?"

"Car died," Fang said. "Dead as an old nag."

"Uh . . . what do we do?" Liu rubbed his eyes and stared at the infants in the back. His foundling was waking up from the sorghum-induced stupor.

"Those fellows down by the trucks might be able to help," said Fang. "But we've got too many babies."

"What shall we do with them?" Liu asked.

"Hide them in the trunk," Fang replied. "Two of them."

Liu raised his eyebrows. "How are they going to breathe?"

"The same way you do, my friend. Don't worry, there's ventilation."

Liu flashed a skeptical look, and Fang proceeded to unhinge the back seat, remove one section, and shove it into the cavity of the trunk. He covered the gaping hole with a blanket.

The old broker directed Liu to grab two of the babies. The twin girls, still sedated, went into the trunk. Liu's infant started to fuss in the back seat, and the male infant stirred a little.

"I had that custom-made," Fang said, patting the remaining cushion.

"Do you . . . uh . . . often keep them in the trunk?" asked Liu.

"Only in the city," Fang replied. "If a policeman stopped me, I'd be better off having a crowd of dancing girls in the car than all these babies."

IN THE LAP OF THE GODS

A car rounded the bend, whizzing by close to the men. Fang told Liu to push the car to the shoulder while he steered. He would have preferred the dancing girls, but the scavenger was earning his keep.

• • •

NOW THAT Liu was alert, he could feel the sting of the wind, which came in brisk, unpredictable gusts. He was impressed by the old man's ingenuity. But Fang was in command of the situation once again, and Liu felt uneasy about that.

"You stay here," Fang said. "I'm going to head down to those construction workers. And when I come back, don't say anything, you hear? I'll do the talking."

Liu nodded, shuffling his feet in the gravel.

After some time, Fang returned with a bulldozer driven by a construction worker in a bright yellow vest. The bulldozer blazed toward Liu, spraying clouds of gravel from its enormous tires. It was a monstrosity, with a golden claw that could devour a donkey.

Or a man, Liu thought. He remembered old Wushan, flattened to rubble by pickaxes, sledgehammers, a thousand sticks of dynamite. He wanted to back away, to run, but he stiffened his legs instead.

The construction worker, a scruffy fellow with mirthful eyes, hopped out of his vehicle and surveyed the scene. He heard one of the babies whimpering and peered into the back seat.

"Who are these critters?" he asked, folding his arms across his bright vest.

"The baby boy is my grandson. I'm taking him to the city for an operation," said Fang. The fellow stared at the infant's cleft palate. "The girl belongs to Liu here. His wife lives in Wanzhou."

The fellow seemed to buy the story. It wasn't unusual for parents to be separated from their children when one or both had to find work in the city.

Liu said nothing. He had this strange feeling that a new identity had been created for him. He could be a father of that baby girl, cursed because she was a girl and left to die because of it. She was helpless, but even in the course of a day she had asserted her needs,

39

and was now asserting some small place in his life, even if it was a fabricated one.

The construction worker could not fix their car, but told them that his boss would be showing up for an inspection. The manager might be able take them to Wanzhou, the closest city. The bulldozer kicked up a swirl of gravel and disappeared down the lonely highway.

Fang laid out their plan—they would leave the car for now, catch a ride with the construction worker's boss, and take two of the babies with them.

"What about the other two?" asked Liu.

"You're going to take them to that little village and leave them by the road."

Liu was aghast. "You mean, abandon them?"

Fang grabbed Liu by his collar. "Listen, if you play savior now, we're all going to be in deep water." He whisked two fingers across Liu's neck.

"Maybe you can come up with a good story." Liu shuddered as the old man released his grasp.

"What, two men running a day care? No fool's going to believe that. We're going to stick with the alibi, hear me?"

Liu nodded. He resigned himself to the situation, and pushed his resentment into the shadows. Since he was younger and stronger, he would have to take the babies to the little village while Fang guarded the vehicle.

"What if someone sees me?" Liu asked.

"Drop down, or drop dead," Fang replied with a sinister grin.

Liu braced himself; it seemed that danger was constantly at hand. He moved along with little protest, taking his orders from Fang with a somber nod. But his mind remained vigilant. I'm as good as a criminal on the run, he thought.

He took a deep breath, picked the twin girls out of the trunk, and tucked them under his arms. The village was a good stretch away. The buildings appeared like specks no bigger than his thumbprint. Liu pushed forth and felt everything around pushing him back—the strong gale sweeping across the ridge, the tall grass that entangled his feet, the leaden weight of the babies in their drugged state. The voices of reproach swirled inside his head. *You are leaving them to die. You are putting them out to the wolves. You will be caught. You will answer to the gods.*

Liu broke into a run. He ran until everything around became a blur, a kaleidoscope of wind and grass and sky that heightened his senses and numbed his mind. When at last he approached the outskirts of the village, he took in big gulps of air, but his heart was still pounding. Eyes seemed to lurk all around him, in the stalks of ripened wheat, the slate-colored roof tiles in the distance, the rubble pile by the road.

But no one was watching. The village was quiet in the light of late afternoon. No one was there to contemplate the fate of two young lives. For now, it was up to Liu.

He placed the two infant girls side by side just off the gravel road. He adjusted a stray hood, his fingers brushing against the soft, blubbery cheek. The twin stirred, angling a pink thumb into her mouth. He reached in his pocket and placed a coin against each young breast. "*Tien bao yo*," he whispered, and with the fleeting wish for their safety, he turned and ran all the way back to the highway where Fang was waiting. He was too shaken from the deed to feel anger toward the old man, who demanded unquestioning obedience, as Liu's father once had.

The construction supervisor showed up presently and agreed to take the men and two babies to Wanzhou, where they would catch a ferry back to their hometown. In the car, Liu spoke little, staring out the window to drown out unsettling thoughts of what could come next.

The infant girl sat in his lap, and she was becoming more and more restless. Fang had brought along some milk powder for the long ride, as he could not pack enough homemade gruel for four infants. Now, of course, there would be plenty for the two remaining ones. When Liu's infant began to cry, Fang took a plastic bottle out of his ditty bag and filled it with a loamy mixture of powder and water.

"Here, give her this." Fang handed the bottle to Liu.

Liu fingered the rubber nipple, amused by its bulbous shape. "Is this supposed to look like . . . you know . . . ?"

"Yes, my friend, think of it as a wet nurse. At a fraction of the cost." Fang chuckled. "No need to keep another woman fed and happy."

In Wanzhou, the supervisor dropped them off near the dock, refusing money for his help. Liu was struck by the modern appearance of the town's waterfront. "All new. Beats the old town," the fellow said.

An enormous port building pushed through the veil of scaffolding. Behind it, the assembly of hovels on the hillside seemed out of place, disheveled as beggars. As they descended the long stairway to the quay, a tram chugged alongside down the steep concrete embankment. Liu counted eight beats before the tram finished its journey.

And then it dawned on him that the newly built dock would soon be submerged. A large sign on the embankment marked the next rising of the river in bright blue strokes: 156 METERS. This much he could read, having seen the signs that dotted the slopes of condemned villages. He glanced around at the crowd of waiting passengers, chased by ragtag porters vying for business. "When is all this going under water?"

"In a couple of years." said Fang. "Everything will move up again. Except for those guys." He pointed to the hustling porters, their bamboo sticks strapped with suitcases and boxes. His prophecy gave Liu a funny feeling, a mix of dread and relief. The waters would rise again; everything was temporary, even the new parts of town. But that would mean his scavenging days were far from over.

On the journey back to Wushan, Liu noticed that the clientele had changed dramatically from a decade and a half ago. Gone were the peasants dressed in drab blue Mao suits, smoking their cheap cigarettes. The women wore cool summer dresses that whispered as they walked by. Most of the other passengers appeared to be businessmen, some in dapper suits with stiff collars, quite a few talking into their cell phones in crisp, porcelain tones. The elderly folks were conspicuously absent. It seemed to Liu that modernity had descended over the Yangtze River, and along with the dirt and grime it had swept the shipboard clean of poverty, old age, and infirmity.

Liu carried the baby awkwardly, not wanting to cradle her as a woman would, nor eager to look like a peasant wielding a plow. In the waning light of summer, the rusty brown water of the Yangtze became gray like spent coals. Before curfew time, the babies began to cry again, and each got a share of milk from the same bottle. Liu dreaded the thought of changing the baby's diaper. Fang told him to pad it with paper napkins until they got back to Wushan.

•   •   •

THE OVERNIGHT JOURNEY WAS A SMOOTH ONE, AND THE ferry cut through the subdued waters of the Yangtze like a silent water snake. The Yangtze River itself was a serpent, gliding through an escarpment of limestone. With the swelling of the reservoir, it had chased villages and towns, entire cities up the hillsides and across its banks to higher land.

Liu noticed that the newest buildings near the horizon were gargantuan and uniform, as if the Communist Party had taken the Soviet-style buildings from the early days, scrunched them into vertical blocks, then stacked them together like mahjong pieces. Older buildings, dilapidated dwellings of mud and pinewood, clung to the land above the riverbank.

"All this used to be farmland," Fang said, pointing at the high-rise apartment buildings.

"Where did the farmers go?" Liu asked.

"They got shuffled out to Chongqing, and some provinces as far away as Hubei. The peasants put up a fight. Made no sense to give up all this fertile farmland."

Fang mentioned that the peasants from another village near Wushan had sought his help in claiming their share of the resettlement funds. He had gone to the county office in charge of distributing the funds, where he worked his way up to a chief administrator, who promised to look into the matter.

When it came time to move, most of the villagers had not received their compensation. They surrounded the county building and demanded to be paid. An official told them to go home and pack up. And then the Public Security Bureau stepped in, descending on the crowd with clubs. The peasants left empty-handed.

"Those damned thieves pocketed the money." Fang shook his pipe in protest. "Rotten eggs, all of them."

Liu stared at Fang, curious that the old cheat had attempted to perform a public service, if only for a price.

Fang leaned over and hissed, "those crooks should have been thrown in the river, pockets of gold and all."

Liu imagined the officials, their vests heavy with gold ingots from the county coffers, sinking in the deep waters of the Yangtze.

"Did you get in trouble?" he asked.

"Nope. I kept a low profile after that incident. Don't take on these kinds of cases anymore." Fang extinguished his pipe, just as the lights flickered before going out across the ship.

•   •   •

EARLY THE NEXT MORNING, LIU AWOKE TO THE BABY GIRL'S cries. The first rays of dawn shone through the porthole, diffracted by the dusty panes into filaments of silver light. He was tired, less from the narrow cots they slept on than from her cries during the night. She had demanded to be fed, yet the pulpy concoction of cow's milk did not sit well with her.

Liu grimaced; he would have to change her diaper after all. In the ship's bathroom, he whisked cold water across her exposed bottom. She wrestled with him, her ribs slipping in and out of his callused fingers. Her flesh was as red as a baboon's from diaper rash.

Watery excrement swirled down the drain, and Liu lurched to the side as the ship hit some turbulence. He kept a watchful eye on the baby while washing the diaper, his nose turned away in disgust.

When the baby wriggled toward the edge of the counter, Liu reeled her in and tapped her bare bottom. The baby responded with raucous wails, her cheeks glowing red at both ends.

Should never have found her, Liu thought. All this effort to sell a baby. This baby peddling business made him terribly uncomfortable, but giving her up had been the logical thing to do. Then he remembered the two infants he had left by the village road. A knot seized his stomach, and Liu agitated the cloth diaper feverishly.

He took a deep breath. It was time to diaper her up. As he fussed with the squirming creature, the diaper pin drew a trickle of blood from his thumb. The baby giggled.

Blood streaked across the diaper, mulberry red like the stain of drunken brawls. Liu pressed his thumb against his teeth. He flared his lips at the infant in a mock grimace.

"You little brat," he grumbled. The baby tugged at her diaper nonchalantly. Her chestnut brown eyes twinkled at him, and Liu was suddenly struck by a feeling of affection. How strange, he thought, that this unwanted creature could turn his mood around so quickly.

When he emerged from the bathroom with the baby in his arm, a woman walked by, staring at them with amusement. The diaper was contorted in knots above one leg, and bulged like a steamed bun above the other. An unsavory streak of red showed at the edges. Liu kept his gaze down. As he slipped past the woman, he knocked over someone's thermos, sending it to the floor with an unceremonious clatter.

Fang had already awoken, and was staring out the window. "Look, it's Fengjie."

A swelling in his chest, a quickened heartbeat, these signaled the upwelling of memories that Liu could not suppress. Fengjie was Fei Fei. It was their life together in a sunlit apartment, on a stroll through cobblestone alleyways, on the deck of his father's barge, in a bamboo bed that gave way to his groans of pleasure and her sweet lips. The Fengjie that Liu remembered was a small town with grand old gates dating back to the Ming Dynasty.

His elation was short lived. When he looked through the porthole, he could not recognize the town. The bold angles of Fengjie's buildings gleamed white and silver in the early morning light.

"This is the new town?" Liu mumbled. It left a strange taste in his mouth, like bitter melon seeds.

"That's right. They moved new Fengjie upriver."

"And the old town . . . is no more?"

"It's a pile of rubble at the bottom of the river." Fang looked over at Liu. "I wouldn't go diving in there. Worthless rock. All the good stuff's taken."

The vertical lines of steel and concrete in new Fengjie were not unfamiliar to Liu, as he had seen a similar change in Wushan when the new town sprang up above the old. But the familiar landmarks were gone.

"Where's the city gate?" he asked.

"They took it down and moved it to Baidicheng," Fang replied.

Liu hoped to catch a glimpse of it downriver. When the ferry approached the mouth of Qutang Gorge, he pressed his nose against the glass.

"The cliffs—they seem different too." They were imposing as before, heavily robed with bamboo and pine groves, and threadbare where the rock face rose vertically. But the thickets of maidenhair fern braided into the crevices were gone. The turrets of rock fortresses, the limestone busts of old women gossiping beneath big straw hats were gone. What once lived in Fei Fei's imagination was now underwater.

Liu peeled his eyes away. His heart was heavy, and he sat in silence as the baby grabbed at his shirt with her waifish fingers.

"Cheer up, my friend. Nothing is immortal," said Fang. "You can't believe those old wives' tales."

The thought did not give Liu comfort. Fengjie was gone, and so was Fei Fei. He could not drain the great river to make old Fengjie rise from the rubble, any more than he could venture into the spirit world to reclaim his wife and unborn child.

The infant girl settled down and snuggled against his shoulder. A great commotion seized the ship as passengers prepared to disembark.

"When we get to Wushan, we'll take the babies over to Mrs. Lung," Fang said. "She'll watch them until I get the car back."

Until you collect more babies for sale, Liu thought. He stroked the infant at his breastbone, and looked Fang in the eye.

"No, Fang, I'm going home. I'm keeping this one."

Fang drew a puff from his pipe. "As you wish, my friend." He chuckled, then added, "Just remember, she'll be worth less when she gets older."

6

LIU OFTEN THOUGHT ABOUT THE EVENINGS THAT HE HAD SPENT with Fei Fei in their old apartment, how he had watched her stomach grow, how she carried their unborn child, ripe as a melon, as she bustled about, as gracefully as ever. He had rested his ear against her belly, imagining this blossoming of life inside her, and as he rubbed her belly, he fancied himself bringing form to this shapeless mass. It was a godlike act, this creation of a baby. It mystified Liu, yet it had made him the more practical man.

His wages as a coal porter had been modest. He knew that the family could scrape by on what he earned, but he was tired of struggling. Each load of coal meant another bowl of rice on the table, and a day's work could provide a packet of herbs for his wife's morning sickness, or a new pair of shoes when his old ones became worn out from trudging up and down the dock ten hours a day. But this work could neither put them ahead, nor provide for their child's schooling. Liu wanted his unborn child to get more than a fourth grade education, which had been his lot.

On those evenings, when Liu traced the veins beneath the porcelain surface of his wife's belly, he began to think about creating a new destiny, a new life for his family. He had broken free from his father's grasp, and his departure was also a protest against the old, unforgiving way of life. His grandfather tilled the soil, and his father before him. They were peasants, rooted to the soil, and their lives were an ongoing battle against famine, pestilence, and floods.

As a young man, Liu had his shot at freedom when the nation's leaders announced a tide of reforms that opened up the economy. But the idealism of his youth was quickly tempered in Shanghai. He was a lowly construction worker paid with rice bowl wages. If he complained, the boss would say, No problem, pack your bags and we'll find another guy to take your place. The beggars got an occasional coin from a well-heeled passerby, but he lived in the shadows of the elite, and he was invisible to them. He learned to despise authority, in all its guises, capitalist or communist, petty official or despotic manager.

Now that they were awaiting their child's birth, along with the impending move to new Fengjie, Liu revived his hopes for an unshackled life. He might be able to learn a trade, or apprentice himself to an auto mechanic or a ship repairman. Or perhaps, with Fei Fei's help, he could even set up a roadside business catering to tourists. The crowds had swelled; the tour groups arrived with their uniform caps and flags. They flocked to the Yangtze to gawk at the cultural relics and deep limestone walls of the gorges before the river swallowed it all.

And so, Liu nursed the dreams of an expectant father. But in the eighth month of his wife's pregnancy, the tight web of their life together suddenly came apart. It snapped like the ropes that harnessed a tracker to his team, leaving him to thrash in the waves as the boat inched forward behind the toiling men. The great river brought prosperity and nurtured human dreams, but it could also take away life. When Fei Fei died, Liu found himself adrift, a young man drowning in an old man's sorrows.

It was Fang who had thrown out a branch to the drowning man. Liu met him soon after he moved to old Wushan that winter. He managed to stake out a spot on the hillside leading to town, where he threw up a shack in less than a day using bamboo poles and plastic sheeting.

One night, Liu was shoveling down a bowl of egg noodles at Tai's noodle shop, trying not to think where his next meal might come from. An old man in a distinguished gray vest with brass buttons came in and sat at the table next to his. Liu noticed that the man was staring at him, and for the first time, he looked down at his tattered cotton pants, patched in critical places but falling apart at the seams. Liu tried to ignore Fang, but the old man began to ask him questions.

"Haven't seen you here before. Where are you from?"

"Fengjie. I moved here in January," Liu replied, still gulping down his noodle soup.

"Enjoying your noodles there? Did they just release you from a labor camp?" Fang chuckled.

"No, I work at the dock here. Hauling coal." Liu lowered his gaze. "Work's been scarce lately."

What Liu didn't say was that he wasn't going back to work. Wushan had its rough parts. He had gotten into a fight with another porter the day before. The man was making lewd remarks about the prostitute he had slept with a few days ago. "A woman's good at the end of a hard day, like a good cigarette," he gloated. He then carried on about naughty pleasures with married women, until another porter told him that Liu had recently lost a wife. "Forget her," the man snorted. "There's a thousand pearls in the sea to be fished out." Liu took him by the collar, and when the man spat back in defiance, Liu felt a great fury, the guardian of hidden sorrows, discharge from his chest and pummel the man to the ground.

Liu told Fang he could do almost any kind of manual labor. The old man knew a contractor in town who needed another pair of hands with small construction and repair jobs. Liu worked for the man for six months, but as large segments of the population were being relocated, the work dried up. Old Wushan was being dismantled, and although money could be made from building projects right until the end, the old town would soon meet its demise.

Liu struck up a friendship with Ol' Fang, who frequently ate at the noodle shop, smoking his pipe and reading the newspaper. One balmy afternoon, as the days were getting longer, Liu brought up his work prospects again.

The old man thought for a moment, then said, "You know the big dam that's going up?"

Liu nodded, but he had paid little attention to the news reports.

"Well, it'll flood the Three Gorges, and it's going to send all of us scurrying like beetles to higher ground." Fang thought for a moment. "I know a man in the county office. His job is to manage the resettlement of nearby towns and villages. Well, you can find out when people have to leave, and when they do, your job is to pick up after them."

Liu caught the sly smile on the old man's face, but he was puzzled by Fang's suggestion. He asked if this meant more work for porters. Fang explained that the migrants didn't need help moving; rather, they might likely wait too long and pack up in a hurry, leaving some of their possessions behind.

"You see, this is underground stuff, my friend." Fang leaned in close. "You're not supposed to know what's happening with the new dam. And neither am I. But we'll work together on this. You find the goods, and I'll sell them to the right people and give you your cut."

Liu wondered if Fang was a friend or just a smart businessman. But he could see that the wheels of the seedy old town were grinding to a halt, and this would be an opportunity to generate some income. He did not think about the contradictions, that he would be doing something on the illegal side, with the help of a government official.

"Tell Mr. Wu that I sent you," Fang said.

Liu obtained the documents with little trouble, and the old man helped him decipher the map and relocation plan. He was overwhelmed by the data. There were hundreds of villages in Wushan County affected by the dam, and Liu had little interest in keeping track of the migration of tens of thousands of people. He asked Fang what he should do.

"Stay close to home for now. You'll find plenty of pickings above ground in this old city. When a building is condemned and the people and workers clear out, you can go and reclaim the scraps. Metal, bricks, doorknobs, all of it will be up for grabs. Until they blow up old Wushan to make way for the ships."

Liu became very observant as he wandered around Wushan. He learned to spot condemned buildings easily enough; the blood-red character inscribed against weathered wood and stone was hard to miss. *Tsai*, the command to tear down, appeared like a fiery warrior with sharp blades at the shoulders and below the belt. Liu was hardly literate, but the changes wrought by the dam were providing a practical education. *"Tsai!"* he would say to himself each time the symbol appeared. It was a harsh word, which sharpened his concentration with its high staccato tones. *Tsai.* It was a word that could take down a whole city.

Little by little, old Wushan was becoming a wasteland. Apartment buildings, storefronts, factories, the houses and hotels for the rich—nothing would be spared from destruction. Liu saw families returning to the ragged shells of buildings where they had lived, as if they were spending time with a loved one in the final days. They sat on the broken concrete to enjoy their midday meal or play a game of cards. In the city, Liu was seldom more than a scrap collector. The city folk planned ahead, eager to abandon crusty old Wushan for the higher city gleaming above the hill.

In the fall, Liu began making forays out to the surrounding countryside. Here, especially in the villages along the river, people were reluctant to give up their last harvest, their cash crop of oranges. Some were reluctant to demolish their homes, even if the scrapped materials were valuable. Liu kept his eye on the stragglers, and stepped in when they were finally forced to leave.

Liu accumulated some savings from his prospecting, although he had a feeling that Fang was taking a healthy cut from the dealer who bought the metal scraps. But it was through Fang's connections that he was able to rent a small apartment in the new city of Wushan.

From the blaring TV at Tai's noodle shop, Liu learned that old Wushan would be destroyed in the eleventh month. The rubble would disappear beneath the Yangtze, clearing the way for ships traveling over the sunken city. As the date approached, Liu found himself walking the streets with more than a scavenger's eye, with a kind of fascination and detached curiosity. It was the curiosity of a boy watching a colony of ants scurry about as their anthill was crushed, some carrying their load of grain or seed or dead comrade.

• • •

IN THE LAST DAYS OF WUSHAN, THE REMAINING RESIDENTS shuffled about in a frenzy of activity. Men carried two-by-fours and wooden suitcases stacked up and tied to their shoulder poles. Women scudded along with overstuffed bags, dragging their young children behind them. Liu bumped into a grandmother carrying a baby in the deep wicker basket strapped to her back. She seemed to be the only person moving with a slow gait, and Liu noticed a pensive look in her eyes. When he asked her where they were relocating, she merely replied, "Far away." She blinked, and then stared at him with her tired, sunken eyes. "I would rather die and be buried here, but this will be a town of ghosts."

On the prescribed day, the residents of old Wushan climbed to vantage points all around the city to witness the final demolition. Liu found a spot on the hill leading up to new Wushan. It was a hazy day, and only the sound of cicadas chirping broke the stillness.

All eyes in new Wushan were turned toward the abandoned city. Old Wushan had a lawless, soulless element, and not many seemed sorry to let it go. In its last days, it was as good as the skeleton of a fish, stripped of its flesh and heart and gills, all of which had been scoured and picked clean despite the rot within.

Just then, a few boys darted down the hill, sending up dust and scaring lizards into the brush. The youngest walked up to Liu. "Hey Mister, whatcha doing?"

Liu removed his cigarette and exhaled. "Waiting for the fireworks."

Moments later, a great explosion rocked the hillside. The old city trembled, and then it began to tumble to the earth—tall buildings tottered and fell like drunken men, shells of low-rises crumbled and turned to dust. The resounding roar flushed birds out of the cemetery's trees, their raucous cries drowned in the din of dynamite that shook the entire valley.

Smoke rose from the city in torpid black clouds as explosion after explosion went off. Old Wushan had become a ship tossed at sea, and when the storm subsided, the city would sink into a remorseless, watery grave.

The boys whooped and cheered as they watched the destruction. Liu puffed away on his cigarette, watching the rivulets of smoke trail out toward the valley of dark clouds below. He had little to lose, but an empty feeling gnawed at his stomach, although he had just eaten. He thought of the old woman's words, he thought of Fei Fei and their home in Fengjie, and when he could no longer stand the emptiness, he got up and made his way back to new Wushan.

LIU SAT DOWN AT HIS OLD TABLE IN TAI'S NOODLE SHOP, RELIEVED to get away from the apartment at last. He had found a willing babysitter in Mrs. Song, a widow whose only son lived far away in Shanghai. She had little to keep her busy other than her knitting, a favorite soap opera, and her shameless snooping on the neighbors.

The proprietor, a broad-faced man in his fifties, walked up swiftly to greet him, in spite of a pronounced limp. "Liu, where've you been, ol' brother?" Tai Shongzi sat down with his lame leg out-stretched and patted Liu on the back.

Liu responded with a good-natured punch on the arm. "Well, the new lake caught me in its clutches. I've been swimming for the past week, looking for treasure."

"Come on, Ol' Liu," said Tai. "Tell the truth, what's kept you away?"

Liu trusted his friend, but there were other patrons around, so he lowered his voice. "I found a baby by the riverbank. I carried her away when the water was rising. Ol' Fang was going to take her to the orphanage, but our car broke down. So I decided to keep her."

"You kept her? Son of a gun." Tai slapped the younger man on the knee. "Didn't think you had that father streak in you, taking care of a whining kitten all by yourself."

"Well, she's a handful. She bawls a lot. Usually she's hungry or she needs her diapers changed. She likes to kick just as I'm pinning her up." Liu pulled up his sleeve, revealing a new scar.

Tai reached out to inspect it. His hand bore a scar as well, a two-inch gash. It was old but severe looking, like the burls of an oak tree. "Oh, she's a baby, you say? Just wait till she gets older. She'll be running the show. All women do, you know, and they start at a young age."

Liu was unmoved; he knew that Tai was really criticizing his own wife, who had a sharp, unrelenting tongue. "Yeah, she's a little tiger. But she needs a home. And I guess I can use a little company."

Tai squinted at Liu through his pouchy eyelids. "Sure you don't really need a woman around? Not an old witch like mine, but a good woman to keep you warm at night."

Liu became quiet. His old longings were seldom made known, even to a friend like Tai. He clenched his fists. "Listen, I can manage, all right?"

"Did I offend you, ol' brother? Come on, you're a man. How long can you hold out?"

"It's not a problem," said Liu, looking away. He ordered his usual, beef noodle soup, and lit up a cigarette.

Tai got up awkwardly, favoring his bad leg, and shuffled back toward the kitchen. "Guo, ol' brother, an order of beef noodle!" he called out to the cook. "Fill it up for my friend."

Liu stared after him, his temples throbbing, his fists still clenched. It was a tension he used to feel in his loins, but nowadays, only anger seethed like a low fire. His friend meant well, but couldn't understand what it was like to lose a woman like Fei Fei. She did more than warm my bed at night, Liu thought. She carried our child, my flesh and blood. No, Fei Fei hadn't completely died; her spirit still moved about. And perhaps that's why Rose was more than a test of endurance. The infant girl had that same spark, an unquenchable force that reminded him of Fei Fei. And when death loomed, that willingness to fight tooth and nail for life.

• • •

IN THE WAKE OF FEI FEI'S DEATH, LIU WASN'T SO MUCH A drowning man as a survivor sinking into quiet desperation. At first, he'd sought out the company of other coal porters in old Fengjie.

A round of *bai jiu* or beer, a hair-raising or ribald tale followed by another round of drinks. Those were the things that kept Liu going in the early days soon after her death. They shared stories of surly ship captains and bumbling tourists. They winked at pretty maidens from the countryside, and took pity on the toothless hawkers who sold toothbrushes and chewing tobacco.

When he moved to old Wushan, Liu lost touch with his former buddies, who had scattered to the winds. After his fight with the lewd coal porter, he began keeping to himself. Each subsequent job sank Liu into a deeper state of isolation; construction work did not inspire him to seek out a new set of friends, and scavenging was by nature a lonely affair.

New Wushan was hardly more tolerable. This was a town for the fortunate ones who had wives and children, a future to look forward to. The advertisements in the central square lured onlookers with the promise of new cars, stylish clothes, and sexy women. Liu rarely walked through the plaza, and when he did, he felt a knot of repulsion rather than envy. Hurried throngs pushed past on the main street—women in black stockings with skirts above the knee, men sporting suits and shoes of fine leather; even the cabbies and shoe shiners and storekeepers had a more polished, dusted-off appearance. This was the new face of Wushan, which seemed seductive to everyone except Liu.

Liu could not say that he felt lonely; he had been alone much of his adult life, aside from six years of marriage. He missed Fei Fei, not only as a spouse and companion. She was a kindred soul who didn't care to conform, as much as was possible under the law of the land. She was content in solitude, but when the urge for adventure arose, she could tease Liu out of his stay-at-home ways.

Perhaps scavenging was a way for Liu to keep Fei Fei alive. She had a childlike curiosity for the unknown, and as a little girl she had begged to travel with her father aboard his cargo ship, which carried coal, lumber, and commercial goods up and down the Yangtze between Chongqing and the Three Gorges. The grand old pagoda in Shibao Block caught her imagination; its red twelve-story structure seemed to grow right out of the cliffs, and Fei Fei would rush to the deck whenever she spotted its multi-storied roofs with the corners sloping up, like the wingtips of a hawk pointed toward the sun.

Her father told her that the pagoda was a treasure trove of miracles. Rice once flowed magically out of a hole at the very top, and through another hole in the stone floor, one could toss in a duck and see it reappear hundreds of feet below on the Yangtze River.

"Just like that?" Fei Fei had asked. She was nine at the time.

"Yes, and if the hole were large enough for a man, why, I would leap in too."

Young Fei Fei imagined herself as the tossed duck, sailing down, down through a dark tunnel, then feeling that first slap of water on her wings, which buoyed her on the brown silt blanket of the Yangtze, swift flowing and cool on a summer day.

Aboard her father's ship was a self-contained world of sweaty men with loose tongues and one well-groomed woman. Fei Fei's mother combed her daughter's hair into neat braids and taught her table manners. Don't let your chopsticks cross others. Say thank you. Let the elders go first.

Fei Fei made friends wherever they traveled, among humans and other creatures alike. She adored the Catholic priest in Wanxian, who drew her close to the satin folds of his robe and tousled her hair. In Shibao Block, sedan-chair bearers offered to carry her along without charge, claiming they could lift her high on one finger and spin her around and around.

Her favorite spot was the Little Three Gorges, a majestic set of cliffs in the Daning River, which spun off the Yangtze at the town of Wushan. Colonies of monkeys jabbered and hissed from their perches high above the water. Fei Fei would answer them back and dance around on her thin legs, wishing she could take one by its hairy hands. She knew the verses of Li Po, a wandering poet of the Tang Dynasty, by heart. And then she invented her own songs:

The maid fell asleep under the light of the moon
Till the monkey prince leapt out of the cliff up high
He sang a little song and roused her from sleep
They swung round and round with the clouds at her feet.

At night, she dreamed that she could ride on the back of a dolphin into the Yangtze, and journey to the bottom of Goddess Peak, where she too would become one of the fairy Yaoji's sisters and weave a spell of safety over sailors and sojourners. She would hurl thunderbolts at pirates and foreign brutes. She would steer the ships of young captains away from treacherous shoals. And when trackers battled the terrible rapids of the Three Gorges, she would lead them to safety.

As an adult, Fei Fei had, of course, grown out of her fanciful dreams, but her imagination continued to alight in distant places. The Shanghai of Liu's memory loomed with construction cranes, alleyways filled with sewage, and silent men inhaling their bowls of rice and limp cabbage at the end of a twelve-hour shift. But the Shanghai of Fei Fei's world beckoned to her, and she yearned to live there amidst the soaring towers, colonial-era brick buildings, and old Russian churches.

That day never came. If they had moved to Shanghai, perhaps she would still be alive. And so, Liu held on to her fantasies and stories, and in the past year and a half they had become trusted companions.

•　　•　　•

ABSORBED IN HIS MUSINGS, LIU HAD NOT NOTICED A MAN who sauntered into the noodle shop and sat down at a table nearby. When Tai brought over the order of noodles, he nudged Liu's arm, and pointed to the new customer. "Look, he's got a nice watch. See those little sparkles—they're really diamond, you know," Tai said wistfully.

Liu wasn't the least bit interested, but he obliged his friend and glanced over.

The man wore a pale green shirt of linen tucked into trousers that fell in a neat line to his boots. Made of thick leather and coated with dust, those shoes seemed incongruous with his tailored outfit. And when Tai waved to his customer, the man shot back a hand in return, revealing a dark splotch of sweat on his underarm.

"Mr. Wu, how's business?" Tai bellowed.

The man adjusted his shirt cuffs, as if he was quite pleased with himself. "Fine, fine, Ol' Tai. Will you believe we had ten customers today? A family from Korea, three German girls, and an American lady with her little boy. Oh, the Americans complain! The boy wanted to watch TV. I said, 'No TV. Watch the river, good movie picture, better than TV.'"

Liu figured he was in the tourism business, but did not understand Mr. Wu's broken English. The man bobbed his head up and down and waved his hands in a grand flourish, like an imperious court official.

"And then the lady complained about the toilets at the tourist stop. She was quite plump. Said she couldn't squat very well. And then she frowned her plump cheeks and said the flush didn't work. 'Why need flush?' I said. 'The river take it away.' 'But it stinks,' she said, and wrinkled her nose." The boatman's thin lips curled into a smirk. "I wanted to say, 'You foreigner, eat much meat, too stinky. Stinky foreigner.' But I just pointed at an incense display and said, 'Buy this sandalwood, smell good, nice souvenir for nice lady.'"

The two older men chortled, but Liu remained silent. "You handled that well," said Tai.

"Yes, and I made 250 *yuan* today, not including tips. Think about it, big boss! When I was a farmer, I slaved in the fields from dawn to dusk, and barely saved a *fen*. Now I can pay for my son's education. The other day, I even bought him a *Nin-ten-do*, one of those new-fangled toys all the kids want. Make him smart like an American." Wu straightened his shirt cuffs again. Liu noted the irony in his words, but kept a blank expression on his face.

"Ol' Wu has done well for himself," Tai remarked to Liu. "When he got the resettlement money, he bought a 45-foot skiff, fixed it up, and now he takes tourists around on the Daning River."

Liu did not know what to say; he did not like the man's airs. Liu could see from his leather-brown hands and the lines etched in his face that he came from peasant stock. When Tai introduced Mr. Wu, Liu reluctantly shook his hand; it was rough like splintered wood.

"What do you do?" Mr. Wu asked. His eyes flickered up and down, appraising Liu as he would a tied-up pig on market day.

Liu felt a prickle of heat beneath the simple collar of his shirt. "I've been . . . uh . . . dealing in antiques. But business is not so good now. Everyone wants new things, you know."

"True, true. That's what I always say to you, Tai, that you should get with the times. Give your shop a facelift, my good man!" Mr. Wu looked intently at the noodle-shop owner. "Put some good luck charms on the walls; they're too plain. And your tables—you could use some real ones, not these rickety sticks."

Indeed, the furniture had been transplanted from Tai's old eatery in the Wushan of bygone days. A certain staleness and grime clung to the interior of the shop, along with the fusty smells of fried onion cakes, simmered fish, and pickled cabbage. The tables were chipped and stained with cigarette burns and spilled hot sauce. The walls cried for a new coat of paint, although the patina of cooking grease was less than a year old.

"I'll tell you from experience," Mr. Wu continued, "appearance counts for everything. Get yourself a new sign out front. Put up some glossy photos of your menu items; things that tourists will eat. Take it from me, they're fussy."

Tai nodded. "You're right, Mr. Wu. But a new sign—it'll cost money."

Mr. Wu rapped his knuckles on the table. "Money! My friend—don't you see? You've got to put out money to make money. You don't get rich by hiding in a mouse hole. Remember what Deng Xiaoping said when he opened up the country? 'To get rich is glorious.'"

Liu was repulsed by the man's crass manner, but as he walked back to the apartment in the evening, he kept thinking about Mr. Wu. Liu did not want a diamond-studded watch, or a crisp linen shirt and smooth pair of slacks. He preferred being a scavenger, answering to no one. He couldn't imagine catering to the whims of foreign tourists, who seemed awfully scornful and demanding. Nevertheless, Mr. Wu's prosperity held up a small mirror to his own circumstances.

"Now I can pay for my son's education," Mr. Wu had said.

That night, after Liu picked up Rose from Mrs. Song's apartment down the hall, he began wondering about Rose's future. Little

Rose, perhaps only six months out of her mother's womb. She could want more, need more, than Liu. And if she were smart, had more education like Mr. Wu's boy, she could have whatever she desired.

The baby was quiet tonight; she had already fallen asleep by the time Liu came for her. Rose stirred a little as Liu held her and rocked her, the way he'd seen Mrs. Song do, with the baby cradled between her sagging breasts and apple-round belly. Rose turned her head, heavy with sleep, rubbing against an old gash on Liu's arm. He stroked her velvety head, and laid her down at the foot of the cot. She was no longer a foundling at the brink of death. And maybe, if fate smiled upon her, she would have a future that her ancestors could never have dreamed of.

MR. WU'S ADVICE HAD A CURIOUS EFFECT ON TAI. OVER THE NEXT three weeks, the proprietor of the noodle shop applied a fresh coat of paint to the walls, and brightened up the place with decorative hangings and table centerpieces. The paintings were really paper replicas pulled out from a large calendar of classical art, depicting lush chrysanthemum blooms, mountain landscapes with tiny people and houses in the foreground, cranes soaring over feathery treetops and streams. The roses on the tables were made of cloth and plastic, and the slim vases were purchased on clearance. Some of the tablecloths were slightly soiled, but Tai was happy to get them at a discount from a manager at one of Wushan's three-star hotels.

Liu could not go to Tai's for supper during this time, since Mrs. Song was laid up with the flu. It was nearing the end of June, and despite the sultry heat, he was anxious to get out of the apartment. With Rose in his arms, Liu slid past the smoky Internet parlors where video games hummed, and descended onto the main square. Before he could take the last step, a plastic buggy in camouflage colors whizzed by, with a young boy in the driver's seat and his sister shrinking into his coat. As the little daredevil rounded a corner, other buggies followed suit, a bright yellow one resembling a cartoon cat, a flaming red fire engine, a bulbous gray whale. The children steered their way across the smooth tiles of the square with gleeful and wicked grins, while their parents nodded and smiled on the sidelines. The older children zipped along in smooth contrails, while the younger ones moved in staggering drunken lines. One little dumpling, who was no more than two, had her father guiding her pink Cadillac from behind with a remote control.

Liu held the baby close to his chest, moving with the steady stream of locals and sightseers across the square. Little Rose seemed quite curious and alert to the commotion around her. She stretched out her little fingers, almost grabbing a blond tourist's hair until he swiped her hand away. As Liu pressed on, he felt a sudden thrust, like a small fist, against his thighs.

"Oh, so sorry!" A young woman smiled, pulling her child's wrist away. The boy giggled, stuck his fist in his mouth and stared up at Rose.

"Not a problem," Liu said. "Is it always this crowded?"

"I guess so." The young mother looked at Rose. "How old is your baby?"

"Uh, well, she came along when I . . . we moved from the old town." Liu felt a surge of heat rising up his spine. He found lying uncomfortable, but necessary, even though she was a stranger.

The woman wiggled her fingers at Rose, who shook her tiny arms and gurgled excitedly. "You're a good husband to help with the baby. Wish mine would."

"It's not so bad. Besides," Liu gave a stilted laugh, "this is better than changing diapers."

The mother looked surprised. "Well, you are a diligent father." She bade them farewell and disappeared in the meandering crowd.

Liu leaned against a lamppost and thought about what he'd said. This time, it wasn't Fang who had concocted an identity for him. He was a husband; certainly that had been true at one time. He was a father now. But what did that mean if he had no blood relation to little Rose, nothing binding him to a father's duty, to the endless cycles of diaper changing, feeding, and baby soothing? Liu wondered if he was responsible for her future, like the peasant boatman was for his own son's.

If Fei Fei were alive, would she love this child as her own?

Then again, if Fei Fei were still in this world, would Liu have kept the baby? He might not have found her in the first place. His life would have been transplanted elsewhere, to new Fengjie, or even Shanghai. When his wife was alive, he had neither the time nor inclination to ponder such things. Now, with a baby in tow, his mind drifted down these troubling channels.

Perhaps he needed to go scavenging again. He would have to get those maps from Fang to find prospective sites that hadn't been flooded.

But maybe, he thought, this wasn't a real job. And he wasn't a real father.

Liu shifted his weight uneasily. The heat rose from the cement through the soles of his shoes. He had no answers at the moment. Liu turned back, eager to retreat with Rose to his humble apartment.

When Liu showed up again at the noodle shop, he noticed how business had picked up. Tai rushed over, his limp leg in tow, and greeted his friend with an extra hearty slap. "Liu, pretty soon I should put a little reserved sign on your table, eh?"

Liu looked around at the small crowd of diners. Amidst the native chatter he could hear a foreign tongue that sounded like the pop music blaring out of clothing stores.

"Well, Tai, you might just do that. Then again, I might not be able to afford to come here anymore."

"No, my friend, I'll always keep the noodles on the menu for you." Tai beckoned his friend into the kitchen. "Come here, Liu, come see the new sign I'm going to put up."

Tai pointed to a sign lying beside the freezer unit. Red letters etched into the dark wood spelled out "TAI'S RESTAURANT" across in English. Black, gold-trimmed characters "FAN DIEN" ran down one side, upgrading it from a noodle shop, while "TAI HAO" proclaimed it to be really good, playing on the owner's name.

Liu was impressed. "Well, this will really bring good fortune to your door."

"It cost me 400 *yuan*. But that fellow Wu was right. You've got to put out some money to make more. Don't we all want to do that?"

Liu gave a perfunctory nod. "I guess Wushan's not an old, run-down town anymore."

"No sir, and it's high time for an old fart like me to keep up with the new generation."

The cook hollered to Tai, who excused himself, saying a waitress would be out to serve Liu. A waitress, Liu thought. He's really changed his cheapskate ways.

Soon after Liu sat down at his old table, a young woman dressed in a pale blue blouse and skirt appeared at his side. She had graceful legs, a pretty face shaped like a watermelon seed, and large eyes. Black eyeliner lifted them up at the corners, giving her a coy expression. She handed him a menu and returned moments later. "What would you like, sir?"

"My usual . . . uh . . . the beef noodle soup, spicy." Liu found himself stammering, and noticing this unsettled him more.

"Anything to drink?" The waitress scribbled onto her pad and brushed her long hair back, revealing a small mole on her chin. A beauty spot, the envied mark of movie actresses.

Liu shook his head. Again, he felt an uneasy flutter in his chest, and his voice trembled a little. "You're new here?"

"Yes, does it show?" she asked, with a slight curl of her lips.

"No, no . . . I mean, Tai must be glad for the help."

The waitress reached out for the menu, another feature of Tai's jazzed-up restaurant. Liu fumbled to give it back to her, almost knocking over the jar of hot sauce on the table. Her movements were brisk yet graceful, and her skin smelled like plum blossoms.

His eyes drifted in her direction as she served the other customers. He felt uncomfortable, as if he'd been caught spying on an exchange between lovers. The waitress was quite friendly with several of the patrons, as if they were lifelong acquaintances. Liu found the changes in Tai's noodle shop a bit hard to swallow. He decided to leave earlier than usual, slipping out after he finished his noodles.

That evening, as Liu was rocking the baby to sleep, he thought about Fei Fei much as he did every evening, but images of the young waitress at Tai's intruded on his thoughts. It unnerved him to think about her. The nagging thoughts, insisting that he should move on and find another woman, alighted like bats. They hid in the shadows and flitted out unexpectedly, just as he was tucking little Rose into her cradle, which he had fashioned from salvaged wood.

When Rose had fallen asleep, Liu turned on the television and lit a cigarette. His stomach rumbled; he had been eager to leave the noodle shop and hadn't finished his meal. He felt a vague sense of unease and needed some distraction.

The local evening news featured a special report on peasants who had resettled with the building of the dam. The reporter's tone was measured but somewhat critical, as if he needed to tow the party line but the truth revealed itself anyway. "The residents of Xianghuamen village only had to move fifteen kilometers, and forty families have been successful in establishing their new plots. Higher up in the mountains, the farmers must find new ways to improve the crop yields."

The camera panned to a peasant couple with their young son. "We are grateful to obtain this parcel of land," said the husband, "but we have to make do with what we have. We lost our orange grove, and without the extra income, we may not be able to send our son to high school when he gets older."

"We had a daughter," the wife said, "but she died a few years ago, so we had another child without penalty." Liu wondered if the little girl had really died, or if she had become one of those roadside orphans.

"How have you dealt with these hardships?" the reporter asked.

"Well, for one thing, I have a devoted wife and a good son. I almost lost them a few years ago." The man did not smile, but merely pulled his son closer.

"My wife almost died in that flood," the man continued, looking away from the camera. "She was pregnant with our boy at the time. But *tien bao yo*, with a neighbor's help we carried her to safety."

"Yes, the gods were watching over us," the wife added, clutching their son by the collar. The boy broke free from her grasp and disappeared from view.

Liu turned off the news, and lit another cigarette. He drummed his fingers on the table, letting the ashes fall to the floor. He regretted watching the news, because a new emotion overtook him like a typhoon, and there was no warning.

He was angry. Liu had been adrift for the past two years, since the death of his wife. Guilt, remorse, longing, these became his mistresses, and they had their way with him. Still, he held back the tears. As his outer world crumbled, as all that was familiar disappeared and new towns emerged in the shadows of the old, Liu became even more stalwart within. Now the façade started to crack, and for the first time, Liu felt a helpless rage. It shook his body, coursing through his veins, flooding his temples with a feverish pulse. Liu threw his cigarette on the cheap tile and stamped it out.

He wanted to pick up a chair and hurl it out the window with his grief tumbling after it. He did not have to lose his wife and his child. He could have been like that farmer, a man with a family and a future; now he could only pretend to a stranger in the park that he was a real father, a devoted husband with loved ones, and responsibilities. For the first time, Liu felt resentment toward Fei Fei. She had to die, leaving him stranded on this island. The angry voices reached a crescendo, driving him out of the apartment and into the dark streets.

Liu stumbled downhill like a drunken soul, past prowling dogs and evening strollers, until he reached the fringes of old Wushan. He made his way down the dirt path to the cemetery, which stood intact among the few remaining buildings. He fell on his haunches, leaning against the trunk of a willow tree, as the wind whistled through its leaves.

Fei Fei is gone from my life, he thought. And she will not come back. The tears dribbled down his chin, and he did not wipe them away.

His knees scraped against rock. She is walking in the spirit world, and I have to muddle through this life on earth.

Then Liu pulled himself up, and listened to the scuffling sounds of the wind. He squinted at the mounds where the dead were buried. They did not stir; they were at peace. But all around were shadows of movement: crawling insects, shanty dwellers on the hill, ghosts wandering through the night. There was movement in his body: the tingling in his fingertips, the rise and fall of his chest, a shudder from the cold. His life was still intact. It had been uprooted, not just by her death, but also by his own volition. He would find a way to anchor it again.

Liu wiped the moisture from his face, and stumbled back along the rocky path. In the new town, he slipped past the lamplights like a scarecrow in the night, sleeves and pant cuffs flailing. The tears had dried without a trace; nobody but Liu would know about this moment, when his life began to emerge from the shadows again. His footsteps fell lightly on the sidewalk, carrying him home as a full moon emerged from the clouds.

LIU'S TRIP TO THE CLOTHING STORE WAS A MAJOR EXPEDITION, more daunting than his forays into abandoned villages. He had never seen so much apparel; all of Wushan could be clothed by this one store. The life-sized manikins were all legs, dressed in seductive colors, but Liu merely felt a tingling, creepy feeling on his skin. He bought the first item that caught his eye, a light green linen shirt with a stiff collar. At home, Liu tore up his old shirt, a fossil record of his various jobs, and threw it in the trash.

That evening, the waitress appeared at Liu's side again. She had on the same pale blue outfit. Tonight, however, a white apron set off the mermaid outline of her hips. "Do you come here often?" she asked.

"Well, yes. I've been coming here for a while, since Tai had a shop in old Wushan."

"What was that like?" She tilted her pencil against her lips. Liu followed her movements, then looked away.

"Good food, but not as nice as this place. I guess you're new here. Where are you from?" Liu spoke casually, trying not to appear too interested.

"I'm from around here. Glad to move out of old Wushan. I never felt comfortable there walking the streets alone, even in the evenings when they were filled with street vendors."

"I know what you mean." Liu nodded. "I was rather fond of the *huoguo* stands. I like the dish extra spicy, you know."

"But you can't taste the meat when you drown it in spice."

"Oh, I would drink the broth, swallow a chili or two." Liu smiled. He didn't feel so uncomfortable tonight, but had an urge to impress her.

"Well, I'll have the cook make your beef noodle extra spicy then." She remembered his order from the night before. "But if you start sweating, don't say I didn't warn you!"

"You'll bring me some water, won't you?"

"Well, yes." She crinkled her eyes, the painted dark lines tilting toward her smooth temples. "But I rather like watching a man sweat."

Now what was that? Liu thought. His heart fluttered as she walked away. Liu wondered if her womanly charms were displayed with other customers in the course of her duties, to keep them coming to Tai's. After all, the place was no longer a hole-in-the-wall, but an enterprising business whose owner could change with the times.

When the waitress returned with the beef noodle soup, Liu saw that there were several red chilies floating on the surface of the broth.

"As you like it." She smiled.

Liu thanked her, and raised the bowl to his lips. A firestorm leapt from the chilies into his mouth, stinging his tongue, his lips, taking siege of his vocal cords in a wicked blaze of heat. Liu coughed and spluttered until tears welled up in the corners of his eyes. A bit of broth splattered onto his new shirt, staining it brown and orange.

The waitress's smile dissolved as Liu clutched his throat in agony. She ran into the kitchen to fetch a glass of water. Liu gulped it down and slumped back in his chair.

Liu mustered a faint smile. "You're a woman of your word," he mumbled when he was able to speak.

"And you're one to tell a fib!" She smiled good-naturedly.

"Okay, you called my bluff. Tai will be glad that you keep his customers honest."

"Listen, I'll bring you another bowl, okay?" The waitress took the uneaten noodle soup back into the kitchen.

When she returned, Liu worked up the courage to ask her name. It was Mei Ling.

IN THE LAP OF THE GODS

That evening, Liu rolled her name around on his tongue as he tucked Rose into bed. Mei Ling. *Mei* for beautiful. *Ling*, bright and alert. He wanted to know more about her. He would get over to the noodle shop before it opened in the morning, and have a talk with Tai.

•   •   •

LATE AT NIGHT, AFTER MEI LING RETURNED HOME FROM THE restaurant, she counted up her wages for the week. One hundred and twenty *yuan*. Sharing a small room with two other women, she needed to set aside some of the money to pay rent. Mei Ling would wait until the apartment quieted down to sort out her finances. She loved the feeling of the paper bills in her hands. She stared at the image of Mao Zedong on the notes; it was always the same portrait of the middle-aged Mao with a heavy-set chin, and a certain fatherly but aloof look in his eyes. He actually reminded her of some of the businessmen who had come into the beauty salon in old Wushan where she had briefly worked. These men had eyes that grabbed. In the presence of men they grabbed power. Around women they grabbed attention and admiration, but always with that standoffish air.

When seated, the men would lay hold of her arm, her thigh, or any convenient spot if they wanted to tell her a funny story, which was never that funny anyway. She would swivel the chair away; they would resist. When they got up to go, they brushed against her breasts, never apologizing, just assuming it was their right, by dint of their status.

One day, the salon owner propositioned her about making more money. "Just hand them a card," he said. It was a plain business card with the bust of a woman, all hair, no clothing. "Girls, at your service. Sexual favors. Reasonable prices."

Mei Ling was shocked. She knew that women prostituted their bodies, and got paid well to do it. But she had learned from her father to stand up for herself, and from her mother she learned to be resourceful. Of course, they were simple peasants, and they spoiled their male child, which she resented. *Dzong nan tsing nu*. The son carries more weight than the daughter. Mei Ling was keenly aware

71

of these injustices, but she had decided she would never put up with a bad situation.

So she declined, acting as if her boss's proposal was not unusual at all. And perhaps it hadn't been. The large posters in the windows of the hair salons all depicted women in sexually suggested poses; the models were foreigners with blue eyes, straw-yellow and earth-brown hair, but their Chinese counterparts were simply the back-room part of the equation. Her boss began to treat her differently, snapping at her over trivial things, and diverting customers to the other women. Two weeks later, Mei Ling quit.

That was almost a year ago, and her new job seemed to be go-ing well. She had seen the sign in front of Tai's noodle shop seeking hired help. Mei Ling had never done waitress work before, but she convinced Tai that she knew how to take care of customers. She made him laugh when she said, "At the hair salon, they paid me to take something away. Now I can actually give something to the cus-tomers for their money." Mei Ling told him she had quit in order to find better prospects in new Wushan.

Mei Ling liked her customers. They were an odd mix; more foreign tourists were showing up, but among the Chinese, some seemed well-to-do and others were dressed shabbily, like poor peas-ants. She thought of the fellow who wanted chilies in his soup. Tonight, she had noticed the sinewy coils of his muscles when his shirt sleeves were rolled up. He was rather handsome, although his linen shirt did not go with those old cotton pants. She wondered if he had been trying to impress her.

She put most of her earnings in a small tin box, and shut the drawer. Two 20-*yuan* notes remained on the table; she wrapped them in several pieces of paper, and wrote a cursory note.

> Dear Pa,
>   I hope your first harvest is a good one. Give my
> best to Ma.
> Your daughter,
> Mei Ling

IN THE LAP OF THE GODS

• • •

WHEN THEIR VILLAGE WAS EVACUATED, IN THE SPRING OF 2002, Mei Ling's parents learned that they would all have to move across the country to Guangdong. Her father resisted, but his pleas with the village chief were met with gloomy refusal. "Ol' Chang, I have no say in the matter. Those are government orders."

"We have lived here for generations. My parents survived the terrible famine; my family made it through the floods in '98. We are rooted here," Mei Ling's father said.

"Well, the government is like the Yangtze; she's stronger than you. All you can do is submit to her. If you refuse to leave, you'll simply be drowned by this last flood. And it'll be a big one."

Ol' Chang grabbed the chief's arm with both hands. "I beg you, can we stay in this area? Guangdong is like a foreign country. We can't understand their dialect. Besides, they're wily people; you can't trust them."

The chief shook his head. "Ol' Chang, I don't have a choice, either. Just make the best of it. You'll have a nice little plot of land. You're lucky. The neighboring village got stuck with shabby land up the mountain."

In spite of her mother's wishes, Mei Ling decided she would find a way to stay in the area. She did not want to remain a peasant's daughter, and marry to become a peasant's wife. She could find work in a nearby city. In old Wushan, there were dozens of beauty salons, mostly on the main street. The posters had caught her eye. How could they not, with their life-sized images of stacked breasts and stacked hairdos.

Mei Ling did not tell her parents why she really quit that job. That the hairstylists were expected to perform other services, selling their bodies. Or that, in the last days of old Wushan's existence, the women she had worked with still sat behind the salon windows. They wore a listless expression, as if they didn't care about going under and taking their seedy patrons with them. In her letters, Mei Ling only told her parents how happy she was to live in the city, even a city that faced imminent destruction.

She managed to squirrel away enough money until she moved to new Wushan with her roommates. They were kind to her, splitting the rent between the two of them when she was looking for another job. Pei's waitress job paid decently, and Lan made good money working at a new hotel in town.

In the new city of Wushan, she found work as a nanny for the child of a professional couple. Mei Ling shuddered whenever she thought about the wife, a chatty woman who sold cell phones. The wife was the jealous type, and although her husband worked long hours at the health clinic, she found every excuse to give Mei Ling grief.

"Mei Ling, you forgot to put two napkins in the lunch bag. My son *must* have two napkins. One won't do. Greasy foods makes greasy hands." The doctor's wife was fastidious in washing her hands, even after touching her own child.

"My darling soiled the bed last night," she would say. "I told you that the sheets must be changed immediately." But Mei Ling could never do anything to please the woman. And what if she had been there, in the middle of the night, tugging frantically at the sheets as the accident was happening? She would have been blamed for giving the boy wet dreams.

The final straw came when the wife accused Mei Ling of lying to her. "You wanted to be alone with my husband," she hissed. "You never told me that my friends had cancelled that lunch date. I waited and waited." In fact, Mei Ling had, but the woman continued to fume, stomping around her son's room in a rage, gathering toy trucks and robots in her arms, hurling them like grenades at Mei Ling. The little boy cowered in the corner, and then ran out of the room.

The woman's temper terrified Mei Ling. But she denied the charges, steeling her nerves as the jealous wife screamed and ranted about bad women. Finally, Mei Ling's patience snapped. She couldn't take it anymore.

"Okay, I quit!" she shouted. Her voice trembled, but she fought back tears. "I quit so I don't have to put up with your unreasonable demands! You find yourself another girl, a spineless girl, to take care of your son. I . . . I have more respect for myself than that."

The wife stared past her, like a crazed woman who had been shot up with morphine. Her shoulders slumped; she became the frightened one. Mei Ling grabbed her coat and fled the house, running, stumbling in her flimsy sandals all the way home.

How dare she . . . how dare she treat me like that, Mei Ling thought. She ruminated about the ways she could seek revenge. She could spread rumors about the woman, or turn her son against her. She could poison her husband. She laughed at the absurdity of that idea. Mei Ling decided she would gain nothing from revenge; it would merely be a salve for her bruised ego.

That day, Mei Ling began to think about power. She would learn to grab power too, but in subtle ways, using her feminine charms so that men wouldn't notice. Coming from peasant stock, she was limited to work that serviced the needs and whims of others—customers, tourists, children. But she didn't want to be someone's kept servant. She vowed she would not put herself in that situation anymore. Never again.

When the woman sent over the last paycheck, perhaps in an attempt to save face, Mei Ling wrapped all the money in toilet paper, and sent it to her folks. They were delighted to get the package, and pleased that their daughter was doing so well in the city.

EARLY IN THE MORNING, LIU DROPPED ROSE OFF AT MRS. Song's and hustled over to the noodle shop. The window shades were already pulled up, and the first customers of the day were arriving. Liu headed straight for the kitchen. Here, the pots clattered as they hit the burners of the coal-burning stove and knife blades screeched against the sharpening stone. Large slabs of pork thudded onto the counter for a second slaughter. His friend Tai was too busy to notice him.

"No, listen to me! When the foreign devils want their meat lean, you pull out those fatty pieces, got it?" Tai was shouting at his cook, Ol' Guo. Liu stood in the doorway against its thin curtain, hesitant to intrude.

"And what do I do with them? Feed them to the alley cats? I can take them home, you know." Ol' Guo sucked on a toothpick, which he often did in the kitchen where he couldn't smoke.

"No, no, no! I paid good money for that. You just mix it in with the fried pork dishes, for the locals."

"Why don't you just buy a leaner cut?"

Tai looked exasperated. "Because that's too expensive!"

Liu was about to turn around when Tai saw him. "My friend, what brings you here so early?" Tai's eyes darted back to the cook. "We're sorting through something. Have a seat and I'll be out soon, okay?"

From the dining area, Liu could hear the cadence of their voices rise and fall, with all the melodrama of a Qing Dynasty soap. He could not help but be amused. The voices did not match the roles. The cook bellowed with royal indignation, while Tai spat out his tirade like a rasping eunuch. Tai was the boss, but he seemed unable to get his way.

The noodle-shop owner came out shortly, wiping the sweat from his brow with a dirty sleeve. "Stubborn old goat. Can't keep up with the times. Maybe I should fire him." Tai grunted. "A new cook would be too expensive, though."

Tai launched further into his restaurant woes. All the while, Liu was growing more anxious to broach the subject of the new waitress. At last, he interrupted Tai and asked, "Your new waitress should make things better. So . . . uh . . . Tai, how'd you find her?"

"Mei Ling? Why, she must have seen my ad in the window. She seemed bright, didn't have experience, but you can teach a pretty young woman anything."

"I . . . just wanted to find out a bit more about her." Liu kicked the wooden leg of the table, then looked up sheepishly at Tai.

A big grin lit up his friend's face, and all traces of frustration from the kitchen wars fell away. "Ol' Liu, you never fail to surprise me. First the baby. Now, it looks like you've finally come to your senses."

"Wait, Tai, not too fast. I just want to know . . . you know . . . if she's attached."

"Don't think so. Hey, I don't pry into my employees' business, but she's given to flirting with the customers. Especially the well-dressed ones."

Tai appeared to be delighted that he could attract such customers. Liu, however, was crestfallen that it was Mei Ling attracting them. "Do you think she's married?"

"Didn't say she was married. She did say she has two roommates, I think."

"Don't say anything to her, okay?"

Tai remained silent, his eyes twinkling until Liu punched him in the arm. "Promise?"

"Okay," Tai relented. "You'll have to tell her yourself."

• • •

WHEN LIU ARRIVED AT MRS. SONG'S APARTMENT, HE COULD HEAR the baby wailing. He hesitated at the door, knowing that Mrs. Song would find fault with him again, and he never had good enough excuses for his fatherly ignorance.

"Mrs. Song, I've returned from—"

"Liu, you must take better care of her! Babies are very delicate creatures. She threw up all the egg custard I fed her." The matronly woman patted the baby on the back, and rocked back and forth on her bulbous feet to soothe her. Rose was suspended in a large carrying cloth strapped around the woman's shoulder and waist, like a small watermelon against Mrs. Song's pear-shaped body.

Liu apologized, but Mrs. Song ranted on. "I fed her almost two hours ago, and next thing you know, it all came back out the same end. So I ground up some *po-chai* pills and put that in some water. She spat it out, too!"

"Well, I do appreciate your watching after her."

A huge wave of a sneeze rippled through Mrs. Song's belly, and the baby rose up like a boat on the swells. "Oh dear! I . . . aaaah CHOO!" She hustled to the kitchen sink, turned sideways and blew out her nose. "My nose is stuffed up like a *jian dui.*"

Liu thought the old woman rather looked like a fried dough puff herself.

Mrs. Song collected herself, wiping her cherry nose with the edge of an apron. "Had the flu, you know. Must be the heat. Hot fire rises up the body."

"Why don't I take her back? You can get some rest."

Mrs. Song puttered over to a chair and untied the carrying cloth. "Oh dear, my knees. All this weight is hard on my old bones, you know." She glared at Liu. "You're young, you wouldn't know. Now listen. Take these *po-chai* pills and grind half a vial into some soymilk. Don't go gallivanting off to the restaurant tonight. A father bird's gotta take care of his babies."

"Yes, Mrs. Song." Liu nodded meekly.

Mrs. Song handed Rose back to Liu. The baby sank her head

against his chest. She felt warm and moist when he touched her forehead.

The old woman rubbed her kneecaps and pounded her thighs as if she were kneading dough. "Now all my life I've been taking care of people. A husband, bless his departed soul, but he was cranky. A son, all grown up now, but he's still my boy. Don't think for a minute that they can make a lot of money and forget they had a mother."

"He's a good son, isn't he?"

"Yes, yes, he sends me money." Mrs. Song sat up and gave Liu a stern look. "Now, Liu, you've lost a lot of family, why don't you take on a wife? Somebody who can take care of the baby. Better than this old mother hen, and certainly better than you."

Liu stared at his feet and remained silent. He stroked the baby's head, and shuffled toward the door. Before departing, he said, "Thank you, Mrs. Song, you've been a big help. Why don't I take care of her until you're better?"

"My dear man, I don't mind caring for the child, really."

"No, that's fine. You deserve a break, being sick and all." Liu did not say that Mrs. Song might keep spreading her germs otherwise. That would offend her.

Another prolonged sneeze sent Mrs. Song reeling back in her chair. She mustered a feeble good-bye, and reminded Liu to give Rose those *po-chai* pills.

Over the next several days, Liu was confined to the apartment with his sick infant. Rose cried almost constantly. As she lost weight, the dimples disappeared from her elbows. He was reduced to feeding her soymilk, but she could not keep that down very well. It never occurred to Liu to seek a doctor; his own family had been too poor, and his village too remote, for access to medical help.

The *po-chai* pills helped a little. But fever had possessed the little soul, and even in her sleep, she seemed to be tormented by demons that turned her stomach and set her cheeks on fire. Liu did not get much rest. He was no longer able to distinguish day from night; only her cries would force him into a brief bout of wakefulness, and he would attend to her needs with bleary-eyed diligence. His own had become neglected. Liu had little energy to shave or bathe, or cook more than the dried noodles and mushrooms he dug out of the cobwebs beneath the kitchen sink. Dressed in the same thread-bare pajamas, Liu shuffled about the tiny apartment, marooned in a lonely struggle against the baby's illness.

There were brief periods of calm when Rose napped in the late morning and afternoon. Liu would slump into the wooden chair and draw in his cigarette in long breaths, listening to the hum of the small refrigerator. Even the television seemed tiresome. Every-one on the shows screamed. Ecstatic contestants screamed on game shows. Distressed widows whined in maudlin soaps. News reporters bellowed into their microphones on noisy streets. Liu had endured enough screaming for the past few days.

In those quiet moments, his mind seized upon a strange lucidity. Despairing thoughts arose, feeding upon his dreary existence. He began wondering again, as he did in her foundling days, if he could really keep her, if the responsibility were not too great for a single man. What if she were seriously ill? Could he save her life, as he had done by the riverbank? Or—and the prospect of her death now gripped him with fear—could this fragile life be snuffed out, after all she'd been through, by the gods of fate?

Two infant girls, swaddled in ragged cloths, lying by the dirt road. The image haunted Liu. Two girls, abandoned once and again, cursed by their gender, at the mercy of strangers. He thought of that fateful day, how they had to pick two babies to surrender. Yet he had been a captive in Fang's hands, and had no choice but to leave those two infants at the doorstep of unknown villagers.

Liu still resented Fang for his dictatorial ways. But perhaps Fang had to take control of the situation, and Liu had really been along for the ride. He did not trust Fang any more or less after that un-fortunate event, but he could at least count on the old man to act in a dire situation.

A week later, the baby began to show signs of recovery. She was sleeping more soundly and crying less. She was able to keep down her food, and the feverish glow had left her cheeks.

Liu grew fidgety in the confines of his apartment, shuffling endlessly between the cradle and kitchen. He threw open the curtains to let in the morning air, before the sun could seize upon the smell of *po-chai* pills and baby vomit. He needed to get out and scavenge again. If he couldn't rely on Mrs. Song to babysit, he'd have to pay someone. But paid help might not be more reliable. Doubt crept in again. Perhaps he should ask Fang if there was a childless couple in Wushan who wanted a baby. A baby girl for someone desperate for a child. No, that's criminal, Liu thought, I cannot turn little Rose over to the old wolf.

Liu visited Mrs. Song in the afternoon, first to see if she was reasonably well, and again to leave Rose in her care for a few hours. He bathed with a small sponge, put on his good shirt, and headed over to Fang's house. Squaring his shoulders, Liu braced himself for another encounter with the old broker.

At length, Fang opened the door and gave Liu a hearty slap on the arms. "Ol' Liu, what a surprise! I thought you might have gone after sunken treasure, fed the fish. Some are carnivorous, you know." The old man's eyes twinkled. His smile was disarming, and Liu felt a little foolish about his militant stance.

"Fang, old man, I've been busy with the baby. I had no idea, of course, how much energy a youngster could take up. And she's been sick the past week."

"Yes, you look a bit worn out. If I didn't know better, I'd blame it on a badgering wife." Fang chuckled.

"No, Fang, no woman around. Listen, I need to get out there again." Liu knew the broker could give him the raw end of the deal, but he had no other prospects.

"What is there to scavenge? The old towns are buried under water. And the next round of flooding won't happen for another three years."

"Well, Fang, you said there'd be more to find after June. There's gotta be more pickings out there."

"If I scattered birdseed to the pigeons, or a wad of paper bills to the thieves, how quickly do you think it would get snatched up?"

"Quit talking in riddles, Fang. I need your help." Liu lit a cigarette and paced up and down Fang's sitting room. After the exhaus-

81

tion and delirium of the past week, he couldn't help betraying his desperation.

"Now, now, we'll find you work, trust me. Have I let you down before?"

Liu glared at the old man and said nothing.

"Look, Liu, I'm not your enemy. If you strike gold, why, I'll help you get market value for the goods." Fang waved his pipe in an arc. "Besides, I know you've got an extra mouth to feed. Nothing like fatherhood to turn a man into a real hunter."

•   •   •

FANG SHOOK HIS HEAD AS HE WATCHED LIU'S LANKY FORM disappear down the street. How women make fools of men, he thought. There must be a woman in the picture. Or if there wasn't, perhaps the scavenger was indeed looking for nice treasure, the kind that one could curl up with at night.

Taking out a roll of documents, Fang pored over the county map and schedule for some time, his pipe dangling meditatively from his lips. He had told Liu the truth. The towns and villages along the Yangtze had been submerged, and every human, land animal, and insect in the river's path had been forced to higher ground. It would be risky to rummage through the villages targeted for the next flooding. No farmer would be willing to abandon his home and surrender the fruits of his labor before it was time.

Fang turned his attention to other matters. A contractor had solicited his help in obtaining the permits for a new building in town. He was new to the region and wanted to find out which officials could help grease the wheels. Fang relished these kinds of cases, which were more profitable than small-time deals like baby trading. Whenever he guided a big project through the bureaucracy, he would make an offering at the altar to his ancestors. Fang believed that his father continued to exert a powerful influence on his affairs, even though he had long departed from this world. On the anniversary of his father's death, he would set out bowls of rice, dishes with steaming pork, string beans, and tofu laden with Sichuan spices. He would place crisp paper bills by his father's rice bowl.

It was an unusual gesture, but Fang felt that he was indebted to his father, who had given him a shrewd head for business and a keen sense of judgment about people's desires and vulnerabilities.

Fang kept thinking about Liu's situation. It puzzled him why he would be concerned at all, since Liu's forays had generated sporadic profits. "I've dealt with lots of pigheaded bastards before," Fang said to himself. Was it the lack of pretense, the country bumpkin manners that amused him? No, the old broker felt mostly scorn and derision for his kind. Perhaps something about Liu reminded Fang of his younger self, but the old man couldn't figure out what it was.

By the time Liu returned the next day, Fang had thought of an enterprise to cure the man's cabin fever.

"There is a small city upriver called Fengdu, past Wanzhou where you and I caught a boat, and it may be worth exploring." Fang sat with his arms crossed, holding his pipe with the ease of a *da lao ban*. He stared intently at Liu. "The residents are still being moved out. Find the buildings that have a bit of life in them. Who knows, you might even come across a little stash of opium or heroin. Now that's out of my league, you know."

Liu looked concerned. "It sounds kind of risky."

"My friend, most of the town is dead as an opium den. The enterprising young folk have moved across the river. I think it's pretty much the old geezers who can't afford to move. Just steer clear of the dark alleyways, and you'll be fine." Fang exhaled, sending forth a magnificent swirl of smoke.

"Now, Fang, it's hard to know what's left in a ghost town, but if I come across some valuables, I want to be part of the bargaining, okay?"

"Ol' Liu, you're young and already so cynical. My kind of man." Fang chuckled. "I took you on that trip to the orphanage, remember?"

"Ol' Fang, that was a fiasco. My conscience still haunts me about those two infant girls." Liu leaned forward. "Tell me, what did you do with the infant boy?"

Fang's eyes were placid, unmoving. "Why, I found a foreign doctor who sewed up his lip. They have such pity on us Chinese, you know." The broker grunted. "Now the boy is under orphanage care, if he isn't already snatched up by some eager parents."

"I'm sure you got a little reward for your good deeds. I just don't want to be shortchanged, Fang. Okay?"

"Trust me, I'm an honorable man. My father was an upright businessman, and I am his first born, Fang Shuping. Fang as in *da fang,* generous."

11

IN MATTERS OF BUSINESS, TAI COULD BE AN ENTERPRISING MAN in spite of his stinginess, which was somewhat of an indelible stamp on his personality. But he was not a big risk taker in most affairs, and his advice for Liu was one of caution.

"Go into a crumbling old town, Liu? I think you'll catch a hundred sewer rats before you find a single ounce of gold."

It surprised Tai that Liu would take such a risk, as the younger man had hinted at the sobering losses of the past two years: a wife and child, a real home, and reliable work. Yet his friend had a tough spirit, with a touch of stubbornness. Tai figured there was something besides boredom driving the scavenger toward this new venture.

"Tai, I've been stuck with a sick, bawling baby for a week. I need to do something. I'm used to hard work, you know. No man can stand being cooped up like that."

Liu said he was running out of money, but Tai was still convinced that a woman was at the bottom of this. Perhaps Liu was sexually frustrated. Tai himself was, and his energies merely percolated into his noodle shop, now a thriving business and one of the more popular places in town with locals and tourists alike. Liu had inquired about his new waitress. That was a sure sign. Mei Ling was awakening pent-up desires in the younger man.

Tai decided that it was his duty as a friend to help Liu fulfill those desires. Besides building up his business, Tai began strategizing ways to maximize contact between Liu and Mei Ling. But how?

Liu was too stubborn to take any hints from Tai about inviting her out on a date. And the restaurateur certainly didn't want her to spend her work hours lingering at his table; no, that was not good for his business.

One afternoon, while chopping a batch of cabbages, Tai hit upon a solution. He had his eye on a vacant storefront for lease on Wushan's main street, which would take his business to a new level. He could even secure the adjacent space and turn it into a banquet room. The shop owner there sold hardware and bathroom fixtures, but his business had slowed down after the town's resettlement was completed. Tai figured he could hire a contractor and put Liu on the payroll. Mei Ling would be given extra duties to do the interior decorating. Perhaps she could also tend to the workers' meals, which he would provide to save some money on salaries. It was a brilliant plan.

• • •

A FEW NIGHTS LATER, WHEN LIU RETURNED TO THE NOODLE SHOP, Tai hobbled over to his table with a funny spring in his step. "Liu, I want you to work for me," he declared, explaining the grand project.

Liu took a deep breath. "That's good news. Tai, you don't know how I've been longing to do something with my hands besides changing diapers and mashing carrots. I try to distract myself with television, but that only makes me more antsy."

The baby's recent bout of illness had tested his patience as an adoptive father. Liu had little energy to notice the new sounds she uttered, the way her eyes tracked his movements, how her apple-shaped face mirrored his moods. In the wake of that exhausting week, even her dimpled smiles could not cheer him up.

Liu barely heard his friend's ranting about the cost of hiring five men. But his ears perked up when Tai said, "Just as important for the new restaurant is a pleasing interior. It'll require a woman's touch. I got ideas from another restaurant on Guangdong Street— put up some wallpaper, wood panels, auspicious paintings and such. Oh, and a tank of tropical fish at the entrance."

Liu caught on to his friend's excitement. "Great, when do we start?"

"Next week, my friend." Tai grasped his hands. "Yes, I can use a good pair of hands like yours. And a good pair of hands makes a good catch."

•   •   •

AT THE END OF HIS FIRST DAY OF WORK, LIU WAS GRATEFUL FOR the chance to sit down and eat. The small crew was provided with a makeshift table of plywood on stacked bricks, and a few crates to sit on. Liu did not mind the modest accommodations; his bowl of beef noodle soup went down well amidst the dust and chaos of construction.

Mei Ling appeared at four o'clock every afternoon with a cart of food. She served the four men graciously, but did not pay special attention to Liu. Tai also made a point of visiting the construction site every day, making the trek uphill from the noodle shop when business was slow. One afternoon, he told Liu that he needed his help with the interior decorating.

Liu was puzzled. "What do I know about flower prints and carpets?"

"It's yin and yang, my friend," Tai replied. "A woman provides a warm touch; a man balances it out, offers a cool eye. After all, I won't be hosting weddings and baby celebrations all the time. I expect plenty of businessmen to use the banquet room."

When Liu realized that Mei Ling was the woman for the project, a wild pulse surged through his body. He could not help but feel drawn to her. The waitress's coy smile radiated out to the beauty mark on her cheek. She moved swanlike, as if gliding through water, and in her wake the stern angles of the old hardware store softened. When she served the men, they slid their crates back respectfully, but he could see that they were all caught in the ripple of her feminine charms. In that barren space of concrete and mortar, her arrival was the highlight of his workday.

And yet, joy was ephemeral, running away like a shy child as soon as he noticed it. Guilt was his reliable ally. What would Fei Fei say from her watery grave? "Liu, you have flown away from me." Yes, it was true that she was the one to leave. She had flown into the heavens, but his grief had kept her tethered to earth on a long, taut string. Liu felt it most keenly in the dark hours when he was alone with the sleeping baby.

In the light of day, however, he could walk away and forget the fear that trailed him like restless spirits, without a sound. He relished waking up at the light of dawn, and looked forward to his new project, although he felt some trepidation about working with the waitress.

For her new assignment, Mei Ling began coming over to the construction site in the early afternoon. One day, as they huddled over a book of wallpaper samples, he imagined his hands gliding across her skin, finding their way to her shoulders, her hair, her full, buoyant lips. Those desires were naughty, even defiant, but Liu did not care in that moment.

While he never did carry out those fantasies, Liu found as the days passed that he felt surprisingly at ease around Mei Ling.

On a sunny afternoon, Tai sent them to a store that carried lighting fixtures. Liu had never seen such a galaxy of lights, floor lamps casting golden warm rays, track lighting in orderly constellations, spotlights that shone like moonbeams. They headed toward the back of one aisle, where elegant wall sconces were displayed.

"Liu, what would you do if you had all the money in the world?" Mei Ling asked.

"I've never thought about that. I guess I'm happy enough to have a roof over my head." Liu pondered for a moment. "Perhaps I'd want a grand old house with a courtyard, filled with fruits and an old magnolia tree. There were homes like that in Daxi, where I grew up."

"Did you live in one?"

"No, the best we had was a three-room house that Pa built after the floods destroyed the old one. But I left home soon after that, a year or two later."

"I grew up in a village not far from here," said Mei Ling. "I always wanted to get out, too. My father didn't let me, though." She ran her fingers down the neck of a table lamp inlaid with cloisonné.

"Why?" Liu asked, somewhat distracted by her movements.

"I was the firstborn, and when my brother came along, the penalties for a second child increased. My father decided I should pay those dues by working on the land—as if it was my fault for being born." Mei Ling flashed a look of indignation. "Even when I reached a marriageable age, he wouldn't let me go."

Liu stared at her smooth porcelain features, wondering how old she was. "What happened to the suitors?"

"Well, my father scared them away. He said I was strong willed, that I had no homemaking skills, and couldn't tell a teakettle from a crowing cock. My mother was offended, of course. And it wasn't true, except for the strong-willed part."

"So how long did they keep you at home?"

"Until last year, when I was twenty-three. Our village was moved to Guangdong province. I didn't want to go, so I found a way to move to the city. My parents are having a hard time there, though. They received a plot of land half the size of what we had before. And the neighbors, they treat them like refugees from another land."

"It's good you found your way here. Tai is very glad to have you." Liu was seized by an impulse to flatter her, but could only think of his friend's words. "He said you have a woman's touch."

Mei Ling turned to Liu with a sweet smile. "Yes, I know just how to spice up a bowl of beef noodle soup, don't I?"

Liu clutched his throat. He fell to his knees, hacking as if seized by an uncontrollable cough. The bright lights bore down upon him. Sweat trickled down his temple, and a tickle in his throat almost convinced him the act was real. Mei Ling went along with the ruse, patting his back vigorously with both hands. She uttered exclamations of concern, and when she could no longer keep a straight face, she broke into hysterical giggles.

Liu straightened up, and Mei Ling's hands seemed to linger a moment before falling away. "Can you tell a boastful man from a whistling kettle?"

"No." Mei Ling wrinkled her nose. "But I'll take the crowing cock any day."

By this time, Liu's theatrics had attracted attention from the store clerks. The two hurried through their selection and placed an order. As they walked back to Tai's restaurant, Liu asked Mei Ling what she would do if money were no object.

Without hesitation, Mei Ling replied, "Why, I would be a singer. Not in classical operas, like some dressed-up peacock. I'd be a pop music star, and sing to packed audiences in Hong Kong or Shanghai."

"Do you sing now?"

"Yes, when I go to church. My mother began taking me to Mass several years ago, when I was old enough to understand. She was baptized as a little girl. My grandfather became Catholic, you see, when he lost his wife, my Po Po." Mei Ling's voice trailed off.

Liu remained silent. He thought of Fei Fei, and for the first time, he did not get choked up with despair, but simply felt a rustle of sadness in the space he shared with Mei Ling.

The two stopped to sit on a bench in a quiet square. "Po Po lived through the terrible famine. My grandfather worked all day in the village furnace, stoking the fires to melt cooking pots and plows into steel. Like everyone else, he had to leave the harvests untended. Po Po had three children to feed, and when she went to beg for rice from a merchant in the neighboring town, she . . . she was taken advantage of."

Mei Ling's voice became strained, as if these were her own memories. "So Po Po had an illegitimate son by this man," Mei Ling continued, almost in a whisper. "My grandfather never knew. And when the little boy became gravely ill, Po Po went to the merchant to ask for help, to get some modern medicines for their son. He turned her away, saying, 'That is not my child. And if you insist on sullying my name, I will send bandits after your family.' So Po Po left. Days later, she threw herself in the river."

Mei Ling began to sob, her chest heaving softly as she tried to keep from attracting attention. Liu did not know what to say. He often heard that women were emotional creatures, but he did not recall ever seeing Fei Fei so dispirited. He fished out a soiled hand-kerchief from work, which Mei Ling accepted.

"My grandfather mourned for all of forty-nine days, and as soon as his duty was done, he married Po Po's younger sister. She knew what had happened to Po Po, but never dared to tell him. The little boy soon died, and Po Po's sister bore a son, which was a great joy and relief to my grandfather. After all, he had Po Po's three girls in tow, and nobody to carry on his name."

Liu put a tentative hand on her shoulder. He was struck by the suffering that Mei Ling's grandmother had endured. Those crude comments he used to hear, casually uttered by the coal porters as women passed by, now seemed not only thoughtless, but cruel. A spike of anger arose. He leaned closer.

"Po Po's sister, of course, treated her own son like a little prince. But my mother and the other stepchildren were girls, so they were doubly cursed. My mother married as soon as she turned seventeen. She had a crush on the parish priest, a young foreign man. When she got older she dreamed that a wealthy suitor would sweep her off her feet. But she married my father, a poor peasant from a nearby village."

When Mei Ling finished her story, she dabbed the last traces of her tears with the handkerchief, then returned it to Liu. "Thank you. I . . . I don't know what came over me. I'm sorry I babbled on. We should be getting back."

●   ●   ●

IN THE FOLLOWING WEEKS, LIU AND MEI LING SPENT MORE time together, finding new projects to work on, from designing the entrance décor to picking linens and plates for festive occasions. Mei Ling persuaded Tai that these details were quite important, es-pecially if a couple was getting married or a businessman was host-ing foreign guests. Tai relented, but as the expenses grew, he insisted on wrapping up the work so that he could open his new restaurant.

At last, Liu invited Mei Ling to an outdoor concert in the town square, featuring singers and dancers from a traveling troupe. Mei Ling declined, as her Sundays were filled with church activities. She invited him to join her instead.

Liu had little interest in exotic religions, although he remembered Fei Fei's encounters with the Catholic priest she had befriended as a child. He agreed to go; it was a chance to spend time with Mei Ling outside of work.

• • •

THE FOLLOWING SUNDAY, LIU SHOWED UP AT SEVEN IN THE morning outside the Catholic Church in Wushan. Grander than anything he had seen, the edifice was solid white, as if carved from one immense stone. The church bells chimed in a mellifluous tone like the chanting of monks, and Liu bowed his head instinctively.

"This is a nice place," he said, as he joined Mei Ling inside.

"Yes, it's like a glimpse of heaven," Mei Ling replied. "We're fortunate to have this new church, after the old one got destroyed."

The interior of the church was otherworldly. Every surface glowed with light, the smooth wooden pews, the brilliant panels of stained glass, even the backs of the elderly women kneeling in prayer. A long table at the altar was adorned with fine silverware. Behind it was a life-sized figure of a man suspended on a huge crossbeam of wood.

"Who is that?" Liu whispered to Mei Ling, as she led him down the aisle into one of the pews.

"Why, that is the living Christ. He is the son of Mary and the savior of mankind."

"Where does he live? And what are those things in his feet?" Something about the statue fascinated him: the gaunt Western face, the beads of blood frozen on its temple, the scanty loincloth.

"Well, Jesus Christ lives in our hearts, if we accept him into our lives. He died on the cross, you see, to atone for our sins," Mei Ling said solemnly.

Liu was confounded by her declaration. The statue clearly depicted a human, and how could a dead man also be alive, no matter how great he was? And how had she accepted him into her heart? Perhaps she loved this Jesus. Liu suppressed a tinge of jealousy, and decided he should not ask any more questions.

The priest soon emerged in a magnificent robe. The sleeves undulated in great waves whenever he raised his arms in prayer. The readings and incantations were delivered in Chinese, but Liu could barely understand anything the priest said. The language was elevated, the stories mythical yet different from any of the legends that Liu had grown up with.

At length, Mei Ling whispered to Liu, "Now Father Chong is giving a sermon about how we should live our lives."

Closing the leather-bound tome, Father Chong raised his voice from its steady drone. He delivered a bellowing sermon, full-throated and sincere. His eyes seemed to pierce into the soul of every member of the congregation. He wagged his fingers as if lecturing children, although many in the pews looked like they could be his mother. When he reached an epiphany, the spirited priest pounded his fists on the table, and a tinkle of silverware echoed through the church.

During the sermon, Liu managed to piece together the story about a woman named Mary, with a long last name. She had committed adultery, the priest said, but Jesus forgave her and allowed her to follow him.

What a weak man, Liu thought. I would never forgive a woman for betraying me.

"We are sinners, all of us. And only by giving our lives to Christ will we be saved!" Father Chong stared grimly at his congregation. A bird that had flown in during the sermon banged its wings against the stained glass, but not a human soul stirred.

Liu, meanwhile, was getting uncomfortable sitting in the hard wooden pew. Who was this Jesus Christ, he wondered. If he was a martyr, it was only wishful thinking that the man was still alive. Liu decided he did not like the hollering priest, who, beneath his finery, reminded him somehow of his father. Liu figured that what he really wanted was money from the parishioners. Maybe this priest was as sly as Ol' Fang. As for Jesus, Liu wondered what kind of claim he laid on Mei Ling's heart.

When the singing began, Liu glanced over at his companion. Mei Ling's eyes were shut and a rapturous look set her cheeks aglow.

Her voice floated as clear as silver bells as she sang:

> Christ the Lord is risen today
> Ah–ah–ah–ah–al–leluia!
> Sons of men and angels say
> Ah–ah–ah–ah–al–leluia!

Mei Ling swayed from side to side, her dress rustling lightly against Liu, her entire body, as it seemed, consumed by passionate devotion. And as enchanted as she was with the service, the heavenly music, this martyr on the cross, so Liu found himself under her spell. Her devotion uplifted him; her rapture freed some frozen part of his soul. Her voice, joined with the ethereal harmonies of the organ, rose into a crescendo. "Ah–ah–ah–ah–al–le–lui–AH!"

The waves of music washed over Liu, as if he stood beneath a glorious waterfall sent from the heavens. And when the singing subsided into contemplative silence, Liu glanced at Mei Ling, who smiled at him with her quivering lips and clear, moist eyes. She gave his hand a gentle squeeze.

Liu left the service brimming with energy. He could feel it in his bones, that youthful vigor from his twenties. The strain of his sorrows, the unfulfilled hopes that turned into despair, these now retreated to the shadows. Liu did not attribute this to Christ, the priest, or his church and congregation. It had been Mei Ling; she was his angel of mercy.

12

LIU'S CEREMONIOUS DATE WITH MEI LING HAD ENDED ALL too soon. He had declined to stay for a special celebration after the Mass. But he did so with a twinge of regret, and bade her an awkward farewell by the entrance.

"Come, little monkey." He scooped up Rose in his arms. "Let's take a walk."

She clung to him with her little fingers, her rump firmly seated in his elbow. Liu had not ventured out with her since their trip to the town square. Now he was seized by a primal urge for physical closeness, to do what fathers were supposed to do, to hold one's offspring in one arm, even if there was no one else in the other.

Liu thought of bringing Rose by the church, where Mei Ling was likely cavorting and laughing with her fellow parishioners. But he also imagined them frowning on his presence. And the baby—what questions would they ask of a single man bearing a baby? Worst of all, he feared what Mei Ling would think. This savior Christ, he had learned, was conceived by a virgin, and had no earthly father. Yet in no way could Liu explain his single fatherhood as a divine act.

As they passed by a mother toting her young child along, Rose reached out to grab the embroidered flowers on the woman's dress. He batted her hand away, and she squealed in protest. Little Rose couldn't really be an incarnation of Fei Fei, he decided. The infant girl was water. She was salvaged from the Yangtze's banks, with a temperament as fierce as the swollen river's currents. She knew her likes and dislikes. She consumed egg custard and sweetened rice porridge with gusto, crying for more even when her bird-sized stomach had reached its limit. Mrs. Song tried to cajole her into eating cauliflower and peas, but little Rose refused. The twice-cooked mush would be flung back unceremoniously, landing on the old woman's nose and cheeks, or once, on her glasses.

It was a warm midsummer's day, filled with the fragrance of fresh oranges and baked tofu from vendors' carts. The colorfully dressed woman reminded Liu of Fei Fei. It surprised him that he would think of her, but he was in a good mood, and the thoughts appeared like diaphanous clouds.

Fei Fei would always be air. She had an insatiable curiosity and could rarely sit still. Perhaps that was her undoing, Liu thought. In old Fengjie, he relished the quiet Sunday afternoons in the teahouse where the men played mahjong. It was a respite from the commotion of the street vendors, the din of shoppers haggling over the price of pomelos and plastic shoes. There was a turtle-like quality to Liu's movements at those times, during the one day of the week when he wasn't hauling coal. He always thought that if he could carry on at a languorous pace all his days, he would age gracefully like that serene, bronze-faced Buddha in the ancient temple.

Fei Fei, however, had a restlessness that pregnancy only seemed to intensify. In the early months, she could still fly about from one errand to the other, gathering parcels of smoked ham and vegetables from the outdoor market to her growing bosom. In the later months, she developed a strange appetite for preserved cabbage and fried pork rinds, the combination of which would only turn her stomach. Still, Fei Fei struggled to get out of bed, and no matter how much her belly throbbed or her back ached, she insisted on taking a stroll to the Buddhist temple or the town square. She liked to sit beside the old men with their caged birds, watching the crowds playing badminton or practicing tai chi.

In the temple, she would get down on her knees, wobbly with weight and expectation. She would light sticks of incense, and pray for safe delivery of her child. She asked for the benevolent protection of her ancestors. In her father's lineage of boatmen, many had given their lives to the Yangtze. And lastly, Fei Fei asked for guidance, so that she could be a better wife to Liu, reining in her wanderlust to settle down to the duties of motherhood.

When Fei Fei's grandmother, her Po Po, died at the ripe age of 81, her mother set up an altar in the house, with the old woman's photograph on a paper lotus. For forty-nine days, the altar was resplendent with flowers and incense, and every day her mother set out a feast of her favorite foods: spicy tofu, roast duck, beef tripe, and rice wine. Having lived into her eighth decade, she was commemorated at the funeral with red posters instead of white, red as a symbol of happiness that she had crossed the hurdles of human suffering and lived such a long life.

Fei Fei did not get to live such a long life. White was the color of the posters at her funeral, white for death, an untimely one at that. Fei Fei's mother wailed vociferously; it was not just a matter of tradition but the loss of a daughter so soon on the heels of her own mother. Liu stood quietly beside his in-laws, as still as the eye of a terrible storm, with a calm that belied his shattered heart. The chanting of the monks droned on as the women sobbed; the fierce and overpowering incense swirled around him. All seemed meaningless to Liu.

Small paper notes, lined with gold foil, were burnt to provide money for the deceased in the afterlife. Liu had resisted such customs as a child. Now he felt as if his own soul had been consumed in the fire. Yet nothing came of it; his grief offered no transcendent gift to provide comfort for Fei Fei's soul. And it did not seem to appease the gods of heaven and earth.

All that remained of Fei Fei were charred ashes. The cremation ovens had ground her bones and flesh and organs into a handful of dust. Black, too, was death. The color of mourning garb, the dark circles under her mother's eyes, Fei Fei's ashes at the bottom of a lacquered container.

And when her ashes were scattered to the Yangtze, Liu imagined the entire river turning black, and all the creatures of the deep swimming amidst the remains of Fei Fei's body. As the ashes flew into the wind, to be devoured in the choppy waves, Liu felt his lungs fill with blackness and cloying incense.

Almost two years had passed since Fei Fei's ashes were scattered to the Yangtze. Liu had loved her deeply, but he could not hold her soul captive, and he realized that now more than ever.

• • •

MEI LING BIT HER NEWLY POLISHED NAILS, WISHING THE PHONE would slip through her hands like a coal brick too hot to touch. "No, Father, I cannot visit you at this time. Work is keeping me busy, especially with Tai's new restaurant opening soon."

"Well, when can you come?" insisted the voice at the other end. It was a gruff voice, an authoritative one that turned any question into a statement.

"I don't know. I'll send you more money, okay? Just . . . just give me some time for things to settle down, alright?"

Mei Ling's relationship with her father had long been tempestuous, like a thunderstorm visiting the same stretch of land every growing season. Chang Duoming was outspoken and fierce, exacting as the blade of a sickle. Mei Ling thought that she had paid off her debt, having been born a girl and incurring those fines for a second child. But she would never hear the end of his diatribes. What a useless task it was to raise a girl. Girls got married off, and the hard work of raising one was like planting a field of wheat, only to have a thief show up in the night and abscond with the harvest. No, Chang insisted that his daughter be more loyal than that, even though she was so far away. Mei Ling could not understand why her father wasn't content with a bit more financial support. Why did he want her to visit? They could rarely exchange a few civil words before they got into the usual arguments.

Mei Ling insisted on speaking with her mother. She had nothing more to say to Father, and besides, it was an expensive call. She had borrowed her roommate's cell phone; her parents were using a public phone in the nearby township's offices, a three-mile walk from their home. Yet her father had no qualms about raising his voice in public.

"Okay, here's your ungrateful daughter!" he yelled, passing the phone to her mother.

"Ma! Why can't Pa leave me alone? Why does he still try to control my life?"

"No, dear. He wants the best for you. There is a young man, you see, who comes from a respectable family in the village. He wants you to meet this fellow. He's a neighbor of ours." Chen Weijin's tone was measured; it was not the tone of a mother, but of an obedient wife.

"What?" Mei Ling screamed. "First he refuses to let me get married, and now that I'm finally on my own, he still wants to keep me on a leash. I don't want to be tied to him forever. No, Ma, I wish you were close by, but you know I can't stand Pa's temper."

"Well, Mei Ling, you are like your father. I know it's hard to see that," her mother said quietly. A pause, and then Chen Weijin lowered her voice. "Your father just stepped outside. Of course, I don't exactly agree with your father, but he means well. This man he wants you to marry has four *mu* of good land. He thinks we might be more welcomed in the village with a Cantonese son-in-law."

Mei Ling rolled her eyes. "Well, Pa had better make the deal without me, because I don't want to marry someone whom I can't even talk to. Their dialect sounds like a cock fight, and I don't need more fighting, with Father or anyone."

"My daughter, I wish for you a wealthy husband, who could provide for you. You know that. I lost my chance many years ago."

Mei Ling knew that her mother had once fallen in love with a man ten years her senior. The young Chen Weijin dared not even voice her desires to her father. She was the youngest of the three sisters. "Too many hens in the chicken coop," her father would say. The stepbrother born after her was the spoiled, brazen cock. When her stepmother arranged for her to marry Mei Ling's father, she consented, eager only to get away from that house of invisible demons. When she turned her back on her maiden household, her *niang jia*, Chen Weijin could at last make peace with her mother's death. "Your Po Po could never free herself from her past, but I had to," she would say.

Mei Ling had inherited her father's temper, but she possessed her mother's shrewdness. She understood that her mother had made the practical decision, although Chen Weijin had revealed her regret, more than once, that she hadn't married the man she loved. Mei Ling felt the weight of her mother's secret. It perplexed her that she, too, was expected to put her own wishes aside. She promised her mother again that she would visit them, just not for the reasons her father desired.

•   •   •

AFTER THE OPENING OF TAI'S NEW RESTAURANT, LIU WAS ONCE again out of a job. He thought about working for his friend as a waiter, but the idea of catering to a roomful of demanding diners and tourists all day long turned his stomach.

For two days, he paced up and down the small apartment while the baby was napping. He debated whether he should he go to Fengdu after all. Liu lived quite frugally, and two months of work at Tai's allowed him to coast for a little while. But there were new prospects on the horizon, future dates with Mei Ling, and down the line, school fees, a bigger apartment for their family. Their family. Liu sucked on his cigarette, staring at little Rose in her crib.

What if I proposed to Mei Ling? he wondered. Would she say yes?

Liu resumed his pacing, his footfalls drumming a quiet, urgent call to action. But what if she said no? Could the gods of fate humor him just once—just this time—and allow him to realize his desire for a real family?

There was only one way to find out. Liu asked Mrs. Song to recommend a good fortuneteller, and the next day he set out to visit this woman, known only as Seh Yen, Snake Eyes.

The fortuneteller indeed had eyes like a viper. Her tongue slithered out between cracked lips when she greeted him. She had a pudgy face, and her skin was dark as a roasted pheasant. Mrs. Song said she came from the Tujia tribe, one of the minority groups in the area.

"Come in." Seh Yen gestured to Liu impatiently. Incense swirled about the dimly lit room, furnished with two chairs and a rickety table on an uneven cement floor. Liu lingered in the doorway, seized by a desire to turn and scamper away from her serpent gaze. But it was really that tongue that seemed to be sensing him, uncovering his future.

"You have decisions to make." Seh Yen fixated on Liu's forehead. "Come sit down, young man, and we'll see what fate has in store for you." The fortuneteller had a large lump in back of her neck, as if she had just devoured a mouse meal. Liu noticed with a start that the corners of the room were infested with rodent droppings.

"I . . . want to know if I should get married." There. He had blurted out the question that bothered him most.

The fortuneteller took Liu's right hand and ran her fingernail down the side of his palm. "You have been married before."

"Yes, my wife passed away," Liu said. "But you probably know that."

"No, I don't know everything," she hissed, leaning close to Liu. "But you hold the answers to what is possible in your life. It's in your hands, your face."

Seh Yen traced the branching lines on his palm. The life line curved in a long, steady arc toward the veins in his wrist. The love line and career line meandered, like broken tributaries.

"Isn't it all up to fate?" Liu frowned. "That's how I got where I am." After all, he didn't have any choice in the matter when Fei Fei died.

"Yes, but you can change your fate, too. You have some choice, young man." Seh Yen sat back and folded her hands across her thick bosom.

What kind of fortuneteller was she? Liu had come for answers, not platitudes. "The gods will frown on me if I do the wrong thing. Tell me, you're the fortuneteller, what am I supposed to do? I have no family, no job. All I have is a baby."

"Yes." The serpent woman's eyes flickered. "She is not yours. And you will have to choose whether you will keep her."

Liu was startled by the fortuneteller's comment. He had not come to resolve any lingering doubts about Rose.

"A woman has come into your life. And you will have to choose. . . ." Seh Yen's chair groaned; her ancient hips creaked and a sickly, sweet aroma wafted up, mingling with the sandalwood incense. Liu wrinkled his nose, distracted by the woman as she scratched her lively rump. When he registered what she said, he leapt to his feet.

"So I will get married?"

"Only when you are forced from your home will the wish be realized. But first, you must go sweep your wife's grave."

"But her ashes . . . they were scattered in the river." Liu began to doubt the fortuneteller's powers.

"I stand by what I said. You must pay homage to the departed. She shall not be neglected."

"Or else?"

"Or else you will lose everything you have hoped for," said Seh Yen. "Just remember, you have choice, but life and death are in the lap of the gods. Do not displease them."

13

ON THE FERRY TO FENGDU, LIU STRUCK UP CONVERSATION WITH a fellow who boarded in the new town of Fengjie. Wang Ma had a beaked nose and a pencil-thin neck, like a vulture. In spite of this, his demeanor was pleasant, and his voice soft and unassuming. The fellow said he had once been a coal porter, among the numerous odd jobs he'd taken on after moving to the city.

Wang Ma chewed on a toothpick in his mouth, and shook his head. "Yeah, times have changed. All I've got are this pair of hands." He stuck out his palms, calloused and weathered like broken-in saddles. "But now I need something up here if I want to get ahead." The man rapped his temple with his knuckles.

"What kind of work are you looking for? I'm caught in the same bind, you know. The old jobs are gone."

"Well, I'm going through this training program at night to be an electrician. It's not easy. Guess I'm not as sharp as I used to be. Why, the other day, I got the red wire mixed up with the black wire, and—zap—my body was sizzling like a fish in the frying pan." Wang Ma shuddered. "But if I don't finish it out and get a good job, the old woman is going to stick me on the griddle, too."

Liu perked up at the prospect of getting steady work. But Wang Ma said that the instructions were not always easy to read. Liu figured his chances were slim, as he had dropped out of school in the fourth grade. "I guess all I'm good for is hard labor, pulling heavy loads and such." He did not mention scavenging.

"Well, I was a farmer once upon a time. But things aren't what they used to be. I could barely feed the wife and kids. Every year the harvests got leaner. Poor soil, my neighbor told me. All the good topsoil's washed away."

Liu imagined Wang Ma's children, beak-nosed like their father, their hungry mouths agape and unfed. "You're right, it's a hard life. It's a wonder anyone is living off the land."

"Yeah, considering the good land is under the Yangtze now. Why, we must be floating over someone's old home right now, and their crop of sweet potatoes is stewing in the Yangtze. And it's not just the dam. See those buildings in the distance? That used to be the best land for growing oranges. Big ones, big as a woman's breasts." Wang Ma's eyes gleamed.

The two looked out the porthole, where the Yangtze licked at the loamy shores past Wanzhou. The cityscape loomed gray and heavy in the early autumn light.

"Sometimes I miss the countryside." Liu's gaze fell on the horizon. "I can still remember, like it was yesterday, when I was wading in a rice paddy, catching frogs. Big blubbery things. You grab 'em by the hind legs, and they wriggle like fiends, croaking their frog curses. Once, I stuck a frog on my brother's side of the *kang,* under the blankets. Tied it by the legs so it couldn't get out. When my brother climbed in, you should have seen him. He shot right out of bed like a startled rabbit, thumping his legs. He yelped and pissed in his pants and pointed fingers at me. I got a whipping, but it was worth it."

Liu was surprised how he comfortable he felt talking to Wang Ma, in spite of his gaunt, bird-of-prey features.

"Sounds like you didn't get along with your brother."

"That's putting it mildly. He got me back, of course. I had to clean the pigsty, a job I absolutely hated, and he stuck some gooseberry brambles right under the dirt. He got me good. Those damn thorns dug right into my skin, and I jumped up yelling at the top of my lungs. I backed up into more brambles, and there I was, stomping about like a mad porcupine. The mother pig was suckling her babies. She was so startled she got up, and all those piglets dangled

off her like fat peaches. I don't know who looked sillier that day—
me or the pig."

"Don't know, but you'd make a good electrician," said Wang Ma.
"Good startle reflexes."

"I don't think so." Liu's thoughts returned to his present circumstances. "I don't have the brains to do what you're getting trained
for. Maybe I can be a professional prankster."

"Sure," Wang Ma chuckled. "I know some folks who are a thorn
in the side, and I'd be obliged to return the favor."

•　　•　　•

IN THE MORNING, LIU AWOKE TO THE FIRST RAYS OF LIGHT THAT
streamed through the porthole in diffuse bands of silver and gold.
The light was translucent and ghostly; its blades were solid enough
to cut through darkness, yet ethereal enough to reveal the movements of hulking ships and sleepy passengers, wading ducks and
geese, human figures on the distant shore, wandering like spirits in
and out of the shadows.

Taking the slow boat to Fengdu gave him a chance to think. He
wondered how he would pay homage to Fei Fei, but he needed to
heed the fortuneteller's words. Sweeping the gravesite seemed an
impossible task when her bones were no longer bones but ash, and
her grave was wide as the ocean into which the Yangtze flowed.

As the ferry drew close to shore, Liu caught sight of the deci-
mated old town on the opposite bank. Fengdu was the cross-
roads for the deceased, where their lots were cast for the next
life, where the living would come to curry favor before it was
too late. Fang had told him that only Mt. Mingshan, where the
temples and grotesque statues stood, would survive the next
round of flooding. Liu wondered if the legends were indeed
true, if Fei Fei's spirit had made safe passage through the
netherworld.

"Tickets available for Mt. Mingshan," the announcement came
over the intercom. "Visit the Door of Hell, the Emperor Temple by
boat. Come see the ghosts."

What a terrible fate, Liu thought, to be a ghost in a land of gawking tourists. And then, perhaps the legends were not true. He hoped not, for Fei Fei's sake.

As the boat prepared to dock, Liu spied another scavenger at work, crouching close to the water's edge in a garbage pit. Nearby, in the swirling eddies, plastic bags, empty instant noodle cups, rusted cans, and the rubber soles of flip flops floated out of reach of the scavenger's hands. The fellow had a wide-brimmed straw hat that shielded his head from the sun and from inquisitive eyes. He scuttled along like a crab; his hands were indiscriminate pincers, fishing out scrap metal from the heap of trash to add to his collection.

Was this Fang's idea of a good find? Liu clenched his fists. The old man had gotten the best of him again. What if he returned empty-handed, or worse, with a handful of curses wrought by Fengdu's restless ghosts? Liu took a deep breath and decided it was too late to turn back now.

Disembarking in the new city, Liu hired a peasant to take him in a small raft across the river. "I have some business in the old town," he said.

The peasant stared at him with a quizzical look. "There's old and sickly folk remaining in town. What business you got there?"

"Well, I have an uncle. . . . Need to settle some debts."

"Where does he live?"

"Somewhere over there," Liu pointed to the cluster of buildings he had seen from the ferry.

"Watch out for the cops. Even the ghosts are afraid of them."

When the men arrived in old Fengdu, the peasant stood on the raft, arms akimbo, shaking his head as vendors flocked toward them. Liu held his scavenging bag close and scurried up the sloping concrete dock. A cold prickle crept under his skin, and he sensed that Fengdu's ghosts had gathered to greet him. Before him was the dying city. A massive expanse of land had been reduced to rubble, the jagged remnants of old buildings blasted off their moorings. All the useful parts had been scavenged—doorknobs, window frames, steel fixtures, copper wiring—and the remaining carcasses of concrete carried no trace of the bustling town that had once stood. Along the horizon, however, Liu could make out the tired, old buildings that had refused to surrender to the demolition.

Liu adjusted his bag, where he carried a small pouch with money, a pair of pliers, a pocketknife, two days' supply of cigarettes, a bottle of water, and a light jacket. The overland journey across Fengdu's wasteland took almost two hours. There were few traces of the old roads, only chaotic towers of concrete that traced a rough path into the city's interior. Liu took small sips of water, mindful that his supply had to last for the entire day. In the heat of approaching midday, the mounds of rock seemed to shimmer, and Liu imagined a play land of ghost children, scampering amidst the rubble, crushing ghost ants and beetles, building totems of broken gravel and cracked brick, chuckling as their structures tumbled to the earth. The visions made his legs quiver, and in his haste he tripped several times. The footing on loose rubble was treacherous. Rusted nails, hidden wires, and fixtures as yet unclaimed by scavengers could make any fall deadly. Liu admonished himself to take heed in his steps.

At long last, Liu arrived in a neighborhood alley, where scraggly rows of low-rises loomed on both sides. The smell of urine wafted up from the cracked pavement, and rats whisked across the narrow alley into shadows and crevices. The corpse of a dead cat lay beside the gutter. Here the rats nibbled on its desiccated flesh. Liu recoiled in disgust. Was it an omen? He pushed the thought out of his mind, but imaginary spiders kept crawling down his legs and feet.

The edifices of buildings were blackened by soot, but the wash hung from a few balconies in motley colors, like flags of protest, signifying a refusal to surrender to the decay and squalor that had befallen the remnant neighborhoods of Fengdu.

Liu crept along the silent alleyway, gazing up at the sprawl of apartment buildings. A choking sensation gripped his chest, but the sky was painted only with the ordinary haze of fumes and exhaust from the new city across the river.

The neighborhood was strangely devoid of signs of the final apocalypse—no red symbols shouting "TSAI" to seal the destruction of buildings, no bold numerals on billboards to forecast the rising level of the Yangtze reservoir. Liu stood uncertainly in front of a gray brick building that appeared even more pitiful than the rest. The window dressing of laundry was absent from the balconies; the iron bars across the windows had been scavenged; fragments of broken glass at Liu's feet rested like fingerprints at the scene of a crime. It could have been an act of thievery, the suicide of a desperate soul, vandalism committed by a rogue pack of boys. His muscles twitched. He wondered how he might climb up to that second-story balcony. Perhaps he could scramble up the bars of the window below and throw a rope onto the balcony railings. If only he had rope.

As he stepped back to get a better look, his ankles took a blow from a thin, hard object, and he nearly lost his balance. Liu swung around, his knapsack snug against his ribs, and stared into the eyes of a crippled man whose nose resembled a slab of lotus root above his hollowed cheeks. His gnarled hands gripped his cane like a weapon.

"Aieeee!" the fellow yelped. Shifting his weight, he raised his cane in the air and shook it at Liu. "What are you doing here? If you're here to take me away, you can't!"

Liu ducked instinctively, clutching his knapsack. He fumbled for the pocketknife as he backed away from the man. Heart pounding, Liu flicked the blade, crouching low to meet his gaze.

A cool breeze funneled through the alley, flanked on both sides by the silent sentries of buildings. The man kept his stick suspended in the air, but it was not pointed at Liu like a spear; rather, it flailed like a broken branch in the wind.

Liu shook his head and blinked. Fear had clouded his judgment. How could he possibly be threatened by this fellow, with a lifeless stump of a leg, whose trousers flapped in the wind? Gazing at the invalid's flickering eyes, Liu felt pity for the man. He retracted the blade.

"I'm not going to hurt you," he declared in a flat voice.

"Why are you here then?" The man's tone was still belligerent, although more restrained.

"I came to find my uncle's old apartment."

"Can't you tell that ghosts live here? The dead and the dying. You should leave well alone."

Liu was at a loss. He knew little about the town beyond its rough layout. His alibi did not assuage the man, who kept his cane raised in from of him. Liu decided he would have to try his luck elsewhere, perhaps a few blocks away.

"I'll be on my way then."

The fellow's demeanor softened. His body slumped, and the folds of his shirt bunched up like dead autumn leaves, as if his chest were simply a big cavity.

"If you're looking for someone, might as well ask the authorities. They're stationed a few blocks away. Over there." The man pointed uphill toward Mt. Mingshan. He thrust the tip of his cane into the ground, propelling himself forward with a rowing motion, and disappeared into the shadows.

• • •

AS LIU MADE HIS WAY THROUGH THE FORSAKEN NEIGHBORHOOD, he began to hear the sounds of life inside the buildings, the creaking of rusty hinges, the dull thud of coal blocks fed into stoves, a raspy, uncontrollable cough emerging from an open window. Liu crept along like a stalking cat, scrunching his toes. He tiptoed around decaying garbage, dried spittle, a dead sparrow. Yet he was afraid of being stalked himself, facing off with another angry resident in a town on its last limbs.

The mumbling of voices perked up his ears as he approached an intersection. He turned up the hill in the direction the man had pointed. These were not mumbling voices, these were shouts that grew louder as his footsteps took him past row upon row of old buildings like too many dominoes stacked and ready to fall with the flick of a finger. The shouts pulsed, alternating with the rhythm of Liu's labored breathing.

A small crowd appeared at the next turn. Men dressed in rags, each a stick man with a bruised arm here, a limping leg there. Crumpled leaflets fluttered against the sky.

The voices rose in a din of escalating chants.

"Pay our fair share or we won't go!"

"Punish the crooks! Defend the *lao bai shing!*" These were the old hundred names, the common folk whose families, like Liu's, had tilled the land for generations.

The government building, with a crumbling roof and chipped tiles, was held hostage by the angry crowd. Liu pasted his body against a lamppost across the street, and stared at the rioters raising their fists like rifles.

"No, no, we won't go!"

An official's voice blared from a bullhorn behind a second-story window. "Go home, pack up and leave! You have been duly compensated. There is nothing to complain about."

"Fat cats profit while *lao bai shing* starve."

The crowd pushed closer; more people appeared around Liu. A woman pressed against his shoulder, moving with the crowd toward the disembodied voice. She had teeth like dried corn kernels, and her peppery hair had fallen out of its bun. Liu tried to escape, but could not find an opening through the mass of warm bodies pushing forward.

Arms swayed in unison, like a mass of sea kelp, the bulbous fists of the petitioners rippling in waves of retort.

"Pay our share or we won't go!"

"No! No! We won't go!"

Around the corner, a van lurched to a stop. A dozen burly policemen swarmed around the crowd, and their lusty hollers rang across the square. "Break it up! Go home!"

"No, no, we won't go!" the *lao bai shing* chanted over and over again, in unison. Their unwavering refrain was loud, yet soporific in an odd way, like the voices joined in song at Mei Ling's church.

"Break it up!" A dozen nightsticks swooped through the air in an acrobatic arc before descending on the heads of the *lao bai shing*. All around, heads swayed and bodies crumpled to the ground. The jumble of arms and legs flailed against an indifferent sky.

The nightsticks flew in ten directions. Protesting heads fell silent. Uncombed heads fell into disarray, surrounded by the gleam of silver-capped teeth, and the grizzle of unshaved beards. Frightened heads cried for mercy, but the nightsticks soared into the air and swooped down like buzzards.

A bristly head near Liu sank to the ground, and cracked teeth scattered on cement, bathed in a crimson pool. A wispy gray head, fragile as a dandelion puff, surrendered to the lamppost, as ancient legs fell against Liu's heels. Liu crouched down, wrapping his arms over his head as the air sizzled with moans, screams, the swishing of nightsticks, the crunch of oak wood on brittle bone.

Liu pressed his forehead into the ground, struggling to breathe, but not daring to move. The putrid odors of pus and sweat mingled with the brick-kiln smell of cement. The sidewalk was bright as a revolutionary painting, splattered with blood-stained Mao jackets, blood red for protest, faded blue for dashed proletarian dreams. Nearby, the woman with the unkempt hair bun lay unconscious, her lips parted in an unfinished cry. Liu lifted his head slightly and spied a thick band of jade on the ground, beneath the sprawl of her clothing. Bracing his toes, he propelled himself forward an inch, then another, and his right arm sprang out and snatched the bracelet. A second later, he returned to a fetal position. The screams around him subsided, but Liu sensed that his ordeal had only just begun.

14

AS THE PROTEST DISSOLVED INTO SWOLLEN-LIPPED SILENCE, AN entourage of military trucks rushed to the scene. Two dozen protestors were crammed into the back of each truck. As the unconscious regained their senses, and the injured wrapped their hands over broken jaws and ribs, the riot police tucked away their nightsticks. Their captain ordered the truck drivers to take the prisoners to an empty warehouse adjoining a fertilizer factory that had shut down.

Liu had managed to escape any serious blows, but his lot had been cast with the protestors. He thought of declaring himself an innocent bystander, but that would have aroused further suspicions. Crammed into the center of one truck, Liu felt the bony shoulders of another man pressed against his ribs, forcing his breath out with a jolt as the truck careened down one of the remaining roads. Elbows jostled for space, but there was none to spare. In front of Liu, a man's oily hair smelled like turpentine, and another fellow coughed continuously into his ear.

By the time the prisoners arrived at the warehouse, the sun had sunk low on the horizon. Armed guards hustled the protestors up the ramp of the loading dock. "Move it, come on! We haven't got all day." A burly guard with a broad jaw swiped his nightstick at the prisoners as they passed by.

Most of the men, and the handful of women in the crowd, moved along listlessly, but one fellow swung around and grabbed the nightstick. "What have we done to deserve punishment?" he hissed. "We just want the government to treat us fairly."

"Hey, I'm following orders. Gimme the stick." The guard tugged on his end, but the man wouldn't let go.

A few other protestors chimed in, emboldened by their ring-leader. "Yeah, let us go. We haven't done anything wrong." They swarmed around the guard. As the circle closed in, six other guards swung into action and grabbed the petitioners by their collars, toss-ing them aside like runt piglets. Liu backed away as a tussling match ensued. The rabble-rousers outnumbered their oppressors, shoving, hurling insults, meeting the blows with ragged knuckles and palms.

A single shot was fired into the air. Gunsmoke lingered like a comet's tail, then dissolved in the red glow of twilight. The crowd fell silent. A death sentence had been dealt to their protests.

The prisoners filed solemnly into the warehouse; ninety-six men occupied the main room, while six women were ushered into an adjacent empty office.

The guard who had been the target of resistance fished out his cell phone. "They fought like pigs at the slaughter." He flung them a curse with his bruised fingers.

"Detain them all," came the authoritative voice at the other end.

"This isn't the first time; we gotta teach them a lesson."

"I'll send in some guys to do an ID tomorrow, single out the repeat offenders. Trust me, they won't give you trouble again."

•   •   •

THE NINETY-SIX MEN LINED UP IN THE OLD WAREHOUSE, awaiting the two inspecting guards. Standing in six long rows, they resembled a ragtag army forced into surrender. Skinny men stood next to husky ones; tall and short, hairy and bald, toothy and tooth-less, they were now united by one identity, that of prisoners. The men were told to strip down to their underwear.

Soiled shirts and trousers fell in heaps at the feet of the prisoners as the two guards sauntered down each row. The men reluctantly handed over their good-luck pendants and other personal belongings.

While they were undressing, Liu snatched the jade bracelet from his knapsack and stuck it down the front of his underwear, where elastic bands held it in place. The polished girdle of jade sent a cold tickle through his belly.

When a guard appeared before him, Liu handed over his knapsack. The guard lingered a moment, noticing an odd bulge above his crotch.

"You hiding something?" the guard growled, tapping his nightstick on Liu's hip.

"Nothing sir, just my family jewels," Liu said with a straight face.

The guard smirked and moved on to the next prisoner. An hour later, after their clothing was inspected, the guards told the prisoners to get dressed and threw them some blankets for the night.

The men were kept in the main warehouse, separate from the women. Twice a day, the prisoners ate a thin porridge of rice and cabbage, sprinkled with a few anchovies. At night, they huddled together, two or three sharing a blanket against the cold damp that set in with nightfall. The concrete floors pierced their spines like knife blades, and during the night, mice scurried about in search of food, on occasion nipping a tender earlobe or a ripe toe.

The warehouse had once stored fertilizer, but the place smelled less like manure and soil than like curdled tofu. Liu spat repeatedly, but couldn't clear the phlegm from his throat.

Languishing in their dank cell, the men got used to the squalor. They fell into a somber state, as the guards refused to tell them when they would be released. The police detectives who arrived on the second day pried out their names and residences, threatening to execute anyone they caught lying. Liu's alibi was met with suspicion, but a fellow spoke up for him, saying he was an outsider never seen before in town.

During the evening meals, the prisoners grumbled about the circumstances that led them to protest. They clanked their spoons loudly against the metal bowls so that the guard on duty could not hear them.

Liu's new friend, Ji Nan, slurped his porridge noisily. "Do I want to live in a new city? Sure. But I can't afford rent that's three times what I've been paying."

"That's right. And the government is unwilling to pay," replied a fellow next to Ji Nan. "Why, I haven't received a single *fen*, and I've worked for the government for twenty years."

"What d'ya expect?" said an elderly man with deep jowls and chipped teeth. "Those damn officials skimmed off a big portion of the funds for themselves. Took the wheat kernels and left us the husks."

"I heard a guard say they're teaching us a lesson here," said Ji Nan.

A skeleton of a man fingered his rice bowl. "I lost my wife to cancer and my young boy was born with a bad heart. What else can faze me?" Liu stared across at the widower. He wanted to speak to the man, let him know that he shared his sorrow. But Liu merely choked back his words along with a mouthful of rice.

•   •   •

MRS. SONG HAD REFUSED TO ACCEPT PAYMENT FROM LIU FOR taking care of Rose for a few days. It was her chance to fatten the baby up a little. On the second morning, she felt a sharp pain in her arch. "Oh dear, this old body needs a tune-up."

Rose was awake, and cried to be fed. Mrs. Song had some trouble finding the baby's spoon, and when she spotted it on the floor, she wondered what it was doing there. The old woman felt a nagging ache in her bones; it seemed to spread upward from that bad arch.

While Rose was awake for more hours during the day, Mrs. Song was staying in bed longer. Her energy flagged soon after breakfast. Over the next few days, she spent much time in front of the TV, and took long naps in the afternoon. She never used to indulge in such idleness. No, she did not feel like her normal self.

Standing in front of the mirror above the little sink, Mrs. Song pulled back the gray hair from her face, but she had trouble tucking it into a bun. She did not recognize that face. So wrinkled, almost frail looking. Where had the years gone? She grabbed a dirty sponge and brushed back the gray wisps that strayed from her temple.

When the pain in Mrs. Song's arch finally subsided, she decided it was time to see the herbalist. Dr. Liang could give her something to tonify her system. "My body must be weak after that long bout of flu," she muttered. Glancing over at the sink, she had a fleeting image of some disaster in the kitchen. A fountain of water pooling at her feet. A wet mop. She must have mopped for an eternity. "All that water should have taken the excess heat out of me," she thought ruefully.

Rose, however, seemed to be in excellent spirits. She launched into a chorus of shrieks, her arms waving madly like a sailor chasing away the demons astern.

"Dear, dear, you are a fiery little goddess, aren't you? Now hush, or the fairy's going to turn you into one of her sisters, and like it or not, you'll be silent as the peaks of Wu Gorge."

Little Rose kept up her protests; Mrs. Song would have to take her along. Since she was getting too heavy to carry, Mrs. Song put her in the wheeled cart that she used for grocery shopping. As they meandered through town, Rose clutched the wire mesh, her head bobbing about like a giant bulb of garlic.

The herbalist's shop faced a small square in town where vendors lined up their kiosks during the day. A young man opened the door, and Mrs. Song pushed her cart inside. "Greetings, Dr. Liang, how is business?"

The herbalist's broad face lit up. "My dear Mrs. Song, what brings you here?"

Mrs. Song leaned her elbows on the counter. "I tell you, my energy's not what it used to be. Feeling tired a lot, not sleepy you know, just not my old self. And I've been kind of forgetful. Couldn't find my keys this morning. And my shoes. Looked under the bed, the couch, everywhere. Oh, that was bad on my knees! Oh dear, and a bad arch, too. But that's better now. Oh, what was I saying? Been tired a lot. Maybe because I was sick. Dr. Liang, I need some mending herbs, some nice strengthening herbs to build up my chi."

Dr. Liang listened patiently, then laid Mrs. Song's palm on a small cushion, and felt her pulse. "Mmmm. . . ." He nodded, writing in his ledger with an ink brush. At his bidding, she also stuck out her tongue, and he peered at the cracked lines that covered its surface. "Tsk tsk. . . ." Dr. Liang shook his head, and jotted another note in sweeping strokes.

"What is it?" Mrs. Song asked.

"Too little *jing* in the kidney meridian. I'll fix you just the right combination to boost your energy."

"And throw in some herbs to build up my strength. I had a terribly nasty flu."

Dr. Liang walked over to the herbal repository, a collection of drawers, each the size of a lunchbox, that extended across the length of the counter and up to the ceiling. He laid out six pieces of butcher paper, and opened several drawers in quick succession, doling out portions of the requisite herbs. The little mounds contained chalky slabs of astragalus, gnarled roots, seeds and kernels and ground-up bones. Dr. Liang topped the batches with the empty carapaces of a large cricket-like insect.

"What's that?" Mrs. Song's eyes bulged, following the flutter of the insect shells as they descended, light as rice husks, on each pile.

"It's a secret. Cleans out your system. Now here's some licorice to sweeten the mix. I had a foreigner come in once, for gout. He said the Chinese medicine tastes like coffee grounds."

"I'd drink tar if it would give me my old self back," said Mrs. Song. She paid Dr. Liang, and hung the bag containing her prescription inside the cart, where Rose batted at the white bundles as if they were crib toys.

As Mrs. Song stepped out to the square, squeezing past the throngs of vendors and passersby, she noticed a scarf falling off the side of a kiosk. And then, before Mrs. Song could blink, it all happened in a flash—the vendor stooping to the ground, a hooded figure brandishing a knife, a large black case flying through the air, a gloved hand arresting its flight, a scuffle of legs tearing through the crowd.

"Stop, THIEF!" cried the vendor, whose strident pursuit was no match for the speed of his assailants.

Mrs. Song sprawled herself over the cart to protect Rose, who was jumping up and down amidst the commotion. Harsh words flew all around them like crooked arrows never finding their mark.

"Where'd he go? Where are those bastards?" Fingers flailed about, pointing in all directions. "He went that-away. No—there—I saw him!"

"Oh dear, oh dear," Mrs. Song moaned. She felt for her purse. It was gone. She looked around frantically, then turned to the stunned bystanders. "Have you seen my purse?" Heads shook.

Mrs. Song was too distraught to notice that her foot was aching again. The shouts, the odor of fried garlic and cigarettes and bus fumes, the hubbub of the curious throng, suffocated her. She pressed her way through the crowd, and when she reached a quiet street beyond the square, she found a wallet in her coat pocket. Someone had stolen her purse and stuck in that wallet. Mrs. Song shook her head in confusion over the phantom purse. Still, she was relieved she had money, and decided to catch a taxi home.

Meanwhile, Rose continued soaking in the excitement of the mob in the square, safely suspended inside Mrs. Song's shopping cart, with a bag of herbs to keep her entertained.

• • •

THE PRISONERS FILLED THEIR EMPTY HOURS WITH JOKES AND stories from the old days, but when the cracks of idle time turned into wide chasms, each inmate fell into a silent stupor in which the minutes seemed like hours, and the hours like days. Liu had not had a cigarette for days; his head throbbed and his restless fingers played with the tattered corners of his shirt.

He worried about Rose. He had told Mrs. Song that he would be gone two or three days, but now he had no idea how long they would be detained. He pushed down the gnawing dread that he might be stuck in this dreary prison indefinitely. Liu admonished himself that he should pay more attention to Rose when he returned. Oh, how he had neglected her, spending long days working at Tai's, planting her in front of the television in the evenings when he was tired, or when she cried too long or too loud. He would take her out for more strolls. Why, he would even take her to the restaurant one of these days.

He would try to understand the language of infancy better;

surely, there was more to Rose's cries than hunger, fatigue, or soiled diapers. Perhaps she felt in her bones a longing for her old family, a life lived amidst the ebb and flow of the great river.

As the days wore on, visions of Fei Fei haunted Liu. Like unseen fairies, they played visual tricks on him, turning the exposed calf of a neighbor into the flesh of his beloved, the bare yellow bulbs on the ceiling into her soft breasts, the flicker of a lit match into the spark in her eyes. Late at night, Liu stared at the ceiling where the feeble light had been snuffed out, and sobbed quietly. Although the men around him were asleep, he felt embarrassed and wiped the tears away with a rough hand. He had been selfish in his grief. He had neglected to pay tribute to Fei Fei the past two years on Tomb Sweeping Day, when family members honored their dead. He had moved to old Wushan the month after she died, and moved again. No, that was no excuse. Liu decided that he owed it to Fei Fei to provide her comfort in the afterlife, so that her soul would not wander back and forth like the uprooted peasants of the Yangtze. Perhaps she wanted him to be happy, too, to feel warmed by the hearth of family, to carry on with his life bravely and nobly.

A week into his prison stay, Liu thought of Mei Ling. In his mind's eye, her lustrous hair swayed like windblown reeds by the river's edge. Her lips puckered when she sang, and spread wide like morning glory blossoms when she laughed, as she often did. That evening, as Liu cradled his cold metal bowl of porridge, he remembered how she had delivered bowls of steaming beef noodle soup to his table. Her delicate fingers, tipped with cherry polish, as bright as those wicked hot peppers. Those capable hands, how easily they rested on her hips; perhaps those same hands could cradle an infant with tenderness.

Liu awoke the next morning in a sweat, as if he had ridden a wild steed through the night. He would return home one of these days, and he would ask Mei Ling to marry him. A silly grin crept over his face throughout the day, but the other prisoners barely noticed as they rocked their stiff bodies and brooded over their fate.

That evening, the guards released Liu and most of the other

prisoners, detaining a few they deemed to be the leading trouble-makers. Catching a boat ride with a crew of demolition workers, Liu turned his face into the wind howling down the mighty Yangtze.

• • •

A STEADY STREAM OF PEOPLE PASSED THROUGH THE SQUARE IN Wushan that afternoon—uniformed police, shopkeepers, babbling witnesses, and a string of suspects, none of whom fit the description of the robbers. At last, the waning light and cool of evening quelled the crowd. The shopping cart, with its forgotten cargo, lay in the shadows.

The autumn chill had seeped through Rose's cotton garment and thin socks. Her cries had gone unheard in the bustle of the crowd, and when she had worn herself out, she sank her head against the wire mesh, and fell asleep. It was a middle-aged woman with a shopping cart of her own, full of recycled bottles and cans, who found Rose in Mrs. Song's cart and turned her in to the herbalist's shop nearby.

When the phone rang in Mrs. Song's apartment, she was soaking her sore arch in a small tub, rummaging through the wallet that appeared, after all that fuss, to be hers.

"Mrs. Song, you left your baby behind," said the herbalist. "I'm afraid she's quite distraught, must be hungry or something." Loud wails filled the herbal shop, as if the dust of ground tiger bone and dried reptile organs had come to life.

"Oh dear, when did I do that?"

"Well, you were getting some herbs earlier this afternoon."

"Getting some herbs. . . ." Mrs. Song wracked her brain. She remembered the herbalist's voice; she had heard it recently. He had handed her some crickets. No, it was an herbal prescription. She leapt to her feet, uttering a feeble cry. "Oh my, had I left the child behind? Goodness me. Must be the cold weather settling into these old bones. Dulls the mind. Weakens the chi, you know."

Dr. Liang's assistant showed up before too long with Rose tucked among the bags of herbs in her shopping cart. Mrs. Song stretched out her arms and brought the sobbing infant to her bosom. Her ancient eyes glistened with tears. "Dear little girl, did I leave you? How long has it been? Too long, I'm afraid. Granny will make it up to you."

Rose's limbs felt stiff and cold. Mrs. Song rubbed her little hands until they began to thaw out.

Mrs. Song happily spent the next three days cooking Rose's favorite foods and cleaning up her apartment. She worked diligently to remove a smear on the prized silk scroll that had been painted by her husband. She tried an iron, an old toothbrush, a rolling pin coated with flour, but each attempt sank the scroll into further decay.

One evening, a quiet knock sounded at the door. A strange man with bloodshot eyes and a scraggly beard appeared before her. His drawstring pants hung loosely at his waist, the tattered cloth about to blow away in the slightest breeze. Mrs. Song recoiled, muffling a scream with her hands.

"Hello, Mrs. Song," said the apparition.

"Who. . . ? How do you know my name?"

"It's Liu, do you recognize me? Well, I guess I must not be very recognizable."

The man chuckled, stroking the beard as if he were relieving an itch.

"Liu. . . . Do I know a man named Liu?"

"Why, I'm your neighbor, and that's my little girl you've been taking care of."

Mrs. Song stared at him with a blank expression, wondering where she had seen him before. "My neighbor. . . . How do I know you?"

"Let's see, I fixed your sewing machine once, brought you a sack of sweet potatoes from the market last month . . . uh . . . made a mess of egg custard in my apartment, and you cleaned it up. You've been a big help, Mrs. Song."

Perhaps it was that incident in Liu's apartment that jogged Mrs. Song's memory. Or perhaps it was Rose's response that affirmed the man as her Ba Ba. He stretched out his arms across the room, as if to tickle her, and she erupted in a fit of giggles. He sank down on his hands and knees, and patted the saddle of his back. She bounced so hard on her rump that she nearly fell backwards.

A glimmer of recognition appeared in Mrs. Song's eyes. "Why, yes, Liu. My neighbor. When was the last time I saw you? Rose has been a good little girl, dear little girl. Treat her like my own." She fetched Rose from her crib, and gave her over to Liu.

"Little monkey," he cried, swinging her in wide arcs. Liu brought her close, his bristly face brushing against hers. "There, there, your Ba Ba's back. I won't leave you again, I promise."

The reunion between man and child brought a quiver to Mrs. Song's lips. Liu smiled sheepishly, thanking her once again. "Not at all," she replied, feeling a twinge of guilt. She had been terribly forgetful. She slipped into the kitchen, rummaged through her collection of salvaged containers, and presented Liu with a freshly made batch of custard.

"Warm it up on a low flame. Now don't you set your kitchen on fire again," Mrs. Song said. In a moment of lucidity, she added, "And don't leave your brood for too long. A man's always good as his promises." He nodded, clutching the baby to his breast. She watched as their figures receded down the hallway, beneath the canopy of cobwebs that fluttered in the waning light.

15

LONG AFTER MEI LING HAD FALLEN ASLEEP, HER ROOMMATE Pei stayed up, knitting by the light of the feeble lamp. A stitch broke, and as she tried to hook it back onto the knitting needle, her fingers dropped a few more stitches. She too felt troubled, and Mei Ling's concerns only compounded the problem.

The day before, Pei had run into their neighbor in the hallway as she was returning to their apartment. The woman threw a conspiratorial glance her way and rushed over, her thin arms flying about. Pei had neither the time nor the patience for the latest gossip, but Ah Fan had an uncanny way of hooking unwary neighbors with a fast line, although the bait was often stale.

"Pei, you won't believe it, but our apartment building is condemned. We are all going to be evicted."

"You must be kidding," Pei said flatly. But she had to admit that if there was someone in the know, it was her neighbor.

"These buildings are only a few years old. I heard that some shady deals took place when the apartments were built. Sure, it all looks brand new, but see how thin these walls are?" Ah Fan struck the plaster with her skinny knuckles.

"Can't they spend some money to fix up the building?"

"I don't think it's that simple." Ah Fan leaned in closer and lowered her voice, although nobody else was around. "I'm told it's not just shoddy construction. The ground beneath us is not steady; we're on a steep hill, and if we ever have a landslide, there goes our home."

123

"How could it be? The government put a lot of money into this new city."

"What do you think? We're like ants on a log. If the government shakes us out of our home, for whatever reason, if a business interest crushes us with a giant hand, what can we do?" Ah Fan sighed. "I was glad to leave that stinking old town, but it looks like we'll have to move again."

"Maybe we can appeal to the government bureau, you know, those folks in charge of resettlement."

"Oh, Pei, you're such an idealist! Don't the officials line their own pockets every time a hotel or high-rise goes up? They're as rotten as peaches in a vat of worms."

"You're such a cynic. We'll wait and see, I suppose. One of our roommates is getting married, and I don't know how Mei Ling and I can afford a new place with just the two of us."

Finishing the last row of knitting for the evening, Pei felt an edge of anxiety in her stomach. She cringed at the thought of moving again. The lamp flickered, its golden light illuminating the textured wooden grain of the desk, which was rather homely looking by day. The shadows stretched long tendrils to the edge of the bed where Mei Ling was sleeping.

Their roommate Lan worked the graveyard shift at Jinfu Hotel. She was engaged to a foreigner, a stern-looking fellow from Germany who had stayed there. What would their children look like, Pei thought. She could not imagine marrying a foreigner. In fact, she could not see why a smart young woman would get married at all if she could make her own way.

Outside, the chirping crickets on the hillside sang their night songs with the verve of old women who laughed over the stories they told once and again. Pei opened the desk drawer to put away her knitting. She thought about the neighbor's news. It was probably the gossip of idle women. No need to tell Mei Ling any time soon; she had other worries at the moment.

•   •   •

FANG SHUPING ENJOYED THE MORNINGS WHEN THE LIGHT

flooded his sitting room through the east window. He took a pinch of tobacco and stuffed it lovingly into his pipe. His fingers glided over the ornate label. *House of Craven, London. Fine pipe tobacco since 1863.*

Fang grabbed the newspaper and settled into the sofa. He had picked it out of a catalog of imported goods. The Victorian legs and the blue-and-rose floral design seemed a bit gaudy for his taste, but it reminded him of the loveseats that had adorned his father's quarters, where he would sit as a child, waiting for an audience with the elder Fang.

At last, Fang Shuping was living up to his father's name. Having concentrated his dealings on real estate, Fang had made a sizable profit over the past few months brokering developments in local towns. Fang was tired of selling babies to orphanages and trinkets to pawn shops. The botched trip with Liu. His arrangements for the hare-lipped boy. None of it had been worth the hassle. He had grander visions, bigger pearls to fill up his chest. He relished the thrill of tinkering behind the scenes and then witnessing the fruits of his work spring up around town and beyond. He could truly claim to be the son of Fang Dashong, who had made his fortune as a shipping tycoon.

The doorbell rang, and Fang got up reluctantly to answer it. Most of his transactions nowadays took place on the phone, and he promptly picked up, as he never let a good business opportunity slip by. Visitors were another story; these house calls came from locals like Mrs. Lung or petty traders and scavengers like Liu.

An impatient voice rang out from the other side of the door. "Fang, open up. It's Duo Ruyi."

A skinny fellow, whose body tapered like one of Fang's pipes, appeared in the doorway. He sported a watch chain on his lapel. Duo Ruyi shared Fang's taste for expensive British items, but his look seemed to be a throwback to a different era and a bygone empire.

"Fang, I've had my mind on building a four-star hotel in Wushan, but it's gotten harder to lay a claim on real estate now that the town's established. So, big brother, I need you to pull some strings, help me find a good tract of land."

"Ol' Duo, are you up to your schemes again? First it was the gambling casino in Shanghai. And then the brothel down the street from the joint. When the authorities busted you, they got two eggs and one cluck. Have you wised up?"

"Hey old man, I'm just doing business. What's wrong with rigging some of the roulette tables? Life's a game of roulette anyway. Russian roulette for the hard-nosed Communists among us." Duo Ruyi chortled, sending forth a spray of saliva. The man's lower lip glistened. His cheeks were bright crimson and his breath smelled of brandy.

"All right, what's your idea?"

"Ol' Fang, haven't I always said that information is gold? Well, I hit a gold mine. I learned that a block of buildings in east Wushan is going to be condemned. They say half the town has been built on an old landslide. Matter of fact, do you remember hearing about that slide a year and a half ago? The bureaucrats hustled to shore up their own buildings—the courthouse, police station, port authority. Should have let 'em tumble to hell." Duo Ruyi's arms flailed about as if he were a child destroying a tower of wooden blocks.

Fang jabbed the excited fellow in the ribs. "What do you want to do? Build an amusement park? With a brothel nearby?"

"No, don't be silly. Here's my chance, you see, to land my hotel on some prime real estate. After the residents are evicted, of course. Don't want them loitering around like waifs once I open the doors." Duo Ruyi paced up and down Fang's sitting room, his eyes rolling about wildly. "Now what you can do for me, my friend, is to rouse one of those snoozing bureaucrats from the Urban Development Bureau and wave a 10,000-*yuan* note in front of his face. Say I'll be the first buyer after the old buildings are cleared out." Duo Ruyi paused and grabbed Fang's arm. "Ol' Fang, can you do it? It's the deal of a lifetime."

Fang drew a long puff on his pipe, and stared at the smoke rings as if he could divine the fortunes of the enterprising Duo Ruyi. The fellow's name implied a life of ease where things always went his way. But with eight failed businesses, including a contraband narcotics ring that had landed him time in jail, nothing was further from the truth. Still, Duo Ruyi had managed to amass a small fortune in stocks. And Fang was never one to displease his clientele if he saw some potential in the scheme.

"I'll see what I can do, my friend."

Over the next four days, Fang pulled every string he had. An old friend at the Shanghai port authority used to work for the Three Gorges Project Development Company. The fellow referred Fang to the deputy chief of the Urban Development Bureau, who was far from the sleeping bureaucrat of Duo's estimation.

Fang saw his job as opening the gates, and it was up to the client to step through them. Sometimes, though, he had to grease the hinges a bit, but even the most straightlaced bureaucrat could succumb under his agile touch. To keep his fingerprints off this project, Fang visited the deputy chief, a square-jawed man known as Inspector Mah, after hours. Sitting across from the chief, Fang leaned forward on his elbows and got down to business.

"I hear the apartment buildings on Dong Yang Street are condemned. That must be a big headache—not only to find a new site to build, but to deal with the vacant land. Do you have plans for redevelopment?"

Inspector Mah's granite jaw did not budge, and when he did finally speak, his words were crisp with authority. He had the voice of someone who demanded obedience and never failed to get it. "No. We don't have plans. The engineers say that another landslide from the slopes above the buildings could decimate the area."

"My client is a seasoned contractor. He'll find the right folks to shore up the hillside with concrete infill."

"It'll cost money," replied Inspector Mah.

"Not a problem," said Fang. "My client is eager to lease, and can pay the engineers' salaries as well."

The deputy chief arched his eyebrows, which were overgrown like wild rushes with streaks of gray. "What's the catch?"

"Nothing. He's a shrewd man and he's willing to pay top dollar for this hotel project. And he'll take care of that faulty hillside. Wushan depends on tourism, as you know, and this will bring in valuable revenue."

Inspector Mah nodded his head. "What kind of revenue are you talking about?"

The hinges were starting to loosen; Fang only had to lean in a little more. "Well, he's looking at 120 rooms for a four-star hotel. You can do the math. You can also be assured that he'll provide funds up front for the engineering surveys and work, and for other expenditures incurred by the bureau. And I'm not talking about an extra copy machine. I'm talking about some well-deserved bonuses."

"Such as?" The deputy chief leaned in closer.

"Oh, there'll be compensation for the special efforts made to speed up this process." Fang fixed his gaze on a crystalline paperweight inlaid with an ancient bronze coin.

"We don't want to repeat the disaster we had a couple of years ago."

"Of course you won't. You're dealing with a known quantity here, a hillside, not an entire town. And besides, the dam on the Three Gorges is the new Great Wall, and you have access to the best technology in the world."

A faint smile registered on Inspector Mah's face. "That is true."

"And furthermore," Fang continued, interlacing his fingers, "you'll receive some funds specially earmarked for your efforts. Is that your son?" Fang shifted his attention to a photo of Inspector Mah with a teenage boy with the same square jaw and crew cut.

"Yes, he's in high school, about to take the exams to enter university. He wants to go into business," replied Inspector Mah.

"Ah, college costs a fortune nowadays. He looks like a bright young man; he'll get into a good school."

The deputy chief beamed; clearly, the boy would make his father proud.

"A shame it's so expensive nowadays." Fang added, drumming his fingers on the paperweight.

Inspector Mah set his jaw again. "So what's your part in this?"

"I help to facilitate the deal. Mr. Duo will pay you a visit shortly, and send you the first check. How does that sound?"

"Fine." Inspector Mah got up and shook Fang's hands.

As Fang got up to leave, he turned toward his host once more.

"Your son will do well. My father was a great businessman. He always believed that good *guanxi* would get the job done, and he rewarded his allies generously."

•   •   •

THAT AFTERNOON, FANG CALLED HIS CLIENT TO REPORT HIS success with Inspector Mah. The following week, Duo Ruyi met with the deputy chief at a restaurant several blocks from the bureau office. They agreed that Duo Ruyi would handpick the engineers, and their survey of the hillside would be used to determine the best course of action. The entrepreneur sent the first check to Inspector Mah at his home address, along with a bottle of *wu liang ye.*

On the last day of the tenth month, the bureau sent a notice of eviction to the apartment buildings on Dong Yang Street that stood beneath the overgrown hill.

THE BLITZ OF SMELLS AND SOUNDS IN TAI'S RESTAURANT WOULD have melted down the senses of any other year-old child. But Rose was an unusual creature. Whenever a steaming tray of food sailed past her, she leaned forward from her perch in Liu's arms and clawed at the spice-laden air.

The odor of fried garlic invaded her nostrils like a stifling hug from one of Mrs. Song's friends. It stung her eyes and made her sneeze, as some of the old people did with their ointments of tiger balm rubbed below their noses, which were rather shaped like garlic bulbs.

The sting of spicy red pepper pummeled her senses. It was more touch than smell, like the tingling sensation on her skin when she slapped her father's arm for a donkey ride. The effervescent seeds of pepper crawled through her nasal passages and into her throat until she almost choked from the dryness.

Rose began to cry. Bulky figures crowded around her, and her father thrust a bottle of milk in her mouth. She sputtered, letting the milk dribble, and turned her stricken face toward Liu's chest. Breathing in the sweet, musky aroma of his sweat, Rose found some relief from the onslaught of strangers.

She turned her head slightly and peeked at the chattering adults around her. A gaunt man, whose chin was eye level with Rose, thrust a bony finger toward her cheek. He appeared lopsided, as if his legs were crooked branches, and even his torso and face appeared somewhat twisted. He leaned in closer; his skin was nut brown with thin lines streaming from his eyes and cheekbones. A long gash ran down his cheek. It writhed like an earthworm when he opened his mouth to speak.

Rose was about to cry again, but Liu batted away the man's fingers. The next man to step up was bovine and broad. His shoulders filled the doorway, and the fat on his arms rolled as he approached them from a room filled with even more pungent smells. A blast of heat whipped across her face, followed by the rumbling stench of his breath when he leaned in close. Oh, that breath was inescapable, like the acrid smell of burnt stew. Then Rose realized that it was a stronger version of those flaming sticks that Liu often put in his mouth. Her tiny lungs would flutter in protest, but she had learned to let her tongue fall back, allowing small sips of air when smoke filled the apartment.

This man was twice as thick as the first one, but he didn't scare her. As her tongue fell back, her eyelids lifted up, following the wobbling motions of an object he dangled above her. The furry thing had little claws, and its owner made hissing noises, as if he were a dog sneezing through a mouth full of rice. The man scratched the air with his other hand and growled. Rose giggled. He pawed and growled some more. Rose batted at the object, but he lifted it out of her reach. With steely resolution, she crawled up on Liu's chest and reached out as far as her arms would go. The object leapt once more, eluding her.

Now Rose was angry, and she lashed out at the big man, who couldn't move as fast as his furry puppet. She screeched. The man tottered backward in slow motion, and crumpled to the floor. When Rose looked down, she caught a smile on his ruddy face. She giggled; it was a triumphant giggle, and those gathered around her smiled and clapped, bathing her in a halo of victory.

And then a hush descended on the small crowd. A female figure sailed toward them like a spring breeze carrying the scent of orange blossoms. Her skirt rippled, sending a ribbon of flowers into a frenzied dance, and all around the men seemed to flutter in the electric current of this woman's presence. Like the others, she leaned in, extending a delicate hand toward Rose's cheek. Her eyes were framed by thick black lashes, and her nails shimmered like peach blossoms.

In that moment of contact, Rose felt a wild pulse rippling through her skull. Something familiar. Something forgotten. A memory from long ago of warm breasts, sweet milk, a woman's breath like spring water, unsullied by tobacco and stale garlic. She craned her neck, wanting to linger in that touch, but the hand pulled away.

The woman hovered near Rose but did not touch her again. In the impulse to feel her electric warmth, Rose thrust out her arm, fraught with need and desire. It was innocent enough, and yet her advance caused the woman to withdraw—ruby lips, peach fingernails, bat-like lashes, all retreated in a single swift motion. A lump arose in the soft cave of Rose's throat; something pressed on her eyelids but she could not cry.

•　　•　　•

LIU'S REAPPEARANCE HAD CHEERED HER UP A LITTLE, BUT Mei Ling remained in a despondent mood. Nothing to ward off her father's insistence that she enslave herself to his wishes. That Sunday, she forced herself to go to Mass, more out of habit than out of any strength of will to lift up her spirits.

But the ritual of Mass did give Mei Ling comfort. The hardness of wood against her bones as she knelt down, resting her folded hands on the pew in front. The soft light that illuminated the altar where Father Chong stood, with Jesus Christ the Savior behind him, a wounded but divine guardian. The glow of parishioners' cheeks, wrinkled with age, turned to the light of the Lord.

That Sunday, Father Chong focused his sermon on the Virgin Mary and her willingness to serve as mother of the Lord Jesus.

"Now Mary could have said, 'I don't want to be the Lord's servant. We have no money, no means to take care of the child, and my feet hurt. I can barely take care of myself.'" Father Chong scrunched his eyes, and pushed up his thick glasses. After a pregnant pause, he threw his arms out toward his congregation, imploring, "Could you see the utter devotion that Mother Mary showed her God? To accept the Lord Jesus into her womb. To say, 'Yes! I will be the vessel to hold the child of God, the salvation of the world.' Can you say 'yes' like Mary?" Father Chong's eyes shone, and beads of sweat trickled down his temples.

The crowd murmured. Bellies rumbled in anticipation of the noon meal, armpits and crotches itched; some got relief, others, not. Foreheads tingled; some from the presence of gnats, others with the glimmer of understanding in the wake of Father Chong's poetic plea.

"Can you say 'yes!'"

"Yes!" the congregation replied in unison.

"Yes, Lord, I will accept you."

"Yes, Lord, I-I-will-accept-pt-you." The rest of the declaration was jumbled with coughing and gnat swatting.

Mei Ling put the full force of her breath into those words. She imagined being that vessel, serving her Lord, and she allowed her belly to swell as she took a deep breath to sing the opening verses of "Ave Maria."

Her voice lifted her up, away from Wushan and her troubles, to the heavens. For the time being, her mind felt at ease. At the end of service, Mei Ling thanked the priest for his wise words.

"No need, my child. Just remember, the Lord wants to hear your 'yes.'"

That afternoon, when Mei Ling returned home, she shut her eyes and searched her heart. The face of Father Chong, sincere and pious, appeared before her. Could it be so simple to say 'yes'? What was God really asking for? Surely, He would not want her to say 'yes' to her self-serving father. Mei Ling shook her head vehemently. No, she did not have to say 'yes' to needless suffering.

When her roommate came home, Mei Ling sat her down. "Pei, you know how my faith has been tested by that father of mine? I've decided I can stand up to him. My life is here; this is where I'm supposed to be. It seemed like I had no prospects here, and now this fellow at Tai's has invited me to supper, this coming Tuesday."

In her excitement, Mei Ling took to cleaning their small bedroom. She ran the feather duster lovingly across the desk, as if she were a fairy whisking away the troubles of mere mortals. She pounced on other surfaces, and then on Pei, giving her roommate's shoulder a playful swipe.

Pei neither smiled nor pushed her away. In a quiet voice, she spoke up. "Mei Ling, I didn't want you to worry about one more thing. But I think you should know, because it's no longer just a rumor." Pei thrust a dirt-stained notice in front of Mei Ling. "We have to move out of our apartment, by the end of the month."

"What?" Mei Ling's gleeful expression fell away. "Why do we have to move?"

"The building's condemned; the hillside above us could give in to landslides, I'm told," said Pei.

Mei Ling's foot twitched, as if it, too, could remember. That morning, when she was late for work, she had stumbled on a crack in the sidewalk. She had been in a hurry. She had blamed herself, but perhaps there were indeed forces that moved mountains.

Still, Mei Ling would not surrender so easily. She mustered a note of optimism. "Pei, we'll be able to manage, won't we? I mean, even though Lan is getting married, we should be able to find a decent new place."

Pei remained silent, and Mei Ling felt an impulse to pry the words out of her roommate's mouth. When Pei spoke at last, her eyes seemed clouded over by a strange glaze. "Perhaps I should not have waited to tell you, but I have been talking to my parents about moving into their home in Guangzhou."

Mei Ling choked back her tears. She threw down the duster. "How could you not tell me, Pei? I thought we were in this together. You were the one who brought me to the city in the first place."

"Oh, Mei Ling, I'm so sorry," Pei cried. "I've been really torn about the prospect of leaving this town, leaving you behind. But my family needs me. They are not doing well. My father has some kind of kidney disease; he suspects the water's been poisoned by nearby factories. Father says he needs me to take care of him. I must go. I have no choice." Pei slumped against the wall.

Mei Ling reached out to her roommate. "I had no idea . . . I am staying for my selfish reasons, but my parents don't need me, like yours do." Her anger had melted away, and now guilt crept into its place. Could she have said "yes" if she had been in Pei's shoes?

Pei stood up, squeezing her hands. "I must do my part, too. The village chief is a scumbag. He doesn't care about the people who have gotten ill. He's just stuffing his own pockets. If we're to keep the spirit of the revolution alive, we must fight for the *lao bai shing*. It's capitalism that's killing us, poisoning our rivers, making people sick with the slime from factories." Her plain, creaseless eyes flashed with indignation; the proletarian cause seemed to catalyze Pei even more than did her parents' plight.

For Mei Ling, old revolutions meant nothing. And capitalism was no greater evil than the innate greed that hardened the hearts of people like the village chief. And how was lust different from greed? Her Po Po had surrendered her life because of the man who fathered her child and would not take responsibility. And her mother paid the filial debt of shame, enduring the scorn of the aunt who raised her. Mei Ling had nothing to be ashamed of, but she understood the weight of family sorrows. And her work at Tai's had become tedious. Perhaps she was ready for a change.

"Yes. . . ," Mei Ling mumbled.

Pei stared at her with a puzzled look.

"Pei, I know why you must leave this place. Please don't worry about me. I'm in good hands."

Before leaving for work, Mei Ling pressed a 100-*yuan* note into Pei's hands. "For your parents." She turned toward the door before her roommate could protest.

•   •   •

LIU DONNED HIS BEST SHIRT, HIS ONLY GOOD SHIRT MADE OF linen with a starched collar. He looked in the mirror, an old hand-held thing that dangled upside down above the washstand, pulled the skin of his cheek taut, and drew the razor blade across. A trickle of blood erupted at his jaw line. He dabbed at the cut with a moth-eaten towel.

Liu thought of what he would say to Mei Ling on their date. Would he feel the same ease he had when they were co-workers? He had not seen her for the few weeks since his prison stint. He had worked up his courage to bring Rose to the restaurant. She was delighted to see him, and kind to little Rose. But she appeared distracted, and paid them little attention the rest of the night. He noticed that she moved about with a slight limp, and wondered if it was an ungodly curse from working with Tai. And then, when he saw her again the following Monday, Mei Ling's spirits had somehow been revived. A rosy blush had returned to her cheeks, and she moved about with her old spryness. Mei Ling flashed a buoyant smile at Liu, not only when she was serving him, but throughout the evening. "Would you like to have supper with me?" he asked, and she said yes.

The past week had been filled with Liu's fretting and pacing about, to which Rose appeared to be oblivious. Tonight, he would need to harness every ounce of his *jing shen,* his vitality, and his *chi,* that flow of life energy, to ask for her hand in marriage. Every time he thought of the prospect, his bushy eyebrows flickered. Was he doing the right thing? Did she feel a special affinity toward him? Ah, but those sweet glances—which she had showered upon him for the past eight days—seemed to say so. After all, she had not paid such attention to the other male customers, even the dapper, well-dressed ones. A strange sense of possessiveness seized Liu. He wanted Mei Ling; he wanted to drink in her beauty, her womanly attentions. And he wanted her to love Rose, as a mother would love her own child.

• • •

THEY SLURPED THEIR BOWLS OF STEAMING BROTH, AND LADLED strips of beef and tofu from the hot pot bubbling away on the table. Mei Ling took another sip of Chongqing beer. She could feel her blood rush to her skin, turning her rouged cheeks even redder. She had only drunk a glass, but her heart throbbed against her lungs. Mei Ling considered alcohol as seductive as a man; it charmed and exhilarated her. She could not resist its pleasures, yet it could be deadly intoxicating, a poison to the heart and flesh.

The restaurant was no bigger than Tai's old noodle shop. Around the other tables, the customers dipped into their steaming cauldrons and filled each other's glasses in a ritual of brotherhood. On the walls were paintings of steamships, Chinese junks, and other motifs of a maritime era gone by. The man sitting in front of Mei Ling seemed out of place. Liu was dressed in a linen shirt with a crisp collar and shirt cuffs. And yet, it seemed as though he'd been pulled from the deck of one of those ships, scrubbed clean, and dressed in his boss's clothes.

Both of them felt awkward at the start of the evening, but as their glasses began to empty, Mei Ling gazed longer and harder at Liu's face, noticing the fullness of his eyebrows, the long ridge of his nose. And Liu's eyes lost that shiftiness, which was a sign of bashfulness, not dishonesty, as far as Mei Ling could tell.

Mei Ling sensed that Liu had been trying to impress her. The co-worker she knew labored with his hands, but perhaps there was more to the man. She was curious about his baby, and his job, the unexplained source of sustenance that provided for the two—or perhaps the three—of them. Mei Ling decided to start with the baby; perhaps that would address the other nagging question. Was there a woman in the picture? If there was any hint of deceit, Mei Ling would find some convenient pretext to end the date once and for all.

"Your little girl is darling." Mei Ling smiled. "How old is she?"

"Oh, probably a year old. Yeah, she's one." Liu fidgeted with his glass.

"Do you spend a lot of time with her?"

"Why, yes. Well, it depends." Liu cleared his throat. "Rose spends quite a bit of time at the babysitter's, but I always enjoy the chance to take her for a walk. Gives us a chance to get out of the apartment . . . to get some fresh air, that is."

Swirling her glass, Mei Ling took a big gulp of beer. The rush of cold liquid down her throat soothed her. She leaned forward and her gaze was unwavering. "Where's her mother? Clearly you are inviting me on a date. This is lovely, but of course I'm wondering if you are married or—"

"No, no. . . ," Liu interrupted. "I am a widower. I have no wife. No, she's been dead for two years. If you want to know, this child is my brother's. They lost their lives in a flood, and I could not bear to see Rose given away to strangers."

Mei Ling stared at his eyebrows. How they flickered and danced. But his lips seemed to be telling the truth. "Oh, I'm so sorry. I didn't know. What a terrible loss." She reached out and touched Liu's hand, feeling the sharp ridges of his veins.

Liu did not move his hand, and she did not move hers. And then, as if the plume of poisonous liquor had passed through, Mei Ling pulled her hand back, tucking it between her thighs.

"At first, I could not see raising her on my own. She's rather impetuous, and I often feel like a clumsy father. Or a bad one." Liquor seemed to part the curtains to Liu's soul. "But she is a source of joy. And she was quite drawn to you."

Now it was Liu who gazed intently, almost fervently into Mei Ling's eyes. His sincerity made her uneasy. The heat rose into her alcohol-flushed cheeks. She was seized by the impulse to escape, but her legs felt weighed down by lead. She mustered a feeble laugh. "Well, yes, one girl knows another best."

Liu seemed to notice her discomfort, and his gaze fell on the empty bowl in front of him. "Mei Ling," he said quietly. "I have enjoyed the times we've spent at Tai's, on our walks around town, at the church. . . ." Liu looked into Mei Ling's face, blinked and looked down, as if her eyes were too bright to gaze upon. ". . . And I would like. . . ."

Nearby, three men rose up from their tables after polishing off a bottle of *baijiu*. They stumbled past Liu and Mei Ling, belching loudly. His eyes darted over to the men. He played nervously with his chopstick, striking it against the bowl. He seemed like a confused animal that had strayed far from its den and lost its instincts.

"What were you going to say?" Mei Ling asked.

"Nothing. . . . Oh, it was nothing at all."

They ate in silence, and drank more beer, although it did not seem to release them from the tension of what remained unspoken. Nevertheless, Mei Ling felt a floating sense of comfort, a faith in possibilities, as Liu walked her back home that night.

At the entrance to her building, he bade her good night, leaning forward slightly. An imploring look flashed across his face before he turned and shuffled down the street, stepping across an uneven break in the pavement.

●   ●   ●

DISTRESSED CRIES EMERGED FROM MRS. SONG'S APARTMENT. Liu banged on the door with his fist, then the heel of his hand. The echoes resounded through the dim hallway that joined their homes.

When Mrs. Song opened the door at last, she looked startled and pointed at Liu, as if trying to remember his name. A feeble light emerged in her eyes, a flicker of recognition. Mrs. Song seemed to be a stranger in her own home. This was not the fastidious Mrs. Song that Liu had always known.

Her odd behaviors upon his return had made an impression on Liu. He had started taking Rose with him to the restaurant in the evenings, and while he thought he was merely getting her acquainted with Mei Ling, he realized now that he was afraid of Mrs. Song's erratic behavior. Perhaps she had taken some strange medicine, or maybe that prolonged flu had stricken her brain; he did not know what to do about Mrs. Song, except rely on her services less and less.

The apartment was in shambles. The crocheted sofa covers, the quilt on her bed, the lace doilies that used to sit neatly on her table—all had been moved about in a bizarre manner. The calligraphy scroll on the wall had become an object of contempt; its edges lay in tatters, the interior had bled profusely like a wounded animal. He noticed the pile of dishes in the sink; the smells reminded Liu of his bachelor's apartment. But Mrs. Song was never one to let even a grain of rice fall before she would swipe up the offending kernel.

Liu rushed over to little Rose, whose naked bottom lay on a quilt spread haphazardly across the dining table. The soiled diaper had been tossed aside onto a heap of old newspapers. She had stopped crying when she sensed his presence, but when he scooped her up in his arms, her wails pierced the walls like sharp nails. Her bottom was hot to the touch.

"She's been having the itchies," said Mrs. Song. "So I took a toothbrush to her behind and scratched it right out. I don't know why she keeps crying."

Liu could not believe his ears. This was the old woman who had handed him ointment for the baby's rashes, when he was an ignorant new father. Had Mrs. Song indeed lost her senses?

"Well, she seems okay now," Liu said to Mrs. Song. He wrapped his shirt ends around the baby's exposed bottom, and brought her face close to his. Rose's eyes changed with her moods, and like the seasons, one gave way to the next completely. There was no resentment in those eyes, no fear that she would be abandoned or attacked with abrasive objects, now that she was held in his arms.

Mrs. Song had collapsed onto the couch, her gaze fixated on the ceiling. "My good fellow," she gestured to Liu, "could you turn on the TV? My husband should be coming home soon. Yes, soon. . . . I'll probably fall asleep before he gets back. He shouldn't be leaving his poor wife like this, but at least he seems to like his work."

Liu bent down and turned on the television. There was no husband she could wait for. The horror of unexplained losses drained the blood from his hands. He extended his arm toward Mrs. Song to bid her farewell.

A light came into her eyes as she patted Liu's hand. "Now that's a good boy. Wish I had a son like you."

Her sentiments jolted Liu with anguish. Mrs. Song had a son, but she did not seem to know that anymore. If it was taboo to forget the dead, it was a greater tragedy to forget the living. He waved Rose's hand in a gentle good-bye, knowing this could well be the last time she would see the matronly Mrs. Song.

•　　•　　•

ON THEIR SECOND DATE, LIU ENDURED AN HOUR OF MASS, listening to the priest's pontification on turning the other cheek, which struck Liu as an act of foolishness. That afternoon, the parishioners did not gather for tea, although he would have endured any degree of social torment for the chance to be with her. He had choked back the question earlier in the week. Liu invited Mei Ling for a stroll on the outskirts of town, trying to steady his footsteps amidst the anxiety of his intentions, and his concerns about Rose, who was under the care of a new babysitter, a cheerful, freckly girl from the local high school.

He was waiting for the right moment, when the autumn sun cast its light on her countenance, when the fitful swirls of wind died down, when his heart stood still long enough to allow his tongue to utter the words, inviting her to take his hand in marriage.

Looking into Mei Ling's eyes, Liu could see the fragments of life dancing about them—swaying branches stripped of leaves, a small fire on the hillside, the huddle of gambling men. He waited for the words that came after a long, thoughtful pause.

"Yes," she said, squeezing his hand, then letting it go as the windblown leaves scattered at their feet.

THE DISHEVELED STATE OF LIU'S APARTMENT WAS SOMEWHAT of a slovenly houseguest that refused to leave. As much as Liu tried, he could not clean the surfaces free of dust that gathered in small armies, retreating into the corners when he took a broom or rag to them. The dishes, too, refused to leave his sink; as soon a few had been washed, another set began to pile up. The old pots were cemented with layers of overcooked baby food. Anything made of cloth, the drapes by his cot, the cotton lining of the cradle, and the kitchen rags, had been anointed by liberal doses of baby spittle.

Liu had lived simply, and now he was confronted with a myriad of concerns, from a bed large enough for husband and wife to a source of income that could provide for their family.

He threw away a large pile of cigarette butts, watching helplessly as the ashes swirled about in a small cyclone before settling on the floor. So much seemed beyond his grasp, and he began to wonder if matrimony was an act of foolishness. Yet the fortuneteller had revealed that he would marry again, and nothing indicated that this would displease the gods.

Did he have the means to provide for yet another? He did not have the smarts to be an electrician like Wang Ma, or the skills to run a business like Tai. She's the one with the steady income, Liu thought ruefully.

Liu picked up a stray cigarette butt and tossed it in the garbage.

What kind of man am I if the woman has to take care of me? He shook his head as if he had been slapped.

Rose awoke from a nap and demanded to be picked up. Often, in those moments before she awoke, he would notice a fluttering in her eyes, an anguish that revealed itself in the curl of her lips, the quick contractions of her breath. Liu felt her hot cheek against his shoulders as she writhed about.

A pang of regret seized him. Liu would have to work like a beast again. He had given up a certain degree of autonomy upon adopting Rose, yet nobody dictated that he had to rise to the responsibilities of a wage earner, as long as he could put food on the table for both of them. Marriage, however, was different. A husband's role carried the trappings of respectability. Even as a lowly coal porter, Liu had been a decent man with a job in the eyes of Fei Fei's friends and family.

How would his future wife introduce him to her parents? "My husband, the scavenger who was released from prison?" A hawkish laugh escaped from his lips, waking Rose from her nap.

He ran his fingertips across her temple. "Little monkey, I'm going to get a new job. And you'll get a new Ma Ma. No more walks to the park, and donkey rides. Unless I have a day off." Rose blinked and tossed her head, which Liu took as a gesture of understanding. And then every part of her body calmed, her fluttering lips and chest, even the wispy hairs on her head, as if she had finally awoken from her nightmare.

•　　•　　•

TAI'S WAGGING FINGER HAD A MESMERIZING EFFECT ON LIU, much like the stump of rabbit's foot that Ol' Guo had dangled in front of little Rose. Like the rest of Tai, it was a crooked finger with good intentions.

"My friend, why in the world are you seeing that mastermind criminal again? Can't you tell he set you up in Fengdu?" Tai flicked his finger at Liu as if he were swatting flies.

"There wasn't much else around here," Liu replied. "I knew I was taking my chances. As a matter of fact, he did say something about the police."

"Well, he threw you a scented rag and you followed it like a bloodhound. But even a bloodhound wouldn't be fool enough to go after walking skeletons in a ghost town."

"I did find a jade bracelet," said Liu, staring down at the hole in his shoes. His big toe squirmed, a cornered mouse unable to hide.

"Great. Just make sure the authorities don't get you a second time."

"Tai, listen. I'm a desperate man. I will have to find a job, but I have a wedding to pay for, and a woman to satisfy. You know Big Chen, the antique dealer? He's big on gossip, stingy on deals. I bit my lip and took the bracelet to him. Told him it belonged to my deceased uncle. He offered me 50 *yuan*. Fifty *yuan*? Best I can do is get some baby clothes for Rose. I'd have to show up at my wedding in these old rags." Liu's toe lurched back, but could not retreat down its hole.

"Liu, that doesn't sound like you. When did you start caring about how you looked?"

"Maybe I'm getting older," said Liu in an earnest, pensive tone. "Tai, you know I was locked up with those protestors, and humiliated. As the days passed, their spirits withered, but somehow, my strength returned to me. I thought of my past, my life with Fei Fei, and my future. I breathed in the stink of my own sweat and piss, and I wanted something better than that. I'm tired of being alone, and no woman's going to take a man in rags."

●　●　●

LIU HAD REHEARSED HIS SPEECH A DOZEN TIMES. HE HAD A jade bracelet to sell. He would accept no less than 300 *yuan* for it. He would take it elsewhere if Fang could not meet his price. He refrained from telling Fang about the ordeal in Fengdu. Instead, he got down to business, and thrust the bracelet at Fang. "This is as genuine as it gets, jade with nice, dark veins. What do you say, Ol' Fang?"

Fang turned the bracelet over in his hand and squinted at it through a magnifying glass. "Hmmm . . . not bad."

"I'm taking no less than 300 *yuan*."

"Well," Fang clucked, "you drive a hard bargain. You know I can easily get a specimen like this somewhere else."

Liu clenched his teeth. "Take it or leave it, Fang. Three hundred *yuan.*"

"Okay, my friend, 300 it'll be. But you'll have to come back in a few days."

"No, Fang, I'd just as soon make the swap now." Liu snatched the bracelet out of the broker's palm. The old man had given in too easily. Surely, Fang was up to no good.

"You'd better come back." Fang's tone was imperious.

Liu swallowed hard. Fang could be such a tyrant behind the mask of the avuncular businessman.

"I'm going to be out of town," Fang explained, "to visit an old friend in Sichuan. He needs my help."

"I'll be going then," said Liu, turning toward the door

"No, my friend, wait. I want to ask you something." Fang's tone softened. The old man's mood seemed mercurial, like a gale that kept changing directions.

Fang insisted that Liu take a seat, and after some preparation, he brought out an expensive-looking tray of tea and served it British style with sugar and milk. Liu fumbled with the teacup handle, barely the size of his thumb, and spilled some of the hot liquid. He suspected that Fang was involved in some shady business. Exasperated, Liu set the cup down with a clatter.

"What do you want, Fang?"

The old man put his fingertips together. "I have a friend who lost his brother-in-law recently. The old geezer died with a bloated belly; too much drink, I suppose. This fellow, I'm told, has a daughter who lived not far from here, on the banks of the Daning, in Emerald Gorge. My friend wants to reclaim some of the objects his brother-in-law had given the daughter."

"Why can't your friend go straight to the daughter?" asked Liu.

"He has. Ol' Chu asked his niece, but she claims she had to leave their home in a hurry, as the Yangtze waters were rising up to their doorstep, and she did not have time to take all their possessions."

A sudden nausea overtook Liu. He had been scavenging on the

145

eve of the flooding. From that near disastrous foray into a village house, he had found a few valuables. He was still in possession of a lacquered box. And a baby.

Liu bit his lower lip. "So what can he do now? Everything's under water."

"My friend, you were foraging in the area when the new lake was rising." The old man's eyes glittered. "You were in those houses. Surely, some of those people must have left a keepsake or two behind. Not counting the babies; they don't have to stay in the family."

Liu flushed with anger. "What do you want from me, Fang? I found my girl, and I'm keeping her."

"Relax, Ol' Liu. Nobody's stealing your baby chicks. I'm tracking down some heirloom pieces for my friend. I'll ask him more closely when I see him." Fang got up and took the tea set away. "Tell you what, you look through your inventory, and when I come back we'll settle on the jade, and anything else you might have found. None of it's really yours, you know."

•   •   •

IN THE MONTHS LEADING UP TO THE WEDDING RECEPTION, MEI Ling called her parents several times to invite them to the auspicious occasion.

The first time, Mei Ling's father nearly broke the public phone in town when he learned that his daughter had gone against his wishes. "What a useless daughter," Chang Duoming muttered. "Don't know what's good for her. If she was standing right here, I'd show her how to respect her parents."

The plastic casing of the receiver cracked like a brittle bone. It spiraled in wandering circles, defying Mrs. Chang's efforts to pick up after her husband's rage. She pulled on his sleeve, glancing furtively at the door. "Ol' Chang! Come, come. Don't get the authorities on your back. If we make trouble, we'll wear out our welcome here."

Ol' Chang allowed his wife to drag him out of the building. Once outside, he began his ranting anew. "That no good daughter of yours. Should have sold her long ago. What a worthless girl."

Mei Ling's mother could only shake her head and allow the fires of his rage to burn out. She knew in her heart that Mei Ling had been a filial daughter, providing for them out of her hard-earned money.

When Mei Ling arranged to call again, Mrs. Chang borrowed a cell phone from the village chief, in hopes that her husband would remain subdued in another man's house. The conversation lasted no more than five minutes, and Ol' Chang stormed off, keeping a lid on his temper until they arrived home. That afternoon, terror reigned throughout their little farm. The pigs squealed as if they had been strung up live on the rafters. The hens clucked and rushed around their chicks in a maternal frenzy. The goats bleated like plaintive petitioners declaring they had done nothing wrong.

Ol' Chang stayed in a foul mood for days. The government had claimed a parcel of land to build a wind farm, and his small plot of land would shrink further. Their son was only fourteen, and when he came of age, perhaps there would be nothing left for him. If only he had another daughter to marry off to his neighbor. But if one daughter was worthless, what good would a second one be?

"I will become a toothless, blind beggar on the streets before I depend on an ungrateful daughter," he muttered to himself while chopping wood one afternoon in a small shed.

Chang Duoming had learned to make do his whole life. When he was a child, his family was reduced to boiling tree bark and corn husks during the worst of the great famine. Once, he managed to save a merchant's cart from being raided by bandits. The grateful man gave them a sack of rice. He remembered how his father's eyes had swelled with pride. Ol' Chang knew, at the age of seven, that he could die from hunger unless he kept his wits about him.

In their old village near Wushan, he had been unable to keep his family from being forced off the land. But in spite of defeat, Chang Duoming refused to give up. A battle cry filled his lungs, and when he lowered his axe on a stump of cedar, the wood split with a groan. "No, they'll never run me off the land again," he declared.

Chang Duoming wondered what his daughter's fiancé did. In

147

his disappointment, he had not bothered to ask. If this fellow had some resources, perhaps it wouldn't be so bad after all.

Before the third phone call, the Changs received a package in the mail from their new son-in-law. "Liu Renfu expresses gratitude for the marriage of your daughter," the note read. A box of sweet cakes was accompanied by a small red envelope, which contained two 100-*yuan* notes.

On the fourth call, Ol' Chang and his wife agreed to attend their daughter's wedding reception. The invitation came in a large, calligraphed envelope, and the card was crimson red with gold lettering. An accompanying note from Mei Ling indicated that their actual wedding would be a church ceremony two months before the libations.

Ol' Chang was disdainful of his wife and daughter's religious devotion. He wondered why Mei Ling was so anxious to get married; perhaps the thoughtless girl had gotten herself pregnant. But if this fellow Liu was a man of means, he could provide for not only his wife and son, but the in-laws as well.

•   •   •

WITH LESS THAN TWO WEEKS BEFORE THEIR NUPTIALS, MEI Ling rushed about her days with a glowing, breathless vigor as she combed through stores and catalog pages for wedding attire. There were consultations with the priest and fortuneteller, invitations to send out, and a long list of tasks that only a bride could check off with zeal.

There was also a new home awaiting Mei Ling. When she first laid eyes Liu's apartment, she could tell it had been tidied up and decorated with festive calendars. Yet Mei Ling cringed at the sight of the burned-out pots and the rusted pipes beneath the sink. Frayed curtains hung limply in front of a view of the old cement factory, a gray, prison-like complex. Her spirits faltered, like a young bird pitched from the safety of the nest into alien surroundings.

Mei Ling was sorry to leave her roommates, especially Pei. Their eviction at the end of the month rushed the couple's wedding plans, but Liu was happy to accommodate her need to move.

Hours after her roommate Lan departed for her graveyard shift, Mei Ling continued to sit at the old wooden desk, listening to Pei's soft breathing as she slept. Anxiety crept under her skin at those hours. One night, she let the glossy magazines slip out of her fingers, and rummaged deep into the drawer, fishing out a stone amulet carved by her old boyfriend.

She had almost eloped with him five years earlier, during those terrible storms that seized the Yangtze. Living on the steep banks near old Wushan, the Chang family had cultivated a small grove of oranges, a handful of walnut trees, as well as corn, wheat, and potatoes that were staples they lived on and bartered for rice. When the first storm came, the family huddled in the common room, watching the light of the bare electric bulb flicker and then extinguish as the wind howled and tore through their farm. In the morning, the fields were covered with detritus. The tall wheat stalks had been crushed as if stampeded by a herd of water buffalo. The corn stood like scarecrows with the tasseled ears dangling like broken limbs. The family counted their losses, and with heavy hearts, braced for a lean winter ahead.

A few days later, a bigger storm tore through the entire region. The Yangtze had turned into a bloated serpent, engorged with torrents of rain that emptied the sky of humor and light. Cascades of topsoil rained down the slopes in thick, brown tentacles, moving toward the river. The lattice of stones used to brace the terraced hillside was pried loose and hurled with the force of catapults into the Yangtze. Whatever had remained of the Changs' crops met a watery death.

The terrible rains had destroyed the Chang family's roof, and one after another, their feeble reinforcements gave way—the buckets soon overflowed, the plastic tarp on the roof tore loose and flapped like a howling demon, heavy boards and bricks did nothing to stem the inevitable destruction. When at last a whole section of the roof collapsed under the fury of the rains, the family gathered their meager possessions and huddled under a makeshift lean-to while Ol' Chang drove his donkey to town to secure a government-issue tent. Under its blue and white awning, the family subsisted for a month and a half as they rebuilt their home and salvaged what was left of their cropland.

It was during this time that Mei Ling thought of eloping with her boyfriend, whose home in a nearby village had not been destroyed. She had seethed for years under her father's derisive attacks, and now his vitriol was unbearable. It was Mei Ling's fault that she was not of age to bring income into the family, that she had taken the place of an able-bodied son, that she brought a line of penniless suitors to their door, and somehow, it was Mei Ling's insolence that invoked the vengeance of the gods on their family.

On the night of the planned escape, Mei Ling broke down and told her mother, who prostrated herself tearfully at Mei Ling's feet and promised that she would keep Ol' Chang's wrath at bay. "Don't think of it as a daughter's duty calling you to stay, my child. Think of your mother's love. Be patient; this isn't the time to break away, when the floods have torn everything out of our grasp."

Almost four years passed before Mei Ling did finally leave her *niang jia* to start a new life in Wushan. And now, as she was forced out of her apartment and welcomed into her new husband's home, she wondered why God had taken so long to free her from her father's grasp. Mei Ling turned the stone amulet over three times, as if performing a ritual for the departed, and then released it into a small wastebasket by the desk.

Those were surreal times, and her emotions, once brimming with passion and outrage, now seemed hollow. She had once sought marriage to escape, but there was nothing pressing her now. Her tyrannical father was in Guangdong, and the distance castrated him of his power over her. The eviction was an urgent matter, but nothing could drive her away from home like the onslaught of rain and her father's harsh words. At last, Mei Ling felt that she was free from the stranglehold of her past.

18

On the LAST DAY OF THE ELEVENTH MONTH, THE PARISHIONERS OF the Catholic Church gathered to celebrate the marriage of Liu Renfu and Chang Mei Ling. Father Chong conducted the brief ceremony at the end of Mass that Sunday.

When Mei Ling appeared at the entrance to the church, her radiant presence captivated each old soul in the pews, who sighed and exhaled as if an angel had descended in their midst. A gale of exhilaration swept over Liu, quelling the nervous shake in his hands and the pains in his feet, which were unused to such fancy shoes. Accompanied by an elderly parishioner, Mei Ling strode down the aisle like a great white crane with glorious feathers. A hush descended on the congregation as the escort placed her hand into Liu's.

That moment of contact carried Liu through the strangeness and tedium of the wedding ceremony. All the while, as he listened to the droning chants of the priest, and gazed upon the self-effacing countenance of Jesus Christ, Liu took comfort in the memory of that warm palm pressed into his.

When the moment came for Liu to kiss Mei Ling, he suddenly felt dizzy from the attention of a hundred frail souls. The smell of perfume and smoke from snuffed candles overpowered him. He leaned toward his glowing bride. Her crimson lips loomed like festive lanterns before turning black. And then the darkness swallowed him for a long, painful second. As he crumpled to the floor, the last image etched into his fuzzy brain was that of the priest, his long robe swirling in eddies, pale blue and white, like the frothy waters of the Daning.

A splash of cold water on Liu's forehead revived him, and the elderly women, who had nearly swooned in sympathetic reaction, now fanned themselves and mumbled prayers of thanks. The faces of the priest, Mei Ling, and her escort hovered above him in anxious anticipation. When he got back unsteadily on his feet, Liu felt a violent rush of blood to his temples, the heat erupting through his skin in prickles of self-loathing.

He took a deep breath as he faced Mei Ling again and peered into her deep brown eyes. The gentle pressure of her hands comforted Liu. If there were any dark feelings she harbored, the coal-tinted lines of her eyelashes obscured them.

"I pronounce you man and wife. You may now . . . uh . . . take the bride's hand," Father Chong chuckled.

The couple left the church amidst the thunderous echoes of the organ, past the old women who dabbed at their eyes and careworn brows. A few in the congregation uttered prayers for the young couple, in hopes that the day's mishap would not be an omen of future calamities.

•   •   •

FANG SHUPING SELDOM VISITED THE HOUSES OF THOSE WHO lived in circumstances beneath his. Standing in the courtyard of Chu Longshan's modest home, he lingered before knocking. He had set out early in the morning, heading west with the sun, to make the long trip to Lanping village. He could hear the chickens scratching in the dirt outside the compound. The brief moments of solitude allowed him mastery over any house, not just his fine brick bungalow on the outskirts of Wushan.

Chu Longshan had been his only friend during his stint of commune life in Sichuan. In the thirty-five years since, Fang had amassed a small fortune. His real estate dealings over the past few months buoyed him up from the shadowy realms to a new level of respectability. His friend Longshan, however, had remained a common peasant. After the large commune was disbanded, Longshan saw his meager fortunes slip away as he struggled to defend his land against natural disasters and human schemes that grew like weeds in Sichuan province.

When Fang arrived, Chu Longshan's eyes lit up, and he pumped his old friend's hand vigorously. "Fang ol' brother. It's been too long. Come in, come in. Your hands are cold. Let's warm you up."

Longshan told his wife, a pretty woman whose gray hair showed at the edges, to throw wood into the stove and make some tea.

Fang stared down at his leather boots. The floor seemed cold and dirty, and he did not offer to remove them. He glanced around the common room, which contained only a dining table hewn from pine and rickety low chairs that could easily be mistaken for kindling.

Longshan invited Fang to sit down. "Please make yourself at home."

"I was pleasantly surprised to get a letter from you. Why, the last time we were in touch was . . . let's see . . . ten years ago."

"My son got married," said Longshan, "and you came to the wedding."

"Ah yes. And now your brother-in-law has died. How is your sister faring?" Fang asked.

"She is making the best of it. So sudden, you know. The poor man's heart gave out, and we were too far from medical help."

"Yes, a shame. But I suppose the gods take us when it is our time." Fang fingered the rough edges of the mug that Longshan's wife had filled with tea. He was not truly sorry to hear of his death. This man had laid claim to the one desire that eluded Fang more than half his life, the consummation of his love for Longshan's sister, Chu Sulin.

When Fang's affair with Sulin was discovered, her brother had remained a staunch ally. But that did not matter in the elder Chu's eyes. A capitalist's son was a capitalist's son. Fang was an enemy of the revolution who had disgraced the daughter of a brigade leader. Chu Longshan questioned the peasants' indictment and begged his father to spare Fang's life, but to no avail. His sister pleaded and bargained, then threatened to take her own life. At last, their father relented.

Years after his exile from the commune, Fang learned that Sulin had married the son of a prominent Party official, to whom she was betrothed. He had been driven to despair, but his ravaged heart knew that she must have loved him still. Fang sensed that his fortunes would change again. And yet, there was no other woman like Sulin.

•　•　•

"WE HAVE BEEN PREPARING FOR MY BROTHER-IN-LAW'S FUNERAL," said Longshan, "and I'm afraid there is not enough to pay for a proper burial unless we find some items he had given his daughter."

"Yes, you mentioned in the letter. What are you looking for exactly?" Fang asked.

"My brother-in-law gave his daughter a gold pendant shortly before she gave birth, about a year ago. When she had a daughter, he was quite disappointed, and asked for it back."

"But she refused?" interrupted Fang.

"Yes, but she says that she no longer has it. Says the river claimed it when their home was flooded six months ago."

"Silly girl, should have kept the gold and given up the child."

"It's a long shot, but I thought you might know some authorities in the area. Someone who might have inspected the houses before they were destroyed."

"No, my good man, I'm afraid those bastards won't get their boots dirty, unless you hold their firstborn for ransom. There's a scavenger who worked for me, however. He combed through the area where your niece lives. Where was that again?"

"Suchien village, down a ways in Emerald Gorge. Has your man been there?"

"Perhaps. It rings a bell. I'll pursue the matter with him more closely. If the fellow has the goods, he'll cooperate. He's a thirsty pig at the watering trough, just getting married himself."

Fang lit his pipe and offered his lighter to Longshan. The two men smoked in silence for a while, and Fang noticed with irony how their fortunes had been reversed, how Longshan's carriage and garb stood in stark contrast to his own. Fang's attire was befitting of his new status; even a cross-country trip called for a wool sweater and tweed pants, topped with his favorite black overcoat. His friend was dressed in a Mao suit in faded blue, threadbare from years of heavy labor. It seemed less a political statement than an act of necessity.

Longshan sat hunched over in the hard wooden chair, with his elbows against his knees, as if pondering a difficult decision. His brows were knitted together out of habit; he appeared to be constantly scrutinizing his whereabouts. The worry lines only deepened when he broke into a laugh.

"You know, Ol' Fang," said Longshan, "I never did like my brother-in-law. He had a foul temper, and bad breath from eating all that garlic. It's a wonder that Sulin could stand being near him long enough to produce children."

"Maybe she'll forget the old goat in time."

"Well, you never married. But old couples get used to each other's ways, even if they can't stand them." Longshan's wife appeared in the doorway and shot him a steely glance. "Not you, my dear. You're perfect," Chu Longshan added with a chuckle.

"Ol' Chu, I must be going. I've got some business in Chengdu tomorrow. But if I find those heirloom pieces, I'd like to take them myself to Sulin."

"Fang, you old steed. I would wait a bit. At least until the mourning period has passed. You never know what old fires you might rekindle."

"And how tragic is that?"

"Well, it could break a poor widow's heart." Longshan arched his brow. Clearly, he would allow nothing to threaten his sister's welfare.

Fang backed off. "Of course, she must grieve the full forty-nine days. Well, give it another thirty days or so, eh? I've waited as many years."

•　　•　　•

THE DAY AFTER THE WEDDING CEREMONY, MEI LING PACKED up her things to move into Liu's apartment. Her roommate Lan had moved out a week earlier, and the good-byes were perfunctory. Matrimony had cast a spell on Lan, although the prince of her dreams spoke only semi-coherent Chinese, and she could croak out no more than a few garbled words in German. It was much harder for Mei Ling to part with her friend Pei.

"He seems like a good fellow," said Pei, putting down one of the boxes she had packed for Mei Ling. "I'm happy for you."

"I got two for the bargain, including a baby," Mei Ling replied. "Liu is quite mild tempered. But that child is a hotheaded one, quite willful."

"At least you don't have a mother-in-law to worry about," Pei chuckled.

"Thank God, no. My crabby father is enough to handle, and he's hundreds of miles away."

"Well, if my folks start driving me crazy, I may just show up on your doorstep one of these days."

They stood in the doorway, surrounded by the few boxes and keepsakes they would take into their new lives. Mei Ling leaned into her friend's bony shoulder, which had provided her support unfailingly, without question or judgment. The two women hugged in silence; no words would come out of Mei Ling's lips. At length, she wiped her tear-streaked face and mumbled, "Be well, dear Pei."

"Mei Ling, do not hesitate to call, all right?" Pei spoke in her usual, no-nonsense way, but her eyes betrayed a tremulous light. She paused for a moment before adding, "And don't look too far for happiness, my friend."

•   •   •

RISING ON two tiny feet, Rose braced herself against the legs of the chair. She wanted to crawl beneath its protective frame, but curiosity got the better of her.

On the other side of the room lay a stack of cubical brown objects. A flurry of activity had filled the apartment earlier in the day, when Rose was napping. It had disrupted her rest, and now she felt a pressing ache in her temple, but she could not lie down again. The perfumed stranger had shown up in her house.

She had come in after the last of the boxes, and her powerful scent became intermingled with the dust ushered in from the city streets. The woman seemed to notice her only when Rose sneezed loudly, causing her to lose her balance and land on her padded bottom. A succession of discomforts ensued—a jolt to her sit bones that shot down her thighs, a tinkle of laughter from the stranger, a tightness in her chest swelling like a feverish head or a tummy ache.

Her daddy scooped her up in his arms, and uttered soothing sounds. His laughter was gentle, familiar. He approached the strange lady and held Rose's arm toward her.

The scent of lilac engulfed Rose like a hot mist. The woman's lips parted into a wide smile. They seemed unusually crimson, like her father's cheeks when he smelled of something fermented and grainy. Rose allowed her fingers to touch the woman's cheek, which was cool and smooth, with a powdery layer that smelled of the same perfume, but more muted.

Rose felt herself lifted away from her father's chest, and for a moment she was suspended in space as she waited for the woman to receive her. And then she felt herself slipping from the woman's grasp. She arched her back to stay afloat, her breath coming in shallow gulps. Fussing and soothing noises erupted from her daddy and the woman. When she was settled into the woman's arms, Rose felt her father's rough hands stroking her hair, now long enough to tickle her ears and the fretful space above her brows.

She felt soothed by her father's touch, but the intimate presence of the stranger confused her. The woman's bosom was delicately curved, unlike the bulbous mass of the old lady or the smooth, hard plane of her father's chest. She sensed a restlessness in that bosom, like a cold prickle on the skin. She was afraid she would be dropped again.

Terror filled her heart, a formless memory of cold and hunger seized her in its grip—the scratch of rough wicker, a damp chill in the air, the straitjacket of musty cloths binding her. She howled ferociously, but could not shake the sensation of aloneness and vast, empty space. Where was the wrinkled woman with the round belly and bosom? The cloth cradle which lulled Rose into slumber against a beating heart? The nose-tingling smells of chicken broth and medicinal bark?

The stranger's frame felt hollow and light. Rose remembered a feminine body like hers, whose milk ran thin like water, and then ran dry. Rose had displeased her mother somehow, at a time when memories were but wisps of sensation. Without warning, the warmth of that bosom, and its shelter from wind and cold, were snatched away one day.

She began to wail. She sensed hungry birds about her, circling with great beaks and bloody eyes pointed toward her cold flesh.

Rose was inconsolable. Her perch in the woman's arms became precarious. She twisted about, and as she began to slip once more, she allowed her weight to become heavy, sinking to the ground. Her father took her back and stroked her chest with his big, bony hands. His eyes twinkled with light, and his liquid voice broke through her misery. She soon fell asleep, but when she awoke, the apparition of a gaunt, barren-breasted figure hovered in the room. It evaporated with the taste of rubber and milk, but her anxiety lingered. The perfumed woman had taken its place.

●　　●　　●

THROWN INTO THE DUAL ROLE OF WIFE AND MOTHER, MEI Ling found comfort in filling her mornings with projects to beautify their little home. She found new drapes with a grainy, thick weave that allowed in light, but disguised the hideous views of Wushan's less seemly parts. She filled the one-room apartment with light, covering the table, bed, and crib in vibrant colors. New towels graced the kitchen and the little sink by the bed. She bought a lovely set of plates and bowls etched with ornate borders. In the center of each piece of china was a blue carp, like the ones her father used to catch in the Yangtze. Strangely, this seemed to upset her new husband a great deal, although he had not shown any displeasure toward her, or a finicky sense of taste until then. Liu mumbled something about the shape of the rice bowls, too delicate for his clumsy hands. Blinking furiously, he picked up a plate and traced the image of the carp as if he could divine some message in those lines. Mei Ling did not know what to say, but figured it was prudent to take back the china set without pursuing the matter further.

Aside from the dishes, Liu was generally easygoing about household matters; the baby's mercurial moods, however, occupied much of Mei Ling's attention. At best, Rose was curious and eager to touch Mei Ling's hair or tug on her sleeves, as if she were a plaything for the baby's enjoyment. But when Mei Ling attempted to pick her up, or feed her, or act in any way like a parent or caretaker, little Rose would revolt against the attention. One day, while Liu was out, she threw a small plate of peas to the floor, chattering like a monkey as Mei Ling wiped up the mess. "Little Rose, what's the matter? Why do you act like this?" Mei Ling sighed, exasperated.

The infant squirmed to get off the wooden chair, her legs fluttering like kite tails. Mei Ling caught her under the arms to prevent a fall. Rose struggled to free herself, and tottered two steps forward before falling on all fours. She waddled toward the crib, then sat down beside it on her haunches, sucking her thumb. Mei Ling noticed the infant's eyes following her, trained like a hawk's on every movement. As she cleaned up the last of the peas, she felt weariness in her legs. She missed the freedom of her life before marriage. She wondered why she had not learned more about this insolent child before she had accepted Liu's proposal. Mei Ling felt reduced to the nanny she had once been, except this time the jealousy was manifesting in the child. She wondered if she could learn to love the child, one that wasn't her flesh and blood. Yet Liu himself was not the father, but an uncle, as he had explained, who adopted her in the wake of her parents' death.

Mei Ling washed her hands, and sat in the chair that Rose had vacated. "Little Rose, I'm not your mother, but you'll have to learn to live with me."

The infant stared at her with round, innocent eyes. She jingled a bell on her crib, thumping her legs in delight. Mei Ling sensed that the girl felt safe at this distance.

When Liu came home, Mei Ling told him about the incident. A look of worry flashed across his face, and he reached out to console her. "Give it time, Mei Ling. She's not afraid of strangers, but you're more than that now. You're her new mother."

Was that a role she had chosen to take on? Mei Ling was torn by the sense of duty, and a simmering, nameless desire that stirred in her bosom. It confused her, but she did not want to alarm Liu by telling him. They were still getting acquainted, yet somehow expected to share the intimacies of married life. "Well, she doesn't want me to come near her," Mei Ling said quietly.

Liu turned toward the baby, who was anxious to be picked up. "Little monkey, can't keep still, can you?" He lifted her high in the air, and she screeched as she came down. "Now when you see this woman, what do you call her?"

A jumble of syllables spilled from Rose's lips: *ba-ba-ga-ga-ma-ma.*

"See here." Liu sidled close to Mei Ling. "Ma Ma. This is Ma Ma."

Perched in Liu's arms, the baby flashed a smile revealing several crooked teeth. "Ba Ba!" little Rose cried, hitting her palm against Liu's shoulder.

Mei Ling's chest heaved. Soon she would be going to work. As she hopped on the mini bus, pulling her winter cap down around her ears, she wished that she were traveling to a warm, convivial place far away from her new home.

•   •   •

SEATED IN THE LIVING ROOM, LIU STARED AT THE LARGE PORTRAIT of Fang's parents while his host served tea. The old broker had a fancy couch, but it was hard on the sit bones. Liu took a deep breath, irritated once more with the meaningless gestures of hospitality.

"Liu, ol' boy, what great treasures have you brought for my appraisal?" Fang lit his pipe in a leisurely manner.

"Well, Fang, you know we've made a deal over the jade. You remember, right?"

"Yes. Anything else? Anything from Emerald Gorge?" A hint of eagerness tinged the old man's voice.

"I did find a few trinkets during the flood several months ago. Almost forgot about them." Liu tried to sound nonchalant, although he had less than two months to generate enough cash for the wedding banquet.

A lacquered box emerged from Liu's knapsack, containing an embroidered pouch. He lifted out the gold pendant and handed it to Fang. "This is clearly an heirloom, left behind by one of the villagers on the river bank."

Fang seized the pendant and twirled it in his fingers, mesmerized, as if it were an amulet with magical powers. "This would have been given to the parents of a newborn, yes? Fantastic." Fang was talking to nobody in particular and no longer seemed to notice his guest. Liu fidgeted with his teacup.

"Okay, Fang, what will you pay me for it? I'll take it to Chen's if you—"

"My dear man, you have produced a fount of good fortune. For you and me both, that is, for my friend who is looking for this very piece of metal I'm holding in my hands." Fang peeled his gaze away and eyed the lacquered box. "And what else did you find?"

"Nothing, really. Just an old photo."

"Let me see it."

When Liu handed over the photo, he noticed a curious change in the old man's countenance. As Fang fingered the worn edges of the photo, his breath came in short, raspy bursts. All traces of cynicism, etched over the years into his brow and jawline, disappeared. Instead, a strange light glowed in Fang's eyes, and his mouth hung slightly open, vacillating between a nervous twitch and a smile. Liu did not think Fang could be capable of such a smile, one that radiated pure, guileless joy.

"You like that photo?" Liu asked.

"I suppose you could say that," Fang answered at length.

"Do you know them?" Liu pointed at the faded image of the man and his wife seated next to him.

"I knew this woman, a long time ago, before you were even born." That strange glow lingered in Fang's eyes, and Liu sensed that if something could hold the crusty old man in its grasp, it had to be the love of a woman. He did not want to pry. And yet, for the first time, he knew that Fang did not have the upper hand.

"So you want the picture. I might be able to throw it in. But I've got a wedding reception to pay for, and perhaps I'll get a better price from Big Chen for this pendant. No middleman costs." Liu put the pendant back in its pouch, and reached for the photo.

Fang leaned back in his chair, guarding the photo with his hands. "I'll take the whole package. Just name a price."

"That's not like you, Fang. Come on, I know you too well."

"Try me."

"Okay, 1200 *yuan* for the gold. And 400 for the bracelet."

"It's a deal."

Liu could not believe his ears. The blood rushed into his temples, roaring in his ears like waves cresting and falling. He fidgeted with the pouch as Fang went into the study, still cradling the old print in his hands. When the old broker returned, he counted out sixteen bills in crisp, 100-*yuan* denominations, and handed them over with a playful slap. "For your lovely bride. It's a joyous occasion all around."

As he escorted Liu to the foyer, Fang added, "Even an old bachelor like me can find happiness again."

19

SIXTEEN HUNDRED *YUAN* WAS A LOT OF MONEY IN LIU'S eyes. In his coal-hauling days, that kind of money would have taken at least four months of backbreaking labor to earn. And now, through a stroke of luck, and some twist of fate that Liu did not fully understand, he had come to possess this windfall of money through relatively little effort.

Yet the money did not put Liu at ease. What started as genuine passion, as the reawakened desire for a woman's love and touch, had somehow become weighed down by the obligations of marriage and family life. Of the 1600 *yuan*, 200 went toward repaying Tai for the gift to Mei Ling's father. Rose had fallen ill again, and another of those bills went toward medicines. She had not taken as well to Mei Ling as he had hoped, and between keeping peace and tending to Mei Ling's desires for upgrading their home, he could not even think about long-term work. Mei Ling did not ask about the source of his funds, and Liu was content to keep this a secret. Still, as he sat in Tai's restaurant in the evenings with little Rose beside him, Liu felt ashamed that his wife was the industrious breadwinner and he had become the de facto househusband, and his skills at keeping house were quite poor at that.

Although he and Mei Ling were now joined as man and wife, Liu could not forget a certain unfinished task. It nagged him, dragged him back to the past, to his life with Fei Fei. He still had to pay respects to the deceased, and it was the fortuneteller Seh Yen who had admonished him to keep this obligation. The previous year, his scavenging work had taken him far and wide, but not to Fengjie. And besides, old Fengjie no longer existed. No, that was no excuse. He had to admit that his grief had actually kept him from Fei Fei, from the murky realms of the departed, until his ordeal in Fengdu opened that door. It took imprisonment to free him, to kindle his hopes for a second chance at life.

Liu had told Mei Ling that he was a widower, but it would be a delicate matter to broach his intended visit to Fengjie with their wedding reception so near at hand. It was unspeakable to convey happiness and sorrow in the same breath. And it was unthinkable to pay regard to glorious beginnings and tragic endings all at once, and so close to the lunar New Year. For days he waited for the right moment to approach Mei Ling about the matter.

One Saturday, Liu brought home half a dozen steamed buns and smoked sausages made by one of the local peasant families. "Liu, these sausages are my favorite. What's the occasion?" Mei Ling asked.

Liu had few qualms about shading the truth to avoid friction, particularly in explaining his adoption of Rose, but the matter at hand was too urgent. "I'm glad you like them. Mei Ling, I've been wanting to talk to you about something, but since we've been caught up in all these preparations, I haven't asked——"

"What is it?" Mei Ling bit into a plump sausage, spiced with dried red chilies and star anise.

"The anniversary of my wife's death is approaching, and I must pay my respects. I'll need to go to Fengjie for a few days."

A cloud passed over Mei Ling's countenance. She threw down her chopsticks. "What do you mean, your wife? I thought *I* was your wife."

"I mean my old wife; she's been gone for two years, and I've not had the time to do my duties, to help ease her journey as a departed soul. Might be good for us, too."

"I see. . . . " Mei Ling's jealousy, which had flared so quickly, frightened Liu, but she seemed to be reassured by his explanation. "Perhaps you can pray for her. Let us do that in church tomorrow, shall we?"

"Yes, but in keeping with her practice, I should visit the temple by Fengjie."

"And how will we take care of Rose?" Mei Ling asked, a pensive look flitting across her eyes.

"Well, it may take some time for Rose to get used to things around here, but she's been sick lately, so I don't think I should take her along." He made a silent wish that she could warm up to Mei Ling while he was away.

"I don't know how she'll handle your absence. Why, you go out for half an hour, and she gets fussy and starts to throw a tantrum unless I give her a little toy or treat. I can't just keep bribing her to keep her quiet for a whole week."

"It's too bad that Mrs. Song can't take care of Rose anymore, much less herself," said Liu. "Don't worry, we'll find someone to care for her while you're at work. And I'll only be gone for a few days." At this, the baby screeched, as if she understood that her father was leaving her behind once more.

•   •   •

THE DAY BEFORE HE LEFT FOR FENGJIE, LIU TOOK ROSE TO PAY Mrs. Song one last visit.

The landlord had announced that a new apartment in the building would be available, and it was Mrs. Song's. When her son learned of her dementia, he decided to put her in a senior home in Shanghai, a new facility with the best medical care in the country.

A nurse answered the door and ushered him in. She had been feeding Mrs. Song, and quickly wiped the old woman's lips and nostrils as Liu stepped inside. Mrs. Song's robust face now appeared gaunt, and her plumpness sagged, hanging onto her arms like dumplings. Her round belly was deflated beneath the crinkles of her embroidered vest. Still, she seemed to be in good spirits, and a faint light appeared in her eyes when she saw Liu.

"Mrs. Song, it's Liu, your neighbor, and little Rose. You remember Rose?" Liu sat beside Mrs. Song, and Rose leaned toward the old woman, reaching for her bosom.

"Rose . . . what a pretty name. Your child?"

165

"Yes. You took care of her for many months. See how she takes to you?"

"A darling child." Rose was placed on Mrs. Song's lap, and she held onto the child with limp hands. Somehow, though, her hands seemed to hold a glimmer of recognition, and she repeated, "Darling child. She has a good appetite?"

"Yes, you were a big help in fattening her up. She was a skinny thing just six months ago."

"What does she like to eat?"

"Why, she likes your custard, and the mashed peas and carrots, and porridge with shredded pork."

"Well, let's make her some." Mrs. Song turned to her nurse, and in a moment of lucidity, she asked for her purse and coat for a trip to the market.

The nurse looked uncertainly at her charge, then at Liu. "She's not supposed to go out."

"It's the last chance she'll have before they take her away," Liu said. "It'll be all right. There's two of us to watch her."

That afternoon, the four descended a long series of stone steps to Wushan's main street, stopping often for Mrs. Song to rest. The nurse held onto Mrs. Song, and Liu carried Rose with one hand and braced his neighbor's arm with the other. At length, they arrived at the open market in a side alley. Here, tucked between the gleaming modern storefronts that rumbled with pop music, was a vestige of old Wushan.

The market bustled with the morning activity of shoppers. A long row of vegetable vendors streamed down the middle of the alley, their wicker baskets overflowing with *bai chai*, onions, and lettuce. The gnarled surfaces of bitter cucumber and green pepper glistened in the hazy winter light. Fragrant smells of fried bean curd wafted from stalls to their right, and on the other side, the little shops overflowed with wrapped candies and peanuts. Liu pulled his daughter's hand away from a mound of chestnuts, where a customer was haggling with the irate seller. An old woman hefted two large baskets of oranges on her carrying pole, giving her the appearance of a weighing scale as she crossed the alleyway, steadfastly keeping her balance. Porters looking for work sauntered down the main street with their bamboo poles slung over their shoulders, the tangle of carrying cords hanging loose like an empty fishing net. They reminded Liu of his days hustling for work in a town that no longer existed.

"Stop here!" cried Mrs. Song. "I want to get some cabbage and snow peas for supper. And a cut of pork ribs." She pointed to two shanks of cured meat hanging off a vendor's pole. "I'll make a stew tonight. My husband will enjoy that."

The nurse looked at Liu, and they gently pulled Mrs. Song away, saying that it was still too early to shop for supper.

"Where's Ol' Jing?" Mrs. Song turned toward a shop, slipping out of their grasp. "He sells the best *baijiu* in town, and my husband likes a glass of it with his cigarettes in the evening."

"His shop is closed," Liu said, thinking better than to tell her that the rest of the old town had sunk with it into the Yangtze.

When they returned to the apartment, Mrs. Song waved her guests off with a cheerful, "Come visit me soon." Liu grabbed little Rose, who seemed reluctant to leave, and with a nod and forced smile, he shuffled away, only to linger in the hallway long after the nurse closed the door.

•   •   •

ALONE WITH THE BABY, MEI LING WONDERED HOW SHE COULD endure four days with the fussy child. Little Rose was an impish, peevish baby, and she managed to get into enough mischief in their tiny apartment to sully her baby clothes quite often. She crawled across the kitchen while Mei Ling was getting dressed for work one afternoon, and the sleeve cuffs that were clean in the morning now had a fresh coat of cigarette ash and food crumbs.

"Oh goodness." Mei Ling grabbed a fresh pair of sleeve cuffs. As she pulled the soiled ones from the baby's elbows, the creature struggled and kicked with all her might. "Now hold still." Rose yelped in protest, shaking her head in a fit of defiance. Mei Ling grabbed her tiny wrists and gave them a hard shake. "Stop it! Your daddy's not here, and you'd better behave."

The baby howled, her half-drawn sleeves flapping like ragged kites in the wind.

Mei Ling lifted the creature, a writhing mass of displeasure, and set her down in the crib.

Sinking to the floor, Mei Ling buried her head in her hands. Once again, she was no better than a servant to the whims of others. She was caught in a hopeless situation, rejected by a child who wasn't hers. And what if she had wanted to have one of their own? A second would incur a hefty fine, and in the city, there was no escaping the government's notice. In the countryside, at least one could give the unwanted offspring to relatives.

Mei Ling flashed upon an idea. The girl was adopted after Liu's brother died. Perhaps she could be passed on again, even if she was a girl. Yet it was clear that Liu adored that child, and with the reception coming up, now was not the time to bring up such a proposal. In the meantime, Mei Ling was going to find a way to make peace with the little devil.

The next day, Rose tottered into the kitchen as Mei Ling was getting dressed. Her steps were rather unsteady, so she fell on all fours and scampered into the recesses of the counter. A jungle of wondrous objects surrounded her—a hulking sack of rice, a large jar of pickled vegetables, and dried anchovies with a briny smell that tickled her nostrils. On the floor was a small bone, a tendon-covered joint of pork, no more than two days old. It was the kind Mrs. Song used for making broth. Rose stuffed the bone in her mouth. She rolled it around, her teeth not quite able to grasp its rubbery contours. And then, in the next instant, the bone slid down her throat and lodged against her trachea. Rose opened her mouth to scream, but nothing came out. In vain she tried to suck in air, but could only flail her body against her cramped surroundings.

When Mei Ling heard the commotion, she rushed into the kitchen, and upon seeing the pallor in Rose's face, she scooped up the baby and tapped her briskly on the back. Not a peep of sound came out. "Oh dear," Mei Ling muttered. She stuck her finger into the child's mouth, wincing as she ran into the nubs of new molars. Mei Ling thought of her brother; a similar thing had occurred many years ago when he was a baby. A wise old man in the village had rushed over, seized the boy by the ribs, and given several sharp thrusts with his fists. Bracing herself against the wall, Mei Ling administered the same treatment, although with less force. A heave, and the baby's head lurched forward. Another, and then another, and out came the offending bone. At last, Rose could cough and fuss like her old self. Mei Ling exhaled a deep sigh, and sat with the baby against her bosom, until she remembered she was due at work.

Mei Ling hoped that their domestic life would be a little easier now, and perhaps somewhere in the child's young brain was a glimmer of gratitude. The creature now settled down whenever Mei Ling held her, as she did that afternoon, against her bosom. And yet, while she was perfectly willing to let go of the battle of wills, Mei Ling could not as yet surrender the deeper stirrings of her heart to motherhood.

•　　•　　•

THE PORT of Fengjie was busy this time of year, as many migrant workers, students, and traveling businessmen were returning to their families for the lunar New Year. Liu carried a small black bag with some overnight provisions for his stay with Wang Ma, the fellow he had met on his foray into the ghost town of Fengdu. That trip, Liu had sworn, would be the last of its kind.

Besides paying respects to Fei Fei, he hoped to find prospects for work in town. Yet his body was no longer youthful, and his muscles had lost suppleness, if not strength. Liu wondered if his unorthodox life in recent times had made him too soft.

New Fengjie was not too different from where he lived. On the hill were endless rows of high-rises; below, the river town bustled with the activity of merchants, porters, and shoppers. Liu climbed into a small minibus, already crammed with half a dozen passengers. Whenever it lurched to a stop, the impossible would happen. Another fellow would pile in, scrunching his elbows and ribs; another load would be shoved in the back, already overloaded with rice sacks and boxes of merchandise. Fengjie seemed to be more prosperous than Wushan. If the place reminded him of Fei Fei, it was in name only. He figured the old town had really died with her; indeed, it had found a resting place downstream beneath the tamed Yangtze.

The minibus headed along a highway and across the bridge to Baidicheng, the White Emperor City, where the famed temple stood on a small peninsula. From the side of the road, Liu made his way down the overgrown hill, past peasant homes that dotted its steep slope. After climbing the long stairway to the temple's front entrance, he was told he needed to pay 50 *yuan* to enter.

"But I'm not a tourist," protested Liu.

The gatekeeper stared at him. "You're the first one to show up today. And you expect me to let you in free?"

"I'm paying respects to my wife. She died not far from here."

The man squinted his eyes. A soft breeze rustled the trees inside the compound. Liu said nothing more, enduring the agony of silence. At last, the man gestured him through the gate.

Inside the grounds, Liu wandered past stone tablets of ancient writings, a grove of bamboo, and a fetid pond surrounding a nearly life-sized statue that had seen better days. He remembered the name, Liu Yuxi, a venerable poet of the Tang Dynasty. "From the Liu clan," Fei Fei had once told him, smiling. In the inner square, past idle vendors playing cards, Liu found the sanctuary where a monk greeted him languorously. He, too, seemed to be off duty and enjoying the absence of human traffic.

"Sifu," said Liu, "I have come in the memory of my wife, who passed away two years ago."

"Ah, your sorrow must be great," replied the monk. "Come, light three sticks of incense and kneel before the Buddha."

At the monk's direction, Liu bowed three times, and placed the incense in a large urn.

"Arise, and follow me," said the monk, leading him to a small table, where they sat. The monk gazed at Liu's countenance, and began to pontificate in words he could not understand. Liu was neither devoted nor educated, as Fei Fei had been. It was Fei Fei who found comfort in the chants and ritual prostrations when she was alive.

In the Lap of the Gods

At length, the monk began to speak to Liu's situation. "You must learn to let go of the past. Only then will you find peace, and be free from suffering of the heart."

Liu nodded. Indeed, he had come to grips with Fei Fei's death, and the anguish of knowing that he could have prevented it—if he had been more stern with her, if he had kept her from venturing out in her eighth month of pregnancy.

"What you once had is gone. And you must not be apathetic, for this world is impermanent. What you find comfort in will be taken away, and where you seek solid ground the earth will always be shifting. In the ways of work, you must be diligent, so that you can provide for those in your immediate circle. In human relations, you must be wary, as no person is to be fully trusted when they have their own selfish motives at heart."

"What about those close to me? I am married again," Liu added, feeling somewhat ill at ease.

"You have chosen to share your fortunes with another, and for both to prosper, both must also suffer loss."

Liu started, unsure what the cryptic words meant. "But I have lost already," he cried. "I lost a wife once before. Please tell me, kind master, that I won't have to go through such terrible loss again."

"As the Taoist masters have said, 'Praise and blame, gain and loss, are all the same,'" the monk replied, his demeanor placid and unwavering. He seemed oblivious to Liu's growing distress. Finished with his sermon, the monk stood up and pointed to the donation box before ushering Liu out of the sanctuary.

Liu stumbled outside, trembling as he fell to his knees. His intuition had been to do his duty, out of loyalty and love, and the upwelling of grief caught him by surprise. Surely, he had honored her, spared her more suffering, forgiven her, and sought her forgiveness. What more was needed?

Still agitated, Liu pulled himself up the high wall that sheltered the temple compound. He peered over the edge into the swirling eddies of the river. He could see how Fei Fei had died. She had gone to visit a friend in Shibao Block, and on the way

171

back the ship entered Xiling Gorge, where the rapids had been treacherous.

It had been a strangely windy day, with the gale coming from all directions. The waves sloshed around the small boat, pushing it toward the naked outcropping of rock close to shore. The wind picked up and the waves danced in unison, lifting the boat high in the air. Hollers from the crew forced the passengers inside. She clutched her seat and chanted silently to herself, beseeching the Buddha of infinite wisdom. "*Ami tuo fuo. Ami tuo fuo. Ami tuo fo.*" The boat struck rock, and the splintered wood and passengers fell away. The ancient dragon of the Yangtze swallowed them all. That day, when Liu was expecting her return, Fei Fei and their unborn child were taken away. The bodies had drifted toward shore, but her spirit remained beyond the grasp of his sorrow and his futile hopes.

Staring into the murky waters, Liu cried out, "I lost my family. I cannot bear to lose again."

He wondered if any attempt had even been made to rescue Fei Fei. It was considered bad luck to go after a drowning person, even if she was pregnant and close to bringing a child into the world.

"What a cruel world this is." Liu sank his head into the folds of his jacket, and rocked himself until his trembling body could not cast off any more layers of grief. He drifted into a delirious slumber, and when dusk fell, he roused himself and clattered down the ancient stone steps to return to Fengjie.

•   •   •

THE NEXT DAY, WANG MA TOOK HIS VISITING FRIEND TO HIS favorite hot pot restaurant in Fengjie. He sensed that Liu was in a despondent mood, and did not ask him about his visit to the temple in Baidicheng.

The two ate in silence for some time, as Wang Ma added more slices of raw beef and tofu to the bubbling pot on their table, encouraging his friend to eat. "Ah, being an electrician isn't so bad after all," Wang Ma said, "now that my hair no longer stands on end."

172

"Any prospects for a fellow like me? Not much schooling, just willing to work."

"There's not much industry here in Fengjie. The cement factory shut down. All the state-owned businesses, as you know, have failed. Why, I worked for a linen factory for fifteen years, always thinking that the government would take care of me in my old age, like a good son takes care of his father. When it tanked, we were given a small amount of severance pay, and turned out to the streets."

"I could never stay in jobs working for some big boss," said Liu. "How does someone like me find decent work? I'm not good at being a cog in a big wheel."

"A big wheel it is. See all those men carrying loads? They're really not necessary. If this town could afford new technology, they'd be gone in a heartbeat. That's why there aren't any more coal-hauling jobs for us; highways and trucks are better any day than a hundred men scampering about the dock. And if enough people could afford electric and propane stoves, who would have any use for these dirty blocks of coal?" Wang Ma pointed to the kitchen where a woman shoved a pan of coal nuggets into the stove.

"I suppose we'll never be able to keep up," said Liu. "The world changes too quickly. And then there's the rich people who come to a poor city like Wushan, to ride in a peasant's raft up the Little Three Gorges."

"That must be where the jobs are, in tourism."

"I suppose so. My friend Tai has done quite well catering to that crowd."

Wang Ma leaned back and lit a cigarette. "You gotta keep up with the times. Can't hold onto the old ways. I've got pictures of my great-grandfather. He wore his hair in a long queue. Who could ever question the Manchu rulers? They'd get their heads chopped off. Nowadays, only a rebel would sport a pigtail between the ears. China's come a long way, my friend. Our clothes are modern, our cities light up at night thanks to the wonders of electricity. We have TVs and computers, comfortable hotels. See how the foreigners come to us?"

Liu thought of Mr. Wu, the farmer who turned into a ferryman, boasting of his newfound success. He shuddered to think of catering to foreigners; they must look down on Chinese folks, just as Mr. Wu looked down on them. But the man was making a good living going up and down the Little Three Gorges, and perhaps it wasn't such a bad thing after all.

20

FANG COULD NOT BELIEVE HIS EARS. "SHE REFUSES TO SEE ME? I'm not asking much. I've laid my hands on the Chu family's jewels, and all I want is to take 'em to her. What other man would go to the trouble of turning up the relics of a woman's dead husband?"

Chu Longshan stared into his teacup. "Fang, I cannot account for my sister's behavior. All I can think is, the past is the past, and she doesn't want to dig it up."

"What did I do to wrong her? What burns in her memory still after thirty-five years?" Fang paced up and down the length of the room, clutching the pendant that Liu had scavenged. He knew Chu Sulin to be a determined woman, and a stubborn one who would harbor no regrets. His desire, fervent as it was, would consume him before she ever relented.

"I know she loved you, Fang. But when your affair was exposed, it took all her strength to stand up for you, and after you left, it was as if you . . . you had died. She never spoke of you again. I had to work up the nerve to tell her you were coming here."

"What did she say?"

"You can imagine her shock. She could only whisper your name. And then, after a long silence, she said, 'I have lost my husband. I cannot handle any more grief.'"

"So she makes me out to be a dead man with flesh still hanging on my bones."

Fang swung around, and looked his friend in the eye. "Ol' Chu,

175

you've been my staunch ally. Surely you're not pulling one over on me. I won't hurt your sister. I have no designs on her. Why, if she had any on me, just to get my money, I'd be flattered."

"I know you don't mean any harm," said Longshan. "She's got a lot on her mind. I'm sure that's why she's kept her feelings in check."

"Well, she was never given to melodrama, that's for sure. She would as soon gouge out an eyeball than shed a tear. But her sharp wit was unmatched." Fang let out a hoarse laugh.

"Look, Fang, we're dealing with some troubles . . . with the government. It's preoccupying her, and all of us."

Fang's thoughts were still centered on Sulin, but as his friend spoke of plans for a dam along the Songdu River, he realized that Longshan might have had another agenda for his visit.

"The government wants us to move. Not just our village, but all the townships of Longmen County. The dam's supposed to generate all this electricity, but none of us will see the benefits. And I'm told we're moving to the hinterlands, way north of Chengdu." Chu Longshan shook his head. "I'm too old to move. As far back as anyone can remember, my family's worked the land here. And now they're telling us to leave."

"Well, the government will pay for a new house, won't they?"

"Yes, there's talk that each family will receive 5000 *yuan* per person. But you can bet the local bosses will stuff their pockets first."

"That's all—5000 *yuan* a head? You'd have to pad the numbers, buy yourself some children to get a decent house." The old broker laughed, but his friend's weathered face was expressionless. "Did you know the villagers of Loishan, in the Little Three Gorges, got 10,000 *yuan* each, but it still wasn't enough to get one of the new brick houses? And they all had to move up the mountain where the soil's no good."

"How do you know about these matters, Ol' Fang? Surely the big bosses don't allow these things to get into the news?"

"I was consulted on that case. Didn't come to anything," Fang grumbled. "That was when I realized the limits to my influence in the matter."

176

"Our village is trying to petition for a better settlement," said Chu Longshan. "Fang, you have connections. You have always been a capable man. Can you help us?"

Fang removed his pipe and turned toward his friend. This was the kind of business he did not want to get his hands into. He had learned his lesson from that earlier fiasco.

But Chu Longshan was his long-time friend. And Chu Sulin, his sister, had once been the love of his life. They had only spent six months together, but the memories survived the void of three and a half decades apart. In spite of his successes, his growing reputation in real estate, he never did forget Sulin. He still longed for her. Their separation had caused him great pain, which no one but his friend knew and Fang would hardly admit to himself. He realized that his intervention in this affair, even if the prospect of victory was slim, could bring them together once again.

"Yes," Fang replied. "I'll do what I can, whatever lies in my power."

A grateful Longshan shook the old man's hand, and promised to put Fang in touch with the village chief. The two friends parted in anticipation of things to come, one with a wish for just recompense, in the wake of losing his ancestral lands, the other with a fervent desire to reclaim the past.

●　　●　　●

MEI LING'S REFUSAL TO HOLD THE WEDDING CELEBRATION AT TAI'S had been a source of friction between the newlywed couple. But the windfall of money from selling off the jewelry gave Liu some reassurance, and he consented to renting a banquet hall in the Fu Huang Hotel in Wushan, a three-star affair that saw its share of drunken guests and debauchery.

On the heels of the lunar New Year, bright red posters graced the walls, inscribed with the character *fu*. These were intentionally hung upside down to discourage the impulses of evil spirits trying to thwart good fortune.

Mei Ling appeared after the second course, dressed in a long turquoise gown embroidered with delicate floral patterns in red and gold silk. The slim gown hugged her frame, giving accent to her breasts, which swelled like graceful peaks. A long part in the dress revealed the slimness of her thighs. The men took a deep breath, almost choking on their liquor. The older women smiled approvingly, while the young hopefuls adjusted their too-tight blouses with a downward glance and flutter of their eyelids.

Mei Ling's father was engrossed in conversation with Tai. Since Liu was estranged from his relations, he had seated his best friend, who was neither kin nor venerated elder, at the head table with Ol' Chang.

As the old man became more drunk, he blurted out whatever rumbled in his head, to the point of rudeness.

"So how much money do you make every month?" Ol' Chang asked.

"Oh, enough to pay my staff." It was not an unreasonable question to ask, but Tai was more discreet than most. "Mei Ling is an excellent waitress. Always patient. And smiling. I think she's helped to bring in more business."

"Really? Even if she scares away the men? I used to do that for her, you know. Didn't want just anyone to marry the girl."

"No, of course not."

"So how did Liu snag her? Does he have a small fortune?"

Tai glanced over at Liu, who was heading toward another table with his bride. Liu appeared uncomfortable in his finery; his face was flushed and he cracked a stiff smile with each toast, as a dozen glasses rose up in unison.

"Oh, I don't know," Tai replied at length. "But he does well enough by her and the child."

"So did he inherit the child and the money from this brother?" Chang persisted.

"Brother? Oh yes, his brother." Tai noticed that the couple was approaching their table, having finished their rounds. He got quickly to his feet, and mustered a deep "Ganbei!" from his gaunt frame. A flurry of shouts erupted. "May you have good fortune, health, and the blessings due to a deserving couple!" Tai beamed at his friend, and for the first time, Liu's face softened into a genuine smile.

Chen Weijin nudged her husband as he continued to ask his impudent questions, but he paid her no heed. Ol' Chang seemed determined to find out exactly how prosperous his son-in-law was. Tai figured Chang wasn't doing so well after moving to Guangdong.

When Chang struck up conversation with a guest at the next table, Tai gratefully turned back to his heaping plate, tuning out the senseless chatter of their wives. When he glanced over at the next table, he was surprised to see Ol' Fang. The wealthy old codger was dressed in his British best, with an elegant vest over a Shetland wool sweater, and a gold watch chain that distinguished his rank among the guests. As he ate, Tai amused himself with the snippets he overheard.

"I'm Chang Duoming, the bride's father. And how are you related to Liu?"

"I'm an old friend. And a business partner, partner in crime, you might say." A chortle erupted from the old man's lips.

"Crime, eh? Any kind of business must be lucrative nowadays."

"You take me seriously, sir. We're not talking about the underworld here. I'm a business broker, and I've put a little heat into the real estate in this town."

"And what does Liu do? How does he make his money?"

"Can't account for all of it, but the fellow did recently produce a few gems for me. You know all these towns that have fallen to rubble? There's more than old bricks and wire to be salvaged. He finds me things that other people have left behind."

"I see."

"Are you from around here?"

"Yes, my family moved out of the area almost two years ago."

"If you were smart, you'd have taken all your valuables. But not everyone does. I tell you, there's a gold mine out there. Of course, most of the treasure is underwater now."

"You mean, my son-in-law steals other people's stuff?"

"Only if it's unclaimed. Is it a crime if people are careless enough to leave their keepsakes behind?"

"This fellow . . . this bastard my daughter married, picks through people's *trash*?" Chang Duoming's voice rose into a shrill rasp.

At this, Tai turned to the two men, anxious to defend his friend. "I've known Liu for a long time, Mr. Chang. He is a decent, upright fellow. Why, he even worked on my new restaurant; nobody could drive a nail as straight and true as Liu."

"So he does manual labor, and rummages through people's trash." Chang Duoming shook his head. "I was hoping my daughter would marry a fellow in the city who had more brains than that."

"Liu is a bright fellow," Tai interrupted. "Why, he had the good sense to marry your daughter."

Those words fell on deaf ears. "*Lao Po*," Chang snapped at his wife. "We're leaving. We have truly lost a daughter. The foolish girl decided to marry a common laborer, and a trash digger." His voice rose sharply on the last phrase, and nearby heads turned in the couple's direction.

Mei Ling's mother protested, but Ol' Chang grabbed her by the wrists and hustled her toward the doorway.

When Mei Ling discovered that her parents had left, she hurried over to the head table and pressed Tai about their disappearance.

Sweat trickled across his forehead. "They . . . felt a bit uncomfortable here." He wanted to lie, and say that Mei Ling's mother wasn't feeling well, but the truth would soon be found out. "It was your father . . . he wanted to leave."

"Why? What's the matter?"

Tai lowered his voice, keeping an eye on Liu, who sat twenty paces away. "He was surprised that Liu worked for me. And that he scavenges for a living."

The color drained out of Mei Ling's cheeks. "Scavenges? Why, I never asked Liu, but how in the world did my father find out?"

Tai cast an incriminating glance at Fang, who was savoring a glass of wine he had ordered.

"Who is he?" Mei Ling whispered. And then she seemed to remember her role as the guest of honor. She straightened her gown and backed away. "You tell me later. I'm expected to keep the party going."

For the rest of the evening, Tai watched the couple with an attentive eye. Never once did Mei Ling waver in her smiles, nor hesitate to drink in acknowledgement of the guests' fondest wishes. In fact, she seemed to drink too much, and as the evening wore on, Liu had to support his bride as she wobbled toward the stage and dropped her head on his shoulders. Under the miasma of lights and cigarette smoke, Tai saw her whispering in his ear. Liu smiled, appearing content and comfortable at last. Soon, however, he would discover the truth.

•   •   •

A SOBER LIU SHOWED UP IN TAI'S RESTAURANT TWO DAYS AFTER the reception. Liu glanced up at his friend, a flush of hot shame arising. "What a spectacle I must have been. The penniless son-in-law. And I never caught on that evening. Mei Ling didn't say a word, until the next day."

"It was your so-called friend Fang. The blabbermouth told your father-in-law that you were a scavenger. Nothing could shake the old man back to his senses."

"Fang, that bastard." Liu shook his head violently. He lit a cigarette, remaining silent for some time. A bitter taste seeped into his throat. "You know," he continued, "Fei Fei's parents didn't think I was good enough for their daughter. And then . . . then they grew to tolerate me. Even the mother did. The father came to like me after a while. Now I know nothing about this fellow Chang, but you'd think the bridal gifts would have warmed him up a bit."

"Yeah, probably inflated his expectations, too," said Tai. "Listen, it doesn't matter what he thinks, right? You're married to the daughter; she's yours now. And they're far away, although I know she was sending money to them."

"Mei Ling asked me about the scavenging. I pretty much told her the truth. I wasn't committing a crime. She seemed okay about it. Told me her father is a hard-headed man."

"Yeah, I don't think they get along too well. Listen, you just focus on making her happy, all right?"

"Which means I gotta get a decent job. No matter what the old man thinks, it's time I step up to my duties as a husband."

As the two men discussed Liu's options for work in Wushan,

which were rather slim, the subject of Mr. Wu and his ferry business came up. Tai said that he would contact the fellow, and ask if he needed good help. Liu cringed at the thought of working for someone, especially a pompous man like Mr. Wu, but it would be a necessary move. He could learn the ropes from the ferryman, and find the means to operate his own boat one of these days, just as Fei Fei's father had done. Liu had never been the enterprising sort, but his friend's enthusiasm was contagious. Tai's business was doing quite well; those newfangled marketing ideas had worked.

"I wonder why my father-in-law's opinion of me matters so much," Liu said.

"You marry the girl, but you inherit the rest of the family," said Tai. With a rueful smile, he added. "At least, I have no kids to pass on my misfortune."

Liu turned toward the soft glow of the wall sconces, which he had picked out with Mei Ling. "I left my own family years ago. And here I've created another. Stitched it together, as a matter of fact. Failed the first time, but I might as well make the best of it this time around."

21

MEI LING WAS PLEASED WITH HER FLORAL ARRANGEMENT AGAINST the brocade of silk, transforming their hideous table into an object of beauty. Pei had embroidered the tablecloth in stealth, in the dim light of their old apartment, and given her the wedding gift just before moving. Whenever her spirits sagged, Mei Ling longed for the comforting presence of her old roommate. She stared at the long stalk of peach blossoms in the vase, fluttering in the early spring breeze. She took a large gulp of chrysanthemum tea and picked up her pen.

> Dear Pei,
>
> I wish you could have come to our banquet. But it's just as well that you missed the little scene my father made.
>
> Pa learned that night what my husband does for a living, and he was so ashamed that he stormed off with my mother. I know what you might say, that I stepped into the marriage with my eyes shut. It doesn't bother me that Liu made some money scavenging in the deserted towns. But my mother is just as disappointed that I did not marry a rich man.
>
> It's been more of a shock to me that Liu still cares for his first wife. Only weeks before the reception, he left town to pay his respects. I was very

angry with him. It wasn't that he deceived me; he told me about her before our marriage. But I don't think I fully have a husband if some place in his heart will always be devoted to this woman that he loved. He doesn't say much about her, but Liu seems to go about things with this quiet resolution, and I cannot change his mind. Pei, what should I do? If you tell someone to forget a past flame, they can break off all contact, tear up the old photos, move out of town. But can I ask him to forget a dead woman? And how can I be jealous toward her? Surely I hope I will not bring bad luck by thinking like this.

The baby is beginning to accept me. You can't imagine how much I have wrung my hands over that child. And now that there's more peace in the house, I can't bring myself to talk to Liu about giving her to other relatives. He isn't too close to his family; it seems odd, as he somehow managed to adopt the child when his brother died.

How little I know about this man! I married him because he seemed like a decent fellow, and if I hadn't made the choice, someone else—my father— could make that choice for me. You may think my fears are unfounded, Pei. But I would rather live with the mystery of this man who is now my husband than suffer a forced marriage.

A last bit of news—I walked through the neighborhood where our old apartment used to be, and the building is gone now. As a matter of fact, the whole city block is a construction site. A worker told me they were building a new hotel. Well, you can imagine my indignation. To think, we got evicted on some silly pretext that the mountains would fall on us.

I do miss you Pei, and I know you are making the

best of things. Your father is in good hands.
Your devoted friend,
Mei Ling

•   •   •

FROM THE UPPER REACHES OF WUSHAN, LIU COULD SEE THE gray silhouette of the Yangtze in the distance. Taking two steps at a time, he descended the *Bai Bu Ti*, the Hundred Steps Ladder running down the steep hill on which the city was built. A brisk wind whipped across his face. The city was slowly awakening, as street vendors stirred life into their feeble coals, and a stream of lights flickered on across beauty parlors, clothing shops, and eateries boasting a storefront.

Liu was a working man again, eager to take on whatever Mr. Wu had in store for him on the first day. He wondered what Mr. Wu's customers were like. Were they wealthy, privileged people who looked down on workers like him? Did the men belch and spit in public like normal folk? If not, the upper crust must likely be a constipated bunch. Other worries swam through his head; in particular, his absence could breed trouble between Mei Ling and their adopted child.

But a self-respecting man who worked outside the house was the most important thing for peace in the home, Liu decided. Better an absent father with a job than an attentive one without the means to support his family. Liu was going to be the father his daughter would be proud of one day.

When the last flight of stairs ended at the public square on Guangdong Road, Liu continued at a half trot down a winding street that led past remnants of the old town. The low buildings appeared in the distance like slabs of mud that lined the gullies after a heavy rain. Most of old Wushan had been blasted away a year and a half ago, and Liu was surprised that anything remained to be salvaged. Down the hill, Liu could see wiry men digging up pipes beneath the concrete foundations. Lean, short-legged men with eyes fixed askance trundled past like mules, hauling old doors on their backs, one by one, up the rocky path. The materials were assembled neatly at the top of the hill, doors in one pile and pipes in another. It reminded Liu of a photo he had once seen, where mounds of gold-capped crowns and jewelry were collected by a mass gravesite.

Liu had no regrets about giving up the scavenging life. He had been a puppet in the hands of Fang, a man who gambled with the lives of abandoned children. Rose was spared only through Liu's intervention. Fang had sent him, gullible as he was and desperate for money, into the netherworld of old Fengdu. Surely the old broker could not have set him up for prison, but Liu began to think that Fang was capable of anything, any act that robbed the common man of his dignity. It rankled him that Fang had incited the sudden departure of his in-laws at the wedding banquet.

For Liu, this day marked a milestone along the path to rebuilding the crumbled foundations of his life. Perhaps there was little to salvage from his former life, and if so, Liu walked forth with a sense of purpose stronger than anything he had felt since Fei Fei's death, except for the rescue of an abandoned baby girl on a foggy summer's day.

At last, Liu reached a quiet stretch of the waterfront. He descended down the sloped embankment to the water's edge, where Mr. Wu's skiff was moored.

"Liu Renfu? I've been waiting for you. Climb in." The narrow interior of the skiff echoed with Liu's halting footsteps. The boat was pod-shaped, with a steel hull painted white. Inside the cabin, two planks for seating ran along each side, and an assortment of ropes and puffed-up vests lay in the recesses. "What are those for?" Liu pointed at the orange vinyl heap.

"They're life jackets for the passengers. Not that anything could happen on this calm lake. But foreign tourists can be so squeamish, you know. 'Course there won't be passengers today. It's still the slow season."

Liu was surprised, and somewhat relieved, to hear that they would be transporting cargo rather than passengers today. Their first stop was a village where peasants had formed a collective to grow and sell chestnuts. Liu and his new boss climbed a short distance up the hill to fetch the goods. He hoisted a crate on his shoulders and nimbly skirted his way down the steep, pebbly path. Sweat trickled down his back, but his muscles held firm. He relished the pulse of energy that carried him back and forth between the boat and the waiting cargo.

When the cabin of the boat was filled to the brim, Mr. Wu fired up the engine and headed back to Wushan. Passing through the deep canyons of Misty Gorge, Liu gazed out languidly at the passenger ferries and barges laden with coal that sputtered past, creating feathery ripples in their wake. A sliver of sun appeared behind the clouds, casting a trail of sparkling emeralds on the vast ribbon of water.

The cliffs loomed like ancient terra-cotta warriors along this stretch, their slopes so steep that no traces of cultivated crops or human disturbance were visible. The motor hummed noisily, and Mr. Wu scooped up a pan of river water to cool off the engine every so often. "You think this is an easy life? Wasn't always this way." The boatman stared at Liu, who was leaning against the cabin wall, lulled into drowsiness by the rhythmic slapping of waves against the boat.

"When I first got into this business, the water had not yet risen, and in places the river was no deeper than that thing." Mr. Wu pointed to a bamboo pole, perhaps six feet long. "You could see the pebbles in the water, and rocks so sharp they could slit a man's throat."

Mr. Wu got to his feet, grabbed the pole and began to demonstrate. Liu watched the display with torpid interest. "I hired a couple of men back then to push against the swift current going upriver. The waves would sweep the bow of the boat upwards, and I'd holler to the passengers, 'No tip boat—over here!' and sometimes if they didn't move quickly enough, the propeller would scrape against rock on the bottom. I keep this pole around to show my passengers how tough it used to be.

"Now don't think I'm paying you to sit around like this all the time. It's the slow season. You'll need to help me drum up some business."

The next morning, Liu met up with Mr. Wu at the main wharf. A steady crowd stampeded down the floating dock, whose rickety joints creaked under the weight of passengers lugging burlesque suitcases and enormous burlap sacks.

Mr. Wu handed a stack of small flyers to Liu, each about the size of his palm, and instructed him to hand them out to tourists. "Are these tickets?" Liu asked.

"No, fool, it's advertising. I learned this trick from an American who runs a shop in the red-light district."

"How do I know who the tourists are?"

"They're the ones dressed better than you, and they shuffle along looking lost and confused."

"I'm not a good judge of people," said Liu.

"Just hand 'em out to the passengers with luggage. By noon, I want you to come back empty-handed, okay?"

When a crowd of passengers arrived on the fast boat from Wan-zhou, Liu wedged himself against the railing and croaked in a raspy voice, "Day trip—Little Three Gorges."

The human wave broke for shore, and all he got in response were some suspicious glances. A pretty woman hesitated, then hurried past as the leaden contents of her shopping bag jostled Liu in the thigh. He watched the *bang-bang* men, the porters who lurched toward passengers with their bamboo poles, cajoling and pleading with them to carry their bags. It intrigued him when an able-bodied passenger relinquished his suitcase to the stranger. Perhaps that's what I need to do, Liu thought.

Summoning a courage he had not known he possessed, Liu darted through the crowd that morning, hot on the heels of prospective passengers. By and large, the hurried masses responded with indifference and disdain. Perhaps a dozen people took his leaflet, now crumpled in his sweaty palms. "Get out of my way," a man grumbled. "Got a cigarette?" another asked. One fellow, with a wormy scar beneath his shaggy beard, stuck out his hand at Liu for a flyer. The man held it up to his chin, and hawked a green cesspool into the square of paper. "Police've been trying to arrest me for spitting," he said, tossing the pulpy mass into the river.

Mr. Wu berated Liu for returning with most of the flyers that afternoon, and told him to fix up his appearance. The next day, Liu hovered at the edge of the dock again, this time in a black jacket over his linen shirt, the one he had bought to impress Mei Ling. By mid-morning, Liu had given away a thumb's length of flyers. Pleased with himself, he folded up the rest like paper bills, stuck them in his pocket, and headed toward the roadside stand for a pack of cigarettes. A pack of boys bicycled past, setting a swirl of dust into the vaporous air, and as Liu turned to avoid them, a flurry of fists scratched and pummeled the side of his jacket. He reached into his pocket; the flyers were gone, along with a small cloth bag where he had kept 15 *yuan*. Liu shook his head in disbelief. The misfits chose to pick his poor man's pockets, but a rich man dressed in rags would have been left alone. He sucked on his cigarette for the rest of the morning, tamping down sparks of ash into the cracked earth.

He told Mei Ling about the incident that night, but allowed Mr. Wu to think that his efforts had paid off, as business was indeed picking up with the change of the seasons. As the chill of winter gave way to mild southerly breezes, Liu settled into his role as helper, bag schlepper, soother of frayed nerves and screaming children. Most of the time, the tourists were busy snapping pictures of the sheer cliffs of Dragon Gate Gorge and Misty Gorge. But Liu developed a keen sense that responded to, and even anticipated, a shift in the winds, the small dramas that played out in the confines of the forty-five foot skiff.

Once, in the stupor and exhaustion of late afternoon, a curious tot wandered toward the stern of the boat when the mother wasn't watching. The boy's cigar-shaped body dipped toward the water, and started to teeter over the edge. Liu jumped up, caught the child mid-yelp, and delivered him safely back to his mother's arms. She was so grateful that she tipped Liu 200 *yuan* on the sly, more than a week and a half's worth of wages. The deed made a favorable impression on Mr. Wu, who allowed Liu to take the helm once in a while, schooling him in the ways of seamanship.

Mr. Wu deviated little from his standard tourist trap lingo. He addressed Chinese tourists in the lilt of the local dialect, telling him how his father was a boatman who plied the Yangtze, fishing with cormorants. The man had six rangy birds strung out from his boat, their necks arched like jug handles, with a ring around each. The fish they caught sailed down as far as the pinch of the throat, until Ol' Wu pried the catch from the cormorant's bloated beak. Of course, the birds got their just reward at the end of the trip: small fish that passed through the copper rings of their leash.

Nothing was further from the truth. Mr. Wu spun these stories from ancient lore and the river life that streamed past their old village, where they grew rice and vegetables. When Liu asked about his fib, thinking lies were meant only for awkward and life-threatening situations, Mr. Liu told him that it brought in business. "Even the foreigners. They hear my broken English, and to them it's quaint, it's the strange life of a Chinaman, so primitive and fascinating." And that story, too, was a long stretch from reality. Mr. Wu's new house, a four-room structure of brick and white tile, was supplied with electricity and running water. The kitchen had a newfangled electric stove because he could afford one now. The children watched television channeled in by satellite, and spun CDs like whirling tops when they weren't playing Hong Kong pop on the stereo.

In the evenings, when Liu returned from work, he stayed at home more often while Mei Ling worked at the restaurant. The drone of the television lulled him to sleep shortly after supper, with Rose curled up on his lap.

Throughout the spring and summer months, not much rocked the calm waters of their marriage. And yet, a silent rift was pushing the couple toward opposite banks, as each became absorbed in his or her own concerns and unseemly desires.

An introvert by nature, Liu enjoyed those quiet hours when the chatter of strangers' voices became a faint echo in his mind. As Liu gained more skill in managing the skiff and its daily cast of characters—the squeamish ones and the thrill seekers, the overbearing spouses and bosses—he dreamt that one day he would be the *lao ban*. Not even a *da lao ban*, a big boss with hired help to chase after tots and purses tumbling overboard, but simply an independent one.

Mei Ling began to spend more time with girlfriends, and wrote often to her old roommate. Once, Liu had gotten home early and spied the crinkled parchment of her letter on the table. When Mei

Ling emerged from the bathroom, she bolted toward the table, snatching at the letter as if it were intended for a secret lover. Liu backed away, apologized, and wished for once that he had the power to decipher those cryptic characters, and beyond that, to understand the passions of his wife, who professed an unquestioning love for the strange gods of the West, but seemed rather lukewarm to the intimacies of the flesh.

Yet Liu was too spent after a day of battling wind, water, and the storm of human activity to express much zeal himself, and the milestones of Rose's development slipped by unnoticed. Around the anniversary of her rescue, she began to walk unsupported, and Liu had only a moment to marvel at the waddling of her ungainly legs before his worries about money and Mei Ling took over. By summer, she had cut a new set of canine teeth. He was dimly aware that she clung to the comforts of what was hers: the tattered tails of her blanket, the thumb that soothed frayed nerves, the puppet monkey made from an old sock. While still curious and alert, she had begun to distrust the motives of strangers.

Rose uttered colorful words with the glee of the innocent—*pi dan*, naughty egg; *sa gwa*, silly melon; *san ba*, tattletale. These she must have picked up from Mei Ling. And when the girl finally uttered the softer syllables *ma ma*, recognizing Mei Ling as her mother, Liu was too exhausted at the end of a day's labor to notice.

22

FANG APPROACHED HIS MEETING WITH THE VILLAGE CHIEF of Lanping with his usual swaggering confidence. The chief lived a stone's throw away from Chu Longshan, in a cluster of houses clinging to the hillside, where the chickens and ducks and snot-nosed children ambled and played in close quarters. In Sha Tong's living room, the customary portrait of Mao Zedong graced the walls, but a scroll of equal size hung next to it, a poem in calligraphy extolling the virtues of hard work and patience. The chief wore a humble coat the color of wheat. Its spare cut and butterfly clasps harked back to an era when blue Mao jackets were worn all over the land, in the cities as well as the countryside.

As they shook hands, Fang cringed at the rough texture of the peasant's palm. Sha Tong turned toward an elderly woman with a sweet face, wrinkled like dried tofu skin.

"This is my mother," he said. "She is 79, sharp for her age. Wouldn't you say, Ma?" The elderly Mrs. Sha parted her lips, a mere crack in the masonry, revealing a few teeth that had survived famine, misfortune, and poor hygiene.

"So, Mr. Fang, how is it that you can help us? We are but poor villagers, it's true, and I do not expect those in better circumstances like yourself to take pity on us."

"I am a business dealer, although I'm not here to make a profit off your misfortune. I'm doing this more as a favor, for a friend."

The village chief shot a skeptical look at Fang. "Do you know that this involves more than our humble little village? This scheme, the Gaoshanlu Dam, will flood thousands of hectares, and in seven townships the residents are grumbling about how the officials are treating us."

"I'm told they're offering 5000 *yuan* a person."

"A miserly amount, for taking away our land. Well, I suppose it's not *our* land, but my great-grandfather, and his father before him, farmed along the Songdu River. We're asking for 8000. Even this isn't anywhere near enough."

Fang stared at Sha Tong, whose shrewish eyes read of hardship, a life of squinting into the harsh sun. "So who's calling the shots? Whom should I talk to?"

Sha Tong shook his head. "You don't understand, sir. This is a difficult situation, and many officials are involved. Each time a different one shows up in a slick suit. They are all cut out of the same fabric, but no one takes full responsibility for this thing."

"Yes, but if you toss carrion to a pack of hungry wolves, the leader's going to stick his muzzle out first. Give me the name of the development company and I'll go from there."

Sha Tong's mother, who had remained silent, flashed a toothless grin at Fang. "This young man is a fighter, after my own heart. The ancestors of Sha will watch over you."

Fang extended a hand toward her with a flourishing gesture of respect. "And I will not disappoint them, madam."

When he thought about her words afterwards, the shadows of his old life flickered before him. He remembered his old college friend, who had died a needless death in a needless revolution more than three decades earlier. He did want to help Chu Longshan in his fight, not just for his sister's sake. But I'm no revolutionary, he thought. And yet, Fang knew he was a match for any bastard who boasted of wealth and power.

Over the next three weeks, the scent trail led Fang from the Dalong Power Company, the Big Dragon with ambitious plans for the Yangtze, to various officials, petty and self-important, to the chairman of the Provincial Development Planning Committee in the capital of Chengdu.

His office was grander than anything that Fang had seen inhabited by a public official; even Inspector Mah's office at the Urban Development Bureau back home was a hovel compared to the palatial suite where Chairman Jiang reigned.

A secretary ushered Fang into the office, and Chairman Jiang waved him in with an imperious hand. His eyes darted like a rodent's. Fang felt a little uneasy.

"I am Fang Shuping, a skilled facilitator of numerous business developments, here to address some unresolved aspects of the Gaoshanlu project."

"Sit down. No need to give me your card. I can't keep track of all you peddlers. What about Gaoshanlu do you want to know?"

Fang leaned forward. "I understand that this is an important project, as it will generate billions of kilowatts of power for Sichuan province."

"Yes, 12.6 billion, to be precise." The chairman's steely gaze seemed to stifle further discussion, but Fang continued in his most professional voice.

"The good people of Lanping village, in one of the townships nearby, will need to relocate far away to the north of Chengdu. As you can see, this involves a huge economic loss; the land they farm now may be steep, but yields of rice and sweet potato are quite high there."

"And what does this have to do with you? You look too smart to be one of the poor peasantry. Do you wipe the asses of big government officials? Are you a lawyer? We make sure they're castrated before they come deal with me." Chairman Jiang snorted, and his fat knees rattled against the frame of the mahogany desk.

"No." Fang cleared his throat, and then continued. "I am a broker. I make deals."

"Tell me," said Jiang, "what do you think you can do as a third wheel in this project? The company's starting construction next month; the people have been promised their money. What more do you want?"

"That you request 8000 *yuan* per person for the relocation

funds, including—of course—overhead and extra fees for your office. The villagers can't move otherwise."

"Nope, can't do it. Compensation's been set at 5000 *yuan*."

"Ah, but I can help bring in some extra money. Listen, I'll hook up your partners at Dalong Power with my industry friends, and they'll be guaranteed more than a few investors." Fang knew he had seized on the soft underbelly of this scheme, as Dalong was a high roller, pulling off a speculative enterprise with many promissory notes.

"I see. You have a lot of balls to be in this business, if you are who you say. Tell you what, let's draw up a deal, shall we, with the chief financial officer at Dalong. You'll like each other. He's the son of an old capitalist bull, like you." Chairman Jiang chortled. He snapped his fingers, and the secretary ushered Fang out of the office.

Within a month, Fang had secured three sizable investors and a handful of small players who shored up the construction funds for the Gaoshanlu Dam. But when he brought up the money for compensating the villagers, the chairman cast him a blank stare, denying a deal had ever been made. That was the part he rubber-stamped, he said; there were people higher up in the government who controlled the purse strings.

Fang was infuriated that Chairman Jiang had taken advantage of his good will and offered nothing in return. In fact, the chairman claimed to be doing his investor friends a favor, as the affected counties, and indeed the rest of Sichuan province and China, were starved for new sources of power for their growing cities. The old broker had encountered someone more wily than himself. In the unspoken ethics of wheeling and dealing, here was a man with the scruples of a two-headed snake.

His original desire to see Chu Sulin face-to-face had not been realized, so at this point, Fang decided to take a different tack. He was not about to speak to more committee chairmen and bureau chiefs, Party secretaries or their underlings, as each could simply pass the responsibility on to another. How simple it had been, in all his years of money-moving schemes, to allow the murky waters to run their natural course. Each of his deals deposited a rich layer of silt on bureaucratic shores, smoothing the way for the next. Fang could not admit he had been stumped, but an extra 3000 *yuan* for each peasant meant little to the power brokers and traders. It was simply less padding for their pocketbooks.

•   •   •

CHU LONGSHAN HAD GOTTEN INVOLVED IN THE INTERVILLAGE Council for Relocation Affairs, which, in spite of its formal name, was a scrabble of incensed peasants from the various townships, who met once a week in the abandoned sorghum liquor factory to discuss their plight. When Fang approached him about attending the next meeting, Longshan was quite surprised. "You're going to great lengths to warm up to my sister," he said.

"It's more than that," insisted Fang. "That Chairman Jiang is a slippery bastard. If I can't trap a weasel by the paw, then I'll get him from the rear by his tail."

Twenty-six men gathered that night, sitting on stone benches in the courtyard of the old factory. Spring filled the air with fragrant blossoms, and a gentle breeze rippled through the nearby laurel trees. A full moon beamed down, illuminating the pockmarked surfaces of stone like ancient tablets. Chu Longshan spoke in a clear, resonant voice, his torso rocking forward into the light. The others listened attentively.

"Comrades, we can't allow ourselves to be strung along like this. They tell us we'll have land as good as what we've got right now. Can we believe the bureaucrats? I think we're too smart to fall for hearsay. We ought to demand a visit to the new site. Get the officials out there, perhaps a reporter from the *Zhongxi News*."

A hush fell over the crowd, and the crickets seemed to fire up their chirping to fill the void.

"I'd like to go." A peasant with a canine jaw and big teeth spoke up. "But I don't know about the press. That might send the wrong message, you know."

"Yes, but if the officials are up to no good, we've got somebody to document this," another man replied. "Look at us. Who are we but a bunch of sniveling farmers to those big shots? I tell you. We gotta keep them honest." He pumped his fists in the air, his lumber-jack arms swinging as if they could fell a tree.

Heads nodded in agreement, and then a scratchy, thin voice rose above the murmuring. "Now I know we've got our best intentions here, and me, I've got grandchildren who farm the land. We've got to move carefully, yes we do. Don't think for a moment the government's become soft on us *lao bai shing.*"

The elderly peasant coughed a little, and then continued. "I was only a boy during the revolution that created the People's Republic. I remember when soldiers showed up at the village, ragtag as us kids, snot running down their noses, too. My mother, good soul that she was, bandaged their wounds with a poultice of wild herbs. They had nothing to lose then. They were fighting for a cause and if they lost the shirts on their backs, they still had two arms and their wits. If they lost an arm, they could steal the enemy's weapons and fight until there was nothing left but a bloody torso.

"Folks, it isn't like that now. The government's got everything to lose; they know when they've failed and they won't say, but they refuse to fail now, to give anything up. And to them, this land is rightfully the property of the State. We're the ragtag soldiers now, you see, but we've got nothing to arm ourselves with. They won't stand for us staking a claim to this land, and demanding fair payment for it. No, sir. If we try to stir up too much attention now, you bet they're gonna put us down. I say we see what kind of land we're offered, no reporters, and if it's decent, we live with it."

"And if not?" the buck-toothed man asked.

"We petition to Beijing," Longshan declared. "In the meantime, I think the old man's right; we shouldn't cry foul now. But I still think somebody should take notes on this trip, if we ever need to take it so far as Beijing." Longshan glanced at Fang. "I have an old comrade here from back in the commune days. He is the best educated among us. What do you say, Ol' Fang? Can you be our scribe?"

Fang appeared to be uncomfortable with the idea, shifting his weight until the shadows obscured him in the pitch of night. "I'm not a reporter, you know. I'm a businessman."

"You need not do anything except keep your eyes and ears open, jot down some notes afterwards. I'll help you. And I'll handle things from there."

Chu Longshan gazed intently at Fang, and his eyes said the unspoken. *Your help will come with its rewards.* At last, Fang nodded his head, and the peasant with the overgrown teeth slapped Longshan's friend on the back, offering him a cigarette from a leather pouch rank with sweat from the day's labor.

•　•　•

ON THE NIGHT BEFORE THEIR VISIT TO THE NEW HOMESTEAD, Fang had to make do with the lean provisions of Chu Longshan's home. Standing over a wooden bucket in the yard, he scrubbed his stubbly face with a coarse washcloth. Flecks of skin fell into the inky pool like rice husks. Goose bumps swelled alongside the spider veins on his arms. He thought of those days spent on that commune in the Sichuan mountains. How young and headstrong he had been. Perhaps he could not have survived the scalding summers and cold winters, the blistering journeys to fetch firewood up in the mountains, if it had not been for the grit and sheer ignorance of his youth.

In the morning, Mrs. Chu shoved firewood under the stove and offered Fang a mug of tea, wiping away the soot of her fingerprints with a rag. She coughed, heaved, and spat into the ashes. Fumes from the stove leaked into the sky through an opening in the roof, their tendrils dark and coiled like serpent tails.

Fang gathered with the village representatives by the bridge on the eastern banks of the Songdu River, where a van arrived to take them to the new site. As their vehicle bounced across mountain roads, he watched the river undulating below, smooth as dragonfly wings along the wide stretches, frothy and venomous in places narrow enough for a boy to leap across. Chu Longshan sat beside him, fingering a set of papers detailing the resettlement.

When the river disappeared from view, Fang settled back in his seat and lit up his pipe. "How long till we get there?"

"Another hour and a half. We'll meet up with a busload from three other villages, and a car with some officials from the county."

Chu Longshan paused before adding, "My sister will be there."

Fang turned toward his friend, his sit bones creaking. A light sweat collected on his forehead. "Your sister. She lives two villages away. It can't be a coincidence. Chu—"

"Don't say anything. She doesn't know yet. I simply told her I was getting involved in negotiating this thing, and she should come along."

"Chu, you sneaky devil." Fang slapped his thighs and chuckled. And yet, he had to admit he felt a little anxious.

When the sun had nearly reached its zenith, the van stopped by the edge of the mountain road, and the villagers disembarked to wait outside. The harsh, dry air chafed the corners of his mouth, but the smile remained safely tucked inside Fang's breast.

The wind rumbled across the ridge, and as it whistled through green foxtail and goat grass, it seemed to whisper that this land could not be tamed. Across the road, a grassy incline led up to slopes as yet invisible, where the villagers would get a first glimpse of their new homestead. The grass grew in scrawny tufts, like an adolescent boy's stubble, and low shrubs clung tenaciously to the soil. To the east, terraced fields draped the surrounding hills like the flags of foreign nations. An inky, threatening nimbus cloud hovered over the rice paddies.

Longshan pointed to the runoff trickling down a nearby slope. "Must have rained recently. I'll bet that dribble of water is pulling good soil away. It's brown as a mule's ear."

Fang nodded, half listening. It was much colder at this elevation, and his teeth chattered as he stared at the empty road, his eyes trained on the slightest movement.

A half hour passed, and when a van lurched to a stop in front of the villagers, Fang felt a flutter in his chest. He had waited this long to see Chu Sulin. Thirty-five . . . no, thirty-six years, to be exact. Now that the moment had arrived, he wondered what he would say, what he had to offer her. A hint of the old passions? An apology for the trouble she'd endured? A gesture of goodwill? *I mean you no harm*, he would say, if she should back away when he approached her.

A dozen men got off the bus before she appeared. Her hips were wider than he remembered, her steps sturdy as a mare's, and she grimaced as the wind struck sideways. She stepped forth as if she could vanquish that wind with a defiant kick. Her broad face had changed little, although it was framed by a speckle of gray, and her once-large eyes had receded somewhat, tassled by fine crow's feet.

Those eyes danced in surprise. Chu Sulin's gaze alighted on Fang, then flickered over to her brother.

Longshan rushed over in an attempt to head off a spontaneous combustion. "Sister, my old friend Fang Shuping—"

"Your old friend," said Sulin. Those eyes flared with old embers, as it were, of anger. "I never thought I would see you again, Fang Shuping."

"The pleasure is mine." Fang spoke in measured, genteel tones. He felt lightheaded suddenly; it was all he could do to keep from crumbling at her feet. "It's been many years; you haven't changed."

"And perhaps you haven't either," said Sulin. Turning to her brother she added, "Now why did you really bring me here?"

Chu Longshan assured his sister that this visit was of paramount importance. His friend had taken an interest in the case, and had the means to advocate on their behalf.

Sulin shot a skeptical glance at her brother. When the officials' car arrived, Longshan reminded Fang to take note of the landscape and the exchanges between the parties, so that he could write down his observations later.

Fang nodded, but for the rest of the excursion, he could not help but fix his attention on Chu Sulin. From the road, the group scrambled up the steep hillside for an hour, using a small clump of white pines as a beacon to keep them moving toward the new site. The wind threatened to carry them away, swelling up the villagers' clothing like useless fins. As Fang plodded uphill, a secret hope emanated from his breastbone, invigorating his cranky old limbs.

At length, the group reached the top, although a few officials lagged, plowing their sedentary bellies onward, spitting and cursing under their breaths.

"The houses will be constructed on a north-south axis," said one official, who appeared to be the leader.

"Where will our water come from?" asked Longshan. "It looks pretty dry up here."

"There is a spring several hundred yards to the west."

"So we'll have to fetch our water. At least there aren't any more trees to chop down for firewood, ease the burden on our women."

Fang missed the irony in Longshan's remark, and the official's mumbled reply. All he could think of was Sulin, thirty-six years younger, her sleek lines interrupted by a massive bucket poised on her shoulder, the glow of recognition when she saw Fang, her fingers releasing the wood handle, clasping his, the whisper of his breath on her hands, her cheekbones, her bosom close to his. It had only been in the quietest hours of the day, in the woods along the lengthy trek to the commune's wells, that the two could be with one another, unwatched and undisturbed.

On these unforgiving slopes, far from anyone's home, the land was too open to dredge up old secrets. And his lover's bosom remained closed. Fang attempted to walk close to Sulin, assisting her as they crossed a gully to take stock of the land. She resisted his help, said little in reply to his questions.

When Fang asked her, exasperated, "Why do you hate me, Sulin? So many years have passed. . . ," she turned her broad, still-beautiful face toward him, with lips that trembled slightly.

"I fought hard for you, Fang. And when I thought I'd won the battle, I was forced to destroy what we had." She flashed him an angry look.

"Because you were promised to someone else?" Fang asked.

Chu Sulin would say no more. She turned away, leaving Fang to clutch at her words like desiccated leaves. All the while, spring was already easing toward summer, infusing the land with the brilliant promise of citrus blossoms.

23

LIU STUMBLED OVER TO THE LITTLE SINK, CAREFUL NOT TO wake up Mei Ling and the baby. This morning he would have to take a mini-bus down the hill, as his legs could not carry him fast enough to meet Mr. Wu's first load of passengers.

Rose had been crying in the night, and the agony of new teeth breaking through her gums roused the adults, filling their dreams with phantom echoes of her pain. Liu was weary from lack of sleep, and in his haste he cut his lip shaving. A nick from the day before had scabbed over, but was still painful to the touch. Just like that last fight with his wife, he thought ruefully.

"You always dote on that child when you should be saving up for us to move out of this cramped apartment," Mei Ling had said.

"I am watching our money," Liu insisted. "It's just a lot easier for guys like Mr. Wu to get ahead, when they ride on the backs of workers like me."

"That goes for your friend Tai, too. The old prune hasn't given me a raise since I started. And I still manage to take home most of what I earn."

"To your father, you mean?" Liu knew he had struck a nerve, and regretted it as soon as he said those words.

Mei Ling had lashed back with angry, incoherent syllables, then called him a hypocrite, among other things, before retreating into a bitter silence that lasted well into the next day.

When Liu arrived at the dock, Mr. Wu glared at him and hustled him aboard. The boat was already filled with the morning's passengers. Liu hunkered down at the stern of the boat, preoccupied by his troubles at home. He craved a cigarette, but had been admonished not to light up, as this was a group of hippy Americans who expected clean air along with spectacular scenery.

An hour later, Mr. Wu docked the boat on a jut of land leading to a flock of vendors. The white awnings and brilliant flags fluttered in the autumn breeze, and the tourists were easily lured ashore. Liu stayed on board while they shopped. When the group returned, he had dozed off in the sun, lulled by the rhythmic swaying of the boat.

As the stragglers boarded with hawkers still nipping at their pocketbooks, Liu clambered onto the makeshift dock and began to untie the ropes anchoring the boat. He could hear the engine sputtering to life like a phlegmatic old man, but a stubborn hitch prevented him from releasing the line.

"Just hold on, Mr. Wu," he called out, his throat scratchy from slumber. Liu lowered one leg into the boat. One more tug; the knot unraveled. And then the skiff broke away from shore with an accelerated roar of the engine.

"Wait!" Liu screamed. His body, straddling water, was wrenched from the dock. He clawed wildly at the air as his free leg sank into the waves gushing behind the skiff. Torso followed leg, and Liu somersaulted into the depths of the slack river. He grasped for the rope, but it snaked away in the boat's wake.

In the span of two heartbeats, the accident had unfolded, and it took another protracted beat before the passengers responded. They, too, had their wits dulled by the morning's excursion. One alert man sprang up, throwing a lifejacket to Liu and hollering to Mr. Wu, who had been deaf to Liu's cries. The others only rattled their jaws and craned their timid necks toward the commotion.

Liu's attempts to dog paddle had failed; the freefalling leg had turned to stone, and if it had not been for the orange lifejacket, he would have succumbed to the river's irresistible grasp. He coughed and spluttered, his shaky hands clutching the slick fabric. Soon the boat drifted back toward him. The quick-footed passenger pulled Liu safely back on board.

• • •

WITH HIS LEFT LEG BOUND IN A COCOON-LIKE CAST, LIU WAS confined to his bed for weeks. He kept his cigarette stash in easy reach, along with the painkillers and an ashtray piled high on the wooden stand. A memory of exquisite pain haunted him, but Liu felt a strange numbness in his torso, as if the frigid waters of the Daning still possessed him.

When Rose tried to climb over that white mound, a sizzle of pain shot up into his hip. He pushed her away, whereupon she burst into aggrieved wails.

Too clouded in his mind by painkillers, Liu could barely mumble her name. "Rose, little monkey, stop."

"Little monkey stop, little monkey stop," she prattled.

His head bobbed from side to side, and he drifted into a delirious sleep, in which demons chased him from all directions, with plaintive voices like a young child's and flaming arrows that pierced his flesh, until a tidal wave overtook him and reduced that leg to smoldering ashes.

The accident had created an unspoken truce between Liu and Mei Ling. Yet she was increasingly sullen as she ministered to his needs, all the while keeping tabs on their headstrong toddler.

Liu had failed the family and once again, Mei Ling was the sole wage earner. He replayed those moments before the accident over and over, sinking further into a deep, nameless well. The broken leg would take months to heal, and Liu wondered if there would be a job for him after all that time. No, he thought, Mr. Wu's employees were dispensable. Neither laziness nor bad luck was an excuse.

The days and weeks crept by in tedium. An unspoken tension built up in the apartment, stirring the tempers of adoptive mother and child. But Liu was powerless in his present state. So he held his tongue whenever Mei Ling snapped at Rose, knowing he could say something he would regret.

One afternoon, Mei Ling returned home clutching a bag of groceries and a letter torn open haphazardly. She sighed and collapsed on the small couch they had acquired after their wedding.

"What's the matter?" Liu asked in a thin voice.

"My mother is terribly ill. Her joints have been aching a lot, and she's running a fever. My father thought she was just sick with the flu, but days later, when she fell, her arm swelled into a big purple patch and she couldn't stop the bleeding. So he took her to a doctor." Mei Ling's voice fell to a whisper. "She has cancer. It's in her bones."

"What are they going to do?"

"She'll have to take some nasty drugs that'll make her hair fall out. It's going to be very expensive," Mei Ling replied, chewing her fingernail.

"They will need your help?"

"Yes." Silence lingered in the room. It was time to let go of old grudges, Liu thought. He would be more understanding. "I'm sorry, Mei Ling. I wish I could be more of a husband at this time."

Mei Ling said nothing. She rose up and tucked the letter into a small wooden chest with a brass lock.

• • •

MEI LING FUSSED WITH HER APRON, TURNING AROUND WHENEVER she thought she heard Tai's lopsided shuffle into the kitchen.

"Where's the old boss?" she asked Ol' Guo.

The cook dropped a large coiled heap of fresh noodles into the boiling water and turned around, wiggling his toothpick between his teeth. "He's haggling with the fishmonger. Got a big banquet coming up."

"I need to talk to him. It's important."

"You want a raise or something? Lots of luck. Like trying to catch a rabbit between your thumb and pinky."

"You could frighten one to death, no problem, Ol' Guo. I'm not asking for a perk. I've got people in the family who are ill." Mei Ling's voice quavered, and she turned away to avoid more questions from the cook.

When Tai returned, Mei Ling smoothed her apron and approached him in the back office. She had rehearsed what she would say. A laid-up husband, a growing child, and now a sick mother;

these were all responsibilities that had befallen her. She needed extra money to provide for all of them, especially her mother, at least until Liu recovered.

Tai assured her that he was mindful of her present demands, but he had debts to pay for the renovation. It was expensive to run a larger establishment. And then there was his wife's spending habit. He didn't think he could offer her much of a raise. "You know all those shoe stores on Guangdong Road? She keeps them in business."

"I have an emergency situation, do you understand? Your friend Liu is housebound. He can't work. All he can do is help keep that child quiet during the day when I'm home. I wanted to find other relatives who can raise her, but I haven't dared to ask. Why does he dote on her so? It's not like she's his flesh and blood."

"No, that's true. She was a foundling, after all." Tai filed away some papers in his desk, and turned toward the kitchen.

"Tai. Wait a minute. What did you say?" Mei Ling cried, her voice shrill and hawkish. She was not going to let him leave.

"What? About the baby? Liu told you how she was found, didn't he?"

"No, you tell me," said Mei. She could feel her throat burning, as if all that was unsaid had caught fire. She had completely trusted Liu's claims about the baby's origins, just as she had put her faith in unseen horizons, beyond the shabby state of the lives they led. And now, this act of deception. Another sign that her marriage had been a hasty decision.

Tai appeared nervous at that point, as if realizing he had betrayed his friend's secret. "Well, he told me that she was . . . uh . . . abandoned, you see, parents didn't want her. And Liu, he's got a good heart, you know."

"And a slippery tongue. Tai, he told me that the baby was adopted from his brother. So there's no dead brother. For all I know, it *is* his child, and the mother ran off. And who knows, maybe his wife isn't even dead. Maybe he's making all this up."

"No—no—no; it's not like that. Please don't misunderstand, Mei Ling. Liu didn't mean to deceive you. He just didn't want you to get the wrong idea."

"I've been fooled before. I don't know what to think anymore." Mei Ling's breath came in rasping gulps, but she did not want Tai to see her cry. She tied her hair up in a bun with angry, stabbing motions, and carried through the evening with pain rising up her sore feet.

She thought about the lie on her way home. Perhaps the weeks of self-inflicted silence had its advantages. She would not give way to her indignation, not indulge in the darker passions that could set her eyes ablaze, causing even the bravest of men to cower.

What mattered most to Mei Ling was her mother. She regretted that she could not be with her. Perhaps she could divorce Liu and move back home. But she had declared her vow in front of the congregation, and going back on her promise would be unforgivable. Besides, she could not bear being manipulated by her father. After all, he could revive his scheme to marry her off. She could not see herself tied to some peasant, no matter how prosperous, with bad teeth and rough hands.

The minibus sped along, winding up the quiet streets of the city, past the empty sidewalks where vendors squatted into the evening, making a turn toward the church. The bellowers were bathed in golden light, like a beacon in the dark. Mei Ling would talk to Father Chong; he could provide guidance to quiet the tormented rumblings of her heart.

The next morning, Mei Ling waited for Father Chong outside his office, a modest room above the sanctuary. From the balcony, she stared at the diffuse light pouring in through the stained glass windows below.

When she was face-to-face with Father Chong, Mei Ling spoke as if she were in the confessional. The spectrum of her troubles struck every dark chord of emotion. Guilt about being away from her mother while she was ill. Anger that consumed her, making her wish terrible things on Liu, whenever she caught sight of that blasted leg of his. Regret that she had been foolish in her passions.

"Mei Ling, your heart is burdened with so many troubles. Know that if you nurture your faith, the Lord will provide the answers."

"But God helps those who help themselves," insisted Mei Ling.

"I have to support my mother. My parents cannot afford the treatment. Why, they hadn't seen the inside of a hospital until now, until this terrible cancer. And even with the money I'm sending them, they can barely make a living off the land."

"Look outside, Mei Ling." Father Chong directed her eyes to the sanctuary. "Remember how our congregation learned to make do in a crumbling building? And how devastated we were when the old church slipped away in the heavy rains? A parishioner from Hong Kong appeared in the depths of our misfortunes, and built us this temple filled with light. Our prayers were answered. And yours won't go unheard."

Mei Ling nodded; she would pray for guidance, and stoke the fires of her faith. And yet, when she sank down to pray late in the night, her whispers punctuated by the sighing breaths of husband and child, she found her thoughts drifting to possibilities that lay beyond those four walls of peeling plaster.

●　　●　　●

AFTER BEING LAID UP FOR SIX WEEKS, LIU COULD STAGGER around the apartment fairly well with a crutch. In fact, he could walk almost as well as his little daughter now. To entertain Rose, Liu would balance the crutch on his good leg, rocking her to and fro on top of the seesaw. One day, in the midst of frolicking, the rubbery end of the crutch struck a vase. A teetering, then the dreadful crash on bare tile. Liu clutched Rose instinctively to his chest. The bouquet of flowers was scattered like threshed wheat among the shards. That vase had been a gift from Mei Ling's mother. His wife might take her anger out on Rose. Liu glanced around furtively. As his gaze swept past the window, a cat landed on the ledge outside.

Now he had an idea. Liu hobbled to the kitchen with his crutch and snatched a handful of dried anchovies. Opening the window, he offered a plate to the cat. "Come here, you ol' dirty whiskers, you'll save Rose from a scolding." The cat lifted its paws to sniff at the offering, licked its chops, and leapt gracefully onto the windowsill.

Just then, the door opened and Mei Ling walked in, staring at the spectacle. "Liu, what are you doing?"

Liu's eyes darted from the plate in his hands to the mangled blossoms and shards on the floor. "The cat came in and I . . . well . . . thought I'd feed it."

"To keep him coming back? And what about this mess on the floor?"

Liu confessed. He had been clumsy with the crutch, now that he was mobile. He waited for her wrath to descend, waited for her to drag out every shard of resentment from the past two months.

"I'm very sorry, Mei Ling. I'm sorry for disappointing you."

His wife said nothing, and the silence frightened him more than the threat of her anger. With deliberate steps, Mei Ling walked over, extended her hand to take away the anchovies, and shut the window. The cat skittered along the ledge to the neighbor's apartment. And then, in a quiet voice, she said, "After we put Rose down for her nap, I have something to tell you."

Her tone was flat, her face devoid of expression. Still, Liu braced for the worst. Perhaps she wanted to end this marriage. She must be tired of providing for everyone; she needed a better man, a strong and resourceful husband. "Okay," he whispered.

"I've been thinking," Mei Ling began, "ever since I learned that my mother was sick, that I need to find a better-paying job to support her. My father's no help; he still rants and blames her for the condition. If only I could be with her!" Mei Ling's voice cracked, and then she composed herself, staring out the window where a new apartment building rose up. "Liu, let's be realistic, you know your friend's a miser. I won't get much of a raise from Tai."

"He's thrifty with his money."

"A miser," Mei Ling repeated. "And in order to support her—and us—I am going to work in Chongqing. A friend told me that a three-star hotel downtown is hiring."

It came as a load of bricks, squeezing the breath from his lungs. "Mei Ling, isn't there anything closer you can find? Chongqing is so far away. It's two days by slow boat."

"I need to take advantage of this, Liu. I don't think I can make that kind of money here. Besides, I need a little space to think about things."

Marriage . . . Rose . . . disappointments . . . Liu's failings. The possibilities swirled through his mind. "I should recover in another month or two, and then I'll be back to work, I promise. It won't be so hard then, Mei Ling."

"No, Liu. I think this is for the best." Mei Ling rose from the chair and rinsed the food on the plate down the sink.

• • •

THE BREEZES BLEW IN FROM THE RIVER, STINGING ROSE'S cheeks, her exposed throat. She leaned closer to the car window, drawn to the distant clatter of voices and heavy objects, the melding of gray sky with a tinge of blue. The back door opened, and the perfumed woman she called Ma Ma planted her legs on the dusty ground. A loud thump sounded in the rear, and Ma Ma reappeared with a massive trunk. Ma Ma leaned back into the rear of the cab, kissed her daddy on the cheek, then pecked at Rose's forehead, a cool wetness that tingled her skin. A flutter of words, the sound of her name, a tinkle of laughter like bells, and Ma Ma was gone. Then the car tore away from that dusty spot. Pressing her nose to the window, Rose fixed her gaze on the pinpoints of objects and people as they melted into the gray sky and brown water, fading away like memories of fog and cold amidst a swollen river.

24

FANG SHUPING WAS NOT ONE TO GIVE IN TO HIS VICES, BUT when he arrived back home from the countryside, he found solace in his liquor cabinet. At first, it was an extra drink after supper, and then he began to drink during the lull of late afternoon when his will and his energy sagged. He had failed to exercise any influence on behalf of the Lanping villagers, and his most important project—a reunion with Sulin—had failed miserably. Aside from any feelings she could have for her late husband, he wondered why she loathed him so. Sulin had saved his life, on more than one occasion, and now she did not seem to care if he were living or dead.

In the evenings, Fang no longer took pleasure in reading the papers, gloating over political demotions or the commercial developments that he influenced. Bourbon soothed him, and it gave him temporary shelter from the wretched memory of Sulin's words, uttered with such finality on that windswept hill. Fang was ashamed of those feelings, and he wondered how he could be a legitimate son of his father, a man who had multiple wives. They had been utterly devoted to his father, and the great man never succumbed to their whims or ploys to win his exclusive affection.

Chu Sulin had never been one to give in to whims. She had an indefatigable strength and will, and had come to his aid when he most needed it.

•   •   •

IN THE EARLY MONTHS OF 1969, WHEN SNOW BLANKETED THE
land like a stifling cloak, Fang fell ill with pneumonia. By then,
the villagers had learned of his black capitalist background, and he
was assigned to the worst of jobs, hauling buckets of pig manure to
spread in the fields, and made to sleep in a drafty shed. When Sulin
discovered him, he was nearly unconscious with fever. Medicines
were almost impossible to obtain, but she used her father's status
to procure some herbs for Fang. Day and night she watched over
him, fighting the fever with cold compresses applied to his forehead
and feet, and rubbing his back to ease the bedsores. A week later,
he was over the worst of it, and still she stayed with him. She was
not merely taking pity on Fang; she delighted in his wit and intelligence, in the poetry he recited from the bawdy minstrels of the
Tang Dynasty, and the translated works of Tolstoy and Chekhov.
These were bootleg copies he had obtained in the city, read by
candlelight while books were being burned all around.

Seized by the fever of persecution, the peasants were keen to
detect any counter-revolutionaries in their midst. Fang was scru-
tinized in obsessive and petty detail, and only during clandestine
meetings in the woods could he and Sulin allow their feelings to
flow unchecked. Pushing past the limits of what was respectable,
Sulin declared that she had no regrets, that her passions had no
place in the outside world, where they were starved and subjugated
by the duties of a good Communist leader's daughter.

The borders between life and death were tenuous during those
revolutionary years. Almost a third of Sulin's original village had
died in the terrible famine a decade earlier. While their lives seemed
more secure now, the peasants grumbled about their rations. During
the grievance sessions, they recalled the gnawing hunger of those
early years, when they ground tree bark into flour, only to watch
their elders and young children die with bloated bellies. Still, the
stories did not encourage them to work harder under the commune system.

As leader of their production brigade, Sulin's father was respected for his skill and discretion in smoothing over conflicts. But he was never at ease; they had to keep their productivity high, and he would pad the numbers to stay in the good graces of the bureaucrats. In the summer of 1969, he arranged a marriage between Sulin and the son of an important Communist leader, the county's party secretary. Sulin was devastated by the news. She declared her love for Fang, but her father merely told her that she needed to obey his orders. She protested, but her words fell on deaf ears. He sent someone to spy on his daughter and the lover. When their secret trysts were exposed, Fang endured a series of denunciations by the villagers.

On the first evening, the crowd gathered in an old granary turned into a public arena for the struggle sessions. Shackled with rope made of rough hemp, Fang was blindfolded and shoved onto a platform where the peasants heckled him. It was Fang, and his forebears, who were to blame for the injustices they suffered, for the iron hand of imperialism they had lived under for generations. Fang's persecutors did not accuse him of rape; they knew that it was a consensual relationship, and that Sulin was bold enough to dismiss their claims. The scourge of capitalism provided ample fuel for the peasants' ire.

The elder Chu's henchman declared, "Traitor! This man is here to subvert the revolutionary cause. His father was not only a landowner but a major industrialist—do you hear—a capitalist who dealt with the foreign devils and drained the lifeblood of China to force trade with our oppressors. But the People's Republic has risen above this foreign terror, and we must sentence the traitors to death."

Fang had grown numb to the accusations, but this sentence of death seized him with terror. His nerves were already shattered, his will was crumbling from physical strain and hunger, and all that mattered to him was Sulin.

By the fourth struggle session, Fang's fate was sealed. He was sentenced to die by hanging. The crowd cheered, "Long live the People's Republic!"

During this time, Fang was imprisoned along with two other

suspected capitalists in the granary. His only contact with the out-side was through Chu Longshan, the brother of Sulin, who slipped messages for him under a rock by the toilet pit.

"DO NOT FEAR," a note read, two nights after his death sentence was proclaimed. "SHE WILL FIGHT FOR YOU."

And then came the message, "FATHER HAS SET MAR-RIAGE DATE. SHE IS RESISTING." Fang read the note again and again. His hopes of eloping with Sulin had been dashed, his execution was at hand, and what power could a daughter exert over her father, who held the lives of thousands in his hands? Still, Fang took comfort in her steadfastness, and waited.

The day before his execution, Fang read the final note with disbelief. "YOU WILL BE FREED. YOU HAVE ORDERS TO LEAVE THE VILLAGE WITHIN THREE DAYS."

True to Longshan's word, Fang was banished from the com-mune with only the clothes on his back. Years later he learned that Sulin had threatened to take her own life if her father took Fang's. And yet, he had been devastated to find out that Sulin did marry her betrothed.

The long march of decades had not quelled Fang's feelings for Sulin, and he wondered how he could forget her now, after meet-ing her face-to-face. The fiery spark of her spirit enchanted him, even frightened him. He was out of schemes now; she had refused to rekindle that flame, and all he had gained from this venture was a bit of insight into his friend Longshan's plight.

•　　•　　•

ON THE TWENTY-FIFTH DAY OF THE SIXTH MONTH, THE VILLAGERS of Lanping received a notice that their evacuation was scheduled for the coming year, after spring festival. The construction of the dam was in progress, and any families that did not vacate their homes on time would be fined 17,000 *yuan*.

Longshan showed the notice to his wife. "I cannot believe those bastards. Our efforts have been futile. After our visit, I thought we were still talking over the resettlement money, but this letter"—here he slapped the thin parchment with the heel of his hand—"sounds like it's a done deal. We will not have enough funds to get a decent house; we may have to go into this with another family."

His wife sighed. "I expected as much. There is my brother's family. Or your sister, I suppose."

"My sister is upset at me for bringing Fang Shuping on that trip. We'd best leave that stone unturned." Longshan paced across the room, tapping a pencil against his forehead. "The worst of this is that we won't be able to support ourselves. Who can get by on scraps thrown to a dog? You should have been there, Min Yi. There was barely a stand of trees as far as the eye could see. A barren, demon-cursed landscape, that's where our new home will be. We'd have better luck growing crops on the dirt between our toes. I'm going to call an emergency meeting of our council. We've got to do something soon before the government starts sending the construction crews here."

Longshan grabbed his coat and headed for the door. His wife followed him with a fretful look. "Be careful, the walls have ears, you know."

"If nobody speaks up, we might as well be deaf and mute. Heaven knows we've put up with enough."

On the night of the emergency meeting, a temperamental wind blew through the old factory courtyard, cresting over the tops of surrounding peaks, which loomed in the dark like displeased spirits. The village leaders pulled their jackets close to their bodies and braced against the sideways shear of the wind. They spoke rapidly that night, as if their words would be swallowed up in the gale as soon as they were uttered.

"We should march right up to their marble and brick offices and demand that we be treated decently!" said one villager from across the river.

"You can bet the police will shoo us away like hobos!" cried another.

A man with a quiet, dignified voice spoke up. "Maybe we can take this to the courts. We have a case here. We cannot live on that steep hillside. A few *jin* of corn a year, that's all the land will yield."

"Sir, that'd be a fine idea if we had the resources. My sister's village tried to petition the courts over another matter, and it cost them 10,000 *yuan* up front. And they lost anyway. Their land was taken by a power company."

The villagers muttered among themselves. Where could they come up with 10,000 *yuan*? The grizzled old man who had advised restraint at the earlier meetings stroked his beard thoughtfully. "The courts would be an option if the odds were in our favor. But without a lawyer, what are we but a bunch of squirrels trying to hoard empty nuts? No, there are no guarantees if you take things to the courts. We may have laws in this country, but it's the folks in power who will decide our fate."

"Well, if our means are limited, we do have one possible recourse," said Longshan. "And that's Beijing."

The crowd erupted in whispers, like a swirl of leaves caught in the wind. The idea of petitioning in Beijing was met with skepticism, hope, awe, uncertainty, curiosity. Nobody had done such a thing before. And yet, the news relayed by sons and daughters in the big cities indicated that the Party's top leaders did care about the plight of the peasants. Beijing would listen. And Beijing was perhaps the only recourse.

Over the next three weeks, the villagers drafted a petition for their case. Longshan asked Fang to help polish their written plea, and a ten-page document was produced, taken to the post office, and postmarked for Beijing. The clerk gave Longshan a hard look, and asked him to fill out his particulars on a form, without revealing when the letter would arrive in the proper hands, or if it would even make the journey at all.

Longshan checked the postal mail with unfailing zeal, and when there was no sign of a reply after two months, he decided to make the long trip by train to the nation's capital. Fortunately, as Fang had recommended, the villagers had kept a facsimile of the petition, which Longshan braced between two slabs of birch bark and wrapped in multiple layers of cloth in order to avoid any questions or suspicion.

●　　●　　●

TEN DAYS LATER, A DESPONDENT LONGSHAN ARRIVED HOME

with his package still firmly wrapped in a bolt of cloth. He let out a long sigh, took a gulp of rice wine, and told his wife what had happened.

"When I arrived at the government office, I found a long line of petitioners going out the door. Like a wounded animal with its intestines sticking out. I waited for three days, until I finally got to a window. The clerk looked as worn out as the rest of us."

Longshan took another swig of liquor and rubbed his eyes, which were twitchy and bloodshot from travel. "Three days of waiting, hoping, praying silently for somebody to take pity on our case, and what do you think happened? The clerk told me that matters like ours could not be handled. An agreement was in place and the project was moving forward. 'But we didn't sign any contract,' I insisted. The clerk just shook his head and sent me on my way. At least he took down some notes on our case."

As autumn stamped its rusted seal on the land, a vengeful spirit began to plague Lanping and the other communities around the Songdu River. A cousin of Longshan's was roughed up by thugs who claimed there were old debts to settle, although none of them had ever been seen in the villages. The buck-toothed fellow from the council said an intruder had poisoned his pigs in the night. Others had picked up flyers in town proclaiming the benefits of a new dam on the Songdu River. The notice offered a reward to those who dredged up evidence of any dissident activity.

Longshan suspected that their efforts had incited the wrath of the authorities. Yet nothing they had done showed any disrespect or disregard for their power. The debates of the council raged on with the upsetting news that compensation would actually be reduced, from 5000 to 4200 *yuan* per person. It was a sobering blow to their efforts. "Project costs have been higher than anticipated," the letter claimed.

The following week, several villagers were visited by a well-dressed man who carried a police badge, demanding to know the whereabouts of a certain Chu Longshan. Now his fears were confirmed. The authorities had been tracking their efforts after all;

perhaps there was even a spy at their meetings who reported on the proceedings. On the other hand, the petition may have been enough to raise the red flag.

On the first day of the eleventh month, a uniformed officer showed up at the house. He was flanked by two burly men who rested their hands on gun holsters. Longshan's wife opened the door and was brusquely pushed aside as the officer demanded that their suspect appear before them.

Longshan came in from the yard, wiping the soupy excrement from the chicken coop on a rag before extending a hand to the men. The officer ignored his outstretched hand, and stiffly asked if he was Chu Longshan.

"Yes, what is the matter?" Longshan became very still, clutching the rag in both hands.

"You are under arrest, and must leave the premises now." One of the burly men produced a pair of handcuffs.

"For what?" Chu Longshan cried. "Officer, I've been a good citizen. I've paid my taxes. I—"

"You have been obstructing law and order, but we understand you may not be the only one getting in the way of the government's wishes."

"Wishes? What wishes? You mean the Gaoshanlu dam, right? We're only asking for fair compensation. We haven't given anyone any trouble."

Cold metal dug into Chu Longshan's wrists, and the burly men dragged him by the handcuffs toward their waiting car, its engine still running.

The men shoved Longshan into the back and sat on each side of him during the ride to the county jail. Longshan dared not ask any more questions. He thought of his wife, whose brow contorted in fear as the authorities took him away. He wondered what the other village leaders would do; surely, they would learn the reason for his disappearance, but would they step up to the fight? Was there one amongst the council who would be bold enough? And then there was Fang. Could his friend defend him, just as he had done for Fang half a lifetime ago? For now, only one thing was certain: a cold prison cell, where cobwebs shimmered in the damp of autumn, and the company of men who committed crimes of a questionable nature, for which they could only be pitied.

THE INTERIOR of the WAN BAO HOTEL BORE AN EERIE resemblance to the Jade Dragon in Wushan. Now that Mei Ling was employed as the service clerk of the eleventh floor, she would put on her uniform each morning and pack away memories of home, much like the torn, unsalvageable linens tossed into the back of the laundry room.

It did not take long for Mei Ling to learn the mundane duties of her job—greeting customers in the hallway from her station, servicing them with fresh towels or drinks, and providing directions to the hotel's services. "Business Center is open until eight. Computer, copier, and fax available for a reasonable fee."

"The bar? Second floor. This way, *xian sheng*." It struck her now, more than ever before, that she would address a strange man as she would her husband. *Xian sheng*, first born.

While she managed to keep the tipsy businessmen at bay, Mei Ling could not avoid getting into a few scrapes with her supervisor, a tough old bird with a sharp chin and fishhook brows named Lao Hu. Resting on her seniority, Lao Hu kept a fierce, watchful eye over her territory. Nobody could track the movements, the missteps, and failures of each of her underlings as closely as Lao Hu. With the pretty young hires she seemed particularly harsh. Mei Ling's colleagues assured her it was simply part of the backroom drama in the Wan Bao, whose name boasted of ten thousand treasures and held as many torments.

Lao Hu gave her the most onerous of tasks; Mei Ling had to scrape at wine and cigarette stains in the rooms of careless patrons, and she was in no position to refuse on the grounds that these tasks belonged to another class of employees. While she was higher ranked than the custodial staff, Mei Ling knew her place in the pecking order as long as Lao Hu had her claws on the brood.

The sleek skyscrapers of Chongqing's downtown lit up at night, and when Mei Ling finished an earlier shift, she would head out to the streets with a few coworkers. Enormous billboards displaying milky white women and stylish products gleamed alongside the Liberation Monument. A testament to those who triumphed over the Japanese in the War of Resistance, it seemed incongruous with the garish displays of wealth all around them.

At first, her presence in this city of ten million seemed incongruous as well. Chongqing was the size of one hundred Wushans, and even that town had seemed large to Mei Ling when she left her small village two years earlier. Yet she felt a kind of freedom in the big city she had not possessed since her marriage to Liu. She had responsibilities of course—a mother seriously ill, and a husband and child to provide for—but whatever was left over from her paycheck was hers to keep.

At the same time, Mei Ling felt a vague sense of unease about leaving Liu and Rose behind. She had gained some degree of acceptance from the child, and she could not help but hear echoes of reproach in the tottering steps of young children she passed on the streets. *That woman has left her family,* the voices cried; *she only cares about herself. Selfish girl, she has deserted her brood. Mother hens don't do that.*

The incessant buzz of city life pushed away those nagging thoughts. In the dormitory she shared with five women, the drone of the television was strangely comforting. Her skirmishes with Lao Hu, however, were a new source of worry. She had stood up to the witch and refused an unreasonable task, an act that her colleagues looked upon with admiration. Yet Mei Ling was plagued afterward by thoughts that she had been too brash.

When a customer's load of laundry was discovered missing, Mei

Ling was summoned by Lao Hu, whose tongue was sharpened and ready for attack. "Young lady, you were responsible for taking the laundry from 1106 to the wash room, but no trace of the items can be found. Are you so bold as to steal a customer's belongings, or just plain careless?"

Mei Ling denied the charges, but Lao Hu pressed further. "You'll be sent to the basement to clean furnaces if this happens again."

"Well, do what you want, but I don't deserve those accusations. I'll find those lost shirts, and if I don't, I'll spare you the trouble and quit." Mei Ling turned on her heels and stormed out.

She was about to follow through on her word, but later that afternoon the shirts turned up, starched and folded, from the laundromat across the street, where they had been sent on subsequent orders by the customer. Still, Lao Hu blamed Mei Ling for neglecting to keep track of the transaction. Mei Ling was sent to the general manager of the service department to be reprimanded.

As she approached the twentieth floor of the Wan Bao, she prepared for a verbal lashing. She wondered if she should indeed resign and take her chances at finding another job.

The manager surprised Mei Ling by greeting her with a pleasant smile, and gesturing for her to sit down. The light from his desk lamp glowed warmly against the dull gray skyline. He extended his hand toward her. "I am Sun Daimen. And what is your name?"

"Mei Ling. . . . Chang Mei Ling," she whispered, taken aback by his cordiality. She sank into the cushioned seat, which was more decorative than comfortable.

"Mrs. Lao tells me that you've been neglectful in your duties. Is that true?"

"She expects me to do things beyond my stated duties, and I've been happy to oblige, but I really shouldn't be blamed for this mishap," Mei Ling declared.

Sun Daimen nodded as she spoke, and once again, his response surprised her. "Don't worry about it, Miss Chang. You've done your best. Mrs. Lao can be a little demanding sometimes. I'll have a word with her."

Mei Ling thanked him, although she knew it wouldn't be the

end of her troubles with Lao Hu. The manager rose up and shook her hand, sending a warm current through Mei Ling's palms. When she left the office, Mei Ling felt the imprint of the man's hands, which were strong but smooth as pearl against her skin. For the rest of the day, her thoughts kept returning to his demeanor, and she smiled whenever she remembered the glow of his eyes in the golden lamplight.

• • •

CHEN WEIJIN'S HEALTH HAD DETERIORATED SINCE MEI LING'S last conversation with her. Her belly had bloated up, and the hollow of her throat was tender and swollen. She awoke in the mornings feeling tired and dazed, as everything around her swam in a blurry, shimmering mass. The pain in her joints flared up when she bent down to stoke the wood pilings in the stove.

Mei Ling listened to her mother's tired voice with anguish. Her deterioration tested Mei Ling's faith in cruel ways. When she tried to be optimistic and strong for her mother, she would be reward-ed only by bad news, and when she fell into despair there would be signs of renewed health. Mei Ling could only cradle the small phone in her hands, wishing she were there to comfort her mother and ease the pain in her body.

But Chen Weijin was not one to give in to despair, despite the hardships of life in a strange, faraway land, and a husband who had little tolerance for weakness, as he viewed her condition. His cal-lousness repulsed Mei Ling, and drew her even closer to her moth-er. And while Mei Ling could provide her with medicines, and the balm of comforting words, she could not buffer her against his insensitivity.

In a more generous frame of mind, Mei Ling could see that their struggles in Guangdong had taken a toll on his ornery spirit. She had not been on cordial speaking terms with him since the wedding, and only wished to forget the whole sordid affair. And yet, Mei Ling began to wonder if she had married foolishly, out of a headstrong reaction to her father's wishes.

Still, she felt it was her duty to continue sending money to Liu and Rose. She called Liu once a week, while he was at Tai's, and learned of his progress. His broken leg was healing in measurable strides, and in another month he would be out of the cast. Liu's voice was subdued, and she had trouble hearing him above the din of clanking pots in Tai's kitchen.

"You've been good to Rose and me," he said one evening. "I'll make it up to you, Mei Ling."

She bit her lip. His expression of gratitude, uttered with the innocence of a child, not only touched her, but also exposed the impurities of her heart. Removed from the small world of Wushan, she had drifted away from the Catholic community that had bathed her in the sweet affections of the elderly women. She felt far away now, from the women who chanted as they prayed and from Father Chong, whose answer for earthly sorrows was to find faith again in the heavens.

While she wrestled with her misgivings, Mei Ling noticed that the manager seemed to be paying her special attention. He stopped by the eleventh floor on several occasions, and took extra care to ask after Mei Ling. Once, while Mei Ling was stooped over a bathtub cleaning out the remains of an extinguished cigarette, Sun Daimen appeared behind her in the doorway. A startled look must have appeared on her face, and he apologized for intruding. "I'll get someone to relieve you," he said, touching her on the shoulder.

Mei Ling did not cringe from the light pressure of his fingertips. Yet she was somewhat flustered by the encounter in a confined, private space. She curtsied, thinking that was what one did in such situations, and made motions to leave.

Sun Daimen cleared his throat, and in a voice that trickled like tea water, he asked, "Do you like . . . living here?"

"It's nice, yes. I miss my familiar haunts back home, but there's much to explore here after hours."

"Yes, Chongqing is a grand city. I'm originally from a small village near Wanzhou, moved out years ago and never looked back. I've been lucky to work here, and I miss the family, but it's a tradeoff. They're taken care of because I'm out here."

"Do you have kids back home?" Mei Ling asked, vaguely aware that she might have other reasons for wanting to know.

"Oh no, I'm not married or anything. Mother would like me to be." Sun Daimen smiled sheepishly, as if he realized he had said too much.

Mei Ling felt emboldened by his shyness, but resisted the impulse to tease him. Instead, she thanked him for the break from her duties and excused herself.

That evening, Mei Ling stood in front of the washbasin in the dormitory, staring into the hand mirror suspended on the wall. With lingering strokes, she brushed her long hair back from her face. She noticed the wisps around her hairline, thought of her mother, who started graying in her fifties. She began to think about the prospect of getting older, a journey from which there was no turning back and little reprieve from failed choices. She had taken her youth for granted. And yet, the responsibilities and worries that filled her days were slowly robbing her of that youth, like a small rodent nibbling in the rice sack. "Every day, the mouse would steal a grain," her mother used to say, "and the next day another, and there were always so many left that he did not worry. Until one day. . . ." It was a child's story, but the meaning of that tale was impressed on Mei Ling now more than ever before.

Mei Ling wondered what Sun Daimen wanted from her; if he had been making advances, they were barely noticeable. His mother wanted him to marry. Wasn't he the kind of man that other mothers had designs on, if only for their daughters? And if so, why was he not already taken? Sun Daimen looked to be fairly youthful, perhaps no older than his early thirties.

One Sunday morning, after another fruitless trip to find a church in the vicinity, she received a call from her father. "Your mother's back in the hospital," he told her. She fumbled with the phone, nearly dropping in onto the sidewalk.

"You should've seen her," Ol' Chang said. "She was white as a ghost. Couldn't eat, or keep her food down. Doctors said the drugs didn't work first time around. The cancer's back, and they're trying to zap it again." Her father sighed, and for the first time, he sounded humble and defeated. "I'm not one to go to doctors, but this one's beyond me. Never in my days."

Mei Ling managed to reach her mother in the hospital, but Chen Weijin was too dazed and exhausted from her treatment to speak much.

Shaken by the turn of events, Mei Ling could not keep her attention on the job the next day. She dragged herself about her duties, and her legs seemed to be carved from stone. As she delivered a tray of food to a guest, her knee buckled under, and a large bowl of hot soup splashed onto the carpet.

Her supervisor was livid. "Young lady, you deserve more than a reprimand," Lao Hu hissed. "Your blunders are just inexcusable. I'd fire you myself if I had the authority."

Hooked by the elbow, Mei Ling was marched to Sun Daimen's office with a grip so painfully tight she could not have escaped if she tried. Mei Ling was too weary to fight, and resigned herself to whatever her bosses had in store.

The old crow launched into her tirade, firing sharp glances in Mei Ling's direction. Sun Daimen listened calmly and said, "Thank you, Mrs. Lao. I'll take care of things from here."

Mei Ling waited until Mrs. Lao's heavy footfalls had disappeared down the hall. And then she glanced up at Sun Daimen. Mrs. Lao's charges only appeared to amuse him. His face beamed with delight, as if he had been waiting to see Mei Ling.

"You look tired, Miss Chang. Everything all right?" he asked.

At first, Mei Ling mumbled that she didn't feel well, but Sun Daimen was not convinced. "My mother is deathly ill," she said at last. "I came out here to find work to support her, and I don't know what else I can do, if I can do any good at all."

Sun Daimen was silent; it seemed as if her travails had touched some part of him that could know suffering. "Your mother deserves the best, and you're doing all you can, I'm sure."

Mei Ling shook her head vigorously, and the hot tears flowed forth. She turned her head and brushed them away, but a fresh supply materialized. When Sun Daimen offered her a tissue, she buried her face in her hands, embarrassed that he should witness a woman's weakness so nakedly.

"I have a back office where you can stay for a few hours," Sun

Daimen said. "Don't worry about Lao Hu. We'll sort it out, get you a transfer."

Still ashamed of her outburst, Mei Ling whispered a few words of gratitude, and retreated into the small room. An hour later, Sun Daimen appeared with a tray of hot soup and rice.

"To replace the one you spilled," he teased.

Mei Ling had recovered enough to flash a feigned look of indignation. "Are you trusting me with that? No guarantees you'll have a clean tie when you leave."

"I'll take my chances, "Sun Daimen grinned, setting the tray down beside her. Mei Ling was touched that he would deliver the food himself. It was something she could never see her father doing for her mother, no matter how sick she was.

That evening, he stayed with her until the last office employees had left, past the prime hours when the guests dined fifteen floors below, and even after the businessmen finished their deals, lingering in the bar for another round of drinks.

Sun Daimen told her that he had cared for his ailing father in his youth, while his mother sought work outside the village to make ends meet. The man had suffered from a multitude of diseases, compounded by his earlier indiscretions. "Women and drink. It's done him in," he said wryly. As a young man, Daimen had gone away to work in the factories, not long after the market economy opened up. His two older brothers had fallen sick from the chemicals used at the local tannery and could not work. He was the youngest son, but the responsibility had fallen to him.

Mei Ling glanced at Sun Daimen with admiration. Here was a man who had risen up the ranks, and remained devoted to his family. He did not seem to be the kind who gave in to infidelities like other men of means.

The following week, Mei Ling was transferred to the bookkeeping department, where she took to her new duties quite well, often staying into the night to finish a task or take on an additional project. At the end of the evening, Sun Daimen would take her to supper at one of the local restaurants. She could see that while he could afford a fine establishment every night, they both felt at home in the modest noodle shop they frequented. As they ate, they watched the proprietress making wonton at another table. A dollop of ground pork, a pinch of the wrapper, and another dumpling would land on the growing mound while a giant pot of water rumbled nearby.

Mei Ling knew that the other women on staff were gossiping about them, some out of jealousy, others out of curiosity or boredom. Yet she was drawn to Sun Daimen for all the things that Liu could not offer her. Unlike her husband, this man had a position that commanded awe and respect. And his aura cast a wide circle around those under his wing. For that reason, few of the women mentioned him directly to Mei Ling, and none asked where her husband might stand in light of this possible affair.

Sun Daimen was an educated man, but one who grasped the unschooled ways of the human heart. He was not one to rush any declarations, nor force her into the physical intimacies that someone in his position could easily demand.

In fact, Sun Daimen was so much of a gentleman that Mei Ling could allow her fantasies to nestle comfortably in her bosom, unclouded by worries that she could be unfaithful. At the same time, Mei Ling never mentioned her marriage to Sun Daimen.

As the colors of fall blanched toward winter, a deep friendship blossomed between the two. On her birthday, Sun Daimen gave her a painting of two magpies on a single branch. "Something I do in my spare time," he said modestly.

That night, he treated her to a special dinner in town. Perhaps he sensed it was time to drop the pretenses. Or maybe she had exuded a willingness, in the glow of her cheeks, to take their friendship to another level. He was a little drunk; his manner had a touch of brashness that seemed out of character.

"You may not know this," Daimen said, "but your friendship is one I've come to count on over the months. I may be ill at ease with my superiors' demands, or tired and frustrated after a hard day, but seeing you always gives me such joy."

"Oh, you're too kind, Daimen. Don't forget, it was you who pulled me out of a dark hole when my mother was doing so poorly.

I can never repay you for what you've done. And for taking me out of the clutches of Lao Hu."

"No need, Mei Ling. She's got other young hires to torment, I'm sure. But I couldn't let her do that to you." Sun Daimen gazed intently at Mei Ling. "You mean a lot to me."

Mei Ling felt a surge of warmth in her bosom. If there was any shadow of resistance, it melted away in the light of his declaration. She reached over and placed her hand over his, feeling the spark that rushed from one to the other, across skin, in an ecstatic vibration. It was pure desire, seeking to be fulfilled.

"Let me take you to my place, shall I?"

Mei Ling nodded, and the two quickly left, arriving before too long at Sun Daimen's apartment on the waterfront, where the Yangtze and Jialing Rivers met.

The lights from the city below glowed excitedly. Now that the consummation of their desire seemed close at hand, Sun Daimen was a bit clumsy, rattling the kitchen cabinets for a bottle of wine. At length, they settled down on the couch, with glasses in hand, and when he leaned closer, Mei Ling got a whiff of sweat on the nape of his neck. It smelled of straw and earth and bare sun, of a man never too far from his roots.

He moved even closer. She wanted to give herself to those yearnings. She felt the push and pull, the silent pulse that drew them close. As she breathed in the scent of his body, sweet as loamy earth, Mei Ling felt her face flush from alcohol. She leaned toward him, her heart pounding. And then, without warning, a tide of shame overtook her.

Sun Daimen placed his hand on her hair, stroking it gently, but she turned away. "I can't . . . do this. Sun Daimen, I haven't told you, but I'm married. I have a husband, and an adopted child. I've had to take care of them too, and it's given me almost as much anguish as my mother's illness."

She slowly looked back at Daimen. His fingers retracted from the silken mass of her hair to a throbbing point on his temple.

"Are you . . . were you aware how I felt toward you?"

"Yes, but I didn't have the courage to tell you. I can tell you now, though, that I regret I did not meet you first."

"But you are married to someone else."

"Yes."

"Well, Mei Ling, it's up to you, if you choose to be with your husband. I will have to live with it, I don't know how, but you won't have to worry about me getting carried away like this."

That night, as Sun Daimen drove her home, Mei Ling felt an icy chill seize her body. The alcohol had started to wear off. A cruel emptiness remained where their intimacy had been tended so carefully over the months. She had to choose, and she would have to live with the consequences for a long, long time. Whatever she chose would bring disappointment to someone in her life, and she wondered if her happiness mattered at all in this tangled web.

26

STILL IN HIS SILK PAJAMAS, FANG THUMBED THROUGH HIS MAIL at a languid pace. He expected a few business deals to come through this month. The thrill of baited victory had lost some of its luster, although months had passed since his last trip to Lanping village.

A fragile envelope addressed to Fang in large, bold strokes caught his eye. The handwriting was neat, although the hand that penned it had been somewhat unsteady.

> Dear Fang Shuping,
>
> You may think me shameless, to turn to you after I had so flatly rebuffed you. But I must put my pride aside, and seek help from all possible channels.
>
> My brother, as you know, has been trying to negotiate better terms for our villages with this resettlement business. He was detained shortly after delivering a petition to Beijing. Two weeks ago, the authorities came and arrested him again. But nobody will tell us what his crime is, and we do not know his whereabouts. If you have any connections with the authorities or the company involved in this dam project, please consider contacting them on behalf of my brother. If you are able at all to

help, my sister-in-law and I will look forward to
hearing from you.
Sincerely,
Chu Sulin

Fang Shuping put down the letter, and sat drumming his fingers
on his eyeglass case. He had tried to put Chu Sulin out of his mind,
and now his hopes were rekindled once more. But something else
stirred, a wave of indignation that his friend had been treated so
poorly. What could the man have done that was so terrible? What
was so unreasonable about bargaining for a better deal? It was done
all the time in the world of business.

He realized with irony that these villagers had little power in
the grand scheme of things. How was it, then, that he had suffered
such abuse at the hands of peasants as a young man? Those were different times, he decided. Heady times when the poor thought they
could earn a place at the table. They had seized their petty power
with such vengeance. And their cruelty was unforgivable.

"Damn them all," Fang muttered to himself. His anger, coiled
like a serpent, rose up at the memory of the indignities he had endured. Those shackles that bound him had long ago been thrown
off. But if it hadn't been for Sulin . . . he realized that he owed it to
her, and now she needed him as never before.

Rising from his chair, Fang cleared away the clutter of newspapers that remained unread for weeks. Invigorated with a new
sense of purpose, he began to rummage through his files for all the
contacts he had in Sichuan province who could help with the case.
Later that day, he would venture to make the most important call
of all, to Chu Sulin and her sister-in-law, to arrange a visit in the
next day or two.

•   •   •

THE DIM GRAY INTERIOR OF CHU LONGSHAN'S HOUSE HAD
fallen into neglect with his absence. The weathered bricks that
formed its humble walls were caving in to the stresses of wind and
rain. Made of the rich mud that lined the riverbanks, they were

dried in the sun rather than baked and hardened at high temperature. Fang approached the door, scraping the mud off his shoes before knocking.

Longshan's wife opened the door, and her face lit up upon seeing him. "Fang Shuping! Come in, come in. You must be tired after traveling so far. I'll fix some tea. Please make yourself at home."

Through the feeble light, Fang could see Sulin sitting on a small chair by a barrel of preserved eggs. Mrs. Chu went into the kitchen, leaving the two alone. "Sulin, I never thought I'd see you again. But bad news brings us together, I suppose."

Sulin appeared too distraught to put up her usual defenses. "Thank you for coming. I would not have troubled you, but I think the authorities really mean business this time." There was a catch in her throat, and Fang did not know what to say. He stood there awkwardly, beneath the faded picture of Mao Zedong, until Longshan's wife emerged from the kitchen with tea.

Mrs. Chu apologized for the humble offering, then sat down with her hands folded in her lap, recounting the events of the past months. "After he got detained for going to Beijing, Longshan was sullen and untalkative for days. Then he started going out in the evenings, always coming home quite late, after I'd gone to bed. He only told me that the authorities were displeased with our claims. They said we had no grounds. No grounds, indeed! When they're robbing us of our livelihood, not giving us enough to put a roof over our heads."

Mrs. Chu took a deep breath and continued. "Well, early one evening, shortly before he was heading out, the police showed up again and arrested him. It seems like they were watching him, maybe even followed him around at night. Maybe we're even being watched right now." A frightened look appeared in Mrs. Chu's eyes.

"Where was your husband going that night? Fang asked.

"To meet with the others from that intervillage council, that's what we think. Will they know what's going on? Should we ask them?"

"Worth a try," replied Fang. "Did Chu ever mention those guys by name?"

Sulin, who had been listening patiently, replied, "Some of them were on the tour of the new site. There was a fellow by the name of Dong Xiawen from my village."

"Let me talk to the fellow. I'll find out what's going on. We'll get your man back yet." Fang stood up. "Sulin, shall we pay him a visit tomorrow? There's not enough light tonight for me to accompany you back to the village. Don't want to give your neighbors any ideas." He looked at Sulin intently, eager to detect a reaction to his words.

"Mr. Fang, I'm not scared of you," Sulin said coldly. "Tomorrow's fine."

The next morning, after another night on the hard cot in Longshan's house, Fang drove to Chu Sulin's village, across the mosaic of rice paddies and fields, past the chatter of children on their way to a nearby village school. When he arrived at her house, she appeared in a cotton-quilted jacket whose colors had faded to a pale sky blue. But Sulin carried herself with dignity, in the swing of her sturdy hips, the arch of her cheekbones as she spoke. She insisted on being part of the conversation rather than leaving the men to do the planning.

Dong Xiawen was the bucktoothed council member who had once cautioned against including the press in their site visit. Over the past six months, the fellow had grown a small mustache over his teeth, as if to conceal them, but it only managed to make them appear larger.

"The local officials had found out about this Beijing petition," he explained, "and they told Longshan to turn it over. They released him from detention that first time when he agreed. But Longshan only turned over a part of the letter, and he left out the signatures of the leaders from our council, knowing these people would be targeted next. Apparently that did not satisfy them, and now we've lost him again . . . for how long, I don't know."

"What has the council decided?" Fang asked.

"We're not sure exactly. Some think we should demand his release with a united voice, and let go of the resettlement funds for now. He was elected council chair, and he's been leading us through this fight. Others think that we have no choice but to rally against the blasted dam."

Dong Xiawen said that the villagers had not seen a *fen* of compensation, but they still needed to move, or else pay outrageous fines. "They'll turn us into beggars and thieves, I tell you." The peasant sighed audibly, and dug his heels into the earthen floor.

"Of course we want Longshan to be released," said Sulin, "but how can we do that without putting more people at risk?"

"I can look into that," said Fang. "Where I live is no longer part of Sichuan province, and they can't hold anything against me. Some of those guys owe me favors, anyway." Fang spoke with a tone of conviction, yet something gnawed at him inside. He sensed that he was getting into more trouble than he'd bargained for. He glanced over at Sulin, and thought he detected a faint smile on her lips.

Fang knew that an unspoken pact had been made that day. He owed his life to Sulin and to some extent her brother, and now, thirty-six years later, it was time to repay that debt.

Dong Xiawen promised that he would keep them abreast of developments, and swore them to secrecy. As they left, Sulin declined a ride from Fang, saying she would walk home.

"I'd like to walk with you," Fang replied.

Sulin stiffened. "Your vehicle's here. You need not go out of your way, really."

They walked in silence for some time. The clucking and scratching of chickens broke the stillness of the winter's day. And then, much to Fang's surprise, Sulin turned toward him and asked, "So how is it that you and Longshan found each other again after all these years?"

"An act of fate, I suppose. He had written me a few months ago, asking if I could track down your daughter's old house. Told me about the funeral, a certain gold pendant she was supposed to give back to your husband, and never did."

"And you decided to help an old friend, out of the goodness of your heart."

Fang stopped in his tracks. "Sulin, if you're wondering, your suspicions are confirmed. I knew this was my chance to see you again, after all these years. I knew your husband had passed away. But I was not about to throw myself your way, like an ape with a scratchy ass."

Sulin's lips curled; she could not resist a chuckle. "I'm widowed now, that's true," she said, serious again. "But that doesn't change anything."

"Well, fate does work in strange ways. Oddly enough, I came across a photograph of you and your husband. The scavenger working for me had found the photo, along with the pendant from your husband."

"That was his gift to our daughter, for the birth of a new child. When it turned out to be a girl, my daughter was very disappointed. But that is not why she gave the baby up." An angry look flashed in Sulin's eyes.

"Why not? Isn't that why most of 'em are unwanted?"

"No, that child was illegitimate. The real father wasn't my son-in-law, but the son of a Party member in the village. She might have taken her chances if it were a boy. But she refused to keep the girl. I offered to raise the child, but my daughter would have none of it. She's a headstrong girl."

"Takes after her mother," Fang said, stealing a sideways glance at Sulin.

She glared at him, and the gravity in her eyes sobered Fang. He resisted the impulse to tease her further.

"I have hardly spoken to her since that affair," said Sulin. "She claims that she couldn't help the situation, that the man's family is too powerful. But she could have refused, for God's sake; a woman's self-respect is all she's got in this world."

"Spoken like the Chu Sulin I used to know."

"For all I know she's still having an affair with the man. If she gets pregnant by him again, that is inexcusable . . . even if her husband is impotent."

"No worries, someone else will want the kid. That scavenger fellow—he found the baby, and now he's raising her."

Sulin was incredulous. "My granddaughter?"

"Yeah, he took her in. Liu Renfu, he's a scroungy kind of fellow, lost his wife a few years back, so he was doing it all by himself until he got married again. Beats me why he wanted to keep her." Fang thought of his baby-trading days, and refrained from saying more.

Sulin's eyes grew round, glistening like coins in the pale light. "My little grandchild is alive and well. Where is she? I suspected that she'd been left behind. What I would give to have her back in the family! That heartless daughter of mine, doesn't know a mother's sorrow. She has never eaten bitterness, not like us old folks."

"No, the young buds in spring forget what the bitterness of winter is like," said Fang.

•   •   •

TRUE TO HIS WORD, FANG GOT IN TOUCH WITH EVERY LAST ONE of his Sichuan contacts about Chu Longshan's case. In the end, the trail led him back to Chairman Jiang, the wily official who had taken advantage of Fang's efforts without keeping his end of the bargain. Fang was less than enthusiastic about facing the man again, and when Sulin insisted on being present at the meeting, he felt a wave of relief.

When they arrived at the chairman's office, he merely grunted upon seeing Fang. At the sight of Sulin, however, the portly Chairman Jiang rose up from his chair and extended his hand. "Madam, what brings you along today?"

"We know you are quite influential, and you may be able to help us," Sulin replied. The chairman gestured her toward a seat directly in front of him. Fang fetched a chair and sat down next to Sulin.

"Is somebody in trouble? Chairman Jiang asked. "Didn't pay their taxes?"

"No sir," said Sulin. "Our villages are slated to move in a few months, as you know, and we intend to cooperate, but we must appear to be troublemakers, getting in the way of business."

Startled by her concession, Fang began to speak, but she nudged him to be quiet.

"Trouble? No, madam, you folks haven't given us any trouble. Everything's coming along quite smoothly."

"You've done a marvelous job with this new project," Sulin

continued, "and we know that all our villages will benefit from your foresight and vision."

"Why, yes, this project will put these communities on a path to prosperity. All you citizens will be proud that you served the greater good, and obeyed the Party's wishes."

"Yes," said Sulin, "my brother Chu Longshan, most of all. He is a leader among men in Lanping village. Our father, in fact, once managed a large production brigade, back in the commune days."

"Is that so? A loyal Party member."

"That's right. Two months ago, my brother delivered a petition to Beijing on behalf of the communities giving up their land for this project. But he was detained shortly after his return. And now he is imprisoned. Has some mistake been made, Chairman Jiang? He is advocating for the highest values of the Party, for which your father and my father fought so dearly."

Chairman Jiang cleared his throat. "If there is a mistake, we will rectify it. Can you tell me what he was detained for?"

"We don't know exactly. I can tell you that he was standing up for the greater good of the people when he delivered that petition, and the government should uphold his intentions."

"I can tell you that the petition made a very reasonable request for compensation for the loss of land," added Fang.

"The land doesn't belong to those peasants, don't you know? It's the government's right to do as it sees fit," said Chairman Jiang. He glared at Fang. "So what's your part in this? You look familiar. I never forget a face."

"It was I who arranged for several investors to take an interest in the project," Fang replied coolly.

"Oh, right. Well, hydroelectric is the way to go in terms of investments, if you ask me. As for compensation, there are significant overhead costs involved, and whatever has been set cannot be changed."

Too many fellows skimming off the cream, Fang thought, but he merely replied, "You're the man who's in charge. Whatever you say, goes."

"Hey, I have bosses, too. They pay my salary."

"Chairman Jiang." Sulin spoke up in a melodic voice. "You must be incredibly talented and hardworking to have earned yourself a place like this." She looked around admiringly, running her fingers across the wooden arm of her chair with deliberate strokes. "And you certainly must have a great circle of influence, enough to seek my brother's release. Can you, Chairman?" Her eyes pierced his heaving, swarthy figure as she leaned in, resting her arm easily on the desk across from Chairman Jiang.

Fang detected a flirtatious quality in her gaze. He squirmed in his seat, seized by a restless twitch in his legs.

Chairman Jiang watched Sulin intently with his small, beady eyes. The spittle jetted forth from his lips as he spoke. "I have no jurisdiction over those fellows at the Public Security Bureau, Madam," he replied. "If he did something illegal that you don't know about, that's their business, not mine."

"Chairman, I know my brother was arrested because he was petitioning for the welfare of the villagers. What he did was legal. The police knocked on doors trying to track him down when he got back from Beijing. You must surely have friends in charge of the bureau. If one of your family members were in jeopardy, you'd be able to call them up in an instant, right? You are a man of means, I'm sure."

"I would certainly do what I could," said Chairman Jiang.

"Well, this is my brother I'm worried about. He's done no wrong, and I need your help." Sulin's gaze was unwavering, and Fang could tell that the chairman was surprised and somewhat unnerved by her boldness.

Chairman Jiang's eyes met hers for a flickering second. He looked at his watch and stood up, slapping his palm decisively on the desk. "All right, Madam, you've made your case. I'll see what I can do. Now if you'll excuse me, I have other business to take care of."

"I thank you for your assistance. May I call on you again if we need to?" Sulin replied.

"Sure, sure. One of you is enough. I have no time for peddlers." The chairman donned his coat, ushering his visitors out the door.

Fang walked with Sulin back to his car. "I tried to bring up compensation," he said, "but the man has no interest in keeping his end of the deal. I did secure several investors for his project, after all."

"Can't expect people to play fair," said Sulin.

"Yes, but a woman's charms can get you far," Fang retorted. "I saw him looking at you."

"Now don't start getting ideas in your head. I'm an old woman now."

"And beautiful as ever. I was a third wheel in that meeting. But I haven't lost my touch. I'll get your granddaughter back to you yet," said Fang.

•   •   •

ON THE LONG DRIVE HOME TO WUSHAN, FANG KEPT HIS GAZE fixed ahead on the lonely mountain road, but occasionally a small cluster of houses in the distance would catch his eye. He thought of that child Liu was raising, how she could have fallen into unknown hands the day his old car had broken down on the way to the orphanage. If Liu took credit for saving the little girl's life, so could he. And if Sulin wanted her granddaughter back, he would do everything in his power to fulfill her wish.

Fang had gotten into the business of salvaging babies because it was lucrative, but now this project charged him with a sense of purpose, an ardent desire to make good on his promises. And yet, he felt a little sad that while she was spirited as ever, the old Sulin who loved him, who was devoted to him, had allowed herself to be defeated by fate. Was it poverty and hardship that hardened her heart, he wondered? Or was her heart so fickle as to forget what he once meant to her?

Still lost in his thoughts, Fang approached the outskirts of Wushan. Unwilling to return home, where his cherished solitude now seemed devoid of life, he continued driving along the winding streets of the hill city. A group of day laborers gathered in front of a run-down shack, their voices rising in a chorus of laughter. One fellow reached out the willowy reed of his arm to slap his buddy's back. Nearby, an old woman with a dried tangerine face was stooped over heaped baskets of produce for sale. As Fang sailed along, the open-air storefronts where men huddled over their rice and noodle bowls flashed by like a deck of cards, with the same faces in recurring patterns.

The traffic slowed to a crawl, and a dancing shadow pulled his gaze to the coal processing plant. Fang noticed an older man stomping on a massive pile of coal gravel while another hosed down the dust with water. The fellow was about his age, with a pockmarked face, and bags beneath his eyes that radiated out in ripples. Fang wondered if the man had a wife, if someone kept him from the loneliness he bore in his gaunt frame, in his languid dance that never ended, as more piles of coal were shoveled onto his heap, and freshly made coal briquettes were carted away in wheelbarrows from another mound.

The futility of this work unsettled Fang, and he looked away as the traffic began inching along. When he turned from the main drag toward the harbor, he noticed the bright green patches that covered the low hills beneath the new city. Here the peasants had staked small plots of land to grow a few vegetables. Nearby were the remaining buildings of old Wushan waiting to be destroyed before the next scheduled rising of the river.

Fang got out of his car, stretched his legs, and started walking down the rocky path past a small crew of men hacking away at one of the buildings. The trail led past deserted houses of stone and wood, and behind a grove of trees, the old cemetery. On the hillside, black tendrils of smoke rose from the small camps where women and children huddled around the flickering fires.

Fang wondered why he had chosen to come down this path, as he felt quite out of place. Men in dirty jackets looked up from their work, and the swing of their pickaxes hesitated before falling onto hard rock. The trail ended in front of a plywood shack where a mother was tending a kettle of noodles on the open fire. Her toddler squatted and jumped, poking at insects on the ground with his stick. Fang realized with a start that people were living here, and now he felt like an intruder.

The woman had a lean, leathery face, and sooty eyes that did not mask her surprise when he drew near.

"Greetings. What's cooking?" Fang called out.

She hesitated, then said, "We're not causing any trouble."

"Hey, I'm not a cop. Just here to get some fresh air. I've been on the road a while." The wind changed direction, carrying the black fumes toward Fang. "How old's your boy there?"

Quick as a fly, the youngster darted into the shack as Fang approached him.

"Oh, he's two. Shy boy. Just don't like strangers, 'specially the police. But lately, they've been leaving us alone."

"Been here long?"

"Nah, just since we got scooted off the land year before last. It was that summer when the water rose up like a great flood that never settled back down. They said we'd get a bit o' money, move to a new place. The government would give us a house, some land to farm. Ya know what we got?" The woman looked up at Fang, her pupils darting about like little minnows.

The old broker shook his head.

"Nothing!" the woman continued. "We never saw a single *fen* o' the money. And when it was time to leave, we had to decide quick. Starve in a shack somewhere out yonder, or stay here where we can tend our little plot. It's not so bad."

The child poked his head out. His belly was somewhat distended, and his face smeared with dust, but two clear trails skirted down from the corners of his eyes.

"Say hello to Uncle," the woman said. The boy whimpered. She shook her head, and said to Fang, "Gave him a spanking just now. Tried to nibble on bits o' coal. Silly boy. Ain't even that hungry. We feed him alright. Could be worse, I hear some folk go off to the cities, and scrounge in the garbage for food. We don't do that, mister." A fearful look passed across her face, as if she still thought that Fang could turn them in.

"I guess they can't help themselves," Fang said. "Looks like you're doing pretty good. Is your husband here?"

"He's up there with those men," she said, pointing toward a gutted building. "Doing odd jobs here and there. They're still ripping out the old town here."

"What are you going to do a year and a half from now? This is all going under water." Fang looked out at the hillside where the other encampments dotted the verdant slopes like ink stains.

"We'll get another crop or two in." The woman paused. "I dunno. Guess we gotta move again. Wish my boy could grow up quicker, help out the family. I just gotta feed the little piglet, and he's a fussy one." The woman grabbed the child by the hip, and pulled up his pants. He started to bawl, and she shook him hard. "Now you be good! Got a guest here."

Fang stood up, ruffled through his pocket for his wallet, and took out a twenty-*yuan* note. "Here, give the little fellow a treat. Keep him happy for a bit."

The woman smiled, a cracked tooth bisecting her lips. "You're kind, mister. The gods'll watch over you."

Fang made his way back along the dirt path, bracing against a bitter wind that drowned out the child's cries.

•　　•　　•

A WEEK AFTER SULIN AND FANG'S VISIT TO THE CHAIRMAN'S OFFICE, Chu Longshan was released from prison. Longshan decided to call a meeting of the council, in spite of his wife's plea to steer clear of trouble. He knew that unrest was stirring among the peasants, not just in their cluster of villages, but in other places downriver where the Gaoshanlu dam would engulf their land.

In the old factory courtyard, Longshan arose from a stone bench and addressed the group in a solemn voice.

"Comrades, we have been pushed against a wall, and it looks like we have no recourse but to fight back. They jailed me, they're trying to catch you all, but if we band together, they can't stop us from speaking up. We've seen the tractors at work, tearing away at the riverbank. This is our lifeblood, and if they take this land away from us, we've got nothing—nothing to offer our wives and children. You've seen the new site. If we're forced to move there, with the miserable funds they're offering us, we will eventually starve. And some of us remember what it's like to starve."

The council members grumbled among themselves, nodding

their heads. A fellow with bushy brows spoke up. "And we haven't even seen that money yet. What'd they do with it, those scoundrels?"

"Can't say," said Dong Xiawen, hissing through his buckteeth. "We got mouths to feed, and if we can't squeeze out a *jin* of corn from the land, we're good as slaughtered chickens."

"It's not just our people," said Longshan. "There's thousands more in other villages, from other townships. But there's talk of a plan to resist the tyrants. We're going to stand up for ourselves, once and for all. Nobody's getting his fair share until we band together and protest."

"You mean, demonstrate against the government?" said Dong Xiawen. A hush descended on the group.

"That's right. We will stand united for our rights." Longshan's eyes blazed. "On the twenty-fifth day of the first month, we'll gather by the construction site and stage a mass protest. Go home and tell your fellow villagers. Bring your hoes and plows on that day. Show them that this land means everything to us, and we won't give up without a good fight."

"Yeah, let's give 'em a good fight!" a man hollered, rising up. The others stood up and joined him, their shouts piercing through the blustery wind, each ragged voice bolstered by the angry chorus.

"Let's fight for our rights!"

"Fight for the rights of the people!"

When the council adjourned late in the night, Chu Longshan knew that the villagers were primed to stand up in defiance, and this would be the fight of their lives.

27

ON COLD MORNINGS WHEN LIU STUMBLED OVER TO THE LITTLE sink, a dull ache pulsed through his leg. The face that stared back at him in the mirror was mottled with unshaved stubble and a patchwork of fine wrinkles brought on by worry and doubt.

In the darkest months of recovery, Liu's strength and stamina seemed to fail him. He felt like an injured animal, fallen on a barren plain where vultures circled. Mr. Wu had refused to take him back, as the boatman had purchased a much larger ferryboat and hired two men to service the passengers. He was nothing more than an invalid now. Mei Ling was the one propping him up with financial support, and he had little to offer her. Whenever he ventured into the streets of Wushan, he sensed the frantic, almost desperate energy about the men, whether they were porters or cabbies or businessmen. He knew the specter of a failed man lurked behind the visage of the accomplished one. The patriarch who could provide for his family, who had the means and charms to draw friends into his life, was never far from falling from grace.

Liu realized how much of his life as a man depended on physical prowess. He could summon it easily then; strength had flowed from his angular frame with the sureness and speed of a river that cut unimpeded through any obstacle—rock, earth, felled timber. When his energy began to return, Liu still envied the porters who scurried about with their bamboo poles without a thought as to what lurked around the corner of their frenzied days. And he knew that infirmity and death were hidden out of sight, behind doors. These he had tasted, and the bitterness lingered, relieved only by the small joys of his life, the caresses of his little girl, and the melodic voice of his wife, although she was far away.

One afternoon, as the winter sun broke through the clouds, Liu ventured to the dock, descending the Hundred Steps Ladder with hobbling steps. Along the gravelly path to the waterfront, where he had first met Mr. Wang months ago, the cabbies and motorcyclists were lined up to hustle business from the arriving ferry. When the swarm of travelers arrived, the waiting men bolted toward those strapped with luggage and fine goods, hounding them until they agreed to a ride into the city.

His leg twitched, and this time the pain did not bother him. He could make a living doing as those men did. A different kind of stamina was required. Having faced the throngs, he had learned to crack a smile through his shyness, to steel his nerves to rejection. The only problem was, he had no means of transportation. Perhaps he could use Tai's motorcycle; his own moped had been sold to pay for medical bills. If he could make money again, Mei Ling might be able to come home to her old job, and everything would return to the way it had been.

That evening, Liu arrived at Tai's restaurant in renewed spirits. He noticed that the worry lines on his friend's face had deepened, almost into a scowl. A flicker of concern restrained Liu, but only for a moment.

"Tai, I've been thinking about things. Now that my leg's almost healed, I can work again. Can't keep depending on my woman."

"Glad to hear that, Liu, but I think your woman has something up her sleeve. Mei Ling called just an hour ago. Said she wanted to speak with you as soon as you came in. I asked her if her mother was okay. 'Fine,' she said. Her job's fine. Mom's okay. 'So you want to come home to your old job?' I asked. And she didn't say a thing. She sounded really far away, worlds away. Liu, I think she's up to something. These women, can't figure them out. Except my wife; give her a little money for shopping, and she's happy." Tai shook his head and sighed.

"If Mei Ling's worried about money, I've got good news for her." The spring festival was coming, but Liu did not want to wait until she came home for the holidays to tell her.

When the phone rang, Tai gestured solemnly to Liu. "Must be for you." He slipped out of the office, casting a backward glance.

"Hello, Mei Ling, it's been a while," said Liu.

His wife's reply sounded defensive. "Liu, I've been busy here. Don't always have time to catch you on my evening shift. And you can't afford a phone."

"Mei Ling, listen, I'll be able to work again soon. And maybe we won't need a phone for both of us." Liu tried to sound hopeful, and there was much he wanted to say, that he missed her and wanted her back home, but his voice faltered when she remained silent.

"Liu," Mei Ling began after a long pause. "I've been working here in Chongqing for a few months now, and I like it here. I like the excitement of a big city. I miss the church folks back home, but I think my place is here."

Liu was surprised by this turn, but he kept his composure. "Well, Mei Ling, I suppose that we could move up to join you, as long as rents aren't too high in the city."

"No, no, Liu. You don't understand. I want to be here by myself. I need to think things over, too. My mother's been ill, and it's made me realize that I can't keep doing this."

"Doing what?"

"Living my life for other people. I mean, I won't leave you stranded, if you'll be working again."

"Mei Ling, what are you saying? If you don't want to come home, and you don't want me to go where you are. . . ." Tension crept into Liu's voice, and he paced about the small office.

"Liu, I know this sounds harsh, but I . . . I don't think we should be together. I think we're happier apart."

"Mei Ling, I know I've been a burden to you the last few months, and I'll make it up to you, I promise."

"No, Liu, you don't understand."

"Is it Rose?" Liu cried in desperation. "Are you saying that you don't want to mother someone else's child?" The fortuneteller's words, bitter as venom, came back to Liu. *You will have to choose between the wife and the child.*

"I know she means a lot to you," Mei Ling began, "but I just can't see us as a family. I mean, she's really your child, even if she's not. . . ."

An awkward silence ensued, as neither was able to bridge the chasm. Whoever spoke first would take that fatal, unforgiving step.

"But Rose—she's a big girl now. I mean, she's two, and she can walk. . . . She doesn't need too much attention, really."

"Liu, please, I've thought long and hard about this. I don't want to talk any more right now. Listen, I'll come home in a few weeks and pack the rest of my things, okay?"

"Mei Ling . . . I don't understand."

"I'm sorry, Liu, I really am." Mei Ling sighed. Her voice crackled like dried leaves. "I'll call you when I leave for Wushan, okay?"

After she hung up, Liu stood frozen against the wall, still cradling the phone. Tai puttered in on his ungainly legs.

"Liu, what did she say? You look like you've seen a ghost."

"She wants to stay there. And no, she doesn't want the child." Liu stared at his friend with wild, ravaged eyes. "Tai, I've got to choose between her and my little girl. What am I going to do? The gods have cursed me again, and this time they're taking away only one, but it's like losing both at once. All over again."

"Liu, listen, women are fickle, okay? Let me get you a drink and we'll figure this out."

He fetched a bottle of *huang jiu*, and sat Liu down. A few gulps later, the color returned to Liu's cheeks. A hungry, forlorn gaze settled into his eyes.

"Liu, I've got an idea," Tai said. "You got some money stashed away, yes? Take Mei Ling a nice present, maybe a pair of jade earrings, and tell her you'll raise the child, and she doesn't have to lift a finger."

"I don't know, Tai. She doesn't seem to get along with Rose."

"What other options do you have? You want to give up the little girl? Or the wife?"

Either choice seemed stark, and one without the other was

unpalatable to Liu. He nodded his head slowly. "I guess you're right, Tai. Maybe I'll go to Chongqing, make the first move before she comes back. You think I can get someone to babysit little Rose?"

"I'll ask my neighbor. She's a good lady," said Tai. "Never had children; her spouse died young. If that happened to me, I'd be a free man."

Liu watched his friend limp back into the kitchen, wondering if his own longings were a sign of weakness. He slumped back in the chair, resigned to surrender a little more of his manhood.

• • •

ON THE DAY THAT LIU DEPARTED, ROSE FUSSED OVER HER PORRIDGE to get Liu's attention, but he would only give her a quick hug before his eyes darted to a small pile on the bed. She sensed a change coming, much as a wild creature would become skittish when the air tensed and grew heavy before the first rumblings of thunder.

All morning Liu shuffled about. As her father stuffed a burlap bag, Rose detected a medley of scents. The familiar briny smell of her father's shirt. The crumpled socks, which tickled Rose's nostrils like fermented cabbage. An overcoat with baked-in odors of fried tofu and wood smoke.

Soon, Liu gathered his bulging sack and hoisted Rose to his chest, planting a vigorous kiss on her cheek. Outside, where a ribbon of cars streamed past, he held her close and whisked her into a minibus. The passengers tilted their heads toward her, their crooked teeth glistening. At each stop, a mass of arms and legs untangled and spilled out of the vehicle. The whirring kaleidoscope of their ride ended in front of a smoky gray building with blue trim.

"I'm taking a little trip," said Liu. His voice quivered. She sensed in the clammy sweat of his palms that something was astir. It felt both strange and familiar to her.

"*Qu nah?*" Rose asked.

"Why, we're going to Auntie's house," Liu replied. That did not put her at ease. Every woman she had met, except for Ma Ma, was called Auntie.

Liu carried Rose up seven flights of stairs, and after a quick rap on the door, they stepped into a well-lit apartment. A woman with shaggy curls greeted them. She had a set of gleaming teeth that matched the pearly things on her bosom. The apartment glowed, too, with a smooth and shiny floor. The overstuffed furniture loomed like the large animals she had seen on television.

"Panda," the little girl said aloud, pointing to the black sofa with white cushions. She tugged on her father's pants. "Tiger." She gestured at the soft throw rug by the coffee table.

Her father lifted her up, and held out her arm toward the smiling lady. "Auntie," he said, "will take care of you . . . while Ba Ba is gone."

"Ba Ba is gone. Ba Ba is gone." And here Rose uttered a yelp and retracted her fingers from the woman with pearly teeth. All she heard was that her father was going away.

Too many had left her behind in her young life. In her earliest memories, a thin, warm bosom from which milk flowed forth was wrenched away, and in its place a tide of wind and water had rushed in. That bosom never reappeared. And then there was the old lady, round as a dumpling, who fed her sweet rice and egg custard. The woman cradled her in a woven cloth, against a breast anointed with liniment and incense. She had felt secure in that bosom. Once, though, she had endured a cold afternoon in a shopping cart as a crowd swarmed by, cawing like crows. First her Ba Ba, and then the old woman had left her behind. It had been many dark nights before his return.

Rose did not know why the old woman had to go as well. When a new woman appeared beside Liu, the little girl revolted and pushed her away. And then she grew weary of the struggle, and found comfort in her perfumed bosom. Yet this mother, whom she called Ma Ma, whom her father also held to his bosom, had departed as well. And Rose began to fret that nothing would remain constant in her life, that her longing for mother was like grasping at water, cool and silken and always slipping away from her without warning.

When the door shut, and Rose was left alone with the brilliance of white teeth and marbled floors, she howled like an alley cat and did not let up until her exhausted cries gave way to sleep.

• • •

THE JOURNEY FROM WUSHAN TO CHONGQING TOOK THREE days by slow boat, and when Liu arrived in the big city, he sought out the sister and brother-in-law of his friend Wang Ma. It had been a year since his pilgrimage to Fengjie, where he had stayed with the electrician, but there was *yuan fen*, an understanding between the two men that emboldened Liu to ask the favor.

In Chongqing, the couple refused money for his brief stay. He impressed Mrs. Jew with his capable fingers, pitching in to change diapers and feed their new baby while she was occupied. "You'll have to give my husband some lessons," she said.

"I learned the hard way," Liu replied, not mentioning that he had done it alone.

For two days he combed the district of Wangfujing to scope out opportunities for work. Here, porters with bamboo sticks swarmed the streets. Those who were employed for the day or the hour strained under great loads, cargo and furniture and large boxes of merchandise, while the others clutched their sticks with loosely coiled rope to their collarbones, swarming up to every taxi, truck, and storefront for a potential hauling job.

After numerous inquiries, he found a restaurant willing to hire a busboy, but when they asked when he would start, Liu stuttered in reply, "I have to talk to my wife."

Assured that he could find work in the city, Liu at last worked up the courage to seek out Mei Ling. The following morning, bedraggled from his long walk and bus ride, he showed up at the Wan Bao Hotel. Glancing up at its towering façade, where row upon row of silver-framed windows streaked toward the heavens, he was humbled by the splendor of the Wan Bao. Ten thousand treasures. If only he could have one of them.

He wondered what Mei Ling would think of his unannounced visit. Behind the reception desk, the women in their starched, navy blue suits intimidated him. The doorman cast a quizzical look at

Liu, then turned his attention toward an oncoming limousine.

Liu approached the bellhop, a hawk-eyed, lanky lad who appeared to be the most informal of the lot. "I'm looking for my wife. Her name is Mei Ling."

"Mei Ling, you say?" the fellow replied. "Yeah, there's a woman on the eleventh floor by that name. Don't know if she's still there, though. Heard she's been in some trouble with the old woman who oversees those girls."

"What for?" asked Liu.

"Oh, I don't know, probably just speaking her mind." The bellhop leaned in closer. "That supervisor is kind of a tyrant. If you're not the big brass around here, might as well boss around the folks below you."

The bellhop's description did not fit what Mei Ling had told him all along, that she was happy with her job, content with her life here. Liu took the elevator to the eleventh floor, and when he stepped into the hallway, a pretty, uniformed woman at the service counter greeted him. His inquiries were met with that same quizzical look, and the girl mumbled that her supervisor would offer some assistance.

Down the hallway, he approached an older, stocky woman. She adjusted her steel-rimmed glasses, squinting at him. "What do you want?" she demanded.

"My wife, Mei Ling, works here and—"

"She's gone now," the woman snarled. "Can't scrub carpets or tiles. The manager took pity on her and put her in bookkeeping."

"How can I find her?" Liu asked.

"Oh, you can't. They're up on the eighteenth floor and nobody's allowed up there."

"But she's my wife. I came all this way to look for her."

"If she's your wife she can talk to you after hours. This hotel is for guests only. Get along now, or I'll call the cops."

Hollering down to the service clerk, she added, "Now you make sure that young man's going *down*."

Liu shuffled back down the hall, keenly aware he was being watched. He felt like a hunted animal in the Wan Bao. He did not belong, although his wife had found a home here. In the elevator, he nearly collided with the bellhop and his empty luggage cart. The fellow, who called himself Ah Ming, offered Liu a cigarette and the two stepped outside the building. Pigeons strutted on the ledge above the first story; their droppings speckled the inlaid copper plating on the sidewalk.

"She's your wife, you say?" Ah Ming asked. He leaned against the wall and tipped his cigarette at a rakish angle. Liu nodded. "Well, she's a pretty one, the type that men run after like pigeons in heat. Like those things." The bellhop pointed above their heads, where a flutter of wings ensued, driving one of the birds from its perch.

Liu pursed his lips, unsure what to make of Ah Ming's crude remark. "I came to talk to her about moving here."

The bellhop lowered his leg from the wall and stamped out his cigarette. "You're a good fellow. Everyone here cares only about money and status. If you're a man with neither of those things, just be careful. You ain't gonna win." Ah Ming cast a conspiratorial look at Liu. "Me, I'm trying to get out of here. Sneak over to Hong Kong. I'll be okay as long as the authorities don't catch me."

"And what'll you do there?"

"Get a job at another hotel. And when I save up some money, I'll try to go to England or America."

•   •   •

OVER THE NEXT WEEK, LIU CAME BY THE HOTEL WHEN DUSK descended on the city, and waited by the corner to catch Mei Ling at the end of her shift. For days he waited in vain, and Ah Ming told him that he might try the back entrance to the hotel. Here, in a small alleyway, the city's scavengers lurked between their forays into the trash and recycling bins that lined the downtown boulevards. Liu watched them during the day as they scoured through the refuse. It was passionless work, so different from his own forays along the Yangtze, where he had escaped its furious tides and found a few lost treasures, chief among them his little girl.

As night crept over Chongqing, obscuring its gilded surfaces and seedy elements in the same pitch of darkness, he thought of his trip into Fengdu, a crumbling town that defied scavenging, and his stint in prison. Of this he was not so proud. But in that dank, concrete cell, he had finally laid down the stone of grief he had carried for so long. In the confines of prison, he had found the courage to be with another woman again.

And if Mei Ling demanded that he surrender Rose, if their bond only aroused jealousy in her, could he abide that? In the waning hours, as night shadows flitted like bats across the cityscape, Liu felt a wavering in his soul. Perhaps Rose could have a better life if she had parents who didn't struggle with one another and drift apart in the wake of misfortune. What good was a lonely father who couldn't buffer his little girl against life's blows? Mrs. Jew had casually mentioned a friend of hers in the city who was childless. If Mei Ling wanted him back, maybe Liu could find a prosperous, more comfortable home for little Rose. The thought, however, wrenched his heart. He kicked the railing hard, and the pain distracted and calmed him down a little.

That evening, Mei Ling did not appear. Liu resumed his night watch the next evening, but he began to wonder if Mei Ling knew of his presence, and was evading him.

Shortly after darkness fell, a figure in a heavy coat flung open the door. Hurried footsteps clattered down the walkway until Liu caught a glimmer of the moonlit face.

"Mei Ling!" he cried. His body, numb from the cold, angled forward eagerly.

His wife shrieked. "Who. . . ? What in the world are you doing here?" Her eyes darted about, as if there were others lurking, waiting for her.

"I came to find you, of course. I know it may seem strange, but I couldn't wait until you came back during spring festival."

"Goodness, Liu. The cops might think you're a criminal, loitering around like that."

"If they mistake me for a street dog, they'll leave me alone. And I'd just keep nipping at your heels." Liu took a bold step forward. He crouched down and looked up at his wife with rounded eyes.

"Oh, Liu." Mei Ling thrust her arm out, but she couldn't suppress a laugh. "This isn't a place to talk. It's late. I have to get back to my dormitory."

Liu continued in his jovial vein. "Man caught pouncing on wife. It'll be in the news tomorrow."

"Stop it, Liu. Really." Mei Ling tried to push past him, her warm coat brushing against his arms.

"No, please don't go. I've been thinking about things. And if you're willing to give it another go, maybe we . . . I could find a good home for Rose. And I could get a job in town."

"Liu, it's not that simple. And it's not just Rose. I don't think we can resolve our differences."

"Why . . . what do you mean?"

"Well, I've made a life here. And I don't think you'll be happy in the big city. You have simpler tastes."

Liu stiffened up. "I think you underestimate me. But if you're saying I'm not good enough for you now—"

"It's not like that. Please."

"Mei Ling, I just want you to reconsider. It was your choice as much as mine to get married."

In the murky light, Mei Ling's eyes flashed wildly. "Liu, I can't talk tonight. Let's wait a couple of days, okay? I don't work on Sunday. I can meet you at Li Feng's for lunch."

Liu nodded slowly. He took a deep breath, tracking the outline of her dark cloak as it disappeared into the night.

•　•　•

WITH A FEW IDLE EVENINGS ON HIS HANDS, LIU DID NOT WANT to stay in his hosts' apartment. The presence of the imposing Mr. Jew, a well-clad banker, made Liu feel not only awkward and intrusive, but also less assured about his mission to win back Mei Ling.

Instead, he slurped noodles with his new friend Ah Ming, and they smoked their cigarettes down to little nubs until the last customers had left. He felt comfortable around the lad, whose freckled face seemed to convey an innocence beneath his worldly, cynical remarks. Liu told him about the ups and downs of his marriage.

"She's been distant, eh?" said Ah Ming. He smashed the butt of a cigarette into the ashtray. "Did you know, and this may be rumor, that your wife is supposedly seeing another man?"

Liu shook his head. Surely, Mei Ling wouldn't lie to him. "What? How do you know that?"

"I saw them together myself a few times, and I think he even had his arm around her waist briefly once. He's one of the big managers around here. And the witch who runs facilities, Mrs. Lao, still talks about her, calling her the broken shoe who tripped off the eleventh floor."

The blood rushed into Liu's temples. "How long has this been going on?"

"Oh, I don't know. Been hearing the chatter these past two months."

"Why didn't you tell me this before?" Liu cried. His arms descended like leaden weights onto the table, scattering cigarette ash onto the plastic tablecloth.

"Well, it wasn't my business to meddle in another man's affairs. But then I figured you're really going to a lot of trouble . . . for nothing." Ah Ming sucked in his cheeks, and his gaunt face looked even thinner.

Liu stood up, his eyes black as bituminous coal. A hot sweat drenched his palms, and he shook so hard that he rattled the heavy wooden table beneath his hands. Everything blurred before his eyes, and the walls seemed to breathe, but no air came into his lungs. And then, in his rabid, shaken state, he saw the frightened look in Ah Ming's eyes.

"Liu, you'd best take it easy; go home and think it over. Don't do anything rash."

That night, when Liu collapsed onto the couch in the Jews' living room, an angry procession of thoughts marched through his head.

No wonder she had been sullen and withdrawn. Her concerns about Rose were a sham; all she really wanted was to break free from him. And now that she had a wealthy, successful man at her side, Mei Ling didn't need him anymore. But why did she marry him in the first place?

And then a different stream of voices emerged, a calming tide that called for mercy. Maybe she had loved Liu once. She must have seen some promise in him, enough to put up with caring for a child that wasn't her own. After all, she had dutifully sent money home for the last few months. How could he repay her?

He pressed his arms tightly against his face. Maybe she deserved better, and if he could offer her nothing, it was best to leave well enough alone. She would be coming back for spring festival anyway, to get her things. He would not push her anymore. If she wanted to come back, she would make that clear to him.

But what if Ah Ming's revelation was really just a rumor? Liu thought again about the possibility of confronting Mei Ling. If there was no such affair, then he should still believe what she said about Rose. But if there was another man, Mei Ling would deny it anyway. Either way, Liu could not win.

And besides, he was wearing out his welcome in Mr. Jew's house. The decision to do nothing settled quietly in his gut, and he fell into a delirious sleep.

The next morning, Liu asked the bellhop to tell Mei Ling that something urgent prompted his return to Wushan, and he would await her return at the end of the month. Ah Ming spat on the pavement, scattering a few pigeons. "Smart man. You gotta figure that women are like rings. If you got skinny fingers, they'll slip right off. But if a man's got a fortune—oh—they'll cling to him, and he'll have more than a few shiny stones on his pinky alone."

Liu thought about his friend's assessment, and added, "A rich man pulls a lot of people down with him."

"It's every man for himself," said Ah Ming. "It's a new China; old folks like my dad don't get that. If I had a chance to be on top, I'd take it. Wouldn't you?"

"I suppose." But Liu wasn't so sure. Somewhere in his muddled brain, he knew that even a great man could fall down a well as deep as his own.

28

THE REUNION OF FATHER AND DAUGHTER WAS A WELCOME ONE for all concerned. The little girl screeched, tottering toward Liu, who felt a pang of guilt that he had been gone so long. The baby-sitter let out a sigh, sending her bangles and earrings aflutter, and she accepted his small gift of ginseng with a wan smile.

"Did Tai get that electric stove like his wife wanted?" Liu asked.

"I'm afraid he and his wife have moved," she said, fingering her rings.

"You mean, they found another apartment?"

"No, your friend wanted me to tell you that they've left Wushan. Blamed it on a bad investment. Mrs. Tai was very up-set about it." The woman shook her head, and an array of silver jewels jangled against her face and neck. "I told her not to give him such a hard time, but the loss really did put them out. They boarded a ship for Shanghai earlier this week, where her family lives."

Liu clenched his fists, unable to feel anything except for the scratching of Rose's fingers on his sleeves. "Did he leave an ad-dress or anything?"

The woman opened a desk drawer and handed him a small audiocassette. "Here, he asked me to give you this."

He stuck the cassette in his pocket and lifted Rose into his arms. "Say thank you to Auntie." She waved her little hand as if swatting a fly. He scrambled down the back stairway as fast as his bad leg could carry them, the sound of the babysitter's jewels still echoing in his ears.

In their apartment, stale air hung thick as crumpled old bedding. It surprised Liu that little had changed during his month-long absence; the same dishes remained unwashed, the drawers sat gaping with his spare shirt and socks in one corner and the outgrown baby clothes in the other. Liu fussed about the room, collecting Rose's trinkets in a small pile as she watched him, her pink thumb bulging against her cheek.

At last he sat down and stuck Tai's cassette into a tape player he had salvaged from Old Wushan.

"Ol' brother," the recording crackled. He could hardly recognize Tai's voice, which was drowned out in places by a din of activity. "I am sorry I could not say good-bye to you in person, but all this has happened rather suddenly. You know how happy I've been to build up this restaurant. But I felt I could never keep up with my wife's demands, and there was always something better around the corner. So I invested in a local coal mining company. Unfortunately, that turned out to be a bad decision. The coal's no good. It's blown up a few stoves, and I couldn't pull my money out fast enough before the business tanked. I've had to sell the restaurant, and as much as I hate the idea, we'll be living with my wife's family in Shanghai to help us get back on our own feet."

Tai cleared his throat, then continued. "I guess we'll both have to depend on our wives for a while. I'll see what I can do in Shanghai. You gotta keep your wits about you in the big city, but maybe this experience has made me a little wiser."

A sharp female voice rang in the background. Tai let out an audible sigh. "Liu, I wish you the best, and hope your woman comes back in good time. Give my best to Mei Ling. If you ever come to Shanghai, please do look for me. . . ."

Liu wondered how his friend, who had been thrifty and threadbare for as long as he had known him, could take such big risks with his money. And he thought ruefully how his own life had been one gamble after another in the wake of Fei Fei's death. He had taken his chances with Mei Ling. And while the love of a widower flowed along muddier shores, he had felt assured at one time that his heart was strong again. Now he was not so sure.

•   •   •

AN URGENT KNOCK SOUNDED AT THE DOOR JUST AS LIU AND Rose finished their morning porridge. Liu wondered who could possibly be visiting them. He did not expect Mei Ling back so soon, as the spring festival was still two weeks away.

Fang Shuping stood across from him, with a leather briefcase braced against his wool coat. "Greetings, my friend!" A corner of his mouth tilted into a grin, like that of a man picking his teeth. "It's been a while, haven't seen you since your wedding. How's your lovely wife?"

"Fine." Liu stiffened, barricading the doorway, his body rigid and unrelenting.

"Aren't you going to invite me in?" asked Fang.

"It's not like you to pay house calls, Fang. What do you want?" Liu was worried that the old broker had played a part in Tai's downfall, and was here to collect the debt.

"I have a lucrative proposition for you. Now let's sit down and talk about it, shall we?"

Liu relaxed his stance a little, relieved it was only another of Fang's diabolical schemes. The old man looked less menacing than miserly, with his big black case. Little Rose, who was playing with a pair of spoons, shoved one in her mouth when Fang walked in. Liu reluctantly offered him a seat on the couch. It had been presentable at one time, but had become anointed with toddler fingerprints and scratches.

The old man sat down gingerly. "Cozy place you have here. Could use more of the woman's touch; don't tell your wife I said that. Where is your lovely bride?"

"She's working," Liu replied.

"What a great age we live in," Fang chuckled, "when the wives put rice on the table, and the men get to gamble it all away."

"I don't gamble," said Liu coldly, but the allusion to Tai's mishaps bothered him. "I was working for a boatman until I broke my leg a few months ago."

"That's too bad. Now my offer might be just the thing to take a load off the family pressures." Fang leaned forward, joining his fingertips. It struck Liu as a curious gesture, and reminded him of the old women in church who joined their hands to pray to an invisible deity. In an unguarded moment, Liu's curiosity was piqued by the broker's words.

"Now you may remember that the gold pendant you sold belonged to an old friend of mine, to her deceased husband, as a matter of fact. She was grateful to get it back. There is something else that belongs to the family, and a handsome price will be paid for its return. Consider it a reward for the trouble you've taken as a steward, a guardian of precious goods." Fang glanced over at Rose, who had resumed her concert with the utensils, banging them against the wooden frame of her crib.

"What are you saying, Fang?" A cold tremor seized Liu in the chest. Clearly, the old man was up to no good again.

The child's staccato rapping filled the interlude of silence. *Tap.* Fang rose up from his seat. *Tap. Tap.* He walked to the cradle in a slow, deliberate stride. *Tap.* He squatted next to Rose, holding out his palm. She refused to surrender the spoons, and recoiled from the old man's touch.

"This girl's Po Po would like her grandchild back. It is true that the mother had abandoned the child, but her grandmother is willing to raise her. And for your pains in taking care of her, you'll receive a generous 10,000 *yuan*. Not bad for a year and a half's work."

Liu gestured to Rose, who toddled over to her father's side. "How do I know this is really true? What does an old woman want with a young child? And why are you so concerned, Fang? I've not seen you so interested as you are now in other people's welfare."

"Come on, you might not believe me, but you'll have to take the word of a lady at face value. She's as upright as they come. She'll be in town next week, and you'll see for yourself. And this girl looks like her grandmother, too. Look at those wide cheeks."

When Fang bent over to pinch her, little Rose reared back her lips and bit the old man's bony hand. A squeal of pain escaped from his lips, and he pulled back, as if attacked by a rabid dog.

Rose leaned into her father, and Liu put a protective hand across the small of her back. "I don't think so," Liu began on a tentative note. And then the sound of his own words strengthened his conviction, and his voice deepened. "Rose is my little girl now, and she sees me as her father. Her Po Po may want her back, but her own mother gave her up, and you can't change that fact. What'll happen when the old woman dies?"

A strange light appeared in Fang's eyes. He rapped his knuckles against the wooden frame of the crib. "That is none of your business. I tell you, the girl belongs to the Chu family. You will be given a handsome sum of money. Consider yourself fortunate. Why, it's a wonder how your wife can take care of a man and child on her paltry income."

Liu drew her daughter closer, clutching her tightly, worried that the broker would simply reach out and try to seize the child. The old man's rapping became insistent.

"Listen, Fang, that's generous of you to intervene, but I'm not going to give up this child. I almost did at the beginning, and we've been through too much together since then." He turned to Rose. "Little monkey, who's your father?"

The girl looked at Liu, who awaited her answer intently. "You are, Ba Ba."

The old man rose to his feet, and stood over Liu and the child. "You're making a mistake, my friend. This is your chance to be free of debt and burden and return the girl to her relations, where she rightfully belongs. I'll give you three days to reconsider. When you come to your senses, here are the papers to sign, to make this all legitimate, one surrendering the child to her legal guardian, the other acknowledging a payment of 10,000 *yuan* for your services in the past year and a half."

Fang threw the papers on the couch, tucked his briefcase under his arm, and yanked the door shut behind him. Liu stared at the document, a mass of undecipherable scrawls, and a new object of fascination for Rose. She dug her moist, wrinkled thumb into the layers and picked at the rubber band as if she was playing a crude instrument. For the rest of the afternoon, Liu sat there in stony silence. He was numbed by it all, the marital disappointments, the loss of those who mattered in his life, and the reappearance of this swindler who threatened to take away his precious little monkey.

Ten thousand *yuan*. What would a man do for a little peace of mind? If he signed those papers, would his little Rose be in good hands? Would he ever see her again?

No, he was resolved. He would not be seduced by Fang's offer. Ten thousand *yuan* meant nothing to Liu if he had to endure the rest of his days in forced solitude. In his youth he had struck out into the world alone, enduring its tyranny with a stiff upper lip. He needed no family then, and it was only when he found Fei Fei that a new of way of existence revealed itself. She had understood him as a woman could, and her imagination breathed life into his world. These experiences he had sought to recreate with Mei Ling, but now the distance was too great. It was Rose who indulged her father's whims and pleasures, just as he indulged hers. She could not threaten to leave him; the little girl embraced him wholeheartedly in spite of his failings.

When Fang came back, Liu would tell him no. "No, Fang," he'd say, "I am not a fool who falls for your schemes anymore."

And then Liu's gaze fell on the papers; its cryptic text bore the stamp of authority. Doubt seized him now. What if the woman had a legal claim to Rose? What if the authorities could take her away on the pure grounds that he was not her real father? Rose began to claw at the papers; he shooed her fingers away nervously.

He could take Rose far away where nobody could find them. He could live in the mountains with her, seek temporary refuge in a monastery. He imagined Rose as a wild child, playing among gibbons and wild geese. And he thought of the ancient fables that Fei Fei used to tell. In his mind's eye Rose would ride on the back of a tiger, her nimble legs braced against its flanks, her arms outstretched, defiant and straight as a spear. When his thoughts alighted on Fei Fei, Liu felt an old, familiar twinge. He got up and lit and cigarette.

The little girl was chewing on the rubber band wrapped around the documents, and it snapped in two. She screamed, rearing back, and Liu reached out to stroke her cheeks.

Fang's friend had nothing to prove her blood ties besides a faint resemblance across two generations. Rose's mother had abandoned her, after all, and she would not have kept any records that this child existed. He watched Rose sucking on her thumb, soothing herself. Perhaps they did not need to flee.

The next day, Liu took little Rose down the Hundred Steps Ladder, carrying her for long stretches, and when they reached the main street, he whisked her through the crowd until they arrived at Tai's restaurant.

A hazy winter's light illuminated the storefront. He remembered the signboard, which Tai had so proudly commissioned. The red lettering was a little faded, like a smear of chicken blood; the dusty black background now cast an aura of doom and decay. The windows of the restaurant were covered over with newspaper, and a hastily taped notice fluttered against the door. Like the symbol *tsai*, the scrap of paper appeared to sentence buildings to death.

"Who lives here?" asked Rose.

"An old friend," replied Liu. "It's not his home, but my friend lived here."

"Friend lived here. Friend lived here," little Rose chimed.

Liu peered into the dark interior through a torn edge in the newspaper. The furniture was gone; devoid of tables and chairs, the room had a haunted quality, as if otherworldly residents had set up shop, playing mahjong and frittering the hours away. Liu could see the outlines of drooping posters on the wall, a calendar from the previous year with the same dimpled beauty, and the faint halo of smoked glass on the wall sconces that he and Mei Ling had picked out. He thought of the evenings when he had settled into his favorite table, staring at the customers with languid interest.

It must have all been a dream, he thought bitterly.

Liu peeled himself away from the window and shuffled home, dragging Rose up the long stretch of the Hundred Steps Ladder when he was too tired to carry her. Perhaps he was driven by the desire to forget. Perhaps there was nothing to forget, as all that had brought him warmth and comfort no longer existed.

Three days after Fang's visit, there was no sign of his return. Liu was tempted to evade the old broker, but he decided to confront Fang and refuse his offer once and for all. He would tear up those papers, show the man that he could be neither bought nor intimidated.

As the hours slipped by, doubt seeped in once more. What would happen when Fang showed up with the old woman who claimed to be Rose's grandmother? He could refuse 10,000 *yuan* more easily than he could turn away from the imploring gaze of his daughter's Po Po. If she proved somehow that Rose belonged to her, if the little girl fell into her arms with a sigh of remembrance, then Liu would have to surrender the last remaining thing that was dear to him.

The hours crept by with the heaviness of molasses, and the old broker did not return. The anticipation of a showdown became too much to bear. He needed to get out of the house.

"We're going to watch the ships come in," he told Rose. His fingers worked swiftly to bundle her in a warm coat and scarf. The two headed down to Guangdong Road, and as Liu turned toward the familiar winding path to the docks, a small crowd arrested his attention.

In the center of the crowd, three children knelt on the ground, their spines upright like mahjong tiles despite the heft of their backpacks. The trio, an older girl about twelve and two younger boys, kept their heads bowed as the onlookers stood in silence. Periodically, someone would toss a bill or a one-*yuan* coin into the tin can. One or two people would walk off, and another pedestrian would arrive, glance at the poster board scrawled with bold block characters, then throw a bit of money into the collection bin.

Staring over the shoulder of an old man, Liu nudged his neighbor and whispered, "What does the sign say?"

The man replied without turning his head. "This family has been struck by misfortune. These children have lost their father, and their mother has lost her sanity. They have to fend for themselves now."

Liu stared at the children's sunken heads. The girl had two orderly braids, and her skirt was as neatly pleated as her hair. The boys
wore nylon jackets of orange and gray and none of the clothing was
tattered nor riddled with holes. These children did not look terribly
poor to Liu, certainly not like some of the peasants he had seen on
his scavenging forays. But he gave them the benefit of the doubt
and tossed them a coin. He eased his way out of the crowd with
little Rose at his side.

The two arrived home shortly before dark, after a windswept
stroll along the waterfront. The door was slightly ajar, and when Liu
stepped closer, he saw that the lock had been broken. The apartment was in shambles, as if a great flood had swept through it. The
chest drawers sat empty as abandoned rafts, their contents tossed
out like flotsam. The bed sheets were thrown against the crib, and
the thin mattress turned up. The small kitchen was cluttered with
the debris of smashed jars and emptied containers. Rice lay strewn
all about the floor, mixed with fragments of glass.

Liu picked his daughter up to keep her from diving into the
shards in her curiosity. He planted her on the couch. "Stay there,
little monkey."

"No!" She whined in protest, but her father's voice was unusually stern. Rose sat with her legs splayed, sucking her thumb.

As Liu surveyed the damage, he noticed that the stack of forms
Fang had left remained untouched. He waded through the splattered rice and glass, reaching far beneath the counter for an old
tealeaf tin where he had kept his dwindling funds. The can was
nowhere to be found. His search grew more frantic. He ruffled
through the bags of dried goods and containers, tossing them from
one jumbled heap to another. In the dark corners, nothing but
cockroach and mice-infested grains. Liu stood up and turned toward the child, who could contain her curiosity no longer.

"Ba Ba, what's this?" she pointed to a woolen heap beside her.
Rose picked up a ragged sweater and her fingers pierced through
the holes in the fabric. She peered through them at Liu with an
impish grin.

"It's a sweater that belonged to . . . your auntie. The bad guys had no use for it." His voice choked to a whisper as she lifted the old sweater over her head. Swallowed up in the dark blue wool, she resembled a pile of cooked seaweed. Liu thought of the day when he had found her, bound in that sweater and old cotton pants that circled her body twice. He had kept that sweater, although useless, its gaping holes beyond repair.

He took a deep breath, and sat beside Rose. "Little monkey, it's just you and me now. And we have nothing left to take care of us." Rose, even at her young age, seemed to understand. She reached through a hole in the fabric, round as an eye socket, and touched his hands.

Fang was the culprit; Liu was sure of that. The dirty old broker wanted Rose back, perhaps for the sake of a wealthy benefactress, or an old lady love of his. Money and women—what else could motivate that rascal to rob Liu of the last remnants of his dignity? Nothing mattered much to him now; his mind was weary, and the great tide of misfortune had sapped him of his will.

29

THE OLD BROKER DID NOT REAPPEAR, BUT THE APARTMENT manager did come by a few days later to collect rent, as Liu and Rose were eating the last of the dried noodles. His daughter had clamored for eggs, but much of their food had been spilled or ruined by the burglars. All of Liu's money was gone; what he had left in his pocket that day went toward a small bag of rice and soybeans, which Liu rationed carefully. He had swept up the debris in the kitchen, but the apartment was beyond redemption. He dreaded Mei Ling's return; any lingering hopes that she would come back to her life in Wushan had been dashed. He dared not think of calling her or borrowing money; the support she had provided them over the months was a debt he could not repay.

The manager stood in the doorway, fingering the broken lock. Liu tried to plea for more time. "There's a piece or two of good furniture here. Perhaps I can sell them in the next few days."

The manager stood with arms akimbo, shaking his head. "I'd just as soon set a match to all this kindling. Listen, we've got to get this apartment in shape, turn it around to rent out. Next month's right around the corner."

In the twenty minutes he had been given to vacate the premises, Liu stuffed his old scavenger's bag with warm clothing for Rose, a small blanket, a pocketknife, a tin bowl with the remaining rice, a spoon, a bag of dried mushrooms, and his remaining cigarettes. He slipped Tai's cassette into his pocket, although the old tape player had been stolen. Under the light of a nearly full moon, Liu shuffled down the Hundred Steps Ladder with Rose, his scavenger's bag flapping at his side. His mind swam in confusion, going in circles, but his feet carried him from one familiar waypoint to the next. As he left the searching street lamps behind and entered the old town, his pulse quickened.

In the silver moonlight, the fringes of old Wushan still awaited the day of reckoning. Although the daytime workers who salvaged wood and copper had gone home, the nocturnal scavengers were beginning to surface. In the ramshackle cottage where they camped, the mice scurried about, discovering the stray grains of rice in Liu's bags. The ants blazed a trail down the mildewed frame at the entrance, where the door had been plucked away. But there was nothing for him to scavenge from this house, nothing left of value inside its crumbling stone walls.

The wind whistled through the willow trees in the nearby cemetery. It held the cries of unrepentant ghosts, the drowned and disgraced, the unfed, the tired souls who gave up living before the old town surrendered to the dam. The shifting sounds frightened Rose, and she clung to her father as they huddled against the tamped earth floor.

A wave of regret seized Liu. What if he had agreed to Fang's proposition? Would he have spared both of them this ordeal? He looked at his daughter, who had fallen asleep in his lap. "Maybe I made a mistake," he whispered.

The image of Fei Fei, robust in her eighth month of carrying their child, haunted him now. In the gloom of night, her spirit lingered and glowed like embers of incense. She told Liu to have no regrets, to embrace this child against the cold even when everything else was caught in the undertow.

There was one thing he could do, Liu realized, one remaining friend who could throw out a lifeline to a desperate man. It was Wang Ma, who lived a short boat ride away in Fengjie. He would need ship fare to take Rose with him to that promising shore.

THE ROBUST SMELLS OF THE CITY ENTRANCED ROSE. THE fragrance of sweet sesame oil and baked bread wafted down the street, making her quite hungry. After a few meals of plain rice and soybeans, her stomach was left wanting. But the incessant footfalls all around them drowned out the rumbling of her belly. As hulking metal buggies sped by, she huddled close to her Ba Ba on the pavement, putting her hands up to her ears when they burst into a shrill cry. She remembered sitting in a bright plastic buggy in the town square, the thrill of sliding through space with her father running by her side. But now it seemed that the rest of the world was in motion, and she was forced to sit still. It felt like punishment, but it was not her daddy punishing her, for he sat as still as she.

Soon, a few gathered in a small circle around them. Rose could smell what they ate for lunch, the garlic and chili peppers and fried pork, when they bent over to toss a silvery coin in the jar beside her. The tinkling pleased her, and she would reach into the container until her father gently lifted her hands away. It had become a sort of game between them. As the watery light moved across the sky, the coins tinkled, her stubby fingers reached in, her father's big hands chased them away. Coins, fingers, hands moved with one motion, up and down. Their shadows danced. She giggled with each round, but her daddy was silent.

The strangers lingered longer than she liked. They did not touch her, as younger children or dogs would, but they stared at her with great curiosity. The older ones had eyes like chickens, beady and mucous-filled. One boy had eyes like a pig's that bulged behind thick glasses, and he snorted rather like a pig.

She watched as the onlookers' eyes moved from her to her father, and then to a gray square of cardboard scrawled with black marks. When she grew tired of the coin game, Rose began tracing the scribbles with her index finger. She lifted the finger to her mouth and tasted the dark smudge. The bitterness made her scrunch her face, and the boy laughed. She began to cry, big tears rolling down her cheeks. She tasted the salt on her lips, and that made her hungry again.

Her father shooed the boy away, and held her close. She nestled against him, her thumb providing a bit of relief from that gnawing feeling. Now she noticed the prickle of cold cement where she had sat for so long.

In the evening, an old woman appeared with a small plate of chicken and rice. Rose gulped down every bite her father fed her, almost swallowing the spoon. And when the streetlights began to sparkle, and a canopy of stars appeared overhead, they made their way down to the damp old house, and curled up against the musty earth. She watched the beetles skitter along, unearthing little mounds of dirt. Somewhere, a creature shrieked, piercing the darkness with the cry of a baby. Her father called it a bat. He lifted his arms, said it could fly like this, and his hands fluttered against a beam of moonlight. Perhaps babies could fly, Rose thought. She imagined herself flying away, as the heavy blanket of her father's arm lulled her to sleep.

•   •   •

"FOOL. WHAT A SENTIMENTAL FOOL," FANG MUTTERED TO HIMSELF. No, he was not one to make house calls. It had taken him more than a month to track down the scavenger in his shabby apartment, only to hear that the child would not be given up. An impotent man with a child in tow. Fang wondered how Liu's pretty young wife had put up with him.

Fang took a deep puff from his pipe, and fished out the letter Sulin had given him before he left her village. When she pressed it into his palm, her fingers lingered for a moment before they pulled away. A tiny crack appeared in the porcelain calm of her demeanor. He saw how her eyes, filled with a tremulous light, betrayed her longing. He had rejoiced in that moment, even as he had feared what she would tell him.

Fang unfolded the brittle parchment. He had read the letter many times in the past six weeks. He understood now. The revelations had cleansed and absolved him, removing the sting of her rejection.

Dear Fang Shuping,

You must think me cruel to act so coldly toward you all this time while you've been trying to help us. It is true that I have tried to forget the past— our past—but you must understand the deeper reasons why I have resisted you.

What you do not know is that I carried your child when you were sent away. It seems so long ago, but I am never far from those memories. When I could hide the pregnancy no longer, when the bandages and cloths I wrapped around my belly could not contain its sinful secret, I had to confront my father. I was betrothed to another man, as you know. My father's fury was beyond words; I could see the animal impulse to hurt me in his eyes, and I would have preferred a beating, or exile to some forgotten place, to his quiet, measured words. He had too much to lose if this marriage did not proceed. And an illegitimate child would bring scorn to our family, and demote him as a leader among thousands in the commune. I asked to be sent away, but my mother could not bear the thought. Perhaps she was right; I was bold and headstrong, but I could be taken advantage of in my condition. And how could a pregnant woman on her own explain why she has had to fend for herself?

I thought many times of running away, but in the end, I agreed to have the child removed from my womb, although I nearly died at the hands of the barefoot doctor. And yes, I suppose I saved my own life by taking away the one we had created. But in the years ahead, I chose to make the best of things. My husband was a decent man, and I learned to love him. You must not begrudge me my desire for dignity, and I've realized I cannot deny you the right to know the truth.

Perhaps this is why I am dismayed that my daughter left her child, when she didn't have the same pressures that bore down on me. Perhaps it is the vengeance of the gods, to bring the curse of an illegitimate girl upon her. My wish to reclaim the child may simply be a desire to redeem the past. But I must be practical as well. I am still healthy and able to work, but who knows what the future brings, especially when we are forced to move to our new home, where the soil is barren and the springs run dry? When the girl is of age, she could provide some hope for our family, and find work in the cities as my nephew has done.

Again, I thank you for what you have done on Longshan's behalf. I do not want to give you false hopes, and only appeal to the forces of the human heart beyond our own troubled wishes.

Sincerely,

Sulin

The letter revived his fervent hopes, despite Sulin's stated intentions. Two days after he spoke to Liu, Fang wondered if he should sweeten the pot, or threaten him with the force of authority. But the night before his imposed deadline, Fang received a phone call from Sulin.

Her voice had an edge of anxiety, like a *pipa* slightly out of tune. "Fang Shuping, I hate to trouble you, and heaven knows I have asked enough of you, but I fear for my brother."

"What is it? Is he in prison again?"

"No, but his council has plans to bring out a mass of villagers to protest the dam. And this is no small affair. Many people are upset over the terms we have been offered. And since no money has come in, it confirms suspicions that we'll be wrung over by scoundrels who stuff their own wallets. Those are my brother's words."

"So what are they planning to do?"

"Well, the council has been spreading the word to the thirty villages in this area. In a week, everyone will gather at the construction site and stand in resistance. My brother thinks that they'll get thousands of villagers to protest. And people certainly seem angry enough."

"Is your brother leading the troops?"

"Yes." There was a pause at the other end. "And that's what I'm afraid of. He's been detained and jailed twice already. He's one of the leaders, and the authorities will be watching him. What if the crowd turns into a mob, and violence breaks out? There's no telling what could happen."

"What would you like me to do?" Fang asked.

"I'd like you to talk to Longshan." Sulin sighed. "He won't listen to his wife, or to my haranguing. Tells me that business is best left to the men. He's so pigheaded that he'll put himself in harm's way if he gets out there. And the crowd can't protect him."

"No, they can't, Sulin. That little brother of yours was always a stubborn one. A rare family trait, wouldn't you say?" Fang chuckled, and then his tone was serious again. "I'll come right away, try to talk some sense into him. If the chickens keep squawking, only the foxes will come. I've seen it with my own eyes. I once lost a friend to a mob of Red Guards."

"I know you understand how serious this is," said Sulin. "And I'm sorry to trouble you like this. There is only one thing, though. I will have to postpone my visit to Wushan."

"That's too bad." Fang was actually relieved; he had been reluctant to bring up the matter of her grandchild, as Liu still remained an obstacle to his plans.

"My granddaughter—is she well? Is she in good hands?"

"Yes, this fellow's done a decent job. She's a toddler now, on the skinny side, but she's got good teeth. Really strong teeth." There was a sour note in Fang's voice, which Sulin did not seem to pick up.

"I wish things were otherwise, but I think there's going to be trouble. Maybe now is not the time to bring my granddaughter home. And maybe I'm just an old woman bargaining with the gods for another chance at youth."

"There are other ways to reclaim that, you know." Fang knew that he was crossing an unspoken line, but he could not resist.

"Fang, please. Don't start again. I'll let my brother know you're coming. And my sister-in-law will be delighted to have you stay."

The unexpected turn of events worked in Fang's favor. He was given another opportunity to get closer to Sulin. And while she insisted on sticking to her widow's code of honor, her resistance seemed to be melting. Each encounter dredged another layer of subterranean passions, and now Fang could barely contain himself. He hustled about from room to room, packing a small suitcase. He would bring a bolt of silk cloth for Sulin, for her small sewing enterprise at home. At the outdoor market, he would pick up some candied fruits for the spring festival, sweet tangerines to grace the Chu's ancestral altar, and a long branch of peach blossoms. He wished he had a photograph of the grandchild for Sulin to see. Just as well that he didn't; it was one more reminder that his powers to cajole, to wheel and deal, were no match for her woman's touch.

Early the next morning, Fang set out for Lanping village with his suitcase and armload of gifts beside him. For hours he pondered how he would convince Longshan to stay out of the fracas. There was futility in trying to fight the government, he would say. It was like building a dike with deep mud walls against a sunken field. When the floods came, nothing could stop the fierce current from swallowing the land and crops, driving people and animals from their homes.

No, he would tell Longshan, the great modern economy was that tide, and China had been held back and deprived for so long that all she wanted to do was slake this thirst. And the peasants stood as tiny twigs in the face of the tidal wave. If you did not follow the current, you would go down in the water, and the river of progress would simply flow along unimpeded, drowning out those stray voices.

He was a jaded man, he knew, but the contorted truths of the Cultural Revolution had sobered him as a young man.

• • •

CHU LONGSHAN WAS DELIGHTED TO SEE HIS FRIEND, BUT

he knew why his sister had arranged the visit. "Ol' Fang, you are welcome to stay as long as you like, but the situation is getting heated up, and I can't back down now. Our council members have gone back to their villages. On the twenty-fifth day of this month, everyone will gather at the dam construction site to protest."

"That is very noble, my friend," Fang replied, "but I think your sister's fears are well founded. You think the authorities will just let thousands of people sit around under the sun, thumbing their noses at the project? They'll bring in the police, and where there's police, there will be violence."

"I'm not afraid," said Longshan quietly.

Fang launched a steady stream of persuasive arguments, which he did not dispute. Longshan had great regard for his friend, at times envied him for his business smarts. But this was not the China that Longshan had grown up in; this new China heaped prosperity on people like Fang, but denied even the most basic means of subsistence to peasants like himself. And Longshan had seen too much during his time in prison to be tethered by fear.

His friend attempted a last-ditch argument. "Listen, Ol' Chang, I just don't want to see you killed. When I was twenty-three, I lost a good friend in a terrible skirmish. A fight that didn't need to happen. We were only college students, Chiu Wanlong and I, caught up in the insanity of the times. He was mistaken for a rival Red Guard, and they shot him. In one fleeting moment, his life was snuffed out." Fang's voice was strained, and he stared intently at Longshan. "I don't want that to happen to you. Nobody does. Your wife needs you, and your sister is worried sick about you."

"I know what it's like to lose someone close to you," said Longshan, extending his hand toward his friend. "A fast death is painful, but slow dying hurts a lot, too. My father was an important man when you knew him. Now I know you have every reason to hate him, but he was a fair leader, and he did what was best for the collective. About a year after you'd left, the rabble-rousers began to persecute him, caught up in the fever of the Cultural Revolution. In truth, they were jealous. They rounded up the discontented folk, and the dimwitted ones, and they staged struggle sessions against my father. They called him a traitor, a bourgeoisie in peasant clothing, a criminal, and every filthy name you could image. None of it was true. We saw him come home every night, beaten and bruised. At first, he would not allow himself to be demoralized."

"Didn't anyone stick up for him?"

"Yes, some were willing to speak up for my father. But the crooks wanted to unseat him, so they locked him up for three months, and when he returned, he was a different man. I no longer knew this father. He was wild-eyed and emaciated. He began seeing visions of dead ancestors, and he would hit my mother, calling her a vengeful ghost. He had been such a man of principle that he must have felt utterly defeated by his tormentors. He died two years later of a stroke, but I've always thought it was grief that killed him. Grief over a corrupted revolution."

"And you want to vindicate your father?"

"No, what's done is done," said Longshan. "You make my intentions more noble than they are. What we're talking about here is survival, Fang. Sixty thousand people forced off the land. Hard-working peasants who won't be able to feed their wives and children. These are the people showing up next week." Longshan threw up his hands. "We've tried everything. We have no other choice."

•   •   •

ON A STROLL THE NEXT MORNING, FANG TOLD SULIN THAT HE WAS unable to dissuade Longshan from his plans.

"Then I will join him," she declared.

"What? And put your life at risk?" asked Fang. He stopped at the edge of the field, feeling the sharp spikelets of wheat poking against his shin.

"He's my brother. Longshan stood by me when the rest of the family seemed ready to disown me." Sulin pursed her lips, and turned her face toward the sun.

Fang impulsively grabbed her hand, and Sulin did not resist. "Then I will be there as well."

Li Miao Lovett

"Why?"

"Because I want to make it up to you, for the times I did not . . . could not stand up for you."

"The past is the past," said Sulin.

The old broker traced the well-etched lines on her palm, and he imagined reaching into the past with a brush that could blot out the cruelty of abrupt endings, aborted lives and hopes. "And it lives on," Fang replied. "It lives on whether we like it or not."

30

ON THE TWENTY-FIFTH DAY OF THE FIRST MONTH, THE VAST floodplain of the Songdu River overflowed with the peasants of Longmen County. From the mountains, they trudged from sunrise until noon, across woodlands and fields, crossing gullies and dried creek beds, until they reached the gathering spot. From high above it appeared as one mass migration, but the human creatures were slow and meandering, yet surefooted. Hawks soared beneath the clouds, circling around the luminous peaks, their prey obscured or frightened away by the moving specks that blighted the land like an invasion of locusts. Here and there the blade of a hoe or a sickle gleamed, but for the most part, the peasants were unarmed.

Like slow-trickling water the people moved across the rich soil of the floodplains, and then they defied the natural flow of water and moved uphill toward a canyon to the east of the river. Here the ravages of time and human tinkering left their mark in ravines and gullies chiseled with a woodcarver's precision, in the deep gashes left by tumbled rock, in the bald patches where wooded stumps remained amidst the pine and cypress.

At the base of the canyon, the forward movement stopped. Sporadic shouts reverberated in the alcove of the canyon. A man seated high above the steel jaws of an earthmover choked his engine to a halt. "What's going on?" he yelled to a few peasants down below.

"The government's gotta pay us, or we're not letting this dam project go any further."

The driver chuckled to himself. "Hey, I don't make the rules. Get outta my way, or I'll call my boss."

Like underground rhizomes, the discontent of the peasants had spread, at first through a few daring souls from a few villages. Then the news had radiated out, and the fervor grew to embrace fifteen thousand men and women from various communities along the Songdu. And now, the ire of the bosses would be ignited by their dissent. The workers alerted supervisors who alerted company bosses and party cadres and committee chairs. Soon, a convoy of vehicles appeared in the distance, ramming through rough dirt roads until they, too, gathered at the edge of the canyon.

The armed officers of the Public Security Bureau flanked the men in dark navy suits whose starched collars were stained with sweat. Their questions were demands. "Who are your leaders here?" The rabble of peasants parted to make way for half a dozen men who stepped forward, Longshan among them.

"And what do you think you're doing, disturbing the peace?" an official said.

"We are protesting peacefully, gentlemen," a council member replied. "We will stay here until the government fulfills its promise." The ragtag leaders waved their papers, stained with dirt and disintegrating slowly in the sun.

"You are disrupting order. You're keeping these workers from their jobs." The official tipped his cigarette at the team of construction workers, comprised of a few skilled drivers and a crew of leather-skinned men with shovels, now surrounded by the throng of peasants.

"We have no intention of causing trouble," Longshan said, "but we'll have no work ourselves if we move without getting our resettlement funds. The government can't abandon its poorest citizens."

"That's not my responsibility," the official replied. "I've got a job to do, which is to make sure the work goes on." He turned around and gave a signal, and the navy-suited men went back to their vehicles. "All right, you have two hours to clear out of here."

He scanned the massive gathering. A ragtag collection of

peasants in faded cotton, blurring into the specks of people in the distance. Here and there, a small group had erected a tarp for the elderly to keep out of the sun. But the great fabric of gathered humanity was seamless, fifteen thousand strong, stretching from mountain ridge to valley floor, on the eastern shore of the Songdu.

"Two hours," the official repeated. He turned on his heels and left with his small entourage.

But the cops from the Public Security Bureau remained, and waited. The leaders talked among themselves, shaking their heads as they spat in heated debate. Two of the men proposed that they disband the protest. "We have too much to lose. Look, these cops are armed, and they got their sights on us."

But Longshan and the others did not want to back down. "We have everything to lose if we give up now." Longshan leaned in toward the huddled men. "Look, I've told some people from the Hong Kong press about this. They should be here in a couple of hours."

With each passing hour, the mood of the crowd changed. The presence of the officials created a buzz of speculation, and in each nexus of gathered villages, the peasants whispered to their neighbors.

"Will they hurt us?"

"They can't arrest us. Look how many there are of us."

And when the worried remarks and rumors had run their course, the leaders made their way across the thicket of protestors to rally them in chants.

"Pay our fair share, or we won't go!"

"PAY OUR FAIR SHARE OR WE WON'T GO."

"If you feed us lies you starve our children!"

"IF YOU FEED US LIES YOU STARVE OUR CHILDREN."

In each cluster of villages, the chants radiated out like spokes from a magnetic hub. And unified voices from each of these groups rippled toward the others, like interlocking wheels. Together, the crowd chanted, one massive piece of machinery in which no visible center was found, only inter-moving parts, intertwined voices.

281

The forklift operator and the driver of the earthmover watched with languid interest. The workers who shoveled gravel sat and hugged their knees, their sweat from the morning's labor long dried. The elderly began to tire, and they leaned against their grown sons and daughters under the tarps.

As the sun began to slip behind the mountains, the chanting subsided, and another round of ruminations erupted. "Those cops aren't gone yet. I hear there may be trouble."

"I heard that reporters will show up. They gotta listen when the news gets out."

"Rumors! Who can believe anything you hear?"

And then, as the cool breeze of late afternoon crossed over the ridge into the valley, a convoy of trucks appeared in the distance.

● ● ●

FANG SHUPING HAD NOT EXPECTED SUCH AN ORGANIZED gathering of peasants. Their coarse features and garlicky odors repelled him, and they thrust their fists too close when they chanted. He could not dodge their curious glances. But as the afternoon wore on, the women of Sulin's village lost interest in inquiring about this new friend of hers. When the officials showed up, Fang stayed close to her as the crowd gathered around Longshan. He felt a strange sense of envy toward his friend, a leader of the masses, who was emboldened, not defeated, by the succession of obstacles thrown his way. Fang began to think it was a foolish idea to join the rabble-rousers, but Sulin had become as committed to sticking by her brother as he was to standing up for their cause.

At first, Fang did not join in the chanting, but as the protracted hours of the afternoon crept by, he took part to relieve the monotony. Sulin did not pay him much attention beyond an occasional reminder to drink some water or rest his feet. *I'm following her like a faithful dog,* he thought ruefully, *and all she has to do is throw me a few scraps.*

He scanned the crowd to pass the time, his eyes alighting on the faces of women, the occasional colorful garb, the hoes and sickles that lay on the ground. And he remembered the woman who lived with her little boy in a shack amidst the ruins of old Wushan. She had a broad face like Sulin's, but her nose was bulbous, not so handsome. Maybe she didn't really have a husband. Did she wind up in her present state because she was too homely? But maybe she was telling the truth after all. Perhaps her village had fought a losing battle against the dam that held back the Three Gorges, and she had been left with nothing but a poor husband and child.

A fellow with a small gray goatee offered Fang a spot beneath his tarp, and the two sat smoking as the leaders led the crowd in another wave of chanting. Longshan stood on a large outcropping of rock at the base of the canyon, his cries as blunt as the cawing of a crow, his voice growing hoarser with each round.

"We are here for our children. And our children's children!" he shouted. "And we cannot disappoint our fathers, who fought so hard for a better life, a better China."

"Long live China. Down with the despots!" The crowd surged into a frenzy of renewed chanting.

It was then that Fang gleaned a moment of understanding, that the same China that sought to destroy his father had offered bold promises to her humblest citizens, those who tilled the land. And in the swell of voices, acrid and potent and reeking with garlic and spice, Fang saw that these people did not want to eat bitterness anymore. He could not forgive his own oppressors who had taunted him and driven him from Sulin thirty-five years ago, but he was beginning to grasp the plight of the villagers.

At a quarter to six, Fang spied the first of a long line of trucks. Creeping along like a giant caterpillar, they approached the canyon where the people were gathered. The People's Liberation Army had arrived. Tension hung in the air, and it threatened to erupt in angry blisters. The men picked up their farm tools and turned toward the advancing convoy. Seven trucks arrived, stopping where the dirt road fed into the base of the canyon. Two dozen soldiers filled each of the truck beds, their taut bodies as rigid as rifles.

A thick voice sounded through a bullhorn. "GO HOME. Be good citizens, and there won't be any trouble."

All around, Fang heard anxious whispers, and then the croaking of peasant voices broke through the echoes of the PLA bullhorn. A hundred yards away, Longshan called for the people to stand their ground.

"Stand your ground!" the deputy leaders repeated throughout the crowd.

"Stand your ground!" their voices echoed defiantly. The swarm of villagers rose to their feet.

On cue, the soldiers charged forth with their shields and tore the crowd asunder.

Longshan did not move from his post. "Be brave, people! We've done nothing wrong!"

"Stand your ground!" the deputy leaders cried. But some of the peasants began to duck and run, jostling those who were frozen to the spot. The men with their rusted hoes and spears pounced on the charging soldiers, pummeling a few to the ground. Fang, who had been huddling with the goateed neighbor, felt their tarp topple amidst the chaos, covering them in a mass of canvas. He fought free, and saw Sulin moving through the tangle of arms and legs toward her brother, who was still rooted to his stump, staunch in his cry of peaceful resistance. "Courage, people! Courage!"

Fang rose up, grabbing the shirt of a peasant to avoid being thrown to the ground. All around, sharp blades and spears danced in defiance, as the men shouted and spat and hurled insults. The khaki-colored soldiers fired tear gas, and protestors crumpled to the ground like drunken bees. A spear whisked through the air, crashing with a thud on a smoke-colored shield. A cry punctured the air, and then choked words, a dying groan.

Fang pushed forward, and the tide pushed against him. The sweat trickled down his nose, his dirt-smeared face, but all he could fix his eyes on was the gray blouse of his old lover. He pushed harder, finding a strength he did not know he possessed, grabbing a short stick to prod the tussling torsos and thighs out of his way as he crept along like an animal toward Sulin, toward the raised stump where Longshan fought valiantly. The peasant leader was braced behind the shield of a felled soldier, warding off the rubber bullets fired at him.

"Brother, get out of here!" Sulin cried as she approached Longshan, with Fang close behind her.

"Courage, people! We shall not be defeated!" the defiant Longshan croaked.

Fang called out Sulin's name, but she could not hear him through the din of clashing bodies, metal, and Plexiglas. He groped his way forward. His eyes were glazed with dust, casting the world around him in a murky underwater light.

And then he saw her hand reaching up toward Longshan. In the next breath, a hulking khaki-colored arm seized Sulin. And just before Longshan could thrust his fist from the shield, before two more men could rush to her defense, before she could utter a cry of resistance, Fang leapt on the soldier's back and clenched him around the throat. He felt the bristle of the young man's crew cut, smelled the stench of sweat and blood, and still he clung on as the soldier bucked like an unbroken horse and pummeled Fang with his fists.

And then it was over. A fatal blow landed on Fang's temple, and another, and another, until the old man fell into a lifeless heap beside Sulin.

•　　•　　•

FANG'S BODY LAY IN A SIMPLE COFFIN OF SALVAGED WOOD IN her workroom, beside an unfinished heap of baby clothes Sulin had been sewing for her neighbors. In the three days since the protest, she had refused to let the officials take him away with half a dozen other casualties. She would have to arrange for a proper burial or cremation soon, before their deadline to move. The troop reinforcements had come in two more convoys that day, and in the end, the protest had been quelled.

As Sulin pushed the pedal of her old sewing machine, its needle sailed in a chopping motion along the silk like a steady rudder. When the last row of stitches was completed, Sulin held up the scarf, embroidered with tall pines in dark green, a bubbling brook of pale blue, two small figures like black ants. This had been their secret hiding place. She remembered how she loved the woods in summertime, with its fragrance of pinesap and camphor wood. She draped the scarf around Fang's bosom, carefully lifting his head. And then she rested her hand on his chest beneath the embroidery, as a long, slow tear fell on the old man's chin.

31

MEI LING COULD NOT BELIEVE HER EARS. SHE HAD DONE EVERYTHING she possibly could to move forward with her life. She had initiated plans to divorce Liu; although he had not shown up that following Sunday, she intended to lay it on the table when she returned for the lunar New Year. She had made her choice, and risen to Sun Daimen's challenge. And now that she was ready to start anew, he dealt a bitter blow to her plans.

"You can't continue this because you're *betrothed?*" She blinked, incredulous at the idea that this man was betrothed, set aside and claimed by another. She heard the shuffle of Sun Daimen's feet under the table. He appeared repentant, but it only provoked the anger seething in her bosom.

"Mei Ling, I really didn't know how to tell you this. And please believe me. . . . I never meant to deceive you."

She glared at him. "So I'm supposed to believe whatever you're going to tell me."

"Please," Sun Daimen implored. "Just give me the chance to explain. And then you can hate me if you wish. I was not attached to anyone when you and I started getting to know one another. And when I asked you to make a choice, little did I know that I would soon have to make one myself. The woman whom I grew up with, whom my family has doted on since we were young children, has come back into my life." Sun Daimen lowered his voice. "She was arrested in a student uprising fifteen years ago, in Tiananmen

Square. She was thrown in prison, and released when her father sought help from a high-ranking Party official. But they worried about her safety, and she has been living in exile in France all these years. I never thought I would see her again."

Mei Ling saw the wistful look in the man's eyes, and yet she could not let her heart soften. She lowered her gaze as he continued.

"Her father is an important business leader in Chongqing. And he knew that with the right connections, he could clear up his daughter's record, wipe her slate clean. It took quite a few bribes, going through the right Party members, to erase the record of her involvement in the student revolt."

"How can the government do that? It's like they're changing the past." Her curiosity, for the moment, had gained the upper hand.

"With money you can do anything," said Sun Daimen. "Now don't get me wrong. There are many in China who will carry a black stain for the rest of their lives from the uprising. But Mr. Zhang is a powerful man. He helped me get where I am today. He was the first to rise up from the terrible poverty in our village, and make something of himself. And Zhang Wei, as different as she is from her father, remains an idealist." His voice fell into a hushed whisper. "She said she joined the revolt, not because she hates China and its patriarchy, but because she loves China."

"And you've missed her all this time?" Mei Ling asked, the irritation creeping back into her voice.

"Yes," he said, not looking at her.

"Well, I should be happy for you, Sun Daimen. Your true love has come home to roost. And what we had, I'm sure, meant nothing to you." Mei Ling's voice rose into a shrill pitch. "I sacrificed what I had. You asked me to choose, and I gave up my marriage to be with you. And what am I left with now? A big bag of lies!"

Heads turned as Mei Ling snatched her purse and stormed out of the noodle shop with Daimen close behind her. She fluttered down the street in high heels, but could not outpace the man who had jilted her.

"Mei Ling, please understand. I thought long and hard about this. I've had nothing but respect for you, and I care about you. But

I couldn't turn away from the woman who has been such a big part of my life."

"But that was half a lifetime ago. How do you know that she hasn't changed? That she doesn't find this place too backward?"

"I never meant to hurt you," Sun Daimen pleaded, circling around to face Mei Ling. "Maybe I am a bad man, but I guess I'll have to take my chances."

"Just you wait," said Mei Ling. "This will come back to haunt you." She turned away, avoiding Daimen's pitiful glances, then broke into a wobbly run down the sidewalk.

In the dormitory, Mei Ling wept bitterly as she packed. She had come to depend on this man. And had devoted herself to him. The months she had squandered felt like years. And her marriage, she had thrown it away like a worn shirt. Everything I've touched has turned to dust, she thought.

On the long boat ride back to Wushan, Mei Ling noticed the presence of nearby couples with a mixture of envy and scorn. Her life had been frittered away, and she would have to start over once more. She could ask Tai if he would hire her back. As petty and unrelenting as he was in his ways, she would be willing to work at Tai's again for the time being.

And then there was Liu. Would he take her back? Did she want to return to a family that did not feel entirely hers? Yet her own father swore that Mei Ling must have come from different stock. "We found you in the fields," he would tease her when she was young. She would run crying to her mother, until Chen Weijin assured her that—no—she was indeed made from their flesh and blood. She had wished for a different Ba Ba, one who wasn't scornful toward girls. Boys were precious gems to be sifted out, he used to say. And girls were mud in the river that would flow away in time.

Her husband's lie about Rose had made Mei Ling furious. It was one more act of deceit in a long trail of lies she had heard from the men in her life. She might arrive home in Wushan and find that another woman slept in their bed, ate from their dishes, even dressed from the clothes she had left behind. She might find the little girl's mother, or Liu's wife mysteriously returned from the dead. And then she had a vision of the various women crowded into their humble abode, with a self-satisfied Liu in their midst. It was an absurd image, but it fed her sense of indignation. May God send them all to hell, she cursed them silently.

But what if there was nobody else but the little girl? What if Liu had told the truth in every other way? He was a reserved man, not one to declare his love for her in so many words, but his actions were steadfast enough. He had made the long trip to Chongqing to win her back. The separation had never been made final. Liu was a simple man, bred of the rough-hewn character of the countryside, but he could be more reliable than all the fickle men who made their fortunes in the big city.

And the prospect of taking care of Rose, perhaps that wasn't so bad after all. The little girl had been warming up to her before she left. She could find the spirit of generosity in her heart to care for the child, who was, after all, another lamb of God put on this earth for a purpose.

She dared not think what her own purpose was, as she had not fulfilled the dreams tucked deep inside her bosom, those that remained in spite of the betrayals and cruel turns of fate. Mei Ling knew she was no longer a maiden; she was too cynical and wise to the world now to fall for the illusions of youth, but the secrets of the seasoned woman still lay beyond her grasp. She only knew, from her mother's experience, that time did not necessarily dull the pain of old regrets.

•   •   •

THERE WAS NO ANSWER WHEN MEI LING KNOCKED ON THE DOOR. Liu and the child must be napping, she thought. She fished out her key. No luck there, either. Mei Ling stared at the chipped paint on the door, the faded numbers, then ran upstairs and found the manager's apartment.

"Sir, I have been away working for some time, and my husband must have changed the locks to our apartment." When Mei Ling told him the unit number, the manager's face clouded over.

"Your husband moved out a week ago," he growled. "He was late on his rent. Couldn't pay up when I went to collect it."

"Where did he go?" Mei Ling asked, not wanting to believe what she heard.

"How would I know? I just told him he had to go. I don't know what kind of shady business you folks have gotten into, but a fellow came by saying that Tai's Restaurant owes a lot of money, and your name's on one of the bills. And then your apartment gets broken into. Cost me to change these locks, straighten up the place."

"But I don't work there anymore. I'm just trying to—"

"Listen, lady. We've got new tenants coming in, and there's nothing you can do now." He shut the door unceremoniously.

Mei Ling stared at her feet, speechless. A wave of panic swept over her. It was all she could do to keep from dissolving into a lifeless heap on the manager's doorstep. When she came to her senses, she rushed back downstairs. The neighbor next door told her about the eviction, and had her own theories about the burglars.

"I hear there's a rash of crime 'cause of poor folk coming into the city. Must be from Hebei. Peasant trash." The woman wrinkled her nose. "They can be so uncouth, you know."

Mei Ling was not interested in those rumors. "Were there women going into the apartment over the last few months?"

"Don't think so. Never saw a woman on the premises. And Liu was gone a while, too. Said he was going to visit you. I pressed him, but your husband doesn't talk much."

Mei Ling deflected the flurry of questions and hastened outside, where the wind and dust from nearby construction assaulted her senses. She had one more chance to find Liu.

She caught a minibus to Guangdong Street, and spied the flimsy newspaper plastered across Tai's restaurant. She read the notice on the door, its loose edge still flapping like a broken wing. It was beginning to make sense now. The unpaid bills. The burglary. She called Tai's number; it was disconnected.

Mei Ling turned away from the deserted building. Uttering a cry of bewilderment, she tore down the street toward the outdoor market. She asked every vendor who could possibly recognize her husband if they had seen him.

"Liu Renfu, you say? Has a 2-year-old girl with him? Don't know such a man." Their answers were innocent enough, but their puzzled glances seemed to say, *You can't find your husband? What kind of woman are you to let go of a good man?*

A good man. A disappeared man. The thought threw her stomach into knots.

She stared at the faces of the lean men with bamboo poles across their shoulders, wondering if Liu was among them. She approached a porter with an elfish, leathered face, and asked again.

"Well, I do remember seeing a man with a young girl the other day." The fellow pointed down the street. "Yes, he was sitting right around there, with the child, and a crowd was milling around them. He kept his head bowed, but the girl was a bouncy one, kept sticking her hand in the donation jar."

"Have you seen him since?"

"Why, no. Seen some old geezers selling trinkets and fortune-telling books. That's about it."

Mei Ling swallowed hard. Her husband had been reduced to begging, because she had been coldhearted toward him; she had chased happiness only to bring misery upon them both. She glanced wildly at the stands of squatting vendors, the gleaming storefronts, the silhouette of high-rises on the hill.

Every trace of Mei Ling's life in Wushan had disappeared.

Except for the church. She was unworthy, she knew. But Father Chong would offer up her prayers, and her repentance. Her mind had been clouded by desire. Her body had fallen to lusting for another man. It was painful, but she had to face the truth now. She felt the weight of her sins, a heavy coat that had robbed her of dignity. She was ready to give it up and start anew.

"The Lord bears witness, and the Lord forgives," Father Chong would say across the dark curtain of the confessional.

When Mei Ling arrived at the Catholic Church, a nun greeted her in the hallway. Mei Ling almost did not recognize Sister Liang, despite the familiar gray blouse and skirt. She asked to see Father

Chong. "It's rather urgent," Mei Ling added.

"I'm afraid Father Chong won't be back for several days. He is attending a convention in Wanzhou," Sister Liang replied.

Mei Ling stared past her at the vacant office. She raised her trembling hands to her lips, as if to suppress a scream. The puzzled look in the nun's eyes pierced into her flesh, and she turned and ran down the stairs, her heels clanking against polished stone. She skittered down the winding street, unable to escape the thunderous voices in her head. Perhaps she did not deserve forgiveness. She had strayed too far. Soon her feet gave out, and she collapsed against a lamppost. A motorcyclist stopped, eyeing her tailored dress and heels, and offered her a ride.

When they reached a quiet section of the waterfront, Mei Ling asked to be let off. The motorcyclist seemed puzzled by her request, but he pocketed the money and drove away.

A concrete ramp sloped down to the water's edge, where peasant rafts stopped to pick up their cargo and passengers. It was late in the afternoon, and the place was deserted. Mei Ling took off her heels, squirming at the gravel beneath her feet. She tiptoed to the edge of the ramp.

A thick belt of fog bathed the Yangtze, swallowing the two bridges in its midst. In the near distance, a cruise ship sailed languorously with the current. A passenger ferry signaled its arrival at the main dock. Small flies alighted on Mei Ling's feet. She descended down the uneven surface of the ramp, ridged like sandbag mounds. A distant hum, clear as church bells, sounded from the hill above.

Her toes touched water, and the flies buzzed away. She stopped for a moment.

It would be so easy, she thought.

She took another step. The water was quite cold, soothing to her sore ankle.

A car rattled along the gravel road behind her. Mei Ling crouched low to avoid being seen. When it passed, she straightened her limbs and sank deeper into water, the pleats of her dress billowing in the wind.

WHEN THE FERRYBOAT DOCKED AT FENGJIE, LIU AND ROSE disembarked with the swarm of passengers returning home for spring festival. Shoppers scuttled past with bags of fruits and meat to prepare for their loved ones at home, both living and deceased. Red lanterns adorned the shops to welcome the lunar New Year. Merchants hawked their wares from open-air stalls, their sing-song chants ending on an operatic lilt. "Oranges, eight *jiao* a *kilo*! A buck and a half for *two*!"

Liu stood on the sidewalk, holding Rose by the hand, watching the passengers climb into sedans and minibuses. The taxi drivers swarmed around the others, but left him alone. He was a pauper reduced to begging for their ship fare to Fengjie. He could smell the sour odor of his sweat beneath the jacket of lumpy cotton batting. But little Rose, with her red wool cap, appeared to be a bright flower against his withered stalk, lighting up the women's faces as they passed by.

This was my old home, Liu thought. And then he remembered it was his home in name only. Old Fengjie lay downriver beneath the Yangtze, enshrouded in a layer of silt. A fleeting image of Fei Fei flitted through his mind—Fei Fei, dressed in crimson with blossoms in her hair—but the din of spring festival activity tamped down his thoughts.

On the street, car tires screeched and turned in a fitful dance with wayward pedestrians. Summoning his courage, Liu tried to flag down a minibus just as the first drumbeats of an oncoming parade echoed through the streets. BAH-ba-da-DUM. BAH-ba-da-DUM. The band strutted past in bright regalia, young men in satin pants, young women with a swirl of red and white ribbons wriggling about them like water snakes. And then the fiery golden dragon appeared, its bulbous head rising and falling in time with the drums, its eight human legs shuffling in centipede fashion through the crowd. The ears dropped, two bulging orbs blinked, and the massive jaws opened as shreds of lettuce sailed through the air and fell into its trap.

Rose shrieked, clapping her hands, stirred by the rhythm of the blaring drums. And then the firecrackers blazed in a mad string of explosions. Sparks of light flickered and danced around the tangle of legs. The dragon writhed and snarled. The little girl launched into cries of terror as her father muffled her ears with his bony hands.

"Little monkey, this is a good day, a happy day. The firecrackers keep the monsters away."

But little Rose continued to cry. The dragon continued its spirited dance, and the monsters did not go away.

•   •   •

THE WATER LAPPED AGAINST MEI LING'S CALVES, SENDING shivers up the back of her legs into her spine. It calmed her, and drew her toward the frothy swells that licked against the concrete embankment. She moved forward in a trancelike state, one sluggish step after another, until a holler punctuated the silence.

"Lady, you all right?" a man called out from a peasant raft. The wind billowed against his loose cotton shirt, and his motor idled like a growling mastiff.

The waves swirled around her knees. The peasant's gruff voice warbled in the wind. She could be underwater. The world could be underwater. Still, she was breathing, and the cool air assaulted her nostrils and lips. She felt an impulse to jump, then to turn and run. But Mei Ling did neither. She merely stood there until the boatman pulled ashore and asked her again. "You need a hand, lady?"

"No," Mei Ling mumbled. "I'm okay."

He stared at her with kindly eyes. Her legs were shivering. "You must be cold." He reached into his cabin and handed her a nylon jacket. "Sure you don't need a hand?"

Mei Ling shook her head, and the man throttled his engine, aiming the prow upriver, and sailed away.

When the boat disappeared into the Yangtze, Mei Ling stumbled toward the gravel road where her shoes lay. With the jacket draped around her, she sank to the ground, watching as the fog swallowed the boats sailing beneath Longmen Bridge. It was the

Dragon's Gate, and the mist was the dragon's breath, which had pulled her in and expelled her in the course of an afternoon.

That evening, in the dim light of a noodle shop, Mei Ling hesitated before calling her mother at the hospital. What would she say? That she couldn't do it? That she had to break the curse? That God had showed His mercy after all she'd done?

Mei Ling took a deep breath. She told her mother the truth about Sun Daimen and her decision to leave her husband, about Liu's disappearance. Mei Ling waited for her mother's reproach, but the judgment did not come.

"Mei Ling, you didn't know it would all happen like that. How could you possibly know?"

"But Ma, I've wasted my life. I've done everything wrong, everything that I could to ruin my chances for happiness. And I've disappointed you."

Chen Weijin's voice fluttered with infirmity like brittle autumn leaves. "When I learned that I was sick, at first I resisted. I fought so hard to deny it. I am a poor woman, and perhaps if I had been wealthy, if I had gold ingots instead of mud bricks, there would be another chance at life. But even the rich cannot escape their fate. And even if I had all the riches in the world, I would not be happy if my children were miserable."

Her mother's words trailed away. The surge of blood rumbling inside Mei Ling's temples drowned out that parchment-thin voice. "Ma, I almost couldn't go on. I could see nothing, feel nothing but the weight of my mistakes, and what they'd done to Liu. He was forced out to the streets. And heaven knows where he is now."

"He is a grown man. He can fend for himself. And what's happened lies in the past. All the times your father lost his temper; that's in the past, too. He has been good to me, now that he knows my time here is limited."

"Ma, you are better than me. I don't know that I can forgive myself any more than I can forgive my father. Or my grandfather. You know what it did to Po Po, the shame of being ravaged by a man. She couldn't go on. She couldn't live with the shame."

Chen Weijin sighed. "No, she didn't have a choice. But you do,

Mei Ling. You must carry on for me."

Her words, although meant to comfort, aroused Mei Ling's worries. "You're getting better, aren't you, Ma? Surely the doctors are wrong. And Father's just being an old pessimist?"

"No, I'm afraid it is God's will."

"Then I will come home, Ma. You must wait for me." Mei Ling bit her lip. She held back her tears; she would be strong, so that her dear mother might find comfort in her last days.

Chen Weijin spluttered, her cough rattling like loose stones. It sapped her strength, and she could not speak further. The wretched sound tore at Mei Ling's heart, and she merely whispered a hasty good-bye, with promises of a quick return.

She would return home to a village where she'd never lived, a dialect she could not speak, a mother who was dying, and a father who had changed his ways, whom she no longer knew. His newfound attentiveness toward her mother could not make up for all those years, and it frightened her as much as his old angry self.

Mei Ling would not call the place her parents lived her *niang jia*. Her home, where her maiden self had lived, no longer existed. It had been carried away by the swollen river of summertime, and the torrent that ground dreams to dust.

She would go home for her mother's sake. And when her weary heart regained its strength, she would go on again.

•   •   •

IN THE evening, Liu sank his tired frame into the plush vinyl couch with Rose beside him. Wang Ma offered him a cigarette, and his lips quivered as he lit up. It had been a wild ride, from the dank mud floor of a hovel to Wushan's streets, from a cramped berth rolling on the Yangtze to the creature comforts of his friend's home.

He had bathed earlier, then sat Rose in the small plastic tub, ladling steamy water around her ears and down her back. How quickly the smell of musty soil and the cloying fumes of the city had evaporated from their skin. And yet, in the warmth of this man's home, the bitter taste of homelessness lingered.

He sucked on his cigarette, the smoke curling around him like mist, insulating him from the blare of the television, the restless tap-tap of his daughter's foot against his thighs. His friend was lost in the dazzle of beauties that paraded across the screen, the shimmer of their dresses under the stage lights. They leaned into the microphone with moist lips, their lusty voices bolstered by the cheering of the crowd.

He remembered how Mei Ling's voice soared to the heavens in church. How it lifted him, for the moment, to the realm of possibilities. Liu wondered if she had returned to Wushan. Her last words had been hasty, uttered in the cover of darkness. "Take care of yourself, Liu." It was her declaration of freedom.

He had seen pity in her eyes, and also a glimmer of relief. He clenched his teeth, tasting the bitterness of tobacco. All his life, he had tried to escape the clutches of poverty. Perhaps she had been doing the same, and had finally succeeded.

Liu stared at his hands. The thick calluses formed over years of hard labor were now cut by deep cracks. He could not fault Mei Ling for wanting more. Perhaps, in this lifetime, he could never do enough to please a woman like Mei Ling. But he had a daughter to provide for, and this gave him the impetus to do better. If it were not for Rose, he might have languished in the abandoned stone house at the edge of old Wushan, until the rising tide swallowed him, much as it had swallowed Fei Fei years ago.

He ran his fingers through the wispy strands of Rose's hair. Like Wang Ma, she was caught up in the glitter of bodies that crooned and swayed to the upbeat tempo. She was perched against Liu's breast, with one thumb cradled in her mouth and the other playing against the butterfly clasps of her little jacket.

He could not promise that she would never again suffer from the cold. And yet, Liu knew that he would do everything in his power to seek higher ground. He would work hard again, not to bolster the pride of a man once and again defeated, but for his daughter's sake. She was the nymph spirit that had kept him from giving up.

32

LIU CELEBRATED HIS DAUGHTER'S THIRD BIRTHDAY, WHICH was really the anniversary of her rescue, with a trip to Fengjie from their village. He brought along extra money to treat Rose to an excursion on the river. She donned a pair of leather shoes adorned with sparkling stones and bells, a gift from the shoemaker whose small enterprise had provided Liu with a modest but reliable income for the past year and a half.

Along the bustling commercial strip, the dishes of blue carp for sale, the fleeting passage of birds, the slate-colored statue of Buddha on a widow ledge reminded Liu of his former life with a woman who had loved him without question or expectation. Time had tempered his grief around Fei Fei's death, and the old misgivings had given way to an acceptance that what was could never be again.

And yet, his flight from Wushan and the unresolved matter of his second wife nagged at him. It distracted him, drawing his fingers too close to the sharp needle of the sewing machine punching through tough leather. It made him cough—the chain-smoking irritated his lungs as never before—when a stranger asked about the child's mother. With the passage of seasons the sting of Mei Ling's rejection had dulled, but curiosity and longing did not loosen their grip. As they waited beneath an awning where the steam of wonton soup wafted forth, he shifted his weight from one restless foot to the other. He felt compelled to go back and find her.

"Rose, how about we take a trip to our old home down the

river?" He knelt down, grasped his daughter's fingers, a pleading, almost demanding look in his eyes.

The little girl leapt up in her rubber-soled shoes. "Where is the old home?"

"That way." Liu pointed beyond the canopy of fruit and deli stands toward the river. "We'll get there before evening."

He hoisted her up against the rough hemp of his shirt and joined the gaggle of passengers alighting on the dock.

•   •   •

DUSK FELL ON THE TERRACED CITY OF WUSHAN AS THEIR FERRY approached. Liu gazed past the concrete flanks of high-rises to seek out that familiar steeple, but it eluded him now. In the minibus, Rose squirmed in his lap, each sharp curve of the road throwing her toward a stony-eyed passenger or the sack of oranges at their feet.

"Ba Ba!" she whined, fingering her nose. "I don't like this. When do we get off?"

"Soon, little monkey." Liu tried to hush her, but she batted his hand away with an angry flick. Her simian fingers recoiled when he reached out to grab them. He took a deep breath, knowing he'd have to resort to a bribe.

"A big bowl of *chao shou* for supper, if you keep hush a little longer."

"No!" she cried.

"And a buggy ride in the square."

The little girl's eyes glistened, issuing her consent. The bus lurched to a stop across the street from the Catholic Church, whose bell tower lit the rain-streaked night in soft golden hues. Liu led his daughter toward its imposing edifice, his heart thumping softly.

A woman in a gray jacket and skirt introduced herself as Sister Liang. Her movements were spare, her manner austere, but she doled a generous smile on Rose, who fidgeted and wrapped her arms around Liu's quivering thigh.

Liu hesitated, scrunching his toes against the smooth granite. "I'm here to look for someone. She's a loyal member of your church, a woman by the name of Mei Ling. Chang Mei Ling."

"Why, yes, she used to come to Mass every Sunday. It's been a while now since we've seen her."

His heart sank. She would not forsake the church, certainly not if she had returned to Wushan. A more lucrative life must have led her back to the big city, to her lover. He bristled at the thought. His voice quavered. "She . . . she was my wife. A string of unfortunate events pulled us apart. Do you know if she's stayed on in Chongqing?"

"No, the last I heard she is living with her parents in Guangdong."

"Really? I didn't think she got along with her father." He winced. He had said too much, but Sister Liang did not seem bothered.

"She did come by the church. Twice, as I recall. She seemed quite perturbed the first time. Wanted to talk to Father Chong. When she came again a few days later, the minister had not returned, and she took me aside to relay her news."

Liu sensed that Sister Liang was weighing what she would reveal to him. He did not want to appear too eager, but he had waited all this time, battling the ruminations.

Sister Liang gestured toward a narrow hallway, and led him up the stairs into the belfry. The silhouette of Wushan's edifices rippled in the gilded light. Liu counted seven long chimes of the bells suspended above them. Sister Liang spoke softly, her words alighting like doves before the wind carried them away.

"Your wife was kind to make a donation to the church before she left. She was sorry that she had not found a community in Chongqing, said she had fallen out of the graces of the Lord." The nun cleared her throat, as if she had spoken too much this time.

Liu held his breath, waited for her to continue. But impatience overtook him, and he said, "Was she happy in Chongqing?"

"I do not know. Mei Ling had been such a radiant presence in our parish, with her youthful energy. The woman who returned from Chongqing that winter seemed to have the light snuffed out of her." She glanced at Liu. "Do not fear. The Lord provides a beacon to even the most troubled of souls."

Liu did not want such reassurances. He knew that something had gone awry in the big city, but he felt little sense of victory in his wife's defeat, if there had indeed been another man. Instead, he was seized by a paternal wave of concern. "She is okay now?"

"From what word we have received, yes. She sends occasional cards from Guangdong. Her mother has died, and her father relies on her now that he, too, has fallen ill."

"I am sorry to hear that." Liu glanced down at his feet, and in a fervent heartbeat his fantasies unleashed. He would find his way to Guangdong where Mei Ling would welcome him with open arms, and Rose would seek the bosom of her adoptive mother, so that their lives would be stitched together again after such unraveling. And then the night wind sobered him, brought his attention to the cold grip of his hands on the railing, the clawing of his daughter's fingers at his hip. Sister Liang stared contemplatively across the canvas of the darkened city, her hands tucked into her sleeves.

As quickly as the futile hope had arisen, it scampered resolutely back into the shadows. He could offer her no prospects for a better life. And the idea of living under the same roof as her father was rather unappetizing. No, Liu and Rose had established their little nest outside of Fengjie. It was not to be.

The little girl's tugging became more insistent. "I'm cold, Ba Ba. I want to go eat."

"We must leave," said Liu. "Thank you for indulging my questions. I'm afraid that Guangdong is too far for us to travel, but please let Mei Ling know that I wish the best for her."

"Sir . . . before you go." The nun cleared her throat again. "Your wife had spoken to me about her situation shortly before she left. She expressed her great sorrow at having wronged you. Said that if you were ever to return, you might hear those words and forgive her."

Liu stared into the woman's eyes, honey-colored in the light beneath the silent bells. "She is forgiven."

He seized Rose's hand and lumbered down the steep staircase, turning only to bid a hasty farewell to Sister Liang.

•   •   •

DOWN THE WINDING ROAD TOWARD WUSHAN'S MAIN SQUARE, Liu and Rose trotted along at a clip until a sudden twinge in his leg reminded him to temper their fretful pace. They stopped at a corner where the sizzle of fried potatoes lured them toward a roadside vendor. In the puff of her cheeks and her kindly eyes, shaped like butterfly wings, Liu imagined the countenance of Mrs. Song. A cognizant Mrs. Song who always knew what to do when the baby was colicky or couldn't keep her food down, felt hot to the touch or wet and runny down below. Liu handed the small dish of steaming potatoes, peppered with fried garlic, to his daughter. "Rose, say thank you to the nice Po Po."

"*Xie xie,* Po Po," Rose twittered, suddenly shy, but her eyes held the same glimmer of recognition.

Down the hill they skidded, father and daughter, pulled along by gravity and memory, the footfalls and car horns around them an obliterating presence, shielding them in anonymity. While no one around them could identify him, an ex-scavenger, a man with no wife twice over, a fugitive chased away for lack of resources, he could not help but pick out the eerie semblance of those he once knew and loved in the faces around him.

The taxi driver flicking his cigarette outside the cab window gestured to Rose as they walked by. The crook of his finger, the sharp line of his jaw, his heavy-lidded eyes, were Tai's finger and jaw, those same querulous orbs.

"Need a ride, mister?"

"We're looking for a place to stay. Anywhere will do."

The taxi lurched forward into traffic, and as they sped along Guangdong Street, the kaleidoscopic flashes of an old, familiar life flickered before his eyes. The alleyway where mounds of peanuts and candy vied for attention alongside tubs of fresh produce and baked tofu. The long sidewalks where porters hustled along in the incandescent light of fancy shops, with slabs of pork strung onto their bamboo poles. The open-faced delis where men hunched over noodle bowls. The site of Tai's old restaurant, now a department store, where manikins beckoned to passersby while store clerks huddled in a corner, giggling.

Liu paid the taxi driver, who accepted the fare with tobacco-stained fingers. The Mei Yuan Jiu Dian was a small affair, its name too generous for such a modest inn. It took a few taps of the counter bell to summon the clerk, a young woman with a porcelain complexion and dainty lips, whose pencil-lined brows were arched into an expression of perpetual surprise. When she gave Liu their room key, he felt a rabid impulse to seize the hand that proffered it. He swallowed hard. The knot of muscles in his neck clenched, held him back. He wanted to linger, to learn her name, to find traces of home amidst the dun-colored walls, somber drapes, and stick furniture.

The woman with painted brows was perhaps Mei Ling's age. Did she look past the futility of her present circumstances to a rosier future? She appeared not to care that he loitered, under the pretense of thumbing through magazines he could not read. He wondered why he would be drawn back to his past, one that taunted him with unrequited longings. Liu felt somewhat ashamed of his desire, and when Rose fussed in her sleep-deprived state, he was grateful for the impetus to retreat.

· · ·

A LIGHT RAIN TAPPED AGAINST THE WINDOWPANE IN THE morning, but Liu was undeterred in his mission. He would take Rose back to the place where she was born. Astride his shoulders, the little girl hunkered down beneath a plastic cape as Liu pushed past the crowd of morning shoppers and street hawkers. He was a ready steed, charging into battle toward that one remnant of his former life that could not elude him.

The dock was already teeming with passengers who streamed back and forth in chaotic currents. Liu mustered the courage to approach a small group of travelers.

"A boat to the Little Three Gorges?" one replied. "I've seen 'em dock a couple hundred yards down the road, by that shallow bank."

Liu thanked them, and the two made their way along the gravel road to a quiet stretch of the waterfront. He lowered Rose to the ground and stood up stiffly. "Little monkey, one day you're going to carry your Ba Ba."

"I'm carrying Ba Ba!" The little girl seized his legs and tried to levitate him, to no avail. "Ba Ba is a big goat, a big heavy goat."

Liu kicked up a spray of gravel and snorted at the child, who dashed down the sloped embankment toward the water. Just as he caught her, a small boat chugged into view, steered by a man Liu immediately recognized. It was Mr. Wu, his old boss, a crew of one, whose arrival filled him with a mixture of dread and curiosity.

The boatman who appeared before them was not the pompous Mr. Wu whom Liu had known. He wore a faded jacket with stray threads hanging like unkempt whiskers. His mustache, which had once been groomed to perfection, sported streaks of gray. The leather boots were creased with lines that mirrored the tired contours of his face.

"Mr. Wu, how's business?" asked Liu.

Raking a crooked smile across his face, the ferryman answered, "Not bad. Not bad. Everyone's gotta see the Little Three Gorges before the water crawls up the cliffs again."

"When is that happening?"

"Where have you been, young man? Why, the river is swelling up as we speak. They say it'll fill up to the new level by summer's end, and it looks like we'll get good rain this season to flood it even sooner."

Liu sensed that there was little time to waste, that somehow he had been drawn back before another chapter of his former life became irrevocably lost. But he had worried that Ol' Fang might lay claim to his daughter, have her spirited her away in the dark of night. Enough time had passed to quell his fears, and during their brief stay in Wushan he saw no traces of the old broker, not even in the faces of strangers.

The boatman kept up some of his airs, tipping his cigarette impatiently while Rose tottered along the wooden plank into the boat. Yet Liu felt more at ease around this new Mr. Wu, whose subdued manner harkened back to his old, pre-capitalist self.

"I'm here to take my daughter on a little cruise to her home village. It's already under water, but it's a ways down in Emerald

Gorge, somewhere beneath these rocky peaks shaped like a pair of horns."

"Well, hop aboard. I think you folks are it today. Rain's keeping the others at home."

Father and daughter hunkered down in the cabin, gazing at the silver spray that jetted forth from the prow of the boat as it plied through deeper waters. The engine chugged noisily, but Liu could hear occasional grunts from the boatman's lips as they passed cargo boats laden with coal or produce, a tremendous barge with dried reeds bundled into haystacks. Liu was tempted to ask Mr. Wu about the downsizing of his business. Where was the two-tiered ferryboat that he'd boasted, the extra hands he had hired? And the passengers? Liu sensed that the boatman would be insulted by insinuations that his business had faltered, even if those days of prosperity were over.

It was Mr. Wu who opened up conversation. He squatted on the rim of his boat, hollered into the recesses of the cabin. "You comfortable in there, ol' brother? It's a little musty with all the rain."

"Fine. The child's fine, too." Liu was somewhat surprised to be addressed in this way, with a tone of familiarity that Mr. Wu the boss had never used.

"The rain's let up a bit. View's better out here."

Liu nudged his daughter, who was playing with the straps of her lifejacket, and they emerged from the dark cabin, settling down against its hull.

"Still have family in these parts?" Liu recalled that the boatman had grown up in the Little Three Gorges in rather modest circumstances.

"Yep. Just the sister's gone," Wu replied. "Became a prostitute in Chongqing."

Liu stared at the boatman, who seemed to relish the reaction he drew.

"Ha! Nowadays anyone in the big city's gotta throw themselves into a stranger's lap. She works for a pharmaceutical company. Started as a secretary. Cozied her way up to be a manager." The man winked, but a sinister aura surrounded his words.

"I spent some time in Chongqing, didn't care for it." A sour taste arose in Liu's mouth, and he fished out a cigarette.

"You'd think she'd send some of her money home to the *niang jia*. But no, sir, she's got a good life now. Forgotten her humble beginnings."

Liu was surprised again by the man's revelation. His daughter squirmed, bothered by the chimney of smoke emanating from his lips, and climbed back into the cabin with the straps of the over-sized lifejacket trailing behind. He kept a watchful eye on Rose, and turned a half-attentive ear toward Mr. Wu.

The boatman took a deep breath and exhaled. "Now I can't help the folks much, but she could. Pull 'em out of the hell hole they've fallen into. That's what their village has become. Almost nothing left now." The heavy-lidded eyes squinted shrewdly. "I tell you, the local officials robbed 'em of ninety percent of the resettlement funds they were supposed to get. And then my father, fool that he is, made a stink when he caught a higher-up with his hand in the money jar. What did it get him? Only time in jail. With no end in sight."

Liu stamped out one cigarette butt after another as Mr. Wu relayed the sordid details of his mother's entreaties, the officials' dismissal of their case, the villagers who stuck their necks out simply to be squashed down. It threw a new light on his experiences. The condemned village, once a source of sporadic income for Liu, had been bled dry by corruption. Their residents, who retreated to higher ground with their meager possessions and pickings from the last harvest, fled from home as he once had, but forced flight did not land them on green pastures. Mr. Wu's father was in prison, and his mother, grieving like a widow, refused to leave their forsaken village.

"She's a loyal woman," Liu said, feeling a pang of emptiness that weighed on him like damp cotton.

"I don't know how long she can keep this up. I've tried to talk sense into the woman. The reservoir's rising again. They gotta clear out by autumn, 'cause the water's only going to get higher. And where she's squatting is going to be a big gray fortress of water." Mr.

Wu raised his thick arms in the air, as if invoking a great tidal wave, his eyes blazing in a mixture of awe and horror.

Liu shook his head, disbelieving, except that he had seen such changes with his own eyes. He thought of Father Chong, the blue-cloaked patriarch who, with a great flourish of his sailboat sleeves, claimed that the Lord's people would be saved from calamity. All they needed to do was to believe in their Savior. A curious trick of the mind, that the past would reappear, uninvited. "She'll probably pick up when the water gets high enough."

"No, you don't know my mother. She wants my father back so bad that she's lost her mind. I've tried to bribe the local cadres to tell me his whereabouts, but I'm just a small fly pestering them."

His admittance of humility was fleeting. Mr. Wu snorted, bent over and emptied another pan of river water into the engine. "I would just lift her up bodily and fling her into the boat, but she's mad enough that she'd tear me to pieces like a hungry wolf." Mr. Wu sat up and stared intently at Liu.

"Can you talk some sense into the woman? You're a father. A stubborn old woman's like a stubborn child. You must have a few tricks up your sleeve."

"I . . . I'm not sure I'll have any better luck than you," Liu replied. "And half the time I can't get my little girl to do what she's supposed to."

"Ma's not listening to family. What else can I do? Call in the cops? Ha! Let her drown in the waves?"

The boatman's declaration brought a jolt of remembrance. A deserted shore inhabited by a lone child. Liu's child. The doleful incantations of the Buddhist monk over his first wife's ashes. The cries of grieving women. The drone of ancient voices beseeching the mother of this half-man, half-god Jesus. He had never understood what it all meant. But he understood the impulse to salvage the living from the forces that snatched away life.

"All right, I'll talk to her. And if she doesn't listen, well, I'm not sure, then." Liu threw up his hands. "It'll take an act of the gods, I suppose."

33

THE RAIN PLAYED AGAINST THE EMERALD-GREEN SURFACE OF the Daning, plucking the waves like skilled fingers strumming an *er hu*. The waters heaved, rocked forward then back, drawing Wu's small boat closer to shore. Against the steel hull of the boat, the raindrops pattered insistently in a militant tempo that drove Rose into her father's arms.

While their companion docked the boat, Liu bundled his daughter in her small raincoat, adjusted the hood close, and wrapped his scarf around her until only a pair of saucer-shaped eyes and a dumpling nose remained. He thought of hoisting her onto his shoulders, and thought better when he surveyed the narrow trail, which curved along a hill where cabbages and potatoes grew. They stepped on shore, hands interlaced, and a furious wind swept upon them from behind, lifting the flaps of Rose's scarf in a mad dance. The little girl whined, and Liu pressed her close to him. He tasted grit on his lips, thick as summertime silt. Their lumbering steps left imprints in the mud like sunken cow pies. In the rear, Mr. Wu grunted, his cigarette flickering hopelessly in the gale.

Beyond the vegetable patch, a small shack with a blue-and-white tarp clung to the hillside, surrounded by an odd assortment of stools and low chairs. The wooden ones were missing a leg or a spoke in the back. The plastic stools held a veritable collection of pickled cabbages, limp as soggy laundry. The grizzled head of a woman appeared in the open-faced shack. She tipped the rainwater from the seat of an unused stool, lowered herself gingerly, and stoked the feeble coals of her stove, which was sheltered beneath a broken-up crate.

The woman looked up, and her eyes glowed with the same light from the coal embers. "Back again, you stubborn donkey. Can't leave your mother alone."

Liu had barely caught his breath before the words assaulted his ears. He chuckled silently, realizing that stubbornness wasn't always such a bad trait.

"Who's that young fellow with you?" The woman shifted her gaze toward him. Her red-streaked eyes aroused not so much loathing as a nameless remorse in Liu.

Pulling his daughter close, he approached her cautiously, as if she could combust at any moment, defying rain and human entreaty.

"My name is Liu. Liu Renfu. My daughter Rose has never set foot in her birth village. That's why we're here."

"Is that what brings you to this forsaken place?" She poked at the coals with a vicious thrust, scattering a few glowing nuggets on the damp earth.

"Well, we may not find the village exactly. It's under water now. But your son's good enough to take us around on a day like this."

The old woman glared at Wu, a sorry sight with his drenched mustache and rain-soaked clothes. "He is a troublemaker. First the authorities, now my own son won't leave me alone."

"Ma! What do you want me to do? I've pestered them with wine, soft money, hard money, *hung bao* for their kids. I'm broke, but Pa's still penned up."

The woman threw her stick down and wrapped her arms around her ample bosom, rocking herself on the little stool. Against the ragged tarp, the rain pounded like a stampede of hooves, but the woman showed no signs of retreat.

"Your son means well," Liu broke the silence. He bent over and rested a hand on her shoulder.

She looked up. Her eyes were hungry, pleading. "All he's ever tried to do was keep the petty bureaucrats honest. They've taken it all away. My husband. My house." She pointed to a barren patch uphill. "What they've given us won't even keep the mice alive."

Beneath his rain-swollen hands Liu could feel the current of old sorrows that seized her bosom. At Liu's prompting, his daughter sidled close to her.

"Po Po, don't cry."

The woman seemed far away, and in the throes of her weeping, none of it seemed real to Liu. The rain did not strike ground and the river did not rise, the skeletons of demolished houses did not succumb to greater designs, and the dead did not haunt those who lived on.

The old woman rocked back on her haunches, patted the child's head with a faltering hand. "Child, you do not know an old woman's sorrows. You are young. The gods spare no one."

Liu leaned in where the air rose in a thick, gray column from the sheltered stove. The soot clogged his lungs, but he forced himself to speak.

"This child, she was a foundling. . . . I came across her by the river. And the river would have claimed her if I hadn't."

She said nothing, and Liu wondered if his revelation was made in vain. He watched as the rain crept steadily up the riverbank, consuming the heads of cabbages and tender stalks of *xiang cai* in the summer tempest. He wondered if the gods were angered by human impudence. But it didn't seem fair that only the weak would be punished.

By late afternoon, the storm had given way to fitful gusts of wind and torrential rain that refused to let up. And still they sat. Mr. Wu had retreated in irritation to his boat, promising he wouldn't leave without them. The waters crept higher, the greedy tentacles clawing their way up the terraced land. It seemed as if the river and sky had melded into one, and the meager patch of land beneath them could persist no more than the ethereal outlines of clouds above.

Huddled beneath her cape, in the cave of her father's chest,

Rose soothed herself with little games, counting fingers, toes, stools, sticks, Ba Ba's ribs. She giggled when her father recoiled from the touch, fell into the old woman's bosom and stared up at her with mirthful eyes. She seemed as oblivious as their troubled hostess was to the rising river below them.

The old woman parted her lips. "One, two, three. Three teeth," Rose counted. "I have more teeth than you, Po Po."

"Ba Ba!" Rose cried. "Look how many teeth I have." How at ease Rose seemed in the old lady's bosom, whose ampleness was reassuring even if her mind had been spirited away with grief.

Lightning flashed across a darkened sky, illuminating yellow teeth and white, bloodshot eyes, the bundles of salvaged wood still to be hauled away, the fallen totems of stone that surrounded the fields. Rose leapt from the old woman's lap into her father's arms. In her frenzy she scratched the woman's wrist, but elicited no reaction. Only the little girl's screeches, and the ensuing peals of thunder, upset the rat-tat-tat of rain against the plastic tarp.

The floodwaters curled around Liu's feet. In a decisive moment, he declared, "*Lao tai tai!* We must go. You cannot stay here."

Liu tugged at the woman's wrists, Rose joining in the entreaties. "Po Po*! Quai! Quai!*" Hurry, hurry.

The water poured through the sieve of plywood in the rear of the shack. It coated the mud floor with a gray froth upon which dead insects floated. It amputated the short-legged chairs, consumed the old woman's calves and thighs, and raged through the front opening to pour down the banks into the massive, roiling stream below.

The torrent and sizzle of lightning ignited some vanquished fire in the taciturn woman. A strange light shone in her eyes. "I'm not going! You . . . you have family. I have nothing. My husband needs me. He is coming back, and I must wait."

"He is not coming back here!" Liu cried. "You cannot save him now. You must save yourself."

"No!" She pursed her lips, squirmed until her stool gave way, sinking her waist deep in the mire of floating debris.

The planks of her dwelling creaked, threatening to give way. The spent coals sputtered, their small offering of warmth no match for the frigid tide that seized the encampment. Exasperated, Liu rose to his feet with Rose slung across his shoulders. "I could not save my wife, and I can't save you now. But this child, I will not let her die because of a foolish woman's will."

His shoes sank in the yielding mud. He pushed forward, sank again on the next step. It was all too familiar, this flight from rising water. The gods had put him to the test again, but with the greater burden of years, an older Rose, a loss of not one wife but two, and now, a bereaved woman who stood her ground in vain.

Along the river the rains crashed undaunted against the waves, and on the flooded land the trees groaned with the weight of grasses, shrubs, and summer crops tossed around their trunks. A sharp crack resounded, like the breaking of bone. As Liu turned around he saw the shack crumbling to the ground, its tarp engulfing the old woman. Amidst the rattle of rain-spattered pots and stools, a thin voice croaked. "Don't go."

Liu wrenched his feet out of the thick mud and made his way back to the woman. He yanked her out from the mass of fallen tarp, an apparition of silver hair and yellow teeth. Lowering Rose, he hoisted the woman on his back and wrapped her arms around his neck. He scooped up his little girl and stumbled, relentless as the tumbling rain, across the hillside toward the waiting boat.

"Mr. Wu!" Liu shouted. "I've returned. With your mother."

The door to the cabin unlatched in hasty clicks, and a grateful Mr. Wu ushered the soaked man, woman, and child inside. The old woman was lowered onto a flimsy assemblage of lifejackets, where she fell into a delirious sleep.

Liu smoothed back the rivulets of hair streaming from under Rose's hood and kissed her forehead. The boatman grinned, slapping Liu on the arm. "You pulled her out. You old bastard. You did it."

"No, she found her way out," said Liu. "When there's nothing left to hold you back, you can only move forward."

ABOVE THE SANDSTONE BLUFFS OF QUTANG GORGE, THE FRONDS of willow trees swayed in lazy arcs, beckoning like sirens to the passing ferry. On their way back from Wushan, Liu and Rose disembarked at Baidicheng, where the Yangtze flowed past eroded banks. Enshrouding the ancient temple was the dust of moving earth and construction cranes that loomed overhead.

Liu approached one of the workers and asked what they were building. "A bridge to the other side," the man replied. "What you're standing on here is going under water."

A nameless anxiety seized Liu. Grabbing Rose's hand, he hurried up the long flight of steps to the temple's entrance.

Inside the shrine, Liu burned five joss sticks for Fei Fei and kowtowed with Rose, who stood alongside, mimicking his gestures. He declined the monk's invitation to linger; there was one more offering to make. He swept little Rose into his arms, and they descended the multitude of steps, then skirted around the temple compound to the river's edge. Here a pair of mandarin ducks scudded through the water, a trail of froth falling off their wingtips.

Rose turned her dimpled cheeks into the breeze, and his nose followed hers to the scent of blooming shrubs nearby. She squirmed, her bony frame chafing against his hands. The calluses had grown thick again from his ministrations to leather. Inky patches covered his fingers and thumbs where shoe dyes had been etched indelibly.

Liu released his daughter, and she ran toward the water's edge, where the small waves curled in ribbons and licked at their feet. Reaching into his bag, Liu removed an old wool sweater with both hands, and held it in the crook of his elbows, as if it were the robe of a venerable monk. It was only a sweater, moth-eaten and disintegrating, but it had once sheltered his daughter from the winds raging against a deserted village. That layer of warmth had helped to save Rose's life. Along with other benevolent acts, it must have been an afterthought, hastily carried out by a mother in flight.

IN THE LAP OF THE GODS

Liu Renfu lifted the little girl with the steady crane of his arm. With his other hand, he tossed the dark, woolen mass into the river. The fabric swelled, like a small forest of kelp, almost purple against the gray of sky and water, and sank in two slow breaths beneath the surface.

ACKNOWLEDGMENTS

In my travels to the Three Gorges, I met people in Chongqing, Wanxian, old Fengdu, and Wushan whose stories have contributed to this work of fiction. Having done fruitless searches on Google and in libraries, I am grateful to Xiang Chun for his agricultural expertise and knowledge of the region's flora and fauna. Lin Gu provided his insights while he was a visiting scholar at UC Berkeley. He Qinglian and her husband Chen Xiao Nong helped me to understand the inner workings of Chinese government in the developments of big dam projects. Fang Xin and Pauline Shu shared their knowledge of Chongqing and the region's architecture. The nonprofit International Rivers provided me with a constant stream of news about dams and ecological issues in China that hadn't been covered by the mainstream press. Dr. Steven Younger answered my questions about medical conditions that I inflicted on the characters.

It's been a pleasure to work with my editor, Lisa Graziano, and the folks at Leapfrog Press. A heartfelt thanks to my agent, Joe Veltre, and the others who have gone to bat for this novel, including Jana Robbins, Dawn Yun, and the dozens of folks who read the first three chapters. Gina Davis, Kim Wyatt and others at Squaw Valley Writers Workshop helped to strengthen the early drafts of the book. My husband, Andrew Lovett, has been a staunch supporter throughout it all.

THE AUTHOR

Li Miao Lovett is an award-winning writer whose essays and stories have appeared in the *San Francisco Chronicle*, *Stanford Magazine*, *Earth Island Journal*, and on KQED public radio. She has organized events for Words Without Borders showcasing the works of dissidents and censored writers. *In the Lap of the Gods* was a top-four finalist for the James Jones First Novel Fellowship. Li Miao lives in San Francisco.

About the Type

This book was set in Bembo®, a typeface based on the types of one of the most famous printers of the Renaissance, Aldus Manutius. In 1496 Manutius used a new weight of a roman face, formed by Francesco Griffo da Bologna, to print the short piece *De Aetna*, by Pietro Bembo.

The Monotype Corporation in London used this roman face as the model for a 1929 project of Stanley Morison which resulted in a font called Bembo. Morison made a number of changes to the 15th century forms. Because Manutius did not originally cut an italic for the font, Morrison used that from a sample book written in 1524 by Giovanni Tagliente in Venice. Italic capitals came from the roman forms.

Designed by John Taylor-Convery
Composed at JTC Imagineering, Santa Maria, CA